A RUSSIAN MOTHER

FRENCH · EXPRESSIONS

HOLMES
&
MEIER

A RUSSIAN MOTHER

a novel

ALAIN BOSQUET

Translated from the French by
Barbara Bray

Afterword by Germaine Brée

HM

HOLMES & MEIER
New York / London

Published in the United States of America 1996 by
Holmes & Meier Publishers, Inc.
160 Broadway   New York, NY 10038

Originally published as *Une mère russe*, copyright © Éditions Grasset & Fasquelle, 1978.

Book design by Sara Burris
Typesetting by Stephanie True Moss

This book has been printed on acid-free paper.

Library of Congress Cataloging-in-Publication Data
Bosquet, Alain, 1919-
 [Mére russe. English]
 A Russian mother / by Alain Bosquet ; translated from the
French by Barbara Bray.
  p. cm.
 ISBN 0-8419-1329-3
 I. Bray, Barbara. II. Title.
PQ2603.0628Z4713 1996   94-38053
843' .912—dc20   CIP

Manufactured in the United States of America

To the novelist Boris Schreiber,
who had a Russian mother.

Berthe Turiansky was born in Odessa in 1889. Her father was a Jewish merchant dealing in hides and leather. She studied the violin with Leopold Auer, who also taught Jascha Heifetz. In 1918, after a first marriage which was both brief and unhappy, she became the wife of Alexander Bisk. A civil war was raging by then, and the city of Odessa was continually changing hands. Berthe's second husband was wealthy, but casual and indecisive and given to writing poetry. His family, which came originally from Belgium and Alsace, had emigrated to the Ukraine in the middle of the nineteenth century to build railroads.

Berthe Bisk left Russia in 1918 after managing to save her husband from the OGPU (the Russian secret police), and traveled first to Bulgaria, then to Belgium. In 1940 she went into exile again, settling for a short time in the south of France before crossing over to the United States, where Alexander Bisk, preferring to have as little as possible to do with the outside world, spent his time buying and selling rare postage stamps. Though Berthe did, somewhat late in the day, take lessons from the sculptor Alexander Archipenko, her life by then was chiefly that of a devoted wife and mother, spending most of her time waiting and hoping for a visit from her son, the narrator of this book. After her husband's tragic death, she spent the rest of her life in Paris, where she died in 1977.

Paris, October 1976

You're my mother; you're dead; all I feel is relief.

That line, full of dread and resentment, occurred to me one day as I was leaving you after a pointless scene. All of a sudden, partly involuntarily and partly on purpose, a mass of repressed misunderstandings burst forth from our lips and came crashing down like an avalanche. It was a cold day: a somber autumn wind swept through Paris between rusty leaves below and hurtling clouds above, jostling one another across the uncertain sky like a herd of tipsy cows. The window displays of the stores, first in the rue de Grenelle, then in the rue Saint-Dominique, struck me as cramped and ugly, like the relations between you, the exasperated mother, and me, the impatient son. I felt like pilfering something from outside a greengrocer—an orange, a misshapen apple, a stupid banana—and stamping it to bits on the wet sidewalk; or else going in and buying a doll too horrible to give to any decent child, then gouging out its plastic eyes and foam-rubber innards and dashing them to the ground at the feet of passersby. I'd have enjoyed slapping anyone within reach who looked older or feebler than I was: senility should be a punishable offense, weakness was unforgivable. I didn't try to make excuses for my irritation: I knew I was being unfair and wanted to remain so as long as possible. I figured my mood would probably last until I reached the pont des Invalides. There was one good thing about despairing of you and of myself: it allowed me to despair of Paris too.

1

I rolled my little line of verse around on my tongue approvingly: it fell into three satisfactory parts, it sounded good, was suitably provocative, and its suggestion of suffering was bound to strike chords in other people. Was I being terribly literary? But did I have no other defense against life except literature? As soon as I'd invented the fateful line I did all I could to forget it; but this only anchored it in my memory forever. I spoke it aloud through the mist—muffled by the damp air, it sounded both incisive and insidious. I took the first face that came along: it looked worn and ordinary, and belonged to a woman of about fifty, not well dressed or badly dressed, neither rich nor poor, a social worker perhaps, or teacher at a local school. She had a high forehead and her eyes darted about a lot, as if to counteract her evident diffidence. I stood in front of her for a few seconds, blocking the way, and then addressed my verse to her, pronouncing every syllable very clearly:

"You're my mother; you're dead; all I feel is relief."

The face hesitated. I'd been expecting a shrug of the shoulders, a reproachful look, a dismissive wave of the hand. But my own uncertainty must have been all too obvious, for the woman merely turned meekly away without a word. There was no turning back now, however, and I decided to try out my terrible phrase on another victim: by now it was really weighing down on me, conjuring up all kinds of hideous and apocalyptic images. I had to act quickly to foist the responsibility off on to someone else. The gentleman now coming toward me was wearing a good overcoat and an almost elegant hat; his mustache was by no means ridiculous, either. He must have been about my own age; his bearing was fairly impressive. I spoke, unable to conceal some embarrassment:

"Excuse me. . . *You're my mother; you're dead. . .*"

"Sorry—I'm in a hurry," he said, brushing past. He wouldn't have minded giving me a shove if necessary. So there I was, left high and dry. Then on the opposite sidewalk I saw a little boy of about five or six in a cap several sizes too big for him. I crossed over and took him by the shoulder.

"You're my mother; you're dead; all I feel is relief."

He looked at me with a mixture of surprise and delight, and held out a multicolored marble. I grabbed the sleeve of his jacket and gave him a shake.

"Would you like a mint as well?" he said shyly. "My mother was sick last week. But Dad said she isn't going to die."

I calmed down a bit after that. No one wanted to listen to my elucubrations: I would just have to live with them as best I could. I heaped more blame on my imagination, and on my incurable habit, for the past thirty years, of turning everything into fine phrases. I knew I could take my mind off things by going and having a drink in a bar, or calling up a friend who'd regale me with his own troubles. I was just resigning myself to burying that scrap of verbal poison away inside me and accepting it for what it was—a kind of punishment—when I found myself brought up short by reality. You, my mother, were over eighty-seven years old, and declining physically and mentally; and I was almost sure you wouldn't outlast the winter. I summoned up all my resources—I admit they didn't include much reason. How was I to behave? If I didn't want to be forever at the mercy of innumerable conflicting impulses, I would have to work out a clear and practical attitude toward you. More than ever before, willpower and determination would have to prevail over sentimentality. I revived a decision I'd already come to several years before: I would have to make an effort to dissociate you from yourself, and keep reminding myself that you were no longer the person I'd once loved so much. You looked like my mother still, but you weren't my mother any longer. Perhaps, if I did all this, I might be able to bear your decline.

This led on to various speculations about the future which proved pretty unnerving. I quickened my pace, telling myself my foolish phrase was frivolous, unseemly, but relatively harmless.

You're my mother; you're dead; all I feel is relief.

Was being sensitive to words a way of exorcising the truth they conveyed? I was gradually growing immune to the difference between good and evil. Instead of opting for one or the other, I was the victim of each in turn. When I came to a recently opened movie theater in the boulevard des Capucines I rushed straight in. A second-rate movie would at least take my mind off my troubles—in other words, help to distance me from myself.

You lived on for another four months after I shocked myself with that little phrase of mine.

Lom Pananka, summer 1924

I can still see the scene quite vividly. We're at Lom Pananka on the Bulgarian side of the Danube, which is green as well as blue. The pretty white ships on the river look wryly cheerful: the smoke from their funnels wreathes past their keels and lifeboats, then spreads out over the trees by the landing stage. I gather some bright yellow pebbles from the shingle by the water; they feel so smooth when I hold them in my hand. You tell me I may keep two or three; any more and they'll spoil the shape of my pockets. You tell me the river's very long and goes through several countries, some of them new ones like Yugoslavia and Czechoslovakia. I try to memorize the names: you have to repeat them several times. Alexander, my father, has less patience with me, aged four and half, than you. I'm not any longer a plaything, but nor am I yet someone who can be spoken to normally, without having to have everything simplified or explained. I don't really understand what you've been saying, so he feels he ought to give me a little lecture on contemporary history. There has recently been a long and deadly war which ended in a kind of reconciliation, set out in a contract, with signatures, at a place called Versailles, in France. As a result the good were rewarded and the wicked punished. Whole empires and kingdoms have disappeared, while other once subordinate territories have been unexpectedly transformed into independent countries.

You laugh and say I'll be going through some of them, and they're very beautiful. My father and I are going to sail a long way away on a boat, and I'll see two famous cities—Budapest and Vienna. I won't have to bother about school, and I'll meet my grandfather and grandmother, who'll love me very much. Later on I'll learn all kinds of fascinating things, and when I finally grow up it will be in a civilized country. I don't ask many questions—I'm preoccupied with my pebbles, and with the thought of being seasick; I've heard about that in a story. You reassure me. People never get dizzy on a riverboat, even if the river's as big as this one. My father takes the opportunity to teach me two new expressions: "undertow" and "pitching and tossing." I like the sound of them so much he adds a third: "roller." For a few moments I feel really attracted to the sea, and wonder whether I might decide to be a sailor. You give my father endless instructions concerning my welfare on the journey: I must wear plenty of clothes, be kept out of drafts, and not be allowed to play with children who behave badly. He's to give your love to your parents in Brussels, whom you haven't seen for years. You're going to miss him; you tell him this several times. But the voyage will do him a lot of good, help him get over his recent nervous breakdown. He works too hard, and has never got used to living in exile. And at least he'll have the consolation of getting his son away from this unpredictable country and its uncouth language: that I should have a European education is your own great dream. My grandparents have connections, you say, and more good sense than one might expect.

The boat's filling up. It will soon be time to say goodbye. You take my father aside for a moment, leaving me alone with my trophies. Some grave-looking gentlemen come aboard with a lot of suitcases, which they keep on counting. Cab drivers bow and scrape. I hear a few words of Russian and French amid conversations conducted mostly in Bulgarian. The passengers are greeted by men in white uniforms ornamented with gold braid. The gangway is steep, and the ladies are warned not to let their heels get stuck between the duckboards. Expensive lapdogs run all over the place, yapping and being scolded. A small orchestra is playing a waltz on the upper deck. You put your arm around my father's waist. He pushes back a lock of black hair; you toss your very fair curls. I happen to know you bleach them, some mornings, with hydrogen peroxide. You kiss each other on the lips. As usual, I have to look away.

The orchestra is caterwauling as if the strings of the violins had gotten twisted around the players' fingers. My father says such tasteless contortions must be torture for you, a professional musician. You reply that czardas are not to be taken seriously. I ask you to tell me what "czardas" are—I've never heard the word before. Then I try to say it, and promise you I'll do my best to enlarge my vocabulary. There are lots of knob-headed canes around, and Panama hats; the gentlemen twirl them around as skillfully as circus clowns juggling with plates. The ladies have very short skirts and elaborate veils on their hats. You list more things my father and I have to be careful about while we're on the boat. I have to watch my bowel movements and make sure they're regular; a well-regulated stomach ensures the proper development of the whole body. As for my father, he must learn not to think so much, and to see the future as synonymous with happiness. It's for my own good I'm being sent away: there are certain sorrows I'll understand when I'm older. You kiss me, and I have a feeling you'd like to say something affectionate but that all of a sudden you can't. I'm the one who takes the risk of muttering, "I love you, Mother"—whether I do so out of habit or duty I don't know. Father starts to talk about another, earlier exile: we left Russia soon after I was born, and now here I am, being sent away from Bulgaria, which after all has been quite hospitable. You answer sharply: "We have no choice. . . Only western Europe can make a man of him."

Since I'm going away I decide to give you my pebbles; you'll look after them and return them to me later in that wonderful country where we'll meet again. You hug me. Father, who's serious and perhaps wants to underline the fact, begins to talk about the war again: there was really no need to dismantle the Austro-Hungarian Empire, and Germany, despite all its mistakes, is after all the country that gave birth to Goethe. I try to commit all these names to memory. The farewells drag on and on. A siren sounds, and I wonder if it's the same as at a railroad station: if we're going to be off at once and all the passengers must hurry on board. My father explains that ships aren't so strictly organized as trains: whereas on the railroads the smallest delay may be fatal, navigation on the Danube is very leisurely. The white uniforms come into their own; the orchestra disappears from the upper deck. One or two poodles on leads caper about in a spectacular fashion. Father tells you not to neglect the violin; you won't have so much to do in the house with us away, so you can devote more time to Lalo, Schumann, and Drdla. You answer that art is indeed a great consolation. You admonish me at some length, but very kindly. "Write and tell me what you want to be when you're grown up. . . Grandfather will soon teach you to write. You must forget Russian—French is the language that counts." I'm very taken with the boat, but rather intimidated by all those ladies in extravagant hats and gentlemen with overlong mustaches. With some difficulty I decipher the name written on the prow: *"Der weisse Donau."* My father explains that it's German, means "The White Danube," and is a kind of joke: because of Johann Strauss people have got into the habit of saying the Danube is blue, though in fact it varies between different shades of green and brown. But since the boat itself is white, and named after the river, the color of the one comes to be attached to the other. I don't know whether all this is too complicated for me or if Father's explanation itself is rather muddled, but I feel tired. You hug me again and try to cheer me up: the couchettes are lovely and soft, and bigger than my own bed. I struggle free and throw my last pebble into the water. I believe I see you wipe away a tear, but to my childish way of thinking it's only natural: you're being true to the image I'll be taking away with me.

I've always refrained from exposing this childhood scene to my usual sarcasm. I've probably even gone to some lengths to make it seem as happy and unremarkable as possible. I've cherished that vague and distant vignette for half a century: for me it's come to be an archetypal image of enchantment. Being volatile by nature, with moods of skepticism alternating with fits of somewhat forced belligerence—my own form of self-defense, no doubt—I've always told myself I ought to accept that little picture of reciprocal affection just as it stood. I've never revised it or called it into question till now. But the mere fact of putting it into words forces me, rather uneasily, to analyze it. What kind of a person were you

7

that day beside the gay and carefree Danube? The weeks that preceded our parting had had their share of upsets and enigmas. I can remember quarrels between you and my father: you would weep silently; he, after a few outbursts, would take refuge in a sulkiness you dreaded even more than open anger. I recall doors flung suddenly open; hats crammed down on heads for hasty exits; suitcases being ostentatiously stuffed with dresses, a pair of shoes, and a toothbrush; sealed letters left conspicuously on tables as the writer vanished into the night. Beyond this mysterious maze of histrionic gestures no sooner performed than forgotten, I sensed that awful dramas were taking place.

You'd neglected your music for some months: now you took it up again. You practiced the violin, and sometimes even bought scores with small sums scraped together from the housekeeping. Father turned a blind eye; he knew you were cheating a bit about the price of meat and vegetables. He must have realized you couldn't be satisfied with just his and my love. You used to go to tea parties in town, frequented by a few Russian émigrés and visiting Frenchmen. This small circle, which you never invited to our modest home, encouraged you to perform before audiences of thirty or forty people whom half an hour of good music plunged straight into a romantic past. You were justly proud of your successes. And your friends, troubled by our family's relative poverty, would sometimes pass the hat around, and with the utmost discretion ask you to buy me a new satchel, a pullover, some toys, perhaps even some nice clothes. I accepted these gifts quite naturally, though I had too low an opinion of myself to think I actually deserved them. My father disliked this kind of charity; his job as translator to the Bulgarian branch of the Banque de Paris brought in enough for our needs, and he regarded music as an art rather than a profession.

But were there other reasons for his reservations? You were beautiful, restless, and attractive. You had played the part of devoted mother with resolution and even jealousy, but I was growing up quickly now, and you were free of me two or three hours a day. Not that my presence irked you; you simply took it for granted, and so found it less and less fascinating. And although you didn't actually lose interest in your husband, I believe you felt the need to compare him with other men, men either cleverer or more flirtatious than he. But as I endeavor to puzzle out that period of your life, when marriage had settled down into routine, I can't help feeling my memories are very incomplete. When the two of you quarreled, Father used to accuse you of being too lavish in your use of perfume—in particular the Chanel N° 5 which you regarded as the height of elegance. He thought some of your gowns were too low-cut, and criticized the way you did your hair: a respectable woman didn't wear spit-curls. Did I ever take sides? Shy as I was, I seem to remember agreeing inwardly with my father more often than with you, and you must have suspected as much, even though we never spoke about it. It wasn't unheard-of for you to raise your hand to me if I was too serious or kept staring into space. But almost at once you'd draw back and take me in your arms; you knew you ought to show me affection, and duty got the better of your temper. I concluded that I deserved to be punished, but had been spared because you loved me so much. But such half-memories are misleading; after a few years have gone by, one tends either to distort past events or to supplement them so as to give them a semblance of logic. There's one such recollection which has come back to me often. You and Father had a friend, a garrulous Frenchman who was always telling stories, true or false, about his adventures: the true ones were accompanied by assertions of their veracity and gestures imploring belief; the inventions by an airy wave of the hand, suggesting that the pleasures of fabrication more than make up for some slight infidelity to fact. His name was Victor, and you obviously liked him.

He used to come to our house once or twice a week, and you weren't at all ashamed to show him our two and a half rooms. You liked to say inner riches were more important than the visible kind, thus filling my small mind with anxiety and doubt. Victor was great on promises: he could arrange more profitable concerts for you, and put in a good word with influential conductors: my father ought to have a better job. Victor's loquacity made me uncomfortable, perhaps because he didn't take the trouble to talk about things I could understand; he wasn't really trying to make me like him. But the idyll between Victor and my family lasted only three or four months. One day, in order to make what he called some important approaches, he borrowed what seemed to me a vast sum of money from my father: six or seven hundred leva—enough, according to my calculations, to go to the movies at least fifteen times. After that we saw nothing of him for several weeks, and on his return I noticed apprehensively that he tried to ingratiate himself with me much more than before. One day at dinner my father said grimly, "That fellow is never to set foot in this house again."

You didn't answer, but I saw you could hardly manage to swallow your soup. Usually you were quick to lose your temper and lash out with offensive remarks, but now you were strangely silent.

A few days later I was awakened by the noise of a violent altercation, but this time, instead of listening at the door as was my usual habit, I buried my head under the pillow. The next morning you had a small mark on your forehead, and I deduced that my father must have struck you. But strangely enough it was him I felt sorry for, in a dim kind of way: he must have suffered a lot to be reduced to that. It seems to me now that then, for the first time in my life, I made a deliberate effort to repress my curiosity and disregard all the questions that urged themselves on me. As a result I was weighed down with guilt for more than a week; I reproached myself for being indifferent to the woes my parents were enduring, even if they *had* brought their afflictions on themselves. My father took to staying late at the office, and you played the violin far into the night. You didn't avoid each other completely, but you only exchanged a few words here and there. I too made some decisions, apparently somewhat at random: I'd ask Father to teach me some medieval history and tell me about Byzantium, Julius Caesar and Alexander II of Russia, and I'd ask you to show me the difference between the various notes in music and to tell me what you'd learned from Leopold Auer, who'd been your teacher in Odessa. By this means I would distract you from each other and so soothe away the discord between you.

But I didn't need to put my plans into practice. One afternoon while Father was at the bank, Victor burst into our apartment and you and he fell into each other's arms. Giving me strict orders to stay where I was, you left the house without more ado, and when you came back alone a couple of hours later you looked at once happy and shattered. Father would be home at any moment. I sensed you were afraid I might let the cat out of the bag, but couldn't bring yourself either to cajole me into complicity or to threaten me into silence. Something between us had been broken; from now on our old spontaneity would contain an element of caution and compromise. Did I find this painful? Did I feel you had suddenly ceased to inhabit my own little world and moved out into the vast universe of other men, where all was hostile, serious, and complicated? I think I did perceive there was now a distance between us, and I sought fleeting refuge elsewhere. I started to spend more time playing out of doors with my friends, and even took to talking to boys who were older than I was. Systematically, sadly, I tried to put myself in other people's shoes and to understand other people's feelings.

Hopscotch and blindman's buff prevented me from finding out how our domestic drama ended. Perhaps in the course of the years that followed my own imagination endowed it with exaggeratedly large and melodramatic proportions. On the other hand, I may have missed out on what was a vitally important episode in your life. But other worries, other events, and other intoxications soon crowded in on me: I was at the age when people take themselves seriously and don't know how to live with their own folly. As for you, by then thirty-five years old, you must certainly have been learning to be less impulsive and more sensible. No doubt more hypocritical, too. But then psychology has always run imagination a close second with me; I have a tendency to carry analysis so far it ends up in far-fetched and irrelevant hypotheses. Be that as it may, I never saw Victor again, and my parents' marriage seemed to revert to what it had been before. And yet several important decisions seem to date from that incident. You persuaded my father that he wasn't getting anywhere; the bank didn't really offer him any future. Moreover, it would be better to give up all hope of returning to Russia: the Bolsheviks were now firmly in power, and there was nothing left of the White Russian army. My father didn't actually disagree, but it took him a long time to accept the facts. However, your arguments were weighty and irrefutable; as Russia had to be written off, he owed it to himself to turn to the land of his ancestors, who'd left Alsace and Belgium seventy years ago to build railroads in the Ukraine.

So was it you alone who decreed what was to become of us—your future, mine, and my father's? He didn't say anything. He asked for time to think it over and took all your suggestions seriously, sometimes seeming to weigh the pros and cons with slightly surly intensity. It struck me he was less ready than you to take on a new motherland, probably because he was five years older than you and didn't feel like making a new start. Not that he put up any fierce resistance to your plans—he just let them take their course until they became inevitable. But behind your eagerness to go into exile for the second time, weren't there more dubious motives that I didn't know about? Even as that charming farewell scene was engraving itself on my mind, together with its trappings of idyllic barques, elegant passengers, and intrepid navigators whose exploits were confined to the waters of an absurdly peaceful Danube, I guessed that parting would always strike me as ambiguous. And I never could get rid of my suspicions. But my father wasn't the sort of person one could question without many preliminaries and a good deal of tact. As for you, would you have given me truthful answers, even if I'd asked?

I'm tempted, now, to put that picture-postcard vision of bliss and motherly love down to my own laziness. Wasn't sending your husband off to blaze a trail in the west a good way of getting him out of the way for two or three weeks, while you went off with Victor without having to bother with endless precautions? And, by pressing your distant parents into service to see that your son got a proper education, didn't you escape the curiosity of a witness all the more irksome because his innocence moved you to fits of remorse and pointless anxiety? You were glad to see us go, that day in Lom Pananka. You were about to throw yourself, panting, reckless, free at last, into Victor's arms. The intellectual and other considerations you urged on my father, prudent enough in themselves, were mainly intended to camouflage your desire. But what do we really know about our nearest and dearest? What can I say about your past? To find out the truth one would need to be able to put one's own mother on trial, put her to the torture and not let her go until she'd confessed all. Yet, if I leave out my justified suspicions, any account I give of you is bound to be a kind of hagiography.

But after a moment of madness I come back, humble and ashamed, to my original version: of course, in 1924, you were a faithful wife and fond mother.

Brussels, 1933

"You ought to be top of the class—you're the cleverest."

"I promise I'll try, Mother. But—"

"With your memory you'll wipe the floor with them all!"

"I wouldn't want to be nasty to them."

"Oh, they're just a lot of idiots!"

"Some of them are my friends."

"That's neither here nor there. What matters is getting good marks. You're my hero, and your father's proud of you too, even if he does sometimes pretend not to care."

"The trouble is, I can't get on with math. Or chemistry. I just learn everything by heart. But if there are any out-of-the-way questions in the exam, it'll be a disaster!"

"Would you like some private lessons?"

"No. . . Why do you run down my teachers and my friends?"

"What matters is us—the three of us. We must stick together, defend one another, not let anybody else come between us."

"What about the rest of the world? The universe?"

"It's obvious you're surrounded by dreamers!"

"I have to learn to live."

"I'll look after you. Is there anything you want that you haven't got?"

"I can't model all my behavior on you and Father."

"Do you think we set a bad example? Who can be influencing you, I wonder?"

"I wish you'd invite one or two of my friends around sometimes. Not to check up on them—just because I'm fond of them."

"No, no! They're strangers! Besides, they'll say we're poor and that I speak with an accent!"

"Surely if *I* can trust them—"

"That's only for now. Next year you'll be in another class and have different friends."

"Well, let me go to the pictures with them."

"The pictures! We all know what that means! You end up smoking and ogling the girls!"

"That's why I want you to ask them to tea!"

"Anyone would think your father and I aren't enough for you!"

"Boys my age—"

"What do boys of your age know about anything?"

"Do you want me to speak to Father about it?"

"No, leave him in peace. He has his work to do and he's got enough problems already."

"You're smothering me!"

"Where do you get these expressions from? Go on, then—say your family is a prison! Aren't you happy? You know very well that for your father and me you're our sun and moon, our only hope!"

"I'd still like to see more of my friends."

"I'll have to think about it."

"Is it so hard to understand?"

"So I'm a fool, am I?—that really is the limit!"

"Wait till you see! Leclercq is awfully nice, and so is Livchitz—*he* reads Spinoza and Bergson. Kierkegaard too!"

"Books!"

"Do you know any other way of getting to be top of the class?"

"Not *those* books! They're not required reading!"

"Are you saying the curriculum is all that matters?"

"You have an answer for everything—I don't like it at all! Come here and let me kiss you."

"Promise first that you'll ask Leclercq and Livchitz to tea?"

"Next month."

"No, on Saturday—in three days."

"Madame Meltz is coming on Saturday."

"She smells!"

"She's got a limp, poor thing!"

"That's no excuse for only washing once every leap year!"

"Are you moving your bowels regularly?"

"You're more interested in my stomach than in my brain!"

"Digestion affects the character: when you can't concentrate you're naughty!"

"I don't know what you see in old Meltz!"

"She's suffered a lot. She threw herself out of the window for a man who was unworthy of her. . ."

"There are two sides to every story. She probably made the poor fellow's life not worth living!"

"She loves music."

"And she's lived in Russia, so you can both get together and sigh over the good old days!"

"Go and finish your homework. You're better at books than at conversation."

"I don't call *that* conversation! . . . So it's all right for Leclercq and Livchitz to come on Saturday?"

"Darling, you always get your own way. . ."

"Anyone would think it was a great victory!"

"Well, I don't know when the awkward age begins, but with you it certainly lasts a long time!"

"Wait till you see how learned Livchitz is!"

"Don't forget what your grandmother used to say: 'A good mongrel's better than any performing dog!' The heart! What about the heart? At school they teach you to stifle it. They're going to tear the Russian soul out of you!"

"Russian soul? Russian chaos, you mean!"

"Oh, my little boy. . ."

"That's right—turn the tap on! The usual trick!"

"You're wrong—I'm not going to cry. . ."

"Congratulations!"

". . . but that's no reason to be cruel! Which class is Livchitz in?"

"The one above me."

"He'll end up bullying you, then—that's always the way. What do you get from him?"

"Nothing. Friendship."

"He needs you for a slave, to set him off."

"He lends me Tacitus and Ruysbroek."

"You ought to speak to your father about it. Let him decide."

"You know very well what he'll say: I have the right to choose my own friends. Conflict doesn't exist for him; everything is experience, useful if not actually inevitable."

"I suppose you're saying he's indifferent? He doesn't care?"

"Well, it's a clever strategy!"

"And what about Leclercq? What a name! I suppose his father's a pencil-pusher in some ministry?"

"No. A university professor."

"Oh well, there may be some useful contacts there later on."

"You mean I'm supposed to exploit him? What a horrible idea!"

"Things are difficult, you know. You may not have noticed, but your father works until twelve o'clock nearly every night, and business seems to be getting worse all the time."

"So you accept Leclercq without knowing anything about him!"

"I can't stop you meeting people, so you might as well meet them here. What's he good at, Leclercq?"

"Greek and Latin."

"The dead languages! Hasn't what happened in Russia taught these westerners anything?"

"So they'll both come to tea on Saturday."

"What about Madame Meltz?"

"Put her off. Buy her a bottle of eau de Cologne and hope she gets the message."

"These boys impress you just because they study hard. And so you want to force them on me."

"Not at all. It's just that I don't like hiding my friends. I want to show them to you in broad daylight. It's a proof of filial affection!"

"Now don't start getting too smart, my precious boy! Come along, let's have a laugh, as we did when you were small. Do you remember how we used to drive your father crazy, inventing nonsense language?"

"Gladivadziss. Partadezz."

"Coustoupoufoum balacolass stravidom."

"Mistim falatita."

"Stidirimik varakimil."

"That's seventh-century Turkish."

"No—Irish Greek."

"Martian, in the subjunctive."

"You see! We can't quarrel with each other!"

"Of course not, Mother! Not when you give in!"

"Don't be silly—I haven't given in at all! It's only natural I should meet your Livchitz and your Leclercq. And you're a good boy to introduce them to me—"

"In proper and due form!"

"Etiquette is very important in life!"

"If you're giving in, you might as well make a good job of it. Don't you think?"

"What else do you want?"

"Let me go to the movies twice a week."

"Once is enough."

"I'll work better at school."

"You're already getting on well!"

"I'll let the others beat me!"

"What a little pest you are!"

"The movies are good for my morale. They rest the brain. You said so only the other day."

"We mustn't put your father to more expense."

"He needn't know."

"I suppose I could take it out of the housekeeping money. . ."

"Three heads of chicory fewer than usual! I don't like chicory anyway. You don't cook them properly—they ought to be blanched."

"All right, my darling—I surrender."

"And couldn't you see Madame Meltz a bit less often?"

"Heartless wretch!"

"She offends my sense of the beautiful."

"She's no Greek statue, I grant, but no! A thousand times no! I'm not having you tell me what to do!"

"You could see her in secret. She's too fat and clumsy. And she smells."

"All right, all right—you said that before."

"Paratacampum stacatasis valviron platplatacouss."

"Mistibaldo."

"Moucmoumou."

"Vicoutch. . . So will you be good?"

"If you love me you're bound to think I'm good."

"I adore you, my darling!"

Brussels, 1938

You always encouraged my female conquests, provided they didn't last long and I lost interest in them after a few weeks. You didn't mind some young woman borrowing me for a while if I really liked her, but she wasn't allowed to steal me away. Your instinct served you well, and from such edited accounts of my adventures as I was able to give you, you could always tell the difference between an affair that flattered my vanity and one that represented a real danger for you. If after a couple of months my enthusiasm showed no sign of waning, my friend would be transformed overnight into a rival that must be gotten rid of. Hints were your usual weapon. You were careful not to put my back up; you were just naturally curious, you said—it was for my own good. It would have been in bad taste to ask me to introduce the young lady, but you made it clear you expected me to confide in you. When the details I divulged were particularly spicy—when I rhapsodized about an ample rump, say, or some especially sophisticated sensations—you were relieved rather than otherwise: I was enamored of a skin and a body, and heaven knew there were plenty more where *they* came from. You were more uneasy when my descriptions were reticent and I went into ecstasies over a girl's mind or good nature or bearing—a mysterious look, an enigmatic smile, a turn of the head, an elegant ankle. But even then you would tell yourself that my heart would remain unscathed: once in possession of the physical, what would I care about the mental and spiritual? You took fright only if I started making plans for the future: for instance, if I told you, "I'd like to take her skiing for a few days next winter." Or if I said, "I'm not all that passionate about her, but just being with her is wonderful—the world suddenly seems a more friendly place; it's as if time stood still": then the reaction was always the same. You'd ask endless questions about the girl's background and social status, her brothers and sisters and the house they lived in, her father's political opinions—as if to suggest that though the person of my choice was naturally beyond reproach, the members of her entourage might be second-rate if not downright suspect. The only thing that reassured you was my carnal appetite; what worried you most was for me to derive spiritual comfort from the presence of some young woman.

You didn't know what attitude to take toward Marie-Jeanne Flot. I was quite disappointed by your lack of reaction, by the apparent coolness with which you greeted the news of our affair. Admittedly I'd been particularly lacking that year in family spirit, as you and Father understood it. I'd just finished my secondary education—in modern and practical subjects, as both of you had wished—but felt more attracted to literature than to business. I regarded myself as ignorant of Greek and Latin to all intents and purposes; I remembered only a few ill-digested scraps from when I was eleven or twelve. Now that I was seventeen I dreamed of culture and of History with a capital H, and was starting to assemble in my mind's eye a collection of busts that would represent all I most admired: Beethoven, Rubens, Machiavelli, Hannibal, Rimbaud—together with a few young poets like Jules Supervielle and Paul Eluard. Your nonchalant attitude toward my idols annoyed me intensely. I soon decided our relations must forever after be based on intuition, diversified with a few sentimental reminiscences and the odd anecdote. Could there ever be a real dialogue between us?

Communications with my father were no better. He took refuge as usual in a grouchy neutrality. The most I could ever get out of him when I tried to discuss what course I should take in the future—he regarded my own preferences as too abstract—was the cryptic comment: "To every man his own heaven, to every man his own hell." No doubt he thought I should face up to things for myself, and in particular arrive at a sound view of the past. He may well have considered my intellectual values frivolous and extravagant. But life would either crush me or bring me down to earth. Meanwhile I chafed at the bit and darted here and there according to my whims and fancies; the straight line I'd formerly trod, aiming at staying top of the class throughout all my six years at high school, was now abandoned. The undying friendships I'd struck up disintegrated as the university loomed closer. Now that there were no more exams to act as a restraint, my imagination came into its own. But learning to be free at the age of eighteen called for either a great deal of staying power or an act of rebellion for which I was ill-prepared. I had trouble coping with all my conflicting impulses, but as, whatever other qualities I lacked, I did seem to have some willpower, I soon came to the simple conclusion that I should firmly reject anything I didn't like. I decided I'd never be rich, and I was against ostentatious display of success. Trade, money, business—any kind of calculation revolted me. My aspirations related to other spheres—to the realms of the mind. I would soon choose whether to be a philosopher, a historian, or a writer. But for the time being I put off the decision. I sensed that I still lacked some major experiences and intellectual encounters: all I had going for me so far was a kind of undefined rage and a rather vague determination. I began to have my doubts about Brussels: could I really take on new dimensions there and grow up into somebody worthy of the age I lived in? Leclercq, who had a lot of poise, acted as a corrective to my own intemperance: I still had a lot more thinking to do, I needed to make my hazy ambitions more concrete, and I had to slow down the rush of my ideas if I wanted to give them adequate expression. Livchitz, on the other hand, egged me on: in his opinion it was never too soon to reach for the stars, even if you risked singeing your wings. He regarded excess as a proof of existence, and claimed that to court death was to show a thirst for life. He spoke with passion about the absolute, though he took care not to try to define it.

Was I really at the center of so many conflicts? A more likely explanation is that I didn't have enough to do, and so had time to entertain a lot of half-thought-out notions and uncomprehended desires, together with many hopes that weren't even vaguely formulated. My nerves were bad, and I drank too much coffee. I read left-wing as well as right-wing newspapers, and adopted one short-lived position after another. I was horrified by the assassination of Dollfuss, the Austrian chancellor, yet filled with admiration for the SS, who'd shaken the old Europe out of its lethargy with their bloody and wonderfully barbaric challenge. I wanted to go and fight in Spain: my dignity and my meager pretentions to culture told me the Republicans were right, but my predilection for disaster inclined me toward General Franco. I longed for any kind of action, no matter how rash. I fluttered about, always chopping and changing. Inwardly I was a kind of scarecrow, waving my arms about to conceal the frail wooden skeleton that stopped it from rising up majestically into the air. You looked on in bewilderment at my changes of mood, putting them down to my uncertain digestion or a touch of anemia, exaggerating any small physical ailments despite your doctor's assurance that I would grow out of them all. You knew nothing of the ailments of the imagination.

I often talked about my heroes. You admitted my admiration for Rubens was justified, though painting was never an art that interested you much. You used to say life wasn't lived in museums, and people had to watch out for themselves rather than dream about supermen on canvas. Besides, all those muscles were mere bluff, a show of hyper-virility. Rubens was a champion sportsman before modern athletics were invented, but you had no time for record breakers: his Christs lacked humility and reminded you of the Cossacks of your native land. You were pleased that I liked the romantic composers, because you too doted on Berlioz, Schubert and—of course—Beethoven. You told me he was regarded as a god at the conservatoire in Odessa, when you were a student there in 1912 and 1913, just before the war. But you rebuked me for not liking Russian composers.

"Darling, there's almost nothing Slav about you! If only you could appreciate Tchaikovsky! You can't understand me unless you understand him! His music contains all the sensitivity and despair of the Russian soul!"

"All the stupid sentimentality, you mean, and the most vulgar lack of self-control!"

"Just wait and see! One day you'll be less harsh—you'll know what it is to sigh, you'll realize the charm of the intangible."

22

"Of the soppy and maudlin, you mean!"

"I suppose you'd rather have your precious Hannibal? A complete barbarian, and a failure!"

"He made the whole civilized world tremble! He was within an inch of conquering it when he was defeated. I call that greatness!"

"Don't you be too sure, my boy! Times change, and tastes change with them. In my young days, harmony and happiness were still regarded as virtues. But now, if you ask me, everything's going to the dogs."

"People who can't keep up with their own age always call the past a paradise."

We were always teasing each other, sometimes with a kind of confused sympathy, sometimes with profound irritation. But if the areas of incomprehension between us were a sorrow to you, I was proud of them: they made me feel freer of you, of my father, and of my psychological roots. But on one particular point you were absolutely and disarmingly fair: you didn't object to my admiring young writers you knew nothing about. You said every generation produces new artists of its own, and it would be stupid to try to compare their respective merits. But this argument, reasonable enough in itself, served as an excuse for your own increasing sloth: the fact that you didn't prevent *me* from taking an interest in the avant-garde made it all right for *you* to ignore it altogether. Established geniuses you supported with vague ecstasies, swimming with the tide and joining in the superficial veneration they generally enjoyed. The poets I quoted to you myself you merely acquiesced in, regarding them as seedy adventurers who would fall into utter oblivion when reckless enthusiasts like me eventually dropped them. Right into my late teens I still felt a need for the not always very lucid discussions I had with you, though my friends Leclercq and Livchitz made fun of me for it, the first tactfully, if with a tinge of asperity, the second without mincing his words.

"There's no point in discussing yourself—that's just a waste of time," said Leclercq. "What you have to do is overcome your fears and assert yourself. *Tell* other people, your family included, what philosophy of life you've chosen. Announce it—don't ask their opinion! How can you expect a mother to forget her love for her son when they're discussing something? Her desire to protect him will always paralyze him if it can. Of course, *your* mother is very understanding, I admit."

Livchitz said much the same thing, but with characteristic bitterness.

"History urges us to accept ourselves as we are—I know that's a recent notion, but the German philosophers are always using it. An individual's merely the sum of countless incompatible ingredients. Do you really think you have a right to exist? And that you have any choice about how? You'll turn out to be a shoemaker like your grandfather, or a walking corpse, or a congressman—the chemistry of time will decide. That being so, prepare yourself for what's to come by separating your desires from your dreams. That's where lucidity comes in: in being shit, and being aware of it. I don't know of a more appropriate attitude: it helps you to be a superior kind of shit. Other people! What do you expect them to be to you except distorting mirrors? And the worst of the lot are one's father and the female who gave one birth. They think that because they love you they have rights over you. We should get rid of our mothers while we're young: it's rather cruel, but one finds the strength to get over it. Or else—but *you* wouldn't dare—or else one ought to leave home."

I wasn't proof against this kind of crusade, and one day I asked my father if I could speak to him. I told him that despite my apparent successes my school career had been a mistake, and next year I wanted to go and study Romance philology at the University of Brussels. I wanted to spend twelve months working intensively on Latin and Greek under the supervision of a professor. I realized this would involve extra expense, said I, but was I to ruin my life just because someone else had mapped out a path for me for which I was quite unsuited? Twenty minutes were enough. By the end of that time my father, without either enthusiasm or reproach, had consented to my wishes; he didn't even think it worthwhile to warn me against the probable vagaries of my conscience. He behaved perfectly, and was rather dull. I took advantage of this to explain that I needed a bit of isolation: I'd develop better if instead of living at home I could rent a studio in one of the university residence halls—any small corner with room to think would do. Father listened carefully and reminded me that thirty years ago he too had traveled across Europe from one university to another in search of independence, or at least a modicum of mental liberty. I was just starting to congratulate myself when he added that in those days *his* father was rich, whereas *my* father was not. This pleasantry took the shine off my triumph: it meant I would have to take my new studies seriously and work hard at them. He wouldn't let me thank him, and made it clear the responsibility for my decisions rested squarely on my own shoulders.

You made a major drama out of the pact between Father and me. You hadn't been consulted, you'd been presented with a fait accompli, no one cared about your feelings, we were conspiring to deprive you of my company, we had no use for your services as a go-between, pourer of oil on troubled water, diplomat and devoted humble servant. I didn't need a mother anymore, and your husband had given in to my demands—which probably hadn't stopped short of blackmail—without even asking for twenty-four hours to think it over and share his apprehensions with you. You felt ridiculous, useless, old before your time. I tried to console you by saying I'd come and see you three times a week at least; anyway, the university hostels were only a couple of kilometers away. But you wouldn't be soothed. You refused several invitations to tea with Madame Meltz; you returned (and were reimbursed for) several concert tickets; and you started to inveigh against Livchitz and Leclercq—wicked wretches who'd made me their helpless victim, ready to join in any revolution that was going. You quoted Stalin and Hitler. Finally you accused Father of weakness: he might work all day long but he turned a blind eye to the dangers threatening the family, the only thing in the world that was really sacred. You started neglecting the house, and for the sake of peace and quiet Father sent you to Vichy for three weeks on a cure, though you had nothing whatsoever the matter with you. But rest and reflection only increased your rancor; you came home cynical, harsh, and disagreeable. You didn't trust either of us. He had betrayed you, of course, by letting his affection for me usurp the place of yours, by suddenly trying to deprive you of your privileged position. My own offenses were just as unforgivable: instead of confiding only in you I'd suddenly turned to him, and as a reward for that disgusting conspiracy I'd won the right, without so much as a breath of opposition, to go and live where I chose. As if I had enough sense to organize my own life!

Though you were usually very talkative, you now scarcely opened your lips. And I noticed you'd stopped reading the papers. You didn't actually sulk. You just withdrew inside yourself: you knew that being impassive was a sure way of showing you felt humiliated. But I wasn't a monster, and having gotten my own way I could afford to show magnanimity. I offered several times to take you to the Soignes Forest for the day, and suggested a trip to the seaside out of season—to Ostend, perhaps, or Knokke. I actually missed some get-togethers with friends in order to keep you company, though I didn't talk to you. But your reactions were inconsistent and incomprehensible, and I concluded you must be deeply hurt by my behavior. However, I didn't go so far as to change my mind. Livchitz was right: whatever one's feelings toward them, mothers exploited one. After a month of lukewarm relations and having to think before every word I spoke, my self-confidence was becoming seriously undermined. I was at a crossroads, seething but apprehensive, knowing I ought to make a bid for inner freedom if I didn't want to remain not merely a petty but a positively minute bourgeois, yet incapable of actually uprooting myself. I was sincere, spontaneous, alert, but buffeted about by an avalanche of half-understood and unpleasant truths; and, if the truth were told, I was just as quick-tempered as you were. Your own hostile apathy made me an easy prey for the first excitements that came along.

I met Marie-Jeanne Flot at a dance. I could do a laborious slow foxtrot and a slightly more convincing tango. The big hall, plunged in a semi-darkness propitious to furtive kisses, contained about forty or fifty youths, most of whom, like me, had just left high school. Most of the girls were alone, though some had brought their mothers, all decked out for the occasion. I went for broke and asked one of the protective matrons for permission to dance with a pretty white dress and a blue bow at the waist. In those days I preferred women of about thirty—they didn't waste time on modest scruples, and they took their own precautions without treating the possibility of pregnancy or unpleasant infection as something catastrophic. I was less interested in girls my own age, though I told myself I ought to be able to get just as much pleasure from toppling them. Their clumsiness did in fact add the semblance of a thrill to the proceedings; what I dreaded were their heavy sighs and invocations of eternity. The white dress was slim, with a body both soft and lithe, and the kind of firm breasts I liked. The mass of silk net and lace twirled about airy and untrammeled, and I was quite taken with the saucy velvet bow. But perhaps it was the fragrance emanating from the whole that attracted me, rather than any detail or word. She reminded me of a supple young tree shaken by the wind and forced to shed its flowers one by one. I felt under her arms as soon as we got on to the floor. Did she shave her armpits or pluck the hairs out slowly, one by one, I asked her point-blank, with a nonchalance that surprised myself. Far from taking offense, the white dress promised she'd give me a detailed explanation during the next dance: she was inviting me to go on as I had begun. So a little while later my hands encountered the kind of skin I approved of. It took me a few seconds to get used to a slight whiff of perspiration, which seemed to have a long-distance effect on my salivary glands. Her breath too had curious affinities with my own lungs. I felt I should pass on these observations to the person inside the dress, and this led to the divulging of family name, given names, age, and other particulars. This ruled out one of my usual strategies: we couldn't pretend to be strangers who meet and merge, possess and reject each other, then separate for ever, strangers still. Only one alternative remained: we introduced ourselves in due form, and even had a glass of lemonade with the mother. She was there, no doubt, to ensure that her daughter made as impressive an appearance as possible: matchless, divine, marvelous—and knocked down in advance to the highest bidder.

For the rest of the afternoon my tangos were meticulous, almost mathematical, but that didn't prevent my hands exploring from nipples to groin. I informed Marie-Jeanne that she was going to be mine, and I was giving her two days at the most to think it over. She replied that she was a year older than I was and such delay was torture. I then took possession of her face—I'd almost forgotten about that amid all my tricks and transports. It was a bit bony, but charged with irresistible ardor. I soon decided Marie-Jeanne Flot and carnal dallying offered an excellent and timely distraction from my own ambitions and vacillations. I said as much to the interested party, who made no objection; maybe she thought that in bed, amid morning coziness and exhausted muscles, cynicism would gradually be transformed into tenderness. Two days later my wish was granted and I took her to my studio in the Cité Universitaire: a table, a chair, a radio, a sink, a mirror, a cupboard, and a single bed. She made love the way she danced—with great poise and no stupid nagging. She was freely available, but didn't ask me to make myself so too; so our affair could last until the first twinges of boredom made themselves felt. In other words, probably for about four or five months.

In order to take your mind off your own inner conflicts I decided to keep you informed in detail of this affair. But you didn't pay much attention to my reports, and instead of displaying the fierce fits of jealousy you could produce when you suspected you might have a real female rival, you remained distant and as depressed as before. It was my duty to coax you back to normal—despite your reproaches I wasn't really a callous wretch. I asked Marie-Jeanne Flot around to our place one afternoon when Father had to meet some of his colleagues in town. You were polite rather than interested, and it suddenly struck me my life no longer concerned you all that much. I wasn't quite sure how I felt about this: on the one hand I was getting free of your authority, but on the other I knew I'd miss your dictatorship. I wanted to be both independent and indispensable. Was there going to be a kind of transference by which Marie-Jeanne Flot took over from you a moral influence to which she had no right? But thoughts like this were unhealthy: it was better to act, even rashly. So I insisted on your meeting the girl's mother. You greeted her correctly and confidently. You didn't have much to say to each other: the weather, the news, the dangers of the political situation, the unpredictability of the younger generation. It didn't enter my head that our mothers' courtesies might give an official stamp to our relationship. Were you two idle ladies really likely to put your heads together about farfetched projects like engagements?

You, at least, had other, more selfish aims in mind. Your usual female cronies, recruited among the Russian émigrés, made you concentrate on the past rather than the present. Some still spent their time sighing over the exploits of Denikine, Kolchak, and Wrangel, while others never stopped fulminating against Lenin, Trotsky, and the hopeless incompetents responsible for the tragic end of Imperial Russia. You saw Madame Flot as a westerner, more balanced and less lethargic than your expatriate pals. As she'd never even heard of Pushkin or Chekhov, you fondly imagined she would provide you with a breath of fresh air and some new attitudes to modern times. You exchanged knickknacks and compliments with each other, traded antique spoons and sentiments, serviettes and subjunctives, cloisonné without value and chatter without wit. Your meetings with her were no less humdrum than your meetings with the others, but they made you feel you were being accepted by a westerner, someone who didn't transform facts into terrors and daydreams into ineluctable events. Above all she helped you cast off a culture which was superficial, restrictive, and which suited you all too well. It seemed, after all, that Hugo was as good as Lermontov, and Saint-Saëns and César Franck might be mentioned in the same breath as Mussorgsky and Borodin. In these warm and foolish exchanges, were Marie-Jeanne and I ever mentioned at all, I wonder?

You refused to see my girlfriend as a potential ogress. You were even quite shy with her. Sometimes your attitude was one of languid hostility; sometimes, to avoid displeasing Madame Flot, you were excessively affable. Such aloofness, such restraint: it seemed to me your behavior was more than usually civilized. This had a certain effect on my own attitude: after four or five weeks I too began to wonder about Marie-Jeanne. Skin-deep well-being wasn't enough for me, and eventually it began to irk me that you neither hated nor suspected her. Quarrels between Marie-Jeanne and me grew more frequent, and so did fits of impatience on my part. Marie-Jeanne's first tears only infuriated me. Were my relations with her all that important? It seemed to me that because of her I'd lost something of you. And though this was just a temporary feeling, it had a lasting effect. I was soon making excuses: a heavy workload at the university, imaginary worries. I was gradually distancing myself, and I did so without regrets. Marie-Jeanne would turn her mind to new love affairs, and that was perfectly natural. I wasn't old enough for heartbreak. Our kisses became, quite amiably, few and far between; our caresses soon dwindled to a routine. But I owe Marie-Jeanne one real debt of gratitude: she taught me to play poker. As for the major choices in life—whether to belong to the left or the right, to prepare for war or ignore the threat of it, to be an unsociable individualist or a model citizen; how to choose between utility and art, words and action, religion and opportunism—I thought of such things only intermittently. Perhaps, without admitting it to myself, I was following your example. I tended to change my mind easily; my personality revealed itself through fits of enthusiasm or revulsion rather than in any systematic development. I dimly perceived myself as impulsive rather than intelligent, sensitive rather than solid. Haunted by my own incitements to self-fulfillment but unable to face up to them boldly, I preferred to let my puny, short-term fate rest on whether an ace of clubs or a nine of diamonds turned up on some grimy card-table.

For a while your friendship with Madame Flot survived my breaking off with her daughter. It took me some time to understand your attitude. Your husband preferred his work to you, and put up a rigorous defense to protect himself from your moods. Your son disappointed you with his undemonstrative ways and unpredictable behavior. Your usual friends irritated you with the endless moaning and groaning that was consuming the last remains of their youth. The only thing left to you was to explore the mystery of somebody new. But as the enigma of Madame Flot was not very obscure, she lasted you only six months. The last stage of your friendship was marked by the exchange of biscuits, lipsticks, and anti-wrinkle creams. After that you were free to indulge in the old, familiar soul-warming processes again: you could Russianize yourself once more to your heart's content, and rush quavering with excitement to Madame Meltz's.

One morning when I was at a lecture you got the key to my studio at the Cité Universitaire from the concierge and put up some rather garish mauve drapes. You replaced my makeshift bedding with fine linen sheets, and left me a vase of roses. Just half a dozen—nothing ostentatious. I also discovered enough toilet and shaving soap to last me a year, a bottle of vitamin pills, and, on my pillow, an envelope containing a couple of hundred-franc notes and inscribed with the words, "I wish you every happiness, my boy." All these fine gestures meant that my sins were forgiven and my leaving Marie-Jeanne not objected to. There was also a suggestion that further conquests would be looked upon kindly: only real attachments upset everybody. I puzzled over your magnanimity. I aspired to knowledge and literature, even to politics perhaps, and certainly to fame; but happiness was a passive and ridiculous state which had no place in my projects. But a couple of days later you were yourself again, and resumed hostilities with zest.

"The one thing I can't forgive you for is admiring Machiavelli," you said. "He was a very bad man."

"Without passion," I replied, "no one could ever change anything."

Berlin, October 1945

"Dear Mother and Father,

I've worn three different uniforms since May 10th 1940, and I don't think my war has been any more cowardly or any less stupid than anyone else's. I've seldom had any choice: the most I ever did was insist that first the Americans and then the English should send me to special courses, where I acquired various kinds of technical knowledge and the ability to judge men from a staff point of view. My medals mean nothing: I just happened to be in the right place at the right time—anyone else would have done the same thing. But I do admit that some of the responsibilities I've been charged with, in London and Versailles and finally in Berlin, have led me to engage in some salutary self-examination. I never completed my studies, and my first impulse was to come and join you in New York and go back to school. But I've given up that idea for the time being: because of the sudden withdrawal of the armies there are a lot of vacant posts here, and those who are on the spot will be at an advantage. What we have to do is govern Germany and teach it democracy. I'm being offered good money and a job I don't dislike as liaison officer between the four occupying powers. I'll be working on the Control Commission under a friend of mine, and my main task will be to coordinate the efforts of the various Allies—including Czechoslovakia, Denmark, South Africa, Brazil, and so on—to protect their own interests. Together with other technical officers, I'll be supervising the dismantling of war factories and, most important of all, the repatriation of millions of displaced persons.

"The war shunted me about almost at random. I lost it once, at the outset, with the Belgians, then again with the French in the fatal fortnight. You know what the years 1941 and 1942 were like: what undermined me, even more than the uncertainty, was the impossibility of deciding things for myself. And victory shoved me around no less than defeat had done: what was the difference, apart from the pleasure of watching the thin red line of the front inch forward? Yes—though I really did get a thrill from the series of successful Allied offensives, I never, even then, experienced the pleasure of choice. The work I was doing had been imposed on me by others. But I think it's different now. As—in a manner of speaking—one of the victors, I'll have my share in decision-making and the taking of initiatives. And at the age of twenty-six it's none too soon. As for the details, I shall have a house, a car, and a driver at my disposal: what do you think of that! On the practical level, I'll have to have some Russian lessons; I've never really spoken the language properly, except at home with Mother. And I'll also improve my German.

"I'm to be attached to the War Ministry to start with, then to the Ministry of Foreign Affairs, though people working for the Control Commission have special status. I'll be working for four bosses in turn, changing every month. I find it rather amusing that one of the four will be a Russian. I can just see the horror on Mother's face: isn't working for the Bolsheviks a kind of treason? But it's with the Russians that the world is going to be built, and I'm filled with enthusiasm at the thought that the energy I put into the task will be completely lucid now—not blind, as before. And why shouldn't I, at last, after the war, be in a position of relative consequence? The Germans, whom I've never hated even when I was fighting against them, are going to have to rebuild their country. And while the operation must in the first place benefit the victors, who've certainly earned the right to help themselves to anything that's going, the reconstruction must also help the Germans themselves. They've got the wherewithal to learn democracy—their survival depends on their doing so.

"I'm telling you my state of mind without holding anything back. I enclose some photographs to show you the villa I'm living in at Zehlendorf, well away from all the ruins. The trees are beautiful, and the lawn very well maintained. I suppose I could have made a quick trip to New York to see you. Our last meeting was in September 1943, I believe, and then I was just about to leave for Europe, so no one was very cheerful. That was understandable enough: we didn't know what the future held for us. The troopship I crossed on was full to bursting, and we came close to being sunk when the convoy was attacked by enemy submarines. Our arrival in Northern Ireland was one long wail, with serious casualties and damage of all kinds—I'd rather not think about it. And now I have to take the opportunity that presents itself, sign a contract, get started on an interesting job, and make myself indispensable. But in five or six months' time I really shall be able to come and see you.

"It goes without saying that I'd like to know what both of you make of all this. If Father thinks that, instead of becoming once more the European I've never really ceased to be, I ought to come back to the United States and take over his business, I'll change my plans. But frankly I don't think I'm cut out for it. My future is here, amid the rubble awaiting glorious reconstruction. A bit late in the day, I am young at last. And I know what I want—which hasn't happened since I was still at school. I send you all possible love."

I sent this letter off without reading it over: I didn't want to dwell on its implications for you. It meant depriving you of my presence again, and this time because at last I intended to live my own life, in complete freedom. I'd made up my mind, and there was no reason why I should weaken my resolve with second thoughts and irrelevant scruples. As I saw it, I had three alternatives: I could become the kind of dutiful son who gradually replaces his father because that's the natural thing and devoid of any real risk; I could take a blind leap into literature without bothering about realities; or I could play a part in the future of Europe by educating Germany according to sage and proven principles. And I wasn't being bigheaded: I really did have certainties, though they acted as blinders as well

as armor. In the past, when I'd cultivated an open mind, I'd flung it so
wide open that all kinds of foolishness rushed in; I'd become as recep-
tive as a sponge. But now. . . And now you were another person, just like
any other, on whom I must unhesitatingly impose my will.

Ten days later I received an answer to my letter, written, I supposed,
in one of the fits of sincerity that struck me at a distance as disagreeable, if not downright unhealthy. Your handwriting was even more irregular than usual, with broken downstrokes, straggling capitals, and vowels
that were positively obese.

"Darling," it read.

"We are grateful to you for your frankness. Father agrees with you and
doesn't intend to argue about your decisions. But your mother can't prevent her heart from being wrung. What? That terrible war over and me
waiting to see you—doing nothing but wait to see you, for I have no other
happiness in life except thinking of you and clasping you in my arms—
and you can't even make a little effort and come over right away? *I* don't
know if your decisions are the right ones. I don't know anything anymore,
after all we've been through. You absolutely *must* come—come and explain, come and help me think as you do. Do come, I beg, even if it's
only for a week. Then, if you really have to go away again, you can do so
with an easy mind. Oh, I'd dreamed that you'd rent or buy a little house
on Long Island, by the sea, and that you'd stay with us for a while and
help your father get ready for his retirement. He's in good enough health,
of course, but at sixty I imagine he'd be glad to enjoy some of life's more
peaceful pleasures—nothing special, just what he's amply deserved. And
don't you think it might do you good too? Have you emerged from the
war completely unscathed? Of course I don't want to influence you unduly, dear boy. But something in my heart can't help protesting and saying, if God and fate have brought us through safely, surely it's not just to
part us from one another again? *I'*m getting old, too. I embrace you as
only a mother can."

My first impulse was to reject this mixture of supplication and blackmail, whining and trickery. But after a couple of days I realized your point

of view was quite justified, and that I had emotional duties which I'd allowed my martial activities to erode. With some impatience I went through the necessary negotiations and signed the contract that had been dangled in front of me. Then I hastily set up my office, taking on staff without pausing to check on their efficiency. I had to admit *I* wanted to see *you* too. I also wanted to know peace at last, to savor it solemnly, passively and with delight, instead of already steering it toward future battles. The soldier within me was finding it hard to become a civilian again. I dreamed of light blue suits and silk neckties, of French pastries eaten in a garden to the accompaniment of inane but soothing music, with gentlemen playing *pétanque* in the distance and never giving a thought to the fate of the world. Without telling anyone except my official superiors, I took the plane. The stop-over in Paris, amid the general chaos, was noisy and stressful; the Azores seemed full of soothing poetry; Newfoundland evoked solitude, mystery, and frozen lakes.

When I got to New York I felt an irresistible need to immerse myself once more in that fascinating and beloved city, where there was nothing to remind me of contemporary woes: it seemed quite untouched by the war. Instead of telephoning you right away I walked all the way—six or seven kilometers—from the Bowery to Central Park: through Broadway with its trashcans, past all the city's soft and steaming asphalt, its brightly colored automobiles—vermouth, Pernod, cassis—its faceless madmen, its glass-fronted banks like waiting rooms for travelers going nowhere, its gray churches where gentlemen in a hurry perch on eighteenth-century tombstones to read share prices in swarthy yellow newspapers, its skyscrapers imitating mosques and Turkish baths, its snatches of conversation where echoes of Sicily and chants reminiscent of Lithuanian ghettoes are punctuated with gestures symbolizing the vigor and hope of trade, its sidewalk auctions ("Bankruptcy sale! Twenty-four shirts for the price of one!"), its neon tubes noisier at three in the morning than an army of woodlice, its sausages strewn crushed and groaning over the street, its down-and-outs whom cops take mildly by the scruff of the neck and toss like sacks of potatoes onto the road, its millionaires with shirts depicting naval battles in ten episodes, its ladies' hats trimmed with gardens full of cherries, its ice-creams shaped like Bavarian castles, its accents sharp as the razors used to trim poodles or soft as the chewing gum trapping a pedestrian by the foot in front of a bus just as the lights turn green, its Blacks with foie gras lips and dancing tread, its little girls ordering their mothers around, its clouds whizzing by at sixty miles an hour to be at the office on time, its sky as sudden as a store's steel shutter rattling down at the end of the day, its elegant bridges leading to a God who asks an entrance fee of three dollars and twenty-five cents to enter the Other World, its river where ferocious gulls cut across the blue and white rays emitted by thousand-volt posters.

I checked into the Hotel Astor, right on Times Square. I loved watching the bustle of the crowd. It struck me as at once more mixed and freer than in Europe, especially as to dress and the refreshing vulgarity of language that aims straight at the target: food, work, pay, sleep. I merged contentedly into a humanity that was either sleepwalking or conscious of its own limitations—I didn't care which, for I now felt a vast sympathy for the whole species, whereas in Europe I had to choose, defending some and anathematizing the others. I stuffed myself with hamburgers and pastrami sandwiches. I bought myself some clothes: they might be loose and garish but they were much more comfortable than my uniforms. I went and admired some fabulous buildings, pink and turquoise, which more than made up to me for the scorched ruins of Berlin and the Rhineland. I visited Harlem and went to the Savoy to listen to Duke Ellington, cleaving through the music as agile and haughty as a tiger. I heard Pee Wee Russell playing at Jimmy Ryan's, hissing like a snake or a jungle creeper growing before your eyes. I went to the Café Society Downtown and applauded Fats Waller, who had teeth like a keyboard and plump fingers moving effortlessly over a keyboard like magnificent teeth. One evening when I'd had quite a lot to drink I spent a long time caressing a mulatto girl in her apartment on 133rd Street: she had mauve-tinted skin and fuzzy eyes. Amid the sweat, the orgasm, and the ecstasy, I waged my own war on racism. Next morning my mind called for more familiar food, and I went to have another look at *Guernica* in the Museum of Modern Art. But all I felt was nervous hostility. A few meters farther on, though, the Douanier Rousseau's *Bohémienne endormie, Sleeping Gypsy Woman,* chimed with a poetic excitement that was slowly rising inside me.

And now, sated with pleasing sights and soothing sensations, I was ready to confront you. You greeted me with an eagerness I was too overwhelmed to analyze; I shared your feelings, and even Father entered into the spirit of the occasion for once. You kept letting out exclamations of all kinds to express your joy and prolong the blissful moment. Superlative followed superlative; your determination was contagious. A kind of well-being pervaded the whole apartment, hovering over the divan, the tables and chairs, the lamps, the carpet, and the pictures. There were anemones and petits-fours dotted about the place, gold ribbons and other frills and flounces, as if, two decades late, we were celebrating the birthday of a little boy idealized by absence. We exchanged innumerable anecdotes, not even trying to make them add up. You asked whether the war hadn't left me with secret wounds, with sicknesses or even thoughts that needed a long rest to put them right. Not at all, I assured you: I was no longer a prickly youth pecking at fate like a pigeon that wasn't hungry.

You talked warmly to me about America. You said you weren't living in exile anymore. You'd found friends who more than replaced those you'd left behind in Europe, a continent that went on bleeding and punishing itself and making itself miserable forever. While I was away you'd been taking English lessons, and had even made it a point of honor to improve your French. Your wrinkles were deeper now; you were an old lady. Father didn't say much, but I sensed he was ready now, as he would never have been a few years before, to talk to me man to man. Business wasn't doing too well, but did people like you two need any other riches than reasonably good health? You didn't ask me too many questions. Dinner consisted of some of my favorite dishes: vegetable soup with tarragon, eggplant smoked to resemble caviar, pork brawn seasoned with garlic, and cranberries stewed without sugar. Afterward you measured my waist and saw I hadn't put on weight. Then you undid three or four packages containing shirts either too brown or too yellow, socks that were too thick, and neckties I considered to be in dubious taste. But my gratitude concealed my reservations. I thanked you effusively, and embraced you with an enthusiasm that became genuine sooner than I could have wished.

I was really pleased we'd been able to establish ourselves on such a warm and ordinary footing, and for at least three or four days didn't feel I had to escape. I even went so far as to tell you about my campaigns, only eliminating the harshest episodes so as to leave you with the illusion that for months and months I'd progressed smoothly from one victory to another. When you showed me some of my letters, mutilated by the British or American censors, I was easily able to reassure you: I must, I said, have been waxing too lyrical over the places I was writing from, and might have given away the location of my unit in England, Normandy, Germany, or wherever. You gave me a long look, as if to let me know you weren't taken in by my idyllic explanations. But so what? We were all alive still, and what should be forgotten would be duly consigned to oblivion. You were renouncing once and for all a large part of my past, and I no longer felt the need to reconstruct it for you. We were both agreeing to do without something that had anyway become a fiction.

Father took little or no part in these conversations. The age difference between him and me seemed smaller now; in ten or fifteen years' time, when he was a venerable old man, there'd be real affinities between us, greater even than the ones you sought to establish between me and yourself. I didn't have to make any effort: your happiness was so immense and unreserved. Still, we couldn't avoid speaking of the future. Father loved his work: buying and selling postage stamps by correspondence had become second nature to him, at once a way of making a living and a tranquil passion from which it would be unkind to distract him. I didn't need to worry about him; I had five or six years of freedom in front of me, and after that God would decide our fate. But this way of looking at things was only a stay of execution, and your allusion to some vague and cloying deity irked me. But I didn't make any objection, because I wanted to be beyond reproach. And I might as well go along with your idealized image of myself—it was only for a few days. I claim no credit for this: I was being regaled with mother love in all its forms. When I left for Berlin again, I promised to come back as soon as possible: I'd be able to

39

afford it now, and the time it took to fly across the Atlantic was getting shorter every year. I was surprised to be let off so lightly; I'd expected to be told how much happier and safer I'd be in the United States.

Back in Berlin, as I threw myself into my work, an ambiguous combination of diplomacy and intrigue well suited to my character just then, I made up my mind I wouldn't keep my promise. And I didn't go back to New York until 1949. No, the coming of peace definitely didn't mean you were going to have me with you again.

Normandy, June 1944

The Germans, who were four or five kilometers away, are back again behind the hill. The shells and mortars make holes in the blue of the sky, producing a little thud that I can feel right down to the pit of my stomach. What the colonel has just said leaves me simultaneously amazed and indifferent.

"Burn all the papers!" he shouted.

Should I stop and think? I check that my gun's in working order. Everything is absurd, from the smooth sea spitting out lumps of dirty foam to the tent in which the advance echelon of Supreme Allied HQ has set up its mobile bureaucracy. I'm a pencil-pusher who's forgotten the soldier somewhere inside him. Planning the offensive in the basement of a London department store was tantamount to opting out of the war altogether; army divisions became no more than little flags you moved about on a map, like saucepans hanging up on a wall. The firing is getting closer. I don't mind the smell of burning—there's a perverse pleasure in destroying secret documents whose main contents you know by heart. Thirty meters away, behind a dune too small to be of much use, reinforcements emerge from a landing craft. What annoys me is the disorder. Captain Beatty, whose Oxford vocabulary is usually so elegant and refined, comes out with horrible expressions like: "Get flat on your faces, fuck you! That's an order!"

Atherton, on the other hand, is very cheerful: "No need to polish our boots anymore! In all the sand and blood—and I trust there'll be *buckets* of blood!—who's going to tell the difference?"

Cressaty strokes his mustache, perspires, and murmurs: "All those card-indexes on the coastal defenses, all those photos of pill-boxes—they were sweetly pretty! But now we're seeing the real thing!"

We've been promised we're going to be relieved in an hour or two, but we haven't been given any details. Could anything be more awful than this peaceful chaos, this beach strewn with bits of wood and steel and concrete, and scraps of uniform from which an arm may protrude, a morsel of flesh turned blue by the salt of the sea? My last file goes up in flames.

"Don't pull such a face!" says Atherton. "They've got copies of it in London."

"Yes—we're going to cop it, but others will go on where we left off."

"Not a bit of it! Our job's not needed anymore. In war, one necessity is followed by another."

I can't make it out. Why did our detachment have to follow so close behind the first waves of the landing? Of course, it's a great honor to be on the Normandy beaches on the evening of June 8th! Did some minister in London or Washington want to prove GHQ took the same risks as the rank and file? If so they were making a mistake. They're always making mistakes. I'm short of breath and my lungs hurt, as if they were too big for this damp, cramped, mean sea air. But I'm quite calm. Or am I? All my ledgers and cards, the whole compendium of my knowledge of German fortifications along the Normandy coast—it had become my specialty!—has gone up in smoke! I'm no longer indispensable; I'm only a little second lieutenant who did a worthy job that nobody needs anymore, and now I'm just waiting on a beach to be evacuated. I might as well bury myself here and have done with it: a few spadefuls of sand would do it. All around me the madness is getting worse, with its mixture of truncated visions and stupid magnifications: a gull suddenly becomes an envoy from some distant power, and a piece of leather between two machine-guns conjures up a dead comrade, dead perhaps in some other war long ago, a thousand miles away? Cressaty turns into a youthful marquis from

Limoges, offering two corseted dowagers cups of coffee as strong as that made by the pirates between Formosa and the Kuril Islands in the seventeenth century. I start hating the color of khaki and feeling fond of the blue of the 1914 war: I believe an uncle of mine was killed on the Chemin des Dames. My gullet burns because my indigestible and horribly concentrated K-ration makes me belch. The sky is as low as a Stuka in 1940: yes, even the sky is an enemy, going to bear down and exterminate us one by one. Is my M1 an adequate weapon? Or is it rather, as the hackneyed image has it, the only friend I have at this tense moment, my faithful hound, and of course at the same time my confidant, to whom I shall relate the history of France, always supposing France still exists, under the hail of bullets. Ouch! In this respite, between panic and resignation, my head becomes an attic crammed with snatches of memory and discarded junk fit only for the flea market.

But I get a grip on myself. Captain Beatty inspects the ashes, then checks a document certifying that all the secret and confidential reports have been destroyed by fire after having been duly soaked in gasoline. We're correctly dressed, but the captain suggests that as our rescuers are late and the German advance is experiencing some temporary difficulty, we should, while remaining on the alert, take time off to shave. A fresh-feeling face, a chin that doesn't itch, and a blob of soap on the cheeks is enough to restore a man's morale, at least for ten or twenty minutes. Atherton shrugs, Cressaty smiles disdainfully: since when has a former Lincolnshire schoolteacher, even if he *is* an officer, had the nerve to give advice to a gentleman, who on his own estate wouldn't even let the fellow train his thoroughbreds?

"There are two fighting units, one a hundred and the other a hundred and fifty meters away from us," says Captain Beatty. "You're here to defend yourselves, not to attack. And those are our orders, even if you are in the army. The reinforcements will come along the road, from the right. Don't look at the sea—the main body of the troops is farther away, toward Carentan and Ouistreham."

Do I need to explain? Explanations strike me as vague, incomplete, unconvincing. Why doesn't that semblance of a sand-dune make an ef-

fort and turn into a real one, with a definite outline? Why have the sand
and the pebbles merged into a kind of enormous, soggy soup in which
water and earth are indistinguishable? For that matter, you can't tell the
earth from the sky either, now: the clear blue of ten minutes ago has
turned murky. Is war an inextricable mix-up of all the elements? I can't
feel myself—I might be made of stone or bark. I'm in the grip of a fear
that isn't a real fear yet, but the dread of a fear still to come, a fear that's
almost over the moment I think of it. There are thirty or forty of us, neither in a group nor dispersed: too close together for an artillery barrage
to miss us; too far apart, in case of attack, to offer effective resistance
and survive for a quarter of an hour. My pride as an aware and enlight-
ened fighter is humbled. For over a year I've been trying to make myself
useful in a job which called for knowledge, research, and a certain amount
of thought. Modestly but with jubilation, I've been doing all I could to
prepare for this second front, and I consider *that* to be my business. So
why have I been sent here like this to be hunted down and slaughtered
like a rat, like the mere cannon-fodder I never wanted to be? But even
in Supreme HQ overweening pride must be brought down, and minds too
sure of themselves be punished.

"What do you think, Atherton?" I ask. "Is it all due to a conspiracy,
or only to sheer incompetence?"

"Just one more screw-up. But a special one—one that'll help us win
the war."

"But supposing we lost?"

"Then it would only be an ordinary screw-up."

"What on earth are we doing here, for God's sake?"

"We'll ask Cressaty. Hey, Cressaty, what about a game of poker?"

"You're crazy! When the slugs might start flying at any moment?
Haven't you ever heard of a court-martial?"

"Beatty's too busy being a leader and wetting his pants to come bothering us."

"You never know. It's a comfort to throw your weight around when
you're in a ridiculous situation."

"Have you got the cards?"

"No."

"You're so good and obedient you've burned everything, including the queen of hearts. It'd be funny to stop one and let out your last gasp just as you were saying 'I pass'!"

"You're mixing up poker and bridge."

"Gentlemen, I'm mixing up life and death, which is much more to the point. If a Jerry goes for me I'll show him a hand, tell him to pick a card, and guess what it is: the seven of diamonds. 'Choose your weapon!' 'A joker, sir!'"

There's a violent burst of gunfire fifty meters away. I throw myself face-down on the ground, clutching my M1 against me. Some shells come down, but I don't know how near they fell, and can only guess in what direction. Some cries are borne on the wind, unless it's just the sea. What are the elements conspiring in? I suddenly start to hate the foam, the grasses, the pools of water. Sitting up for a moment, I see a tent on fire. I slither between two hummocks, unsure whether I'm doing so in search of shelter or so as not to be able to see what now seems bound to happen at any moment: the Germans penetrating our weak line of defense and suddenly appearing before us. Where's Beatty? More shells, dotting the landscape with little fountains whose colors range between gray and dark blue, yellow and dirty red. I get down on the ground. I feel a strange hatred toward this wet sand: it's like my own flesh, it yields to my every wish, it protects me, it's obedient, and yet I'd like to tear it off like a skin that prevents me from being myself. In my fear, the only thing for me to do is philosophize, to think about how things and people are transmogrified. I must make up stories, intoxicate myself with images, summon up all my powers of fantasy and abstraction. I must forget who I am, and where, change into another mind and body, transport myself into another place, far away and ever-changing. I must convince myself my fate has nothing to do with myself.

While I am marveling at these vehement resolutions, the detonations seem to be wandering about at random, sometimes quite near, sometimes impossible to locate—hesitant, punctuated every so often with a kind of dialogue between the guns. Still clinging to my M1 as closely as if it were part of my own bone structure, I try to ignore an increasingly unpleasant

45

feeling that's spreading all over me, at once as light as if it changed into a bird every time I breathed, and as heavy as if it were taking on in advance the weight of the lead and the shrapnel now falling nearby. I involuntarily catalog all my muscles and glands, sure in my growing terror they won't be functioning after a few minutes; soon they'll explode, or else they'd rebel and abandon me, unworthy wretch that I am. It's my shoulders I feel escaping first. Yes, my collarbones are trying to break out of that mass of flesh and move about in the air like musical instruments. What a feeble platitude, what a poor literary reminiscence applied to life and death and—who knows?—perhaps survival! Why, on the excuse that a burst of machine-gun fire has just passed within two or three meters of me, are my kneecaps suddenly softening into sponges? If I touched them I'm sure they'd come away in my hands. And my ankles and toes—is it their fault I seem not to have any? But maybe they're still there, only swollen and mauve, monstrous and unable to move. If I had the nerve I'd jab the bastards with my knife to make them get on with their work again. I wonder if my elbows are still working? They must be full of reinforced concrete this afternoon, to pin me down so heavily as I lie hunched up on the ground.

I go on with my catalog. To avoid being obsessed with death you have to be ingenious, regard your body as a maze of caves and miniature landscapes where you deliberately reduce yourself to the size of a germ or an insect which has magically become your own double, and wander about from one surprise to another. I'm a Lilliputian for whom Gulliver is his own anatomy multiplied by a hundred. I have an ego, a counter-ego, and a non-ego. What a relief, to take refuge in the abstract, in the towering foolishness of philosophical concepts which deny my own weight and form! I'm someone I could never otherwise be—a thousand copies of him! I crucify myself with notions I know are ephemeral: they help me to fight against time, to defend this bag of bones wrapped up in their punctured sheath. My forehead has turned into a metronome: from left to right, right to left, it beats out a rhythm telling me that before it has oscillated back and forth fifty, no, forty-nine, no, forty-eight times, my skull will have exploded. I think about Paul Valéry's grenade. That's right, come to the rescue, my favorite authors, and keep me going! With your help I can hang on a few seconds longer. That's right, take up your positions around me, cover my retreat as far as the waves of the sea. First you, Arthur Rimbaud—cuddle up against my stomach, I expect you like doing that, you swine! And you, Baudelaire—looking for my flask, are you? It's all one to you that it's rusty, but you won't enjoy any alcoholic thrill from it, you and your beautiful gaunt face, unless you get me out of here. There's old Hugo, with his flowing white beard—I wasn't expecting him. Yes, dear maestro, do take over command—not just of this sector, that wouldn't be worthy of you: Field-Marshals Terry and Eisenhower, General Bradley and that old fox Montgomery would all be delighted to hand over to you. What the devil are you doing here, Ronsard? Aren't your laurels enough for you? Do you need medals, too, to tell women how much faster than you they grow old? Stand to attention, Guillaume Apollinaire! You at least, as an old gunner, are familiar with this business, and no doubt you think that you, with your poor bandaged skull, have more horrors in your head than I have in mine? The only way I'm better than you is that *I* don't write soppy letters to Lou. And you, my goateed Péguy, perhaps you think I'm not taking this very seriously? Would you like me to hurl myself into the fray full of hope and revenge and with a tricolor up my backside? My dear Lamartine, we're all up the creek on the same lake. Sorry about the dubious joke, but there's no way you're going to get elegance and fine words from someone with a rhinoceros prowling around in his guts. When you're in the grip of a funk as huge and heavy and insufferable as mine, you have a right to do anything, including talking a lot of bullshit to relieve your feelings until you can have a real crap. My apologies for such outrageous language, Mallarmé—you need complication and elaboration and pluperfect subjunctives to express yourself; you can't speak without torturing those dandyish, chesty-little-schoolmasterish syllables of yours.

Something's up. Atherton's clutching his chest a little way off. I can see him only through a tangle of incomplete shapes. If he's wounded, shouldn't I crawl over to him? I try to concentrate; feel my heart with both hands. Is *my* chest still all right? Then I feel my stomach: fear has made a breakthrough there too, and is now laying into my entrails. I'm going to have to make an effort to stop them from dissolving into shit, showing me I'm not a hero but just like anyone else. Semi-intellectual, peasant, bourgeois, or just nothing at all. Or a young man of good family. All the same!

There's a lull, and the setting sun brings me a vague kind of relief. Do I still need to summon up my memories, my legendary characters, my imaginary lives? But would it be wise to remain alone, with this body of mine being gripped by panic as by a giant crab? Never say die—a procession of women's faces files past as if to cheer me up. I wonder what became of you, Cécile Dewaet, with your too-long teeth, your too-nervous hands, your too-greedy lips: you were the first to teach me what pleasure is, in a bathing hut on the beach at Mariakerke. Was it in 1933 or 1934? I wonder how many wrinkles have gathered on your brow, my idol of before the war, of before all wars, for I take pleasure in projecting your image on the sky over Crécy, on the hell of Austerlitz, the ice floes of the Beresina and the lofty galleys of Pharsala. And of course you too, Jacqueline Kolb, can enter my little fantasmagoria—it doesn't commit you to anything. You consoled me during the the summer of 1940 for being a vanquished youth in search of his shadow and his conscience, wounded in his self-esteem and ready, if he only knew it, to enjoy the pleasures of the flesh while Europe crumbled. I remember you talking to me about your native Alsace and the storks that didn't come back anymore; and you showed me other birds too, your breasts like nestlings cheeping for attention. We played at being ten years younger and thinking France was well lost for love. We went and picked blueberries on Aigounal Mountain, and came back drunk with kisses as mauve as the fruit itself. Oh, so many eyes, so many smiles crowd in on me! If I could still remember your names you'd be less dear to me, my little fiancées for a day! Should I line you up between me and the shells so that as if by magic, by a graceful turn of the elbow, you could ward them off? You to begin with, Valentine, the first woman in my life who was younger than I, only sixteen, with your chin and lips not yet fully formed—come over here in the reddening sunlight and tell me how summer follows spring, and serious words succeed light ones. I can't remember now if I met some of you in my arms or merely on the screen, black and white and in two dimensions, though tall as church porches. There's Florelle with her pinched nostrils; Marcelle Chantal, whose armpits suggested one might have comfortable vacations there; Simone Simon, like an eel that gets under your skin and innocently asks if it's not hurting too much; Mireille Balin, volcanic behind the pasteboard bar in a last-chance South American saloon built in the studios at Boulogne-Billancourt; and Marta Eggerth, singing so piercingly that the aluminum stars rain down in pieces from the ceiling! And then there somehow appears a creature part vampire, part goddess, for whom I used to risk damnation there in my six-francs-fifty seat: not wholly Pola Negri, sighing like a lioness, nor exactly Carole Lombard seductive behind her fringe, nor entirely Marlene Dietrich, for whom men offered up their lives and undertook to spy for any country under the sun!

In the midst of this soothing digression, voices approach. How many hours have I been lying curled up like this? Perhaps two or three minutes at most. I'm going to stand up, give my uniform a brush down, straighten my shirt, join Cressaty and Atherton (if he's not on a stretcher somewhere), and put myself at the disposal of the present again. But first I close my eyes: I must make one last expedition, however brief, into my memory. I accord you the place of honor, Mother, and drive out the other incumbents, real or imaginary. You appear to me superimposed upon yourself, at once multiplied and dissolved into your infinite variations. You keep changing all the time in order to become yourself, which nothing can alter anymore. But are you the sum total of all your own metamorphoses, or do you remain unfinished, taking on several forms, each one obsessively precise and at the same time diaphanous, as if you deliberately wanted to disappear, the better to reappear in some corner of the memory which I've neglected? No time or tense pins you down. At one moment you're in Brussels, amid your cushions and fragile furniture, with a book open on your lap, telling me about the walks you went for by the river Preobarjenskaya in your childhood, when the people of Odessa used to stop and gossip and then go and eat cakes in Fanconi's, either standing at the counter or sitting at little round mahogany tables. Or else you're at Knokke-sur-Mer in your forties, still very pretty though perhaps rather plump, and you're telling me to be careful of the waves, which are very tall that day: I shouldn't stay in longer than five or six minutes because the temperature of the water is only sixty degrees, that's seventeen Centigrade. You're talking to your friends Rosa Rom and Madame Meltz, and you turn to look as a mustachioed pianist from Romania goes by. He plays in the afternoon on the terrace outside the Memling Hotel: a horrible shapeless racket like the sound of someone breaking open a safe, but, my God, how all the ladies would like to enjoy his caresses! Finally I see you outside the Frick Collection in New York, in rather poor health and suffering from chronic melancholy, apart from the occasional spasm of cheerfulness. You have too much spare time, you indulge in too many daydreams, elaborate conjectures in which you lose sight of reality. But rather late in the day you've discovered painting, and you feverishly store up scraps of knowledge about Veronese, Toulouse-Lautrec, Braque, Brueghel, Delacroix, and Velázquez, all mixed up any old way. Your prejudiced comments make me roar with laughter.

"I don't like Monet—he makes me feel he's trying to drown me," you say.

I see you, too, at Long Beach, on the rotting planks of the promenade: you can't help shedding tears of joy because you've just had a letter from me, somewhere at the front, in Europe. It's only a note, and doesn't give any details. But I'm alive, and that's wonderful! But then your face clouds over: my letter was written ten days ago.

"The Canadians! The Canadians!" yells Cressaty.

I crawl out of my hole. Death is for another day.

"No need to get excited," orders Captain Beatty.

We're not going to look ridiculous after all. We knew all along the Canadians would get us out of this ambush, because here, just as at the rear, every detail of everything that happens is the product of endless thought, of a minutely prepared strategy. Later on in the darkness we'll discuss the matter. We know high command can perform magic as well as miracles, so they'll see to it that the half-ton of documents—indispensable to the conduct of the war—which we burned earlier, rises again phoenix-like from the ashes.

"The road to Granville is open," says Atherton painfully, holding a rag to his bleeding lung.

Paris, May 1976

The day before yesterday, in your room in the Hôtel d'Argenson, just when my mistrust was starting to abate, you accused me of plotting against you. I was holding you prisoner in a city where there was nothing to console you in your sorrow. You were miles away from your friends; I'd dragged you away from them. My wife Maria was my accomplice in the plot to isolate you, to deprive you of your independence, to let you wither away while pretending to dance attendance on you. But you didn't disconcert me for long. I told you quite calmly you were talking nonsense and were quite free to move if you wished. At first you didn't answer, then you said I was very clever: a person could talk to me for a quarter of an hour and feel reassured, but after a while they'd come to their senses and see they'd been taken for a ride. You looked out through the window at the plane trees in the boulevard Haussmann. You sighed: Father would never see that wonderful sight again. Two little tears trickled quietly down your cheeks: to have him die, burned alive, at the age of eighty-eight! What an awful punishment for you! I told you again you had nothing to reproach yourself with: one can't go on lamenting one's fate forever, and if one tries to do so it becomes an obsession. Then all at once your mood changed, just as wild beasts tearing one another to pieces in a film will suddenly, for no apparent reason, let go of their prey and amble off into the bush. You said I was the only person in the world who gave you any reason to go on living. No matter how one grows used to such about-faces and inconsistencies, they always come as a shock and take one aback. I merely smiled knowingly; I realized you were upset, and hoped that if I said nothing it would give you pause too. For a moment my suspicions returned and I had a feeling you were confusing me with my father. As far as the past was concerned we were quite separate in your mind, but in the present, in everyday life, in little questions of money, shopping, clothes, and transportation the distinction wasn't so clear; sometimes it disappeared altogether. You went on in a kind of listless anger. For such self-control as I possessed you felt an unspoken hatred interspersed with moments of openly expressed affection, for you were ashamed of your own impulses, which you could no longer control. You repeated that I was a thief and a traitor. I found it hard not to flare up in return: you must have seen from my clenched jaw how infuriated I was. I just caught up your hand, planted on it the conventional kiss, and left without another word.

Our meeting yesterday, on the other hand, went off quietly: any tenseness in the atmosphere was neutralized because we were both being so careful. I brought some white carnations with me—only half a dozen, I explained, because I didn't think they were nice enough and hadn't had time to find any better ones. You like to be courted, even if you don't like admitting it. You heaved great sighs of satisfaction, and went into ecstasies when I put the flowers by the mirror over the fireplace—looked at from your bed they were doubled by their own reflection. We talked about all the little things that make up your world, limited now to less than twenty square meters. The pigeons had come and eaten the fruit you'd left for them on the balcony. You weren't going back to the bistro in the place Saint-Augustin anymore, despite the excellent coffee they served there; they'd given you some fish that was very dubious. The manager of the hotel is very nice: she told you she was having a successful love affair with the picture framer in the boulevard Haussmann, but unfortunately he's married and his wife gives him a hard time so they have to meet in secret. Still, you said, it's easy enough in a hotel—the tourists are always out during the day at the Louvre or the Eiffel Tower, and a bed's a bed. . . You asked me to go to the oculist's with you next week: the drops he'd prescribed didn't seem to be having much effect and you couldn't read more than twenty pages without having to rest your eyes. As if answering yourself, you added that most people are practically blind at your age: but it wasn't your sight *you* suffered from most. You'd had quite a good night's sleep, in spite of a nightmare in which, as so often, Father appeared to you. He was reciting a poem by Rilke in an unfamiliar landscape where there were willow trees, a stream and rocks, and some young men on a hill, applauding; but they weren't applauding Father, which was strange. They had their backs turned to him, and seemed to be waiting for the moon to rise. You even gave a timid little laugh—but then you went on: soon after that, Father didn't have a head anymore, and you knew that this image, so close to the truth, was going to haunt you for weeks. Then you suddenly changed the subject. What was the use of half the clothes you kept in your wardrobe and never wore? There was a slightly moth-eaten fur coat you'd be quite willing to sell if you could find a buyer. Unless you simply gave it away—but to whom? The world was full of ingratitude and people in too much of a hurry. I said I was rather worried about all the medicines on your bedside table: there were nearly a dozen different kinds in various forms—pills, bottles, and so on. I was afraid you might get them mixed up. You said if you were to die that way it would simply be because fate had decreed it. And anyway it wouldn't make any difference to anyone, me included, if you did die. Before I had time to think what to say—that you'd soon be so much better you'd be going out dancing, or words to that effect—you had yet another change of mood. You said you were tired, and people shouldn't take any notice of what you said; you knew better than anyone that you were getting senile, though there wasn't much wrong with your head yet. You drew a lengthy comparison between the cane I bought you two or three months ago and the one with a tortoiseshell knob that used to belong to my father—you brought it over with you from America. You venerated Father's cane and were obscurely attached to it, but things were only things, and one had to be able to dispense with them: so you opted for the other cane, crude and rustic though it was. I told you your imitation leather shopping bag was so worn out I'd throw it away if I were you. You faintly protested—you like it better than the others because it's a few ounces lighter. We were trivial, commonplace, matter-of-fact, without malice. But you guessed that this sort of conversation bored me. You began to talk about the news: you'd looked through *Le Figaro, Paris-Match,* and *Marie-Claire.* I told you I hardly ever saw them, which brought me to the question, Would you like a television set? So, you rebuked me, I thought you needed films all day long! What did I take you for? You mentioned vacations and admitted you had difficulty getting around on your own, though there are servants everywhere who'll make themselves useful in return for a tip. You were hesitating between Vittel, which you'd liked last year, and Trouville, which lots of people had recommended. Then came another series of sighs: before the war my father had sent you to stay in Vichy, Karlsbad, and Mondorf. Then back to current events: Did I think Mao was really a great man? You wanted to listen to me for a while, to be taken out of yourself. So I gave you a little lecture lasting a quarter of an hour, making it as easy as possible. For example, I had to clear up certain episodes of contemporary history which you had forgotten. You hated both Khrushchev and Brezhnev, but mixed up their respective doings. You said Nixon was clever and knew how to deal with the Russians. You thought Chiang Kai-shek was a Japanese general. But my explanations distracted you and you forgot your ailments. Then suddenly you begged me to carry a bottle of coramine on me day and night: there was nothing to beat it for sudden heart troubles—if the attack wasn't very serious you recovered in two or three minutes. You told me how fond you were of Gandhi, and I didn't like to remind you he'd been assassinated more than twenty years ago. You told me how much you admired de Gaulle, and you could tell from my sardonic expression that you'd said something wrong. You thought for a bit, then burst out:

"You think I'm crazy—you like to think that! I know very well he's dead, but that doesn't mean he isn't always with us!"

You rhapsodized about Gogol, whom you were re-reading, but told me you couldn't stand Gorky's autobiography, which was lying on the table: nothing but a boor, that fellow. When I left you I was less exasperated than usual.

It's Saturday, the day we go out to lunch together. I take my time, and tell myself at least I'll be doing a good deed. But I manage to seem natural, affable and unpreoccupied, and you're taken in because you want to be; you're an expert at the difference between instinctive duty and duty self-imposed. You make yourself believe my shows of feeling are natural: the less you doubt them, the more likely they are to become sincere. I hold out a box of chocolates: Côte de France are the brand you like best—one of the few genuine pleasures in your narrow existence. You're wearing your blue and mauve dress, my favorite, and your diamond ring, which is massive and too heavy. A wig that's neither brown nor gray more or less matches your skin and makes you look all dressed up. As does the lipstick that seeps into the wrinkles above and below your mouth. You slip your glasses into your coat pocket and make sure your stockings aren't sagging too badly around your now fearfully thin legs. You take my arm and cling to your stick. You can't prevent your own arm from trembling as if it were about to fall off. I wonder about your weight. About ninety pounds? Perhaps even less.

You leave me to double-lock the door: you might leave the key behind if you did it yourself. As we get out of the elevator you smile at the porter and give him a franc; when one gets to be as frail as you are it pays to be nice to people—if you ever had a fall in the lobby you'd need to be able to count on that young fellow to remember what a charming old lady you are and call an ambulance. Taking very small steps we negotiate the intersection of the boulevard Haussmann and the rue de Miromesnil, and go down the latter as far as the rue La Boétie. You say in a cracked voice that the local baker must be crazy, going to all that trouble to make loaves in the shape of bicycles and clowns. You inform me that the hairdresser next door closes up shop between four and five in the afternoon, thus losing a lot of customers; she must have a boyfriend who's free just then. Such is life. Life is gradually departing from you; you have heart spasms more and more often, your arms and legs move very slowly, and when you're out for a walk you have to rest every hundred yards or so. There's a notice posted up in a bank: "8% interest free of tax." You ask me what it means. I answer rather testily that you ought to have learned more about

55

the practical side of life when you were young. Signing a check is a great drama for you because you imagine everyone's trying to rob you—the bank itself, and the person who's going to cash the check for you: me. You stand still and threaten me—if I intend to go on like this you'll go home to bed and never come out to lunch with me again. I give you a little dig in the ribs: if only you really would let me out of that unbearable tête-à-tête! But we walk on, and all of a sudden you say smoothly, almost sweetly, that my father was really responsible for your ignorance: it only went to show how saintly he was—he wanted to spare you any kind of anxiety. Am I going to retort yet again that to deify a dead man whom one loved in a very lukewarm way when he was alive is a form of self-justification? If you felt any remorse you took care to bury it under posthumous adoration.

After a brief pause outside a dairy you've gotten your breath back. You complain about the climate: from that point of view Paris is no better than New York, except that you don't think it's quite so windy here. You go into raptures over the display in the window of a pharmacy—perhaps the exquisite taste of the French, their aesthetic sense, shows itself most clearly in their skill at combining colors and shapes. You observe that butcher's meat is just as expensive here as in New York. My own view is that your memory's getting more and more unreliable, and all these mundane remarks are designed to make me think you're as sharp as ever. We pass a little picture gallery: oh, if only you'd been able to go on with your sculpture, your real vocation! Your hands aren't what they used to be, of course, but you still think about it very seriously. And one of these days, just wait and see, you'll pluck up the courage and get your tools out of the suitcase they're stowed away in. You only need to buy some clay. I wonder if I shouldn't get you some, tomorrow or the day after, so that you can at least potter about and enjoy the illusion of working? On the other hand you're not really up to it, and I wouldn't want to force you into having to acknowledge your helplessness. I haul you across the road and sit you down in a pizzeria which you like because of its chairs and its red candles stuck in the necks of old wine bottles.

We're now face to face, less than a yard apart. I can see your every look, your every gesture. Your forehead is like a crumpled piece of paper that someone's tried in vain to iron flat again. Your nostrils are at once pinched and slack: shapeless. Your ears have aged less than any other feature: they still have so much color they hardly seem to belong to you at all. Could they have been hastily grafted on in a desperate attempt at rejuvenation? Your neck, half hidden by a brown shawl, looks as if it belonged to a chicken. The slackened muscles under your chin quiver and flutter like the sails of a skiff in harbor, cutting a sorry figure compared with great sea-going vessels. Brown spots have congregated on the backs of your hands; your ridged fingernails look as sapped by time and the elements as the battlements on ruined medieval towers. Your dentures are firm enough, but no longer camouflage the impression of ultimate decline. The general impression would be that you're about to fall to pieces if not for the extraordinary mobility of your dark brown eyes. They dart about, then pause. They quiver at the sound of a syllable, look first into the distance, then back into themselves, emerging softer, more insinuating, as if more intent on digesting at leisure the vision they've just been contemplating. No one would guess you're shortsighted. The first thing that strikes other people is your piercing glance, which at first seems like hostility but gradually reveals itself to be perpetual wonder: what's happening? where am I? where can I possibly be?

You grasp your fork and lift it cautiously toward your cross-hatched lips. Is the spaghetti going to reach its destination safely without falling off and making horrible marks on your dress?—your table napkin has fallen under the table. You know I'm watching you mercilessly: as you eat I judge you with a harshness you find more and more unbearable. You pause for a moment, make a stab at buttering a piece of bread you don't want, take a sip of water. You're controlling yourself, I'm controlling myself: there can't be any harmony or spontaneity between us. You tell me, as usual, that I'm behaving like a torturer; I look on at your impoverished, imperceptible, and uneventful slow death as if it were to be taken for granted, as if I were glad there was no cure for it. A quick death would be infinitely better, and you know how to bring one about. The fact that I don't make much of a protest about this naturally proves to you that you've been reading my mind correctly. I say nothing for a moment, then say that these lunches together are the most precious thing we've got now. You laugh sardonically: we've sunk very low if a plate of spaghetti and an onion pizza symbolize our relationship: warmed-up leftovers!

I take refuge in vague and poetic-sounding plans: I'll soon hire a chauffeur-driven car and take you for a ride to Sully-sur-Loire—you liked it so much last year! And I'll show you Lyons-la-Forêt with its wonderful trees, so pure, so Gothic! Words get the better of me, and I launch into a discourse on world politics while you eat a crème caramel. I babble on about King Hussein—one can't help admiring his courage; President Sadat, a great liberal though perhaps a bit talkative; Henry Kissinger, who thinks himself superior to everybody and unfortunately for him is probably right; Alain Delon, with his ambiguous face, whom you always confuse with Yves Montand; and Catherine Deneuve—she can't act, but she's the most beautiful creature of the decade. You come out of your torpor and ask me to get you some photographs of the Shah of Iran: when you take up sculpture again, which will be quite soon now, you're going to make a mask of his face. We're quite serene again now. It's time to take you back to your hotel—no easy matter. You shed a formal tear or two and ask me to forgive you for being so moody. You don't seem able to do anything about it anymore.

Brussels, spring 1929

You comforted me for breaking my third pen in a week: accidents were inevitable if I worked so hard. My writing was improving, and you were very pleased. You said you were satisfied with my school, and the teacher agreed I was intelligent and persevering. Perhaps I could be a bit more careful, though, especially at recess: I teased the other children and called them by funny names I'd found in Larousse. One should never upset sensitive young souls, and calling them duck-billed platypuses and anteaters was hurtful, charming as those animals may be. I kissed you and told you how all the other boys envied my nice new leather satchel—except for Gaëtan Baetens, who was a bully and always making fun of me. You told me to be patient. Young Baetens's family was well off and rather special; his mother had a good job in the city hall, and his father had fought in the Yser campaign and lived in water up to his knees for three years. I confessed I was in love with the hypotenuse, and could see you didn't know what I was talking about. I then decided to be deliberately mischievous and even disagreeable with you. Naturally enough—if you wanted me to be nicer and more careful with my schoolmates, I needed to be able to transfer my rancor elsewhere. And who better than someone who wouldn't hold it against me too much? I exploited what I'd learned at school to ask you questions I knew you couldn't answer. Were Boyle and Mariotte two of the admirals who'd beaten the Spanish into a cocked hat? Was Pepin the Short forty-four or forty-seven inches tall? Was oxygen just hydrogen boiled up in a hermetically sealed pot? Had Gutenberg been excommunicated for adding three chapters to the Bible? Did Louis Pasteur build the Eiffel Tower (which collapsed three times before being given its final form)? Was Impressionism a school of painting for artists who couldn't see very well? Did Australia fall out of the sky in the latter part of the reign of Philip II, sending up great spurts of water and fire? This would explain, among other things, why Australia was inhabited by enormous rabbits and black swans. Were tennis, golf, hockey, and all the other sports for the wealthy invented by Marco Polo? Did Christ betray Judas to Pontius Pilate in order to get some pocket money?

You took a certain amount of pleasure in my pranks, though it was hard for you to distinguish the true from the false, to tell when I was seeking knowledge and when just making things up. You sometimes called my father to the rescue, and he would sort things out, though without actually scolding me. But occasionally he'd admit to ignorance about some historical or geographical fact, and look it up, and this might lead to a little lecture in which truth put gratuitous nonsense in its place. I didn't much like this process, because it made you more sure of yourself. But it irked you too: it showed that your husband was better than you were at coping with your son. Anyhow, I went on playing on your credulity and laziness, and on the immoderate affection that treated my every whim as sacrosanct. You said school agreed with me, but at the same time warned me that home mattered most: schoolfriends are bound to be swept away eventually by life's vicissitudes. The same thing applied to teachers; they're there to take care of the head, which they have excellent ways of filling, but they know nothing of the heart, which is much more important and on which Father and Mother are experts. Such remarks tended to make me surly, so you changed your tactics: you weren't trying to preach at me—just doing all you could to protect me. You then consulted me about the color of my drapes: my room was very small, and you wanted it to be entirely to my taste. I'd worked hard and gotten excellent grades, except in gym and games, and on the whole I was a good little boy. So it was only natural that my world should be arranged in accordance with my own preferences rather than those of my parents, so long as I was sensible and practical.

I didn't devote much thought to your suggestion; perhaps I didn't attach any importance to my surroundings, to furniture and other objects. Vague though my ideas on time and space might be, I found wandering through them in my imagination more entertaining than protesting the tangible conditions in which I happened to live. But you thought the material the present drapes were made of should be replaced by something more cheerful. You were, in short, asking me to join in the game of transforming the tiny space in which I spent a third of my life. To please you I decided to think of it as a ship's cabin or a compartment on a train, and I set off on a journey around it, examining every detail. I observed every nail, every bump in the linoleum, every flower on the wallpaper. And it was true: those drapes were ugly. Their color was something between gray and brown, which meant the dust didn't show and they did't have to be washed very often. I made up my mind: I'd have blue drapes instead—blue with mauve fringes. You agreed immediately, and told me Father's business had been looking up in the last six months. But I wasn't to be satisfied with so meager a metamorphosis: I had ideas of my own about the rest of my ship. I asked to have the ironwork on the balcony painted black, and you assented: the request showed I was concerned about cleanliness, and so shed a favorable light on my mental health.

I went on to make further claims, which you greeted with unexpected delight: if I was as fond as all that of my room it meant I had the right family instincts and would go on loving my parents in the years to come. This display of solidarity cost you and Father a pretty penny, but you both welcomed all my whims. I insisted on having the existing wallpaper removed: I felt crowded by all those overblown hydrangeas. Anticipating my wishes, you presented me with a book of samples. I rebelled: were you trying to influence my choice? I pretended not to like either the plain gray-blue, or the one with little pagodas dotted over a Japanese landscape, or the one with orange rectangles on a dark red background, though that would have gone well with the drapes. You, showing no sign of irritation, said you'd get some other samples: did I have anything particular in mind? Instead of giving a straight answer, I said perhaps it would be best just to have something quiet, that wouldn't strain my eyes; then I wouldn't have to wear glasses later on. For this sage suggestion I was re-warded with more cakes and kisses, though in fact they only put me off. Improvising wildly, I said a green or grayish green wave pattern might be a good idea—they'd suggest the sea, escape, exotic islands, heroic exploits. You fell in with my enthusiasms at once, infusing them with a sincerity I never intended.

But that wasn't the end of the matter. I needed a new oval table. I was always bruising my knees and elbows on the old square one, and the boys at school thought the marks came from beatings inflicted on me by my parents, their affection finally exhausted by my bad ways. My wishes be-ing your commands at this period, nothing was too much for me to ask: once again I got my way. I had to make the most of this! I told you I re-ally didn't like my wooden bed: couldn't I have one with big brass knobs? They felt so cool when you put your hands around them during a heat wave. It wasn't much of an argument, and for a few days you resisted it. This made me touchy, sulky, and unpredictable—I'd weep, repent, and then weep some more for having wept for nothing. Without consulting me this time, you replaced my lamp with two others, more luxurious and equipped with adjustable shades so that I could regulate the area of light they shed. I was delighted, though I did all I could not to show it; now I could set sail whenever I liked for the mysterious isles of the South Seas or the eternal snows of the Andes, and be Livingstone or Savorgnan de Brazza in darkest Africa.

But although the changes to my room did give me some pleasure, as well as the opportunity to wind you around my little finger, I didn't re-ally feel any happier there. I soon became aware of my body in a new and disquieting way. Until then I'd been concerned only with ordinary hygiene: you had to wash yourself at least twice a day, take a bath in the morning, keep your hands and fingernails clean. You had to do some physical exercise in addition to gymnastics at school. Out in the street I should throw out my chest as I walked along, and take deep breaths so the air reached the farthest recesses of my lungs. If I was constipated I must concentrate, and relax my muscles to help Nature take its course. Simple enough precepts, and I followed them implicitly. I knew someone would soon teach me to swim and that I'd have a brand-new bicycle for my tenth birthday. A tennis racket and roller skates would follow in due course if I wanted them. But I was suddenly bothered about my sexual equipment, which I called by various names: my "peenie," my "pecker," my "dong," my "thing." I wasn't particularly fond of my private parts: even their shape didn't amuse me. Perhaps I was vaguely apprehensive; was it all merely funny and grotesque? I grimly compared my member to those of my schoolmates—especially in the winter, in the remoter parts of the school yard. In the matter of length I was neither at the top nor at the bottom of the class. Unlike my friends, I didn't maintain a dialogue with my appendage: each claimed his had an extraordinarily independent, intelligent, and mischievous mind of its own.

Once or twice it seemed to me some change had taken place in me at chest level or in my legs. Had I suddenly started to shoot up? I felt very tired, but I didn't say anything. For a few weeks school was irksome: I kept away from my friends and my grades weren't as good as usual. I couldn't pull myself together: it was if in some strange way every muscle in my body was conspiring against me and my memory. I suffered a few brief lapses, which I kept to myself but which had repercussions on my performance in my favorite subjects, history and geography. I mixed up Brittany and Norway; I made the Rhine flow from north to south, with its estuary in the Alps; I was convinced manganese was a tropical fruit fed to cattle; I said Frederick Barbarossa won the battle of Rivoli; I even maintained there were twenty-two kings of France called Louis. The teachers thought I was making fun of them, and I was in danger of being punished or kept in after school. But though my aberrations were partly due to waywardness, something else was involved too. I found it hard to control my feelings, I was sleeping badly, and I kept breaking out into a sweat. I was afraid this portended some serious illness.

My "thing" kept playing tricks on me: I was conscious of it from morn till night. At night it either made me lie awake or dream of monsters, or of women suddenly taking their clothes off and letting down their hair. Its skin stuck to my groin, and I noticed it kept changing size for no reason, sometimes slack and swollen, sometimes almost tense, as if some strange force were drawing it out of me. I tried to analyze this state of affairs, but was too worked up to get anywhere. I needed advice, but didn't like to confide in you or Father. It took the pair of you nearly a month to notice I was unhappy and preoccupied. You both asked if I had any difficulties at school, and I said I was having trouble keeping up in class. You made me take some cod liver oil, but it didn't do any good. I declared war on my "thing": it was taking up too much of my time, and I railed against it as if it had become a real disability. I was getting more and more anxious, and as you didn't seem able to guess why, you arranged for me to be examined by your doctor. He couldn't find anything wrong with me; I didn't have worms, and my nervousness was only temporary. One day you insisted on taking me to the cinema, then buying me ice creams in a tea shop I liked at the porte de Namur. All of a sudden you'd discovered the cause of the trouble: I'd copied from a friend who was better than I was at chemistry, I'd gotten good grades as a result, and I was consumed with guilt. I had too much imagination already, and there you were, supplementing it with your own, which was usually fairly meager. I wept, and you concluded from this that you'd guessed right. You were very impressed by your own perspicacity. But I'd been so affectionate with you and so ready to admit I *was* sad that in the end you decided something else must be wrong. You consulted my father. His attitude was very sound: if I didn't want to say what was worrying me it must be because I was capable of dealing with it by myself.

One night "my little brother" woke me up with a start: it was hot, sticky, and restless, and emitted a drop of white liquid. I was appalled: had I contracted some disease, was my whole body rotting away? I prodded my body all over to make sure my throat, stomach, lungs, and liver weren't also secreting poison. I couldn't get back to sleep, and the next day didn't utter more than a couple of dozen words. Three days later I found stains on my pajamas, but I had a feeling my nightmares had contained some moments of jubilation and pleasure. I expected to develop spots and blotches; I also made up my mind to confide in you. I rehearsed a whole series of fateful phrases: "Mother, do men as well as women produce milk? Look!" "Mother, I'm sick, and full of all kinds of funny liquids."

"Mother, is it dangerous to have pee that's all white?" "Mother, I think I've got leprosy!" "Mother, there's something wrong with my willy!" But I couldn't bring myself to choose between them, and remained silent. I snuggled up to you several times: you interpreted this as filial love. My eyes kept calling for help, but you didn't notice. I even let out a few little groans, and you thought I was imitating a puppy or a kitten—after all, I was an adorable little pet myself. I was emerging from childhood, but your blindness plunged me back into it again. I couldn't talk to you about my first carnal torments, nor even ask you if I was going to die, as my sleepless nights and my first erections seemed to me to predict.

As I languished in ignorance, I finally decided not to let you into my secret after all. Instead I ingratiated myself with Gaëtan Baetens, whom I hated and who was my most vindictive rival at school; for a whole month I put myself under his protection. I also acted as his henchman, ready to bully the others on his behalf. This strategy stood me in good stead at break and in games, but chiefly in our plots against the teachers. We didn't like them, and used to spring humiliating surprises on them— sponges soaked in ink; chalk smeared with glue from fly-papers; nails in their chairs to snag their jackets or pants; earthworms or frogs on their desks; celluloid turds from a joke shop, laid on the edge of the platform at the front of the class; toilet rolls fixed up in the window so they streamed out like banners in the wind. I showed so much energy and enterprise that Baetens eventually came to respect me, though I was younger than he. Then I told him he was the boy I trusted best in the whole world, and I needed his advice. He invited me around to his house one Saturday afternoon, and I gave him a vivid and fierce account of my affliction, which had to be kept secret even from my mother. He burst out laughing and asked me if I knew the meaning of puberty, sexual development, and the physical attraction of women. I mumbled something to cover my confusion. He congratulated me and told me to be reconciled with my willy. He also gave me a talking-to: if I wanted to stand higher in his regard I must find out what life was all about. He at least had had brothers and sisters to teach him what he needed to know—in particular, how to live on reasonable terms with his own member, which could, without a blush, be called by its right name: phallus, penis, male organ. He warned me the nocturnal emissions would become more frequent, and be followed by others in the daytime. Soon I would want to induce them, and this would bring me incomparable delights. From what he'd told me I deduced with some apprehension that I was going to have to accept myself as I was, including the animal aspects of my nature. He asked to see my penis, weighed it in a hand that trembled somewhat, and said he'd forgive me for being an insignificant little boy, and train me up to perform great and heroic tasks. He didn't specify what they were.

Gradually my equanimity was restored and I was able to sleep again. I contemplated you with a mixture of pity and contempt. You hadn't been able to guess what was puzzling me; your intuition, smothered in useless chatter and exclamations of wonder, had failed you in a moment of real crisis. We resumed our usual games with each other, but more from habit than inclination. I realized I wasn't living *with* you—merely living close to you, under the same roof. Which meant I was really living *against* you, in a kind of fierce hostility. Sometimes I thought you'd seen and understood my distress signals perfectly well, but your cowardice had gotten the better of your impulse to come to the rescue. You loved me—as long as you didn't have to enter into my inner life. It took me many weeks to decide I must exclude you from it forever. I didn't know then that adolescents change their minds, oscillate between spontaneity and calculation, attain self-mastery only by fits and starts. We talked too much about happiness, you and I, but we never arrived at anything more than its superficial and mechanical appearances. One day, irritated by the cloying solicitude I saw as sheer insensibility, I told you my room was a pig-sty, a consumptive little girl's nursery, compared with Gaëtan Baetens' room, which was large, full of plants, and just the sort of place to foster ambition. It was all very well to have nice parents, I said. But it was much better to have rich ones.

Berlin, March 1946

Life's a carnivorous business and I'm not ashamed to show myself as I am: a professional winner. After being tossed about for six years from defeat to defeat, panic to panic, uncertain battle to blind battle, at last I've found a territory on which I can fulfill myself. I've as much right as anyone to take part in the reconstruction of the world, and though such thoughts may be rather intimidating they don't stop me from showing what I'm made of in this ancient capital, where my superiors have granted me a certain amount of authority. I'm not displeased with myself, and I must maintain this attitude, even at the risk of lapsing into demagogy or presumption. I've made peace within myself by accepting a few very simple principles. I don't hate the Germans: it's my job to reeducate them, or in other words transform them, using my own methods. They'll be the raw material I shape in accordance with my own conscience. Only the Russians have won the war, body after body, lung after lung, bayonet after bayonet, skin against skin, breath against breath. Only the Americans have had time to modernize war, coming in, as they did, late in the day. And it's the dollar, properly managed, that will put Europe on its feet again. I admire the English, who very democratically have managed to avoid massacre for massacre's sake, revenge for revenge's sake. As for the French, last-minute guests at the victory, I must admit they have the most subtle ideas. And probably the least practical.

It was I myself who requisitioned the villa I live in. It hadn't been damaged at all, apart from a few broken windows. A fifty-year-old woman was living there with her fourteen-year-old daughter; I gave her three hours to clear out. She'd be placed somewhere else—it was none of my business; that kind of thing was dealt with by another department. I wouldn't let her take any of her furniture or crockery with her—not even her family portraits. Orders are orders, and all she was entitled to take was two blankets, some linen, some cash, and some food. She implored: her husband was a prisoner of war, the Russians had tried to rape her daughter, she'd give me a lot of money if I'd let her stay on and live in the maid's room. She wouldn't be any trouble. But I had no qualms whatsoever about throwing her out: my corporal was there to bundle her off to the clink if necessary. It's not that I'm harsh: I just haven't got time to waste on individual cases. Germany has to be rebuilt, and it's just too bad for the widows. In any case, the Germans won't take to democracy very easily. Old men and civilian women are of no use: only the children, and the five million prisoners, are capable of amendment. All we have to do is give them a new cause: their old one was no good, as we'll have shown them—it brought their country to ruin, didn't it? I know all this sounds rather drastic, but it's more practical to wipe out a whole generation and start again from scratch rather than try to reform such complex kinds of consciousness as existed before.

I'm a liaison officer linking the four occupying powers—in the form of the Control Commission—with the rest of the Allies, ranging from Denmark to New Zealand, from Yugoslavia to Brazil. My colleagues and I arrange conferences, roundtables, discussions and negotiations of all sorts, in which the same problems constantly recur: reparations, compensation, the return of requisitioned property, the search for missing persons and the rehousing of displaced ones. Every day, with my help, things emerge a little further from chaos—a chaos that is gradually turning into a military government, which in two or three years' time will be taken over by the civil authorities. Several times a week I'm called on to act as interpreter at important conferences. These include meetings at the Directorate of Home and Religious Affairs, where the generals and their technical advisers make decisions about what's going to happen to the Germans—demobilization, the return to the countryside, the setting of educational standards, denazification. While I find this aspect of the work fascinating, there's another that is my own specialty. It takes place in my own house, where I gather together the writers and intellectuals destined to take part in the spiritual reconstruction of Germany. Of course they're all hungry for knowledge of various kinds, though I suspect some of them have been wearing blinders for years. But unlike my superiors I don't think all Germans can be classified as either Nazis or anti-Nazis. A whole lot in the middle just did the best they could for themselves in the circumstances. Intellectuals are no braver than anybody else, and some are very lukewarm when it comes to action though their hearts are in the right place. It's my job to kindle their sympathies and direct them away from the Nazis and toward democracy—that vague and sentimental notion which all the victors define differently. Some of my charges have just come out of prison or were even in concentration camps; their ardor is likely to match the zeal with which their jailers burned their comrades alive. But you have to be careful with converts. I must show them democracy needs a good admixture of skepticism.

I send for books from Paris and New York and pass them around. I advise friends of mine to translate them or send them to the few German publishers now just beginning to reappear. In a few months from now the military authorities will establish their quotas of paper, and in the summer of 1947, after carrying out their contracts to print the practical textbooks more urgently needed, they'll be allowed to publish some works of literature. Meanwhile, people's sensibilities need to be prepared, or repaired. I draw up lists that sometimes go pretty far back into the past. Sartre, Camus, Faulkner, Steinbeck, Dos Passos, Eugene O'Neill, Arnold Toynbee, and the two Huxleys aren't enough—we also have to teach what surrealism is, all over again. My copies of Lautréamont and Tennessee Williams, André Breton and Saroyan, are snapped up eagerly, and this encourages me to extend my efforts to other spheres. Wilhelm Furtwängler is waiting for authorization to re-form the Philharmonic Orchestra: next month it's to start giving concerts again at the Titania, a former movie theater in Steglitz. The handful of musicians I stuff with meat and potato salad will have to study composers they should include in their repertoire. It's not enough to banish Wagner because Hitler loved him, or Richard Strauss because he played for other Nazi bosses. Nor is rehabilitating Mendelssohn enough in itself: my good friends must turn their minds to Gershwin, Bartok, and Shostakovich. I intend to put in a word about the theaters' choice of plays too: in particular, I expect Thornton Wilder's *The Skin of Our Teeth* to be a great hit. If it's true Bertolt Brecht intends to come back to Germany, the Russians would enjoy a well-deserved advantage over the West. There's an enormous amount to be done in the field of painting, too. I think it would a be a good idea to confront the people of Berlin with a few Picassos, Dalis, Mondrians, and Tanguys. If it upsets them, so much the better; their insufferable reasonableness and readiness to accept everything could do with a few visions and images from the unconscious! I see cultural propaganda as operating on the highest possible level, and my superiors on the Control Commission approve of my approach. This rather undermines my hitherto excessive respect for them. The great men of this war may be heroes in their own way, but they're also puppets. Sometimes I come in contact with Eisenhower: he talks like a bank clerk turned grocer, and his good humor barely conceals an almost fatuous self-satisfaction. Zhukov wanders around the corridors and attends the meetings where the future of Germany is being decided: but what can he do, trammeled by paperwork and surrounded by the crowds of political advisers who are the sole wielders of power nowadays? I don't suppose either of them has ever heard of Kafka, Joyce, or Proust. Neither, no doubt, has the slippery Montgomery, or de Lattre de Tassigny—the latter, like Cyrano de Bergerac, always ready to duel with his own shadow. So *I* have to work for the glory of Kafka, Joyce, Proust, and the like. I've made my choice between Marshal Ney and Lamartine, Frederick II and Goethe, Colbert and Racine. I must put the Pantheon of my own literary and artistic taste before victorious warriors. If this involves a certain juvenile pedantry, I don't mind admitting it: such decisions are bound to seem immature.

But there's a price to be paid for promoting genius. In order to protect my policy I assume an attitude of unmitigated contempt toward those I have to charm, persuade, or force to share my views. I order my charges to love literature and regard a certain kind of music as important. I have the power to make them obey, and the time at my disposal could be limited: Germany may gradually manage to do without the help of her conquerors. I transmit to a few empty minds some of the principles that are dear to me; I obtain credits, I make choices, people trust me. As the ambassador of St.-John Perse and the special envoy of Stravinsky, I feel entitled to ride roughshod over the sensibilities of the faceless subordinates I win over to what after all is a disinterested cause. Anyhow, that's the excuse I make to myself for my lack of respect for the mob of Germans around me, all busy overcoming their own prejudices. I make use of them, and they are supposed to be grateful for it. This method, which saves me from getting bogged down in subtleties, I also apply to the hordes of women who supply me with pleasure. Physical love at last unhindered by paralyzing scruple. I have no patience with the fools who offer me their bodies before I've even asked, in the secret hope I'll take them on for a while, give them a few useful presents and enough food to let them forget about ration cards. I'm neither good-looking nor ugly, but I am an ideal lover. Could any of the million Berlin females bereft of their mates possibly ask for anything better than an officer in one of the armies of occupation who speaks almost perfect German, who's high-strung and rather disagreeable, and who seems at once authoritarian and uncomfortable? What could be more delightful than a victor whom you yourself can vanquish in one long orgasm? And sometimes calculation is replaced by thoughtless abandon: the women of Berlin are very good in bed, and while fulfilling their feminine needs can show a pleasant forthcomingness which after a few bouts almost makes me believe they're sincere. As I won't be here for long, they think that if I'm downcast it's in anticipation: nothing of all this can last, it will soon be no more than a fading memory. As for my grumpiness and bad temper, what woman of my own age wouldn't hope to be able to cure my surliness by means of the flesh? It's a familiar argument: the warmth and softness of a body eventually contaminates the mind. I'm quite happy to let them try out their theories on me: it brings me lots of kisses and an invasion of the physical self that's sometimes quite intoxicating. But the more I succumb to carnal bliss the more sternly I take my revenge: I cut short any affair that's lasted longer than three or four weeks.

I apply the quota system to friendship too. I invite an author to write an essay about Supervielle. I summon a director and tell him I'd like him to put on a play by Anouilh at the Hebbel-Theater, preferably a comedy. I chat with a town councillor from Wiesbaden. And wouldn't it be a crime not to include some Benjamin Britten in next Sunday's concert given to help rebuild the reception chamber at the city hall? I manipulate people according to my well-defined ideas about my own power. Perhaps I'll become less hard when I'm in my mid-thirties, but for the moment I'm only interested in my fellow humans insofar as they may be made use of. Literature and art are the one area in which I stand out from other survivors of my own generation. It's to literature and art that I owe everything; for them that I feel a devotion I never experienced in any of the martial crusades of the war. At the same time I'm quite clear-sighted: Germany is being pillaged. The mark is worth nothing, and every detail of daily life is governed by the black market. Love, friendship, loyalty, culture, intellect—all of them can sooner or later be converted into cigarettes and cans of coffee.

Anyone can make a lot of money by bringing supplies of these two commodities from the plenty of the United States to the penury of Europe, and no one will think he's doing anything wrong. While Germany may have shortages, it isn't undergoing actual famine. I've no intention of letting my friends suffer from malnutrition: that would just be storing up trouble for myself. I'm a reasonable being: I weigh up the pros and cons of things. I know there are still some works of art and postage stamps around which must be looked on as luxuries, surplus to requirements as far as the reeducation of a nation is concerned. I soon find a formula to deal with this situation. You are to send me cigarettes, I'll sell them, and with the money I'll buy stamps, old ones if possible, for a tenth of their real value or even a good deal less. I explain this little plan to you in several letters, going out of my way to reassure you: I don't want to get rich, I'm not a shameless exploiter, the black market doesn't attract me. Besides, I'm too busy to deal in it—unlike many of my colleagues, who think about nothing else. You answer rather evasively at first, as if you don't quite understand. Our correspondence becomes more heated. I grow emphatic—I need to make my victory a lasting one, and in this cruel world, why should I be any more tender-hearted than all the beasts of prey around me? Should I feel the slightest affection for the Germans? There are times in life when noble sentiments are mere foolishness. Have you forgotten that in January 1944, in Brussels, the Germans rounded up and arrested your own father—to die, for all we know, in some cattle-truck in the icy wastes of Poland? I personally am taking my revenge without harming anyone.

I've hit on a weighty argument. In the past I've never shown much respect for philately as a profession. Isn't my sudden interest in stamps a sign that I'm following in my father's footsteps, perhaps even preparing to succeed him? It's up to you to persuade him and remove any moral objections he may have to my suggestion. For three or four weeks I bombard you with reassurances. No, I won't turn into a horrible profiteer; I have a noble mission to perform, and if I'm to carry it out properly I need to look after myself. My income is fairly adequate, but probably won't last forever. You answer with a mixture of anxiety and reserve. You don't really understand my present way of life, and what does get through to you can't please you very much. I cut your hesitations short: I don't need you, I say—I can get cigarettes and coffee sent over by an export company. My attempt to bring you in was simply proof that I put my family first. My explanations are curt and peremptory. You finally give in, and from then on I get four consignments every week.

I know that as time goes by this chore will turn into a duty, and you'll think you're still playing a necessary part in my life. The devil of devotion, only recently lulled to sleep, will wake up, and you'll feel useful—no, indispensable!—again. I shall cultivate this illusion with careful, affectionate letters. The stamps I buy I can always re-sell in London or New York. I'll put the money in an American bank in your name, for you to do what you like with. It may all seem rather dubious, even unworthy of us both, but there's no need to worry; all around me I see field-marshals, ministers, and ambassadors lining their pockets as fast as they can. Looting is perfectly legal; so-called exchange centers at the various HQs function quite openly. The victors claim the right to bleed Germany white: is that any worse than imposing reparations which deprive a country of its agriculture and its heavy industry for years to come? The Soviet Union takes away a third of our enemies' territory, and that's only fair. France and England dismantle Germany's factories and take over its iron and steel production: don't their own metallurgical industries need building up again as soon as possible? Your son is much more modest, and above all more tactful; by mutual agreement and without the slightest hint of force, he allows a few Huns to eat better in exchange for a few scraps of paper. People can live without postage stamps, and tightening one's belt is very good for the health. We all suffer from bad consciences: I must just learn to turn a deaf ear to mine.

No doubt about it—I'm exploiting you. I don't feel you're at all close to me these days. You're getting old, and I can't detect enthusiasm of any kind in you. You've come through the war unscathed, thanks to a second exile, but you seem to spend all your time in vague lamentation over this further banishment. You've forgotten how to play the violin, you read only for distraction: I don't feel there's any depth to your fragility. I rarely think of you at all except to write a few polite lines two or three times a month to say everything's fine. And to put off my promised return to New York. You're waiting for me to come, of course, but apathetically now. What have we left in common but the ties of blood? Will you ever be able to think of my life apart from the rôle you play in it? Mother love is a monstrosity, a longing for eternal self-sacrifice. As far as possible I stifle any expression of affection; I need to attain an intellectual stature of my own, or at least convince myself my efforts will some day be rewarded by a genuine inner life. And you stand in the way of that ambition. You can still be useful to me. Be useful then, but don't take up any real space in my life.

Boston, winter 1959

I was asked to come to Boston by the poet, Claude Vigée, to teach contemporary French literature at one of the universities here: a six-month interlude in the midst of my life as a writer. I called in at New York on the way, but only for three days. These visits have become variations on a kind of routine. You and I exchanged gifts and smiles that were genuine enough but concealed an insidious unease; we probably had scores of things to say to each other, but each had a feeling the other was concealing hundreds. We expected confidences and emotion, but ended up being shyly polite and feeling more and more alienated. I'd brought you a Lalique vase from Paris, and all over your big divan you'd spread shirts, scarves, handkerchiefs, socks, and neckties. They weren't the sort of thing I'd have chosen for myself, but I'd keep them for my days off, when I didn't have to appear in public. But I noticed considerable changes in you and my father: you'd both had a sudden access of energy. At the age of nearly seventy-five, Alexander Bisk, after a a period of latency going back to the upheavals of the Russian Revolution, had remembered he was once a poet. Literature wasn't quite extinct in him, and now he was trying with genuine ardor to rediscover the vocation of his youth. He'd taken to mixing with other émigrés who had literary interests, and above all he was doggedly bringing himself up to date. He was reading Bulgakov and Yevtushenko's early poems; he was getting to know Vladimir Nabokov—a dreadful cynic, in his view; and he carried on a rather desultory correspondence, by means of postcards, with Boris Pasternak. His behavior was quite natural, given the tenor of his life so far. For more than thirty-five years he'd followed a modest but absorbing profession, which he liked well enough and which had made him one of the dozen or so world authorities on rare stamps. He didn't owe anyone anything, and his old age was sufficiently provided for. He'd never return to Europe, but he meant to enjoy himself: a few authors to dinner from time to time, a couple of cigars a day, a game of bridge once a week, and a movie every day, following his afternoon nap.

This move toward a kind of belated happiness, which I regarded as truer to his real nature than his previous life had been, induced a parallel development in you. You were learning with some surprise that art is the consolation of old age. You gradually stopped rhapsodizing over moral and emotional values, and realized at last that to say someone was good or bad, generous or tightfisted, didn't tell the whole story: a person could also be judged in terms of his or her talent. For a long while you hesitated: people don't start playing the violin again at the age of sixty-nine, especially when they listen to Heifetz, Stern, or Menuhin on the radio several times a day. Your training had taken you too far for you to have any illusions on that score; you knew your fingers were too weak and stiff now to obey you. You wondered whether painting would be more suitable, then decided to take lessons in sculpture. A Russian woman you knew introduced you to Alexander Archipenko, and he agreed to teach you for a modest fee. You managed to strike up a friendship with him, or at least to invite him to cold buffets where the excellence of the zakuski made up for the dullness of the conversation. You did a few clay and plaster portrait busts which caught the likeness pretty well; most of your friends must have sat for you, and they didn't seem to mind doing it. Later on you grew bolder and did a majestic bronze of Don Quixote and some "abstract" statuettes.

You and I were bound to live apart—you had to do something to occupy yourself, and such distractions kept you from perpetually yearning to see me. I was still your chief joy, but I was no longer your only reason for living. And if you ever shed a tear and claimed that I *was*, I could tell you didn't really mean it. For my part I was delighted by these sensible arrangements, and glad you were able to take such a keen interest in modern art. Like Father, you had nearly half a century to catch up on. It was rather moving to see an old-fashioned couple like you two suddenly doing all they could to be contemporary, he reading Sartre instead of Tolstoy, Musil instead of Hauptmann, Orwell instead of Kipling, while you, more eager even than he for change, began to acquire a taste for Duke Ellington and Poulenc. Your talks with Archipenko exerted a crucial influence: instead of devoting your afternoons to Slavic gossip and nostalgia, you visited Madison Avenue galleries, the Whitney Museum, the Museum of Modern Art: the open-air cafeteria between Fifth and Sixth Avenue served very good hot chocolate. Your new acquaintances, though in my view too arbitrarily divided between subjects of ecstasy and objects of repulsion, compared quite favorably with my own. You could rival me in your praises of Brancusi, Klee, and Seurat. Your intuition seldom played you false: you detected a parochial element in Chagall, and thought Matisse had a tendency to value prettiness above beauty. Your observations about sculptors were more subtle; sometimes you even used technical terms. You sized up Zadkine very neatly, deploring a literary streak in his work. You thought Lipchitz was mistaken to go in for religious and ritual subjects, and accused him of being unduly influenced by his wealthy patrons. You'd just discovered González and were full of his praises.

You and Father stimulated each other; he passed newly discovered authors on to you, and you made him go with you to your favorite exhibits. Sometimes the attempted exchanges didn't work, and this would make you both laugh. You didn't like fictional characters to be too anguished, and after thirty pages of Kafka you dismissed him as morbid and degenerate. Father had different limitations: abstract art was for him the work of architects *manqués*, and he always looked for keys and explanations in the images of the Surrealists. But when he couldn't find any such keys in the works of Dali or Ernst, he didn't dismiss them out of hand: he merely said it was all beyond him, and every generation was bound to have a code contrasting diametrically with that of its predecessors. You were now a perfectly presentable old couple, with a veneer of courtliness and pretense you would have regarded as hypocritical thirty years before. But what was there for me to object to? Neither of you knew anything about the United States; you both spoke English haltingly, with traces of Russian and French; your world, to which you were greatly attached, stretched from 100th to 34th Street and from Second to Tenth Avenue. You seldom strayed outside these boundaries. Every year friends took you both out to Long Beach; you claimed the ninety-minute drive was quite enough to keep your finger on the pulse of America. I envied the equilibrium you'd both achieved, naive and ignorant though it was, and sometimes found myself feeling jealous of a serenity troubled only by the odd ailment or a few quite bearable infirmities. Occasionally I regretted the fact that I no longer altogether occupied my old place in my mother's heart, but still. . . I'd turned away from you so long ago, and been so determined to become a true Parisian and a fiercely anti-American European, you'd been forced to do the best you could for yourself.

But Father's influence had been the decisive factor. He'd decided to have a cultivated old age and to emerge from his former grouchy reserve. He still did four or five hours' leisurely work a day; that was enough to keep you both. His old age pension and social security helped make ends meet: neither of you was extravagant, and you both soon stopped worrying about the future. For more than thirty years you yourself had tried to make your son happy whether he liked it or not, but now you were facing the facts; your version of happiness didn't appeal to him. And his aims—fame; power; originality at any price; an intellectual victory every day and a new enemy every week to minister to his own self-respect; outshining and despising other poets; attaining the invulnerable heights of civilized cynicism—all these were irksome to you. Your husband, on the other hand, after a life of self-effacement that had never revealed the slightest spark of imagination, suddenly burst out of his lethargy to resume, in a weaker but still attractive form, the aspirations of his youth. He'd never, as you knew, shown any great talent as an author, but now he was suddenly keen to write a few articles about the Russian language, to deliver a lecture or two about the more prosaic passages in *Eugene Onegin*, to discuss with colleagues the implausibilities in *War and Peace*, to entertain a group of refugee Russian poets, not to encourage their anti-Soviet sentiments but to give them the reassurance of direct and simple sympathy. And he needed help in his new rôle, which involved looking for material in specialized bookshops, raising audiences, making occasional furtive ventures into academia. You acted as his secretary, and cheered him up in his not infrequent moments of discouragement. You revealed yourself as quite a good psychologist. You had to preserve your independence, but at the same time avoid seeming to favor either the left or the czarist rearguard. Sometimes you went too far: one day you advised Father not to take part in a roundtable discussion on Chekhov because Kerensky was one of the speakers: surely they didn't mean to fight the civil war all over again!

You never tried to become my equal; you were my mother, and—at least in your view—that was enough to make you sacrosanct as far as I was concerned. But you had obligations toward my father. And since, in a modest way, he was putting himself once more at the service of literature, it was your duty as his wife to set aside melancholy and the minor cares of everyday life in favor of a more demanding inner discipline. Sculpture came in handy here. And I was surprised at the attention you both paid to intellectuals of my own age, who saw you as wise ancients as nonsectarian—and, even more important, as unpretentious—as could be expected. Even when most sorely tried, you let bores and hecklers down fairly lightly. Father always referred to you as "my wife, the sculptor," and you referred to him as "my husband, the poet." If this met with too much surprise, you might add, "Alexander Bisk, the former poet." (Of course you expected people to object and say, No, no—once a poet, always a poet.) In the midst of this social whirl of mediocrities who seemed quite charming within the illusory refuge of their ivory tower, you forgot about me. It was my father who summoned you back to reality. In front of other people he would exclaim with uncharacteristic emphasis that "the real artist in our family, the real creator, is our son! Here—let me show you some of his books! He's written more than fifteen already!"

In Boston I'd undertaken the sensational or even "terrorist" task of embarking, for the benefit of twenty-five students in blue jeans and ski

boots, on a comparison between the merits of Camus and Cioran, the first
famous in the U.S. as a kind of lay prophet and the second completely
unknown. I relished in advance the reaction of my youthful audience
when I read them some of Cioran's aphorisms: they'd be simultaneously
dazzled and outraged. Then someone told me I was urgently wanted on
the phone from New York. At the other end, Father could scarcely conceal his anguish: you'd been rushed to the hospital and were due to un-
dergo an operation the same afternoon. I excused myself to my class and
caught the first available plane. Less than two hours later I was at your
bedside. There were red tubes coming out of your nostrils; you moved
your eyes but couldn't speak. I brushed your brow with my lips, and you
tried to smile, but it ended in a grimace. I found Father in the surgeon's
consulting room, looking pale and older than his years. After a few encouraging and innocuous words the surgeon came to the point. Four years
earlier you'd had a perforated intestine that hadn't been properly repaired,
and the occlusion you were now suffering from called for positively ac-
robatic skill. The operation would last four hours. The surgeon could
see Father was very upset, and hesitated to go into any more detail. I
asked him what your chances were of coming through this butchery. He
didn't answer for a few seconds. Then, realizing I couldn't be fobbed off
with words, he told me curtly that given your age you had a fifty-fifty
chance. I concluded from this that the odds were much worse—that you
had perhaps one chance in four or five. Father wanted to stay in the waiting room throughout the operation, and I had some difficulty getting him
to come with me to a restaurant, then to a movie. We ate a lobster and
saw an old Jean Gabin film; at least it kept our sympathy for each other
free from useless words and stifled emotions.

When we got back to the hospital they told us you were still on the operating table, but that all was proceeding normally. So as not to leave Father
alone, I slept on the settee in your apartment: he was grateful to me for that.
Next morning they told us you'd come through safely. But your heart had
been overtaxed, and for the rest of your life you'd be subject to spasms,
irregularities, and moments of weakness. In short, the operation had aged
you by at least ten years. They were going to keep you on in the hospital

for another week or so to get back some strength before you went away to convalesce. Father decided you should go to Long Beach, which you both used to visit every summer; the winters there were mild and quiet, and the problem of where to stay was simplified by the fact that only two luxury hotels stayed open out of season. I had to go back to the university in Boston, but I wasn't sorry to have been with my mother through a difficult time. The grudges between us had somehow melted away. You were very clear-sighted, as always in a crisis, and talked to me at length about Father and the metamorphosis taking place in him. He was quite philosophically drifting away from his profession. One postage stamp more or less; whether a client made or failed to make a purchase—what did it matter! You asked me to keep a secret: Father had found some old translations he'd done into Russian of Rainer Maria Rilke, his pre-1914 hero. He'd produced some more translations lately, and even written some sonnets of his own. You allowed yourself a few reproaches: I'd always regarded my father, you said, as rather a dilettante in literature, one of those dabblers who haven't the energy or audacity to commit themselves wholeheartedly to a spiritual adventure. But I was wrong, you'd insist, your already faint voice becoming so strained that the nurse would sometimes decree an hour's complete rest. You spoke as earnestly as if you were telling me your dying wishes.

No doubt Father was rather old-fashioned, you said, but he hadn't had much happiness in his life, what with the revolution in '17, the exile in '19, the invasion of Belgium in '40, and their going to live in America, which he'd never really understood. . . . I told you not to tire yourself going over events we all knew about. You asked for a glass of water and another pillow. Later on you found the chicken broth exceptionally tasty, and the surgeon congratulated you on your courage and good humor: in two or three days' time you wouldn't even remember your operation. So you went on with your lecture: Father had the tastes of his own generation—why should he have those of the next? Looked at in the absolute, all values were equal; how could I be sure mine were right and his were wrong? In matters like that, things were always being turned upside down. I was amazed at your energy and the ingenuity of your case. Then all of a sudden you lost the thread of your argument, became once more an old

lady on a bed of pain, complaining about shortness of breath. Were you
going to faint? The nurse asked me to leave, and not to come tire you
out again until next day. Then I brought you some Parma violets to strew
around you on the bed. You seemed to have forgotten the previous day's
conversation, and rambled on about various memories. Sometimes you
just lay silent, looking at us questioningly, and the surgeon, the nurse,
and I had to explain your operation to you five or six times, with the aid
of drawings. You remained skeptical, however, and observed as if in passing, and with a terrible serenity, that you probably had cancer. Your
mother had died of it too, you said, and the rest of us, out of mistaken
kindness, had agreed to keep the truth from you. Later on, for no apparent reason, you stopped talking about yourself: Father was more important to you. You gradually worked your way back to your campaign in
his favor: he'd read you some of his poems, and you thought they were
very good. Nothing would be better for his morale than to have his work
published. You went even further: to see a book of his in print would actually add years to his life, which he was beginning to enjoy again after
an eclipse of forty years. When I got back to Paris I could, after four or
five months, so as not to arouse his suspicions, write and tell him that
Russian circles there, which were more cultivated than those in New
York, were interested in his work. I could say several Soviet writers passing through had mentioned his name with interest: he'd belonged to the
avant-garde in the days of Babel and Akhmatova, and the younger generation, who were now keen on rediscovering that period, were especially
fascinated by him. I could arrange his poems and translations myself in
one or two volumes, and if we had to pay to have them published you'd
take the necessary steps. You made me swear—which was against my
principles—that I'd act quickly.

For a long time I thought it was wonderful of you to be so concerned
about your husband's intellectual well-being. Then one day I paced the
streets around Roosevelt Hospital and the vacant lot where the first walls
of Lincoln Center were slowly rising up. I had mixed feelings. I was angry with myself for getting so close to you as to be enlisted in your crusades. On the other hand, I'd set your mind at rest: you knew now that I

wouldn't sneak off in moments of danger. You might say to yourself that even though I craved freedom, I still knew my duty. I went and had a *Cuba libre* in a bar on 72nd Street, then an old-fashioned on Amsterdam Avenue. My ideas were confused, but I dreaded anything resembling emotional sloppiness. I was against your project, or rather I wanted it to be aboveboard and without any do-gooding ulterior motive. Of course I approved of Father's return to literature. It was quite permissible for him, without actually saying so, to want to republish some of his old work, together with a few more recent efforts. But it would have been easier just to hand them all over to some printer in Paris, without inventing hypothetical admirers who'd suddenly sprung out of nowhere. I had another drink, my third, but the determination I'd expected from it failed to materialize. I wasn't any more honest and decent than the next man, but why turn a good deed into a trick? However, I soon tired of my scruples. You knew Father's secret desires and weaknesses better than I did, and perhaps, for once in your life, you wanted to provide him with a pleasurable and lasting illusion. I decided to carry out your plot to the letter; after all, how long were you going to survive that serious operation? Without saying why, I cut short my stay in New York and resumed my lectures in Boston even before you went away to recuperate. For a couple of months, in a kind of gratuitous fury, I felt I was playing down the virtues of Montherlant, Mauriac, Claudel, and Giraudoux in order to emphasize my love for more neglected authors. Back in Paris I drew the obvious conclusion from my visit and your illness: you and Father were happy together, and my presence, which you'd always yearned for with such unbearable emotion, had become a luxury you could easily do without. When Father's two books came out, a little while later, it gave you more pleasure than it gave him. Now, in front of a whole coterie, you could express an admiration for him that had in reality been dead for four decades.

Sézanne, Marne, September 1976

"So you kiss my hands now, do you? My hands? I suppose you're afraid to kiss me on the cheek. I do wash, you know. Decomposition—you all think I'm decomposing. It's true—I am. But slowly, much too slowly, eh, my boy?"

"I didn't bring any flowers. You're surrounded with them already."

"Yes. Like in a cemetery."

"You like roses, and there are some magnificent tea roses over by the window."

"What's the use? You know I've lost my sense of smell! And I think gladioli are hideous. So are cineraria. They're all reminders of death."

"It seems as if you're being well looked after."

"I should hope so—it costs you a fortune."

"Have you got everything you need?"

"Medicine, porridge, injections. But the soul—these people haven't any soul!"

"They take only six or seven patients here, and your doctor told me they have the most devoted staff in the whole region."

"Like prison guards!"

"Do you talk to any of the others?"

"Nice day, looks like rain, it's going to be windy—or not, as the case may be. They're sicker than I am."

"You have your own telephone and radio. The television's only a few yards away, in the sitting room. And I'm sure the director would be only too pleased to take you there."

"She's cross-eyed!"

"I think she's nice."

"Because it suits you. You send your mother sixty miles outside Paris, with only nurses and dying people for company, and you don't ask yourself if that's what *she* wants!"

"It was doctor's orders—there was no alternative. You had to get your strength back after that double pneumonia. You're nice and quiet here."

"As the grave."

"Why don't you look on the bright side? The summer vacation isn't over yet. The leaves on the willow tree are only just starting to turn. The hay harvest is in. There's a great plain all around you—you can see for miles. . ."

"See what? You know my sight's failing!"

"I'm sorry."

"I'm sorry too. I'm just a grumpy old wreck. What have you brought me this time?"

"Some chocolates and some kiwis."

"You're the only person I've got left in the world. Where would I be without you?"

"Now, now, Mother—don't cry."

"It's no use saying that—my body doesn't do what I want anymore. My heart thumps like a hammer on a wall. And I have to ring the bell at night if I want to go to the bathroom—just think, only a few yards and I can't get there without help. It's humiliating."

"You'll feel better in a couple of weeks. The doctor told me it would take some time."

"These chocolates aren't what they used to be. Not so much liqueur, and one even had a nougat filling! Everyone cheats these days."

"Would you like to go out on the terrace and walk as far as the kitchen garden?"

"I got dressed up especially for you."

"Some exercise would do you good."

"Everyone wants to do me good—the hypocrites. Pass me my cane."

"Wouldn't you rather take my arm?"

"No, I feel safer by myself. I'm trembling more than usual, don't you think?"

"I wouldn't say so."

"What's in that package?"

"I brought you a sweater."

"Let me see. Camelhair! Why are you so extravagant?"

"That doesn't matter so long as you like it."

"It does matter. I wish you wouldn't. I'm sure it was your wife who chose it. That monster!"

"You promised to moderate your language."

"And what about illness, and old age, and my heart—do you think I can moderate them? I intend to tell the truth for what little time I have left. Especially to you."

"Watch these three steps!"

"The other day I had to sit down on them, right out in the wind—there wasn't anyone to help me up. But will you please stop changing the subject? I don't like your wife, and I don't like what she's made of you."

"If you were a better psychologist you'd know my character's as inflexible as yours, and nobody can manipulate me. I am what I am, independently of anyone else."

"You know how to make your own tale good. How much did you pay for that sweater?"

"What does it matter? Try it on when we get back."

"Anything that you give me is precious. Stop a minute—we've only gone thirty yards and I'm exhausted."

"Last week you couldn't last out half as long. You can't see it yourself, but you're getting better."

"I slept well last night for once. I dreamed about your father. He was tall and handsome. He was reciting poems on the banks of a wide, swiftly flowing river. Oh, I was the one who killed him!"

"You must try to forget all that. It wasn't your fault. I've told you so a hundred times."

"My suffering is my own affair."

"But why add to it?"

"I'm not heartless, like you."

"I have my own way of feeling things."

"You hide everything."

"I don't pour my heart out unnecessarily."

"Why don't you say right out that I'm a savage? You and your wife keep all your feelings bottled up."

"Let's sit down on the bench. The leaves are falling already."

"I don't like the director. She's always counting up what everything costs. Her husband's very nice. Portuguese. Do you see that little wall over there behind the trees? He's going to set up a pottery shop there. He's shown me some of the vases he's made. He's an artist, and he brings me grapes without telling his wife. He lent me a book about all the things you can do with clay. . . . If only I still sculpted. . . But all one's powers desert one. . . ."

"I promise you you'll be able to work as soon as you're stronger."

"A beautiful country, Portugal. He's invited me to spend next summer with his family. I miss the sun and the sea. I'm going to buy a ticket. The journey only takes a couple of hours."

"But you've never been on a plane before."

"You always have to complicate the simplest things."

"You can't start flying at your age."

"I'll discuss it with him. I do want to go to Portugal."

"You're never satisfied anywhere."

"It's like a prison here."

"You can go somewhere else when you're better."

"Tomorrow, the next day, next week. . . Myths!"

"Come now, Mother—be sensible. You can scarcely walk yet, and the doctor's quite definite: it's too soon to think about moving."

"I don't have to do as he says. You're all in league with one another, you and your wife and him. I might as well be under house arrest. There are giant eucalyptus trees in Portugal. Why are you looking at your watch?"

"You stay here—I'll go and fetch the chocolates."

"I want to go to Portugal."

"If the doctor doesn't object."

"You all think I'm going crazy, don't you? But I can see what goes on around me well enough. Including this conspiracy."

"I don't know what you're talking about."

"I've found out what you're up to!"

"If there's anything you need, you only have to say so."

"I want to be with your father again. . .Why don't you say something?"

"The director's quite right—Portugal's a lovely place. They've got some wonderful Bosches in the museum in Lisbon, with priests riding on flying fishes. And Pessoa, one of this century's greatest poets, was born there."

"What if I went to New York? Your father's still waiting for me there."

"You know very well Father's dead."

"I don't have to believe all you say."

"Your favorite pears will soon be in season—the yellow one with a lemon flavor."

"Do you really think I'm losing my mind?"

"Of course not—it's just that you're tired."

"I want to go away."

"It's getting to be an obsession! You can't keep still—after a month or two anywhere, three at the most, you have to move on. You left my place just on a whim!"

"A whim, you call it! What about your wife and her silent hostility?"

"She's not to blame for anything."

"I knew what she was thinking."

"She's never said anything amiss."

"I'd rather she spoke openly. There are certain kinds of looks—"

"You know we shall never agree on that subject."

"Peace at any price, that's you! You're a coward, for all your pretense of being an intellectual and wearing the trousers."

"I can see you're getting better! Don't let's argue."

"We *have* to argue! I'll tell you what I think a thousand times if I want to!"

"Of course. You left the château at Anet without even letting anyone know!"

"It was like a prison! I had to have my meals at fixed times! If I was five minutes late they wouldn't let me have any soup! I might just as well have been in a concentration camp!"

"What about the Hotel d'Argenson? You ran away from there too. . ."

"I suppose I'm allowed to visit your father's grave?"

"Can't you be satisfied anywhere?"

"I don't belong in this world at all anymore."

"But really—aren't you comfortable here? It's so peaceful and quiet."

"Do you call loneliness peace? And what about all my worries?"

"The doctor's given you some tranquilizers."

"You can't tranquilize a person's soul. You all want to turn me into a vegetable that you can do what you like with. But I won't let you! Your father's a saint, and he'll protect me!"

"Do we really have to torture each other?"

"It's all your fault."

"Perhaps I'm not a very good psychologist."

"You can say that again! . . . I haven't got a friend left in the world."

"I've introduced you to plenty of ladies and distant relations here. What about Nadine Krasinski, who used to know you in Odessa?"

"An ex-housemaid who can only talk about the dead! She bores me to tears—you can't expect someone like me to mix with mental defectives. I've got enough to put up with already. I want to see your father again."

"Mother—you must face the facts."

"The past *is* a fact—it's alive, it survives, even though you won't admit it. . . . But perhaps you're right. Do you think I'm out of my mind?"

"No."

"You say that, but you think the opposite. With all these drugs I can't really make things out. . . You must warn me if I seem to be getting confused."

"It's just that you're tired. . ."

"I need to rest! I know! That's what you keep on saying!"

"It's the truth."

"I understand what's going on, you know! And after all, you don't lie to me as much as all the rest. Angel! And to think I treat you so badly! But it hurts me more than you'll ever know. Sometimes I feel as though—how can I put it?—as though I'm in pieces, and that the pieces will never join up to make a real person again."

"You've got problems with your circulation—sometimes your brain doesn't get enough blood. That means you may forget things and not know what's going on. It's nothing to worry about."

"You say that just to reassure me. You're not telling me the truth."

"No. It's just that I refuse to panic."

"You mean you don't care! You're indifferent."

"If that were true I'd take as little notice of your insults as of all the rest."

"My mind may be failing, but you haven't any heart! Go away!"

"You want me to go?"

"At least when you're not here I can imagine you're my beloved son. But you've changed. *Been* changed. And you know by whom."

"Do you want to walk as far as the main road?"

"No, let's go back. Will you stay and have a cup of tea?"

"If you'd like me to. The car's due to call for me in ten minutes."

"I knew you'd fixed the time you could spare me! Three quarters of an hour of my company and you've had enough! The people who bring you to see me are in a hurry! You bring me some trashy little present to soft-soap me, like that sweater, and after that you vanish for a week. Then you phone me to say you have to make a trip abroad. Lies, so that you have to come and see me less and less often."

"Why can't you be a little more pleasant?"

"Your wife's idea of being pleasant is to smile like a snake."

"You know I'm right."

"You're always right, my dear. Will you tell me the truth?"

"The truth about what?"

"Is Father really dead?"

"You know he is—he died three years ago, on May 1st 1973."

"The past, the past! But you'll never take it away from me, the rest of you—I relive it all the time. It's all I have. What do you think of this tea?"

"It's got a nice aroma."

"What's the matter? You look as though you're bothered—as though you want to say something."

"Last Monday you packed your bags. The director told me."

"I had to go home."

"But this is your home. You asked one of the nurses to get you a ticket to Paris."

"The people are so nice at the Hotel d'Argenson. The manager was always very kind."

"You're not strong enough for the journey—you'd never have gotten there."

"So I'd have died at the station—so much the better! Tolstoy died in a railway station. And he was younger than I am. That would have suited you, wouldn't it? Except for the remorse!"

"The director had no legal right to stop you."

"That's right—talk about law and lawyers. Don't forget the policemen as well!"

"You must promise me not to do it again."

"I didn't actually go. . ."

"No, because at the last moment you had a heart spasm. But you always want to run away—you'll never be content anywhere!"

"I suppose you'd rather I pretended! Yes, it would be better for you if I were just a placid old fool—you wouldn't have to worry about me then!"

"To hear you talk, the only thing that gives you any pleasure is giving me pain."

"Take that back!"

"Very well. Another chocolate?"

"At any rate, de Gaulle was better than this Guichard."

"Not Guichard—Giscard. Guichard's only a minister."

"Isn't there some more to his name?"

"Valéry Giscard d'Estaing."

"That's too long for me! Still, he's very elegant. But Pompidou looked more open. I like fat politicians. Still, a face like that would be very hard to sculpt: no lines, and without lines it's easy to fall into caricature. Look at Churchill—an artist's dream. And Trotsky. And the German—what's his name?"

"Adenauer?"

"The young one, with the eyes of a man who enjoys life."

"Brandt?"

"He'd make a marvelous subject. Yes, indeed. But you don't encourage me—you poke fun at my sculpture!"

"You're not strong enough. The doctor won't hear of your making any unnecessary effort."

"And what about the amusement it would give me—the simple pleasure of being useful, of having some purpose beside dragging myself to the bathroom?"

"I'm glad you're not letting yourself get depressed."

"You've brought me some Turgenev—what a gentleman he is. So elegant."

"Not very deep, though."

"What you moderns call depth! You twist everything around, and then you don't know where you are."

"Will you read it again?"

"My memory's so awful now, it sometimes takes me three days to read a single page. I can't take the words in. But why am I telling you this?—you'll only start thinking I'm going senile again! It's true, but you're too pleased about it. I suppose you'll pay the doctor to sign a paper saying I'm not responsible for my actions."

"What on earth are you getting at?"

"I'm not afraid of you, but I am frightened of your wife—"

"Leave Maria out of all this."

"In a few weeks' time you'll put me in an old people's home. I know it."

"I'll find you a nice *pension* near Cannes, with palm trees and mimosa."

"You are sweet. I don't know. . ."

"I'm tiring you."

"That's your diplomat's way of saying you've had enough and are about to go. Your father was so thoughtful! He used to bring me papers, and point out good heads for me to sculpt. The Duchess of Windsor, with her half-smile—it was he who suggested. . . I made at least ten attempts. And Yul Brynner. . ."

"The actor?"

"The shape of the skull was so tempting, and you can't imagine how exciting it is to work on a vein curving around a spherical surface. Nixon too, with that funny nose. What's become of the poor fellow?"

"He's a crook."

"He knew how to handle the Russians. Don't you think Jean Gabin would be a good subject, in old age? Puffy and malicious—what a face!"

"Would you like some photographs of him?"

"Would I like some photographs? Why do you ask? Your father would have come back next day with a whole sheaf of pictures, *and* enlargements, and I don't know what!"

"You're not working at the moment, are you?"

"I'm allowed to dream, aren't I? You won't even allow me any illusions! You want me to be what I am: a helpless old woman who's slowly dying, and you do nothing but rub it in! A typical intellectual!"

"Come now, Mother!"

"If your father could see you he'd die a second death."

"Do restrain yourself. . ."

"I won't restrain myself! He started to mistrust you in his last few years."

"That's not true."

"Of course it's not true. He adored you, but unobtrusively, much too unobtrusively. But I must stand up for myself, mustn't I?"

"You contradict yourself."

"And you try too hard not to contradict yourself."

"We shall never understand each other."

"Serge has abandoned me, too."

"Your nephew? He came a couple of weeks ago—don't you remember?"

"He promised to come, but that was all."

"Have you forgotten? I came with him."

"That's part of the plot as well. You're all going to pretend Serge came—"

"Yes, he came over specially from London."

"—and then get together and have me shut up."

"Do you want me to write and ask him to confirm his visit in black and white?"

"I must have had a mental blank. I'm very comfortable here. The weather's so mild."

"Good! Oh, while I think of it—will you sign your monthly check for me, please?"

"I don't sign anything anymore. You're all robbing me."

"I can't cash it unless you sign. And if I don't cash it, how can I pay the director?"

"How much does your wife pocket out of my pension?"

"Do I have to explain all over again?"

"You're so clever—you can tell me anything."

"Do you want to consult a lawyer?"

"For him to stick his nose in our business? Certainly not!"

"So you must trust me, after all."

"That's my affair. Do I cost you much money?"

"The check covers a third of it—"

"Dying's very expensive. But there's no need to be so precise! I'd rather not be told you're ruining yourself on my account."

"You make accusations, so I—"

"You don't have to answer. Your father would have been more tactful."

"My father never got around to teaching you what a signature meant."

"He protected me."

"We've had this conversation a thousand times before."

"All right, we won't have it again. I'll sign, but this is the last time. Your father used to spare me such trivialities."

"He also wanted to keep you ignorant of his affairs."

"That really is the limit! You surely don't mean to start casting aspersions on his memory?"

"He's as dear to me as he is to you."

"You've never bothered about us much."

"There was the war."

"But you left us before that, to be independent."

"It's easy to distort the past."

"You bring me presents, and all I can do is make your life miserable. You see what I'm reduced to! My heart doesn't function properly. I can scarcely see. I'm full of noble sentiments, but they all turn sour. I'm like a moldy old yogurt."

"I make allowances."

"You mean you're *not* fed up to the teeth with your mother?"

"You must be joking."

"That's right—laugh! It's healthy! Even a mother's deathbed is good for a laugh—it's just a matter of training! I said your father would die a second death if he could see you. And a third death, and a fourth, and a fifth. You keep killing him over and over again."

"Stop wallowing in your own horrors."

"He was a saint."

"You miss him now, so he's a saint."

"You haven't managed to take his place."

"I do my best."

"Halfheartedly. Reluctantly. *He* was always good-tempered."

"You're forgetting his rages."

"I'll forget whatever I choose!"

"Very convenient—you go through your memories, and those you dislike you suppress."

"That's no way to talk to your mother!"

"And I suppose that *is* the way to talk to your son?"

"Your father was a saint."

"You're repeating yourself, but if canonization helps you *I* won't object to it. After all, reinventing Father might be a way of revising your own life."

"You say that so coldly!"

"I'd never thought of it before—therapy through false veneration. You'll end up persuading yourself he was a literary genius, the equal of Goethe and Racine."

"What you're saying is sacrilege!"

"My dear Mother, your logic is perfect. Well done!"

"I can't take any more."

"Imagination can go too far."

"Who can say whether his poems mightn't be read just as much as yours, two hundred years from now?"

"We'll all be forgotten by then—him, me, and you yourself."

"That's an incitement to suicide."

"I apologize for thinking it was possible to have a rational conversation with you."

"Equality's a farce, as you're always the first to emphasize."

"Especially equality with a mother."

"Are you sure you're taking good care of my money?"

"It's in the bank. You can always check it out."

"I'm not like you—I don't spy on people."

"You accuse me of robbing you."

"If you do, I'd rather you did it with my consent."

"I'll never touch your little nest egg."

"Your father toiled away all his life so that I'd never be in want. If I had to count on you I'd be in the street."

"Do you really think what you're saying is fair and kind?"

"You mean you'd prefer me to bow and scrape?"

"The car's here."

"And we haven't settled anything. Why don't you take the money you need for your vacation out of my account?"

"I couldn't do it without your signature."

"It would be all right for you to rob me just a little. Just enough not to be too obvious. Robbing one's mother doesn't really count. I'd forgive you."

"I don't much care for that sort of language."

"Don't play the intellectual with me! Cultural upstart!"

96

"You're determined to make me lose my temper. You want me to do something you have to forgive me for, so that you come out smelling like roses."

"How little you know me! I'm really all heart."

"So you say! Now your chin's trembling—you're going to start crying. Well, it won't work with me."

"May God forgive you!"

"Spare me the histrionics! You don't believe in Him."

"And sometimes I suffer from it. Prayer can bring relief. . . at least, that's what I tell myself sometimes."

"Like pills."

"Go on—you're as much of an infidel as your father."

"Well, at least we've got that in common!"

"You like to belittle him, don't you? But he was a wonderful poet."

"He was almost a poet."

"At any rate, I could understand what he wrote."

"But you refuse to understand what *I* write. You haven't tried to read one of my books seriously for the last twenty years!"

"They're like the times we live in—complicated, disagreeable, uneasy."

"I can't live in any other times but my own."

"You write deliberately so that I can't understand you."

"Of course—even my writing is against you!"

"I don't know how to cope."

"With what?"

"Oh, you must have guessed. . ."

"No, I haven't."

"With death—we might as well call it by its proper name. This waiting and waiting for it!"

"There's no point in getting depressed."

"I suppose you expect me to be happy as a lark? I took two more tablets than I should have done the other night and I was sick as a dog."

"The director told me you'd had an upset stomach."

"A suicide attempt, more likely."

"Come, don't be childish!"

"I'm so clumsy these days—I make a mess of everything! Aren't you going to make me promise not to do it again?"

"Promise if you like."

"You don't seem very concerned. I suppose you're thinking that in five minutes' time you'll be hurtling along the road at seventy miles an hour, and to hell with your poor old mother!"

"I'll come to see you again in a week at the latest."

"So you say. But something will crop up to prevent you, as usual. Anyhow, it's just a chore for you, coming to see me. Look at you—you're more exhausted now than I am!"

"You will try to get well as soon as possible, won't you?"

"You want me to be good, and to rhapsodize over the marvelous life I lead. Listen, someone's honking for you. Oh, I almost forgot—pass me that yellow package on the mantelpiece. You're not the only one who can give presents. I've got one for you. This alligator cigarette case—it's for your birthday."

"It's beautiful. . . But there's another seven months till my birthday. . . You really shouldn't have done it!"

"In seven months' time I may not be here anymore. So I'm giving you your present in advance."

"You'll be strong and up and about again by then."

"Yes, and going out dancing with my handsome suitors! But do you like it?"

"It's magnificent! I'm very touched."

"There, your friend's sounding his horn again. You'd better go. Don't kiss me—it would look as if you're only doing it because of the present."

"Thank you, Mother."

"And tell your wife she's a bitch. Promise?"

"I promise, Mother."

Brussels, autumn 1925

You rushed into your parents' drawing room, and the first thing I noticed was your long brown dress: you hadn't liked brown eighteen months ago, in Bulgaria. You'd put on a little weight, which suited you, and your hair, which was short before, came down to your shoulders now. You hesitated for a moment, not knowing whom to kiss first—your mother, your father, or your son? Your arms flew out, the top part of your body bent forward while your waist drew back, as if emotion were dividing you in two. Then your mother came forward and you threw yourselves, weeping, into each other's arms. You hesitated again: whose turn was it next—your father's or mine? I stood on one side, as if somehow sensing that respect came before instinct in such cases. You embraced your father with a mixture of moderate warmth and solemnity, from which I concluded that you definitely preferred your mother and didn't mind showing it. I drew back a step: I was glad to see you again, but at the same time perplexed about how to behave toward a mother whose absence had made her unreal. I was shy and didn't know what to say. You didn't come across to me right away: to begin with you just looked me over, exclaiming, sobbing, going into ecstasies about how much I'd grown and how well I looked: I was six inches taller, and my cheeks were a healthy pink. I wanted to run over and cling to you, but you suddenly turned away and went back to your mother. The kissing and hugging started up again, with you gasping "Thank you! Thank you!" over and over. Then you went and stood in front of your father and gave him a firm shake of the hand: gratitude took priority over me. Two or three minutes had already gone by before you felt relaxed enough to trip over and kneel down by me so that our faces were level. Then, silently and infinitely slowly, you caressed my hair, my forehead, my nose, my shoulders. My grandparents busied themselves around the table, on which stood an enormous teapot; there was an unpretentious bunch of flowers—poppies and cornflowers—beside every plate. My father, who'd witnessed all these effusions in silence, proffered polite platitudes.

You and I were becoming an island cut off from all the others. The distance between us and them seemed to be growing visibly: it was as if they were being swallowed up in a kind of shadow; we neither saw nor heard them. You went on examining me: my every feature fascinated you, though you still didn't say a word. Then you stood up, held my hand, led me over to the window, opened it, and led me out onto the balcony. Facing us now was the luxuriant foliage of two or three trees, and it was these you took as witnesses of our happiness. Only the horizon could understand how much our reunion meant. You told me to breathe deeply; our lungs filled with space. You didn't want to share your joy with the others, those who were busy over there, in the distance, with drinks, cake, and a few wretched flowers. You didn't say much, and you knew your words couldn't express anything precise. But I was satisfied, and wondered how your coming might change my usual routine. Your mother came and joined us, and I could see from a faint wrinkle on your forehead that you were put out. There were suddenly too many of us to commune silently with the acacias. We were to go in and eat. You put one arm around my shoulder and the other around your mother's waist, as if pleading for a moment's respite. But no, it wasn't done to be so unsociable.

I could only half understand the things you all said to one another. My father's voice sounded deeper to me than it used to be, and I took an immediate dislike to the knobbed cane he kept beside him. My grandparents were careful to use the polite form of address when they spoke to him, and he was equally stilted with them. This all seemed very artificial to me, and I was soon overcome with a feeling of discomfort which the rich cake only made worse. All the people who loved me were gathered together in one great oppressive mass of flesh. My chair was uncomfortable, I had cramps in my ankles, I kept fidgeting. You all went on exchanging compliments, some diffident and brief, some uninhibited and interminable. I wondered which of you was deriving the greatest satisfaction from this gathering of the clans. I gazed at my grandmother. Her whole body was one broad smile; she seemed at once happy and at the same time able to control her joy. Happiness didn't upset her equilibrium; her voice was perfectly smooth and even. My grandfather didn't attempt to conceal his pride: his goatee, pointing up at the light fixture, might have symbolized his noble yet tyrannical attitude. He dominated the others: his age allowed him to interrogate them without bothering to reply to their assiduities. He was conscious of having done his duty. I'd been put in his charge, and he'd made me into a very presentable little boy. According, that is, to the criteria of the bourgeoisie, which likes to see a proper proportion between knowledge and good manners, physical cleanliness and spiritual well-being. As for my father, he looked ill at ease. He was obviously at a disadvantage: he was an exile from Russia, he'd known hard times in the Bulgarian capital, and now he was acknowledging defeat and coming to try his luck in Belgium. Everyone around the table, except me, was sitting in judgment on him. No doubt they'd be very kind and considerate and give him time to make good, but he guessed at very different feelings behind the sentiments they were expressing, and sensed quiet disapproval in every silence.

For me, feelings, people, things, and surprises of all kinds fell into three categories: those I regarded as good, those I regarded as bad, and those which I couldn't classify but which bored or bothered me. For the time being I decided my father was bad: he lacked authority and looked sheepish, as if the sight of what was going on worried rather than pleased him. He gave me the impression that he was being deliberately awkward, giving irrelevant answers not out of natural ineptitude but by way of objecting to what he saw as unseemly curiosity. After all, he had no clear idea of how he was going to make a living for himself and support his family: before coming to any decision, he could surely be allowed to look around and renew his acquaintance with a country he'd almost forgotten. My grandparents, on the other hand, were good:

I admired your father, despite his occasional sternness with me, and I liked the graceful way your mother concealed her feelings. She could convey her emotions without having to put them into words or gestures, and I could understand them without having to puzzle my brain.

I found it difficult to decide whether you yourself were good or bad. I was very torn: innumerable instincts impelled me toward you, yet at the same time, though I didn't actually rebel, I was on the defensive. I felt happy, but I also had a disagreeable sensation, somewhere between my throat and my stomach, that I ought to force that happiness and make it deeper and more intense. Should I throw off my reserve, or did the mere fact that I was asking the question prove that I was slightly disappointed by our meeting? With every minute that passed you were consigning yourself more and more to the class of things, material and moral, which I saw as productive of boredom or bother. It took some time, and another piece of cake, for me to realize this and to accuse myself of being cold and unfeeling. As my qualms didn't go away, and I didn't want to have to reproach myself, I approached the problem rationally. I studied your every gesture, your every intonation. You were jubilant about everything: life was wonderful, and would become even more so now we were all together again. You had all sorts of plans: finding an apartment on the edge of a forest; finding a primary school where I could mix with children of every social class without getting involved with the sons of laborers; offering your services to the people who organized concerts; making friends for yourself in musical circles; helping my father with his postage-stamp business until he could afford a secretary. No one seemed to contradict you. At the most my grandfather looked a bit skeptical, as if to say life would present unforeseen obstacles and teach you not to take things so much for granted. Your mother, however, backed you up with enthusiasm, playing the maternal rôle so perfectly I began to worry lest the solidarity I sensed between you should redound to my disadvantage. I found my father's attitude particularly odd: he kept nodding courteously, he was careful never to interfere, yet behind an air of imperturbable affability he was dreadfully distant and uninvolved.

I asked permission to leave the table, and went and stood by the bedroom door. Something told me all these people, love them as I might, were in league against me. I went over to my cot, between my grandmother's and grandfather's beds; it was rather small, but I felt safe there. A few drops of sweat broke out on my forehead: would I be allowed to sleep in my usual place for another few nights without being suddenly uprooted? My anxiety turned to panic: perhaps the tea had been too strong for me. I went back and leaned against your dress, and asked if I could at least keep my little white bed with its pink pillows. You told me to sit on your lap, then said I was too heavy. You were pleased at this, but wouldn't go back on your decision: the old bed was too small, and I should soon have a room of my own. I went back to what had been my bedroom door, and there my fears increased and multiplied. Would I still be able to go shopping every afternoon with Léontine, the concierge? I knew Brignol's had the best leeks, and that you had to look out for Verstraeten, a drunken crook who cheated on the weight. I liked going to Fritzke the baker's, because Léontine let me play with the dough. I enjoyed the smell we inhaled during our lengthy visits to Delhaize's shop: a mixed aroma made up of chicory, very red pepper, cinnamon, and dried fruit, apricots especially—as delicious as the scent in any perfumery in the world. Sometimes, when there weren't too many customers about, Léontine would take me in to see Madame Dauze, the milliner, who got her patterns straight from Paris and whose garrulous comments on the latest models filled me with delight. Was I going to have to give up all these voyages of discovery? Would I be prevented from sitting on a stool in the kitchen and listening while Léontine, who knew all secrets, peeled the potatoes and regaled me with the epic history of the Belgian royal family?—how poor Charlotte was crazy when she returned from Mexico; how all through the war King Albert stuck like a flag on its pole to his little strip of territory, which the Germans never managed to occupy; how, in the reign of Louis-Philippe, the duc de Nemours intrigued on behalf of his nephew, Leopold II, who very nearly bought the whole of China. . .

Was I going to have to give up Balloon the spaniel, whose owner, a lean old gentleman on the fourth floor, used to take him for a walk at nightfall, just as my grandfather sent me to bed? I was proud of my friendship with Balloon, and of the marks he made slobbering over my jacket. I used to pinch his jowls and rub the back of my neck against his muzzle.

He hardly even growled, and the old gentleman didn't tell me to be careful: Balloon had never bitten anyone in his life. He took no notice of other dogs. Trams were the only things he would bark at, and then he gave only one brief yap. He would lumber from tree to tree, sniffing, lifting his heavy leg, and stepping off the sidewalk onto the street as apprehensively as if he were about to leap into space. Sometimes he'd draw himself up to his full height and press his nose against a store window, misting it over. When I felt unusually brave and Balloon's expression seemed particularly benevolent, I would sit on his back: he'd carry me along for a few yards, then set about shaking me off, the game over. The other children were afraid of him, and I laughed at their cowardice: Balloon never showed me the slightest hostility.

I thought, too, of Adrien Bouvers, whom I used to meet once or twice a week on the stairs. We'd walk along hand in hand, making bets: how many cars would go through the intersection at the end of the rue Masui in sixty seconds? Adrien had a splendid watch which his father had given him for being good while his mother was in the hospital. I didn't pay much attention to his stories, but I was fascinated by his watch. I usually won the bet: thirty-three or thirty-four cars, a convertible counting as two. If it was raining, we used to arm ourselves with paper and pencil and sit on the doormat in the hall, opposite Léontine's lodge. We'd choose a letter of the alphabet at random and give ourselves a minute to list all the cities we could think of whose names began with it. I was especially pleased with myself over V. I'd studied the encyclopedia, and could dash off Vienna, Verviers, Vichy, Vicenza, Volterra, Viborg, Vigo, Vitry-le-François. . . Sometimes, to complicate things, we'd select a consonant and a vowel together, and I'd scribble down, just as swiftly, Valence, Valenciennes, Valladolid, Valparaíso. . . and dream of fabulous cities that suddenly began to fly, like the magic carpets that floated long ago over the minarets of Baghdad. Adrien's wondrous watch acted as referee, and we'd end up with me owing him fifteen marbles or him owing me a bag of violet-scented candies.

You called me over: what was I hiding away for? You were demonstrating that your whole life was a quest for happiness, and to judge from their expressions your family was right behind you. Your words revealed not

mere self-confidence but downright determination. In the past I'd seen
you angry, listless, or anxious about the future; now I was discovering a
new mother—resolute, ready to fight, not only against adversity but also
against her own uncertainties. You challenged Belgium to get the better
of you: with our help you'd overcome all opposition, all weakness, all routine. You didn't bother to make inquiries; action was much more important. No one dared contradict you, anyway. Everyone was your ally, and
you didn't seem in any hurry to probe beneath the surface. You probably thought your mother was going to back you up in all your undertak-
ings; she was in excellent health, and could be called upon for anything.
I supposed that during the eighteen months of our separation you'd won
my father over to your project, which was to build a life of tangible well-
being worthy of you and of me and of the family as a whole. You weren't
asking much, really: all he had to do was agree to go into exile once and
for all, to work ten or twelve hours a day, and to forget about Russia and
his former dreams. Suddenly you gave me an uneasy look. Perhaps my
grandparents had changed me; perhaps my affection for you was merely
mechanical, and absence had made my heart grow less fond. Perhaps I'd
grown too attached to that serene old patriarch, who might well have
stuffed my head with so many abstract ideas about life, religion, and morals that I'd lost all touch with reality. And what about my grandmother?
Had her affection, perhaps, more dignified and undemonstrative than your
own, made me love her blindly, love her more than I loved you? I could
only make wild guesses at what your feelings might be, adding some, sub-
tracting others, bound to end up far wide of the mark.

For a while your loquacity reigned supreme, as if there was really no need
for more detail: you could run our lives as you wanted. Committing yourself in front of everyone like this was, according to your middle-class upbringing, tantamount to a vow of loyalty to your husband, love and devotion to your son, filial respect to your father and mother. I'd grown up a bit.
I'd acquired a certain amount of superficial knowledge, as a child ought,
together with a reasonably wide vocabulary. I might even have learned to
stop seeing myself as an exceptional individual allowed to do anything he
wished. There was nothing seriously amiss; your parents had been equal

to the task assigned to them. All you had to do was break me of a few habits and cut me off from some accidental attachments I'd soon forget about anyhow. I was terrified at the thought of leaving Léontine and Balloon, and, to a lesser degree, Adrien Bouvers. But that dog, those people, those neighborhood incidents were neither unique nor important: and you must have thought I too would quickly realize they were replaceable. You were taking me over, and meant to form me in accordance with respectable, well-defined principles. I was your subject, and if I balked you would let me know what's what with a combination of some firmness and much coaxing.

There was a steadiness about you, an efficiency, that was new to me, and seeing it being exercised at my expense I turned toward my father. He now sat me on his lap. He clearly had no idea how to talk to a child of my age, and began to tell me fairy tales as he might have done eighteen months earlier. I said his legs were too bony, and took refuge in the arms of my grandmother. You gazed at her with a mixture of trust and suspicion; she surely wasn't going to set herself up as your rival in my affections? Grandmother stroked my forehead and told me to go over to you; she was restoring me to my owner. You resumed your ranting: it was very creditable of my father to persevere in a profession which the ignorant dismissed as laughable. Postage stamps were miniature works of art, and it took a specialist, a lover of engraving, to understand them and appreciate them at their true value. Cakes had by now been succeeded by fruit. This created a diversion. Why should you go on explaining yourself when everyone was in agreement? But you had worked yourself up, and it took you some time to notice my grandfather's skepticism. For him the West was no flawless paradise, Belgium no land of milk and honey. He said the meanness and gloom that prevailed in this part of the world were like the perpetually rainy weather. But who really had the heart to destroy your illusions? The homeland of César Franck, Henri Vieuxtemps, and Eugène Ysaÿe couldn't fail to give you a warm welcome: you were now in a world where grateful peoples threw open the gates of glory to musicians.

I saw you tended to overdo things, and foresaw I'd have trouble getting used to your fantasies. You lacked simplicity. For me your return was a disaster.

London, April 1944

In a report that came in this morning one of our best agents, code-name Sebastian K3, reports the setting up of two new pillboxes in the locality known as La Californie, on the edge of the forest of Eperlecques on the D 219, 1,300 meters south of the village of Muncq-Nieurlet. I open my map—scale 1: 50,000—and enter the new fortifications on it by means of the conventional signs. Later on I shall check up in my card index on the state of affairs in the area south of the Somme estuary and along the dunes between Cayeux-sur-Mer and Ault. French sources have informed us there are three rows of mines laid there, half of them possibly magnetic. I have no way of knowing whether this information is genuine; was the informant an engineer working for the Todt organization and thus a reliable witness, or some local with only the vaguest idea of what he was talking about? It's ten-thirty P.M. and I'm very tired. I pour myself my ninth or tenth cup of coffee today. At the desk next to mine, Richards, who's covering the enemy's battle order in the same area, between Dunkirk and Dieppe, is pleased at having identified a couple of SS regiments. Cressaty, whose job it is to find out about any important changes concerning road communications and bridges, observes bitterly that despite the last raid on Rouen, German troops are still passing freely from one bank of the Seine to the other. I stand up, switch my lamp off, stub out a cigarette, and pace up and down for a bit along the squalid corridor in the lower sub-basement of Peter Robinson's at Oxford Circus. The thoughts that visit me transport me a long way away from my work.

I think of you with deep and serious anxiety. Without even wanting to know why, I suddenly need to be with you. I imagine you in your little New York apartment: you're arranging books, absentmindedly but with infinite resignation. Then you look through some old photographs—two or three of them date from your youth in Odessa, just one was taken in Bulgaria, the rest in Belgium. You don't dare let yourself sigh. You get up from your arm- chair or settee and switch off the radio which you were listening to without really hearing, and cautiously open the door leading into Father's study. He's examining the perforation of a stamp with the aid of tweezers and a magnifying glass; unnecessarily, perhaps, but in order to bury himself more deeply in a task he knows is meaningless. Turning slightly, he catches sight of your imploring gaze. Very well then—he comes over, not saying anything. He can guess what you're anxious about and shares your worry, though he doesn't need to express it. One of you goes out to the kitchen and makes tea; you, perhaps, because activity lessens your anguish, but it could be Father if you're feeling too low. You both stir your tea much more than nec- essary; all your gestures are meaningless, anyhow. Finally you exchange a few monosyllables about trivial everyday incidents of no importance to you. The Negro porter of the apartment block is going to retire; he's being re- placed by a Puerto Rican. Roosevelt has gotten very thin, judging by the photograph of him with Stalin and Churchill. Instead of buying whole watermelons, which are too heavy to carry, you'll buy them by the quarter in the future—a quarter weighs only a kilo or two at the most. There aren't many European movies to be seen in New York, apart from Italian ones, and they're too realistic for your taste. The news from Germany is encour- aging. Suddenly you both fall silent, sensing that the conversation's about to come round to me. You're both very worried about what may be happen- ing to me, and have trouble concealing the fact. But it does you good to know you share the same feelings, and this brief interlude cheers you both up. You exchange remarks about the weather, a tap that needs mending, a suit that has to go to the cleaner's, the way the mail delivery is always so late. Perhaps about the neighbor who lives on the same landing and who's just had a telegram informing her that her son has been killed somewhere among the tiny, deathly islands of the Pacific. What you both are and what you both say is deliberately ordinary.

Oh, how thirsty I am for that good, warm banality! Atherton rushes in: there's an air reconnaissance flight going out tomorrow morning—is there any part of the French coast in my sector that I'd like them to photograph? I look through my files: there's a lot of enemy activity around Fécamp, and my intelligence is already three or four months old. Right—we'll ask the RAF to spend some time over that area. I write down the exact references; Captain Beatty will ratify my request and pass it on. Only a few weeks ago I objected on principle to such operations. Here am I in a comfortable bomb-proof office sending airmen out over Occupied Europe so that I can keep my information on Germany's defenses up to date. Out of every ten comrades who go, how many come back? But this aspect of our operations has nothing to do with me, and everyone at HQ considers my agonizing out of place. What my unit has to do is decided by people higher up in the hierarchy, and anyone in my position and with my technical knowledge would act the same way. I'm perfectly replaceable, and the only responsibility left to me by my superiors is that of deciding whether the intelligence details in my records are adequate for the action proposed. Other airmen will fail to return to *their* bases; should I weep for them too? My job's important and calls for attention to detail, but it's relatively easy. I know the positions of light and heavy anti-aircraft batteries, submarine defenses, machine-gun nests, minefields, pillboxes—of all the enemy defenses of every kind wherever they may be, in every village and every meadow, on every sand dune and every hill. On the day Supreme Command decides to land in the sector I'm in charge of, I'll supply them with a list of all the obstacles, and a copy will go to every battalion commander. I'll have been an indispensable element in that furious attack: why should I be any more ashamed of my rôle in a really fabulous intelligence service than an ordinary soldier is of facing up to the fire-power whose position I'll have warned him about?

I try to be less sensitive now. In December of last year I was chosen to work on the preparations for the second front. I've got several English and

American degrees, and I've been on training courses first in Camp Ritchie in Maryland, then in Northern Ireland and Scotland. These prepared me for the job of war technician and bureaucrat—geographer and geometer of terror. I instruct the cannon-fodder: if they're not completely blind, it's thanks to me and the other hundred and three officers and NCOs preparing for the invasion right in the heart of London. Is this task of mine inspiring or monstrous? If I'd been able to tell you about it, you'd have reacted with sorrow or hysteria or a kind of instinctive compassion. Then I'd have had a reflection of my own feelings and the consolation of knowing someone else felt more or less as I did—though I might have been irritated, too, by your solidarity. As it is I go from one extreme to the other. I have moments of pride, when I persuade myself, weak as I am, that I'm taking part in something of crucial importance, the patient organization of victory. At other times I think all this mass of information and intelligence serves no real purpose: the war will be won by millions of ordinary soldiers pitted against millions of other ordinary soldiers in a gigantic confrontation in which food and sleep, warmth and cold, will count more than all the careful preparations of an HQ paralyzed by theories. Other feelings crowd in on me too, overlapping and contradicting one another: determination, despair, exhaustion, enthusiasm. I know the landing is going to take place in the "Neptune" area between the end of May and the end of the first half of June, and I can already see the first battle on my maps. At first light, under a sky full of planes dropping bombs and surrounded by cruisers and anti-torpedo boats, a slow, methodical, inexorable fleet, made up of transport ships moving like cattle and light landing-craft darting about like fish among the waves to lessen their visibility, will ram the Normandy beaches, strewing the sand with corpses, trails of red, patches of black, and the dull iridescence of wounds. The vision I have of it varies according to the elements. Will the sky be clear that day, impervious to the tiny antics of men and thus favorable to the waves of Flying Fortresses, banked one above the other like the score of a Beethoven symphony? Or will it be cloudy, forcing the planes to fly low and in fear of air pockets, those abysses in which height and horizon are thrown into confusion? And how will the sea react? Will it be calm, with only a trace of saliva on the edge of the beaches to show its haughty indifference, or belligerent on its own account, bent on hurling the ships back, attacking some of them, overturning others so as to play its own part in the holocaust?

I feel I'd like to share my moods with you, though I know the impulse would soon disappear if I were actually with you. Whom can I confide in? You would say something hopeful, which I'd find both comforting and silly, feeble but strangely soothing. And you'd tell me to act naturally, to take care of the minor aspects of my body and soul. After a few minutes you'd have made the march of history seem absurd, and the outcome of any war a matter of indifference. I come in unexpectedly and find you in a blue dressing gown and Father sitting with a shawl around his shoulders. There'd be a burst of excitement, and we'd feel very awkward for a few seconds. You'd turn aside furtively to wipe away a tear and try to compose yourself. Father would put his arms around me with an assumed reticence, then, realizing your claim on emotion was greater than his, go out of the room and leave us alone. Your whole body would hesitate between bliss and the pain of bliss. In the end you'd press your lips to the back of my hands as if to thank some deity for having preserved us. Then you'd gradually adopt the easygoing ordinariness that survives all the blows of fate. You'd pass me my slippers, tell me to loosen my belt and make myself comfortable. You'd talk about what we were going to have for dinner, about hygiene, about the best way to avoid catching cold and how to keep one's nerves under control. All this would be so disarming I wouldn't have to mention the fact that a world war was in progress, or suggest that I was in the slightest danger. Your contribution to the war effort would be to pretend there wasn't a war on at all.

I emerge from my maundering. Cressaty suggests we go out for a breath of air. It's been a long day and our work's exhausting. Richards prefers to stay in the office; he's still trying to locate a motorized brigade which he lost track of somewhere on the plains of Hungary and now can't find anywhere. Atherton comes with us. It's wet outside. Is it springtime? Shall we actually have a spring this year? It's 1944, and seems like an eternal November. A fine, deceptive drizzle makes Regent Street look like an enormous graveyard for antediluvian animals dead for thousands of years.

A siren is wailing in the distance. Is it the first, the alert, warning of the return of the Luftwaffe, or the last, the all clear, promising a lull for three or four hours? Numbers 148, 150, and 152 Regent Street, near Bruton Street, are a mass of broken windows and girders burning among charred blocks of stone. Stretcher bearers belonging to the Home Guard come and go; no panic. They hand out blankets, remove a few corpses. We go on our way, indifferent. What we're interested in is not the Germans' offensive against us but ours against them, and our discipline has to be of the simplest. We are full of our own importance, upright in mind as well as body, happy to belong to the small nucleus of men who are indispensable to the cause of the Allies, Europe, and the West as a whole. We don't need to be reminded of the aims of the war, or of the sacred notions of freedom and democracy—we accept all these things tacitly and without constraint. But every night London is being destroyed. And every day the monumental preparations being made for the second front crush the very people who are its silent creators. Every moment, beyond the statistics, one senses the weariness, the nerves strained to breaking point, the doubts and temptations. Why not just drink oneself into a stupor, or fire into the crowd as it emerges calm and heroic from the Underground shelter after an air raid lasting a couple of hours? People like us, the guardians of the future, are bound to be visited by such fantasies. But we're made of steel; our will grows more unshakable with every step.

Here at Piccadilly Circus things are starting to slow down. Time to get some rest, or go for a beer and a sandwich. Cressaty would rather pick up a girl in Leicester Square; they're quick, efficient, inexpensive, and have been satisfactorily educated in the matter of expert caresses by the Free Poles and Czechs. Atherton wonders whether a nice cup of tea in a Naafi wouldn't set him up after three days of constant overwork. We walk on through the darkness. I like the grubby frontages around Covent Garden: their Victorian baroque is still unscathed. We separate after downing a bit of Cheddar cheese on bread that's neither brown nor white, and half a pint of ale that's neither cold nor warm: we're heroes without a trace of heroism. What do I have in common with these knights in the service of military intelligence? Beatty, our impassive captain, used to be a teacher in Lincolnshire. Atherton's father runs a pharmacy in Manchester. I believe Richards was a kind of professional dancing partner, living on his charm. Cressaty comes from a wealthy family, and will one day go and farm his estate in the Limousin. Chance has brought us all together, and a shared fascination with our work creates a camaraderie that would never have existed but for the vicissitudes of war. Perhaps professional secrecy constitutes another bond, a kind of corporate conspiracy; if so, I don't trust it. If we wore colored neckties they'd all be different, and in civilian life half of us wouldn't give the time of day to the other half. For the moment we're friends, and it's not impossible that if one of us was in mortal danger the others would sacrifice themselves to save him. But this doesn't prove anything much. We wouldn't be so close to one another if the fundamental uncertainty about everything that haunts us all hadn't penetrated us to the very marrow. We're united by a quiet terror: where shall we be in a few weeks' time? One may have died stupidly in an air raid, playing the tough guy out in the open in Hyde Park in the company of a white-lipped prostitute. Atherton may have missed the landing because of an attack of dysentery or because he hurt his leg jumping too fast out of the train that brought him to Southampton. Perhaps I myself will be wounded in the head by a piece of shrapnel as soon as I've landed on one of the Normandy beaches. All quite normal and ordinary and without any impact whatsoever on major events. But if I didn't think like this at least four or five times a day I'd be the blindest of optimists. And jeering at death is one of my ways of staying alive.

It takes me a long time to get to sleep. What sort of Europe is it I reign over? Russia has been bled white; the whole of the Ruhr is in flames, and so are the suburbs of Hamburg and Frankfurt; Yugoslavia has lost one man in ten and will soon have lost one in three; Poland is being forgotten; the Nazis are executing anyone who dares to think or to laugh, and will soon execute anyone who dares to breathe. Budapest, Strasbourg, Milan, and Prague are all scheduled to be wiped out; cholera reaps its sinister harvest; the plague's skeletons are happy to gather more partners for their *danse macabre* in the remotest farms of Moldavia and Lithuania. Why shouldn't the blood-swollen Seine sweep away the towers of Notre Dame and the Louvre, toppling the Palais de Chaillot as if it were a mere wooden hut? Why should there still be a France, even?— France, with its music-making orchards; its fields of oats caressed voluptuously by the wind like the hair in the nape of a woman's neck; its footpaths winding from Romanesque porch to Gothic portal, frisky as poachers, austere as widows hastening to milk their cows; its roofs higgledy-piggledy, unable to agree whether to slant to the east or the west; its vineyards which cross on Sunday to the sunnier slopes opposite, and, having for centuries produced black grapes, take a sudden fancy to bear fruit that are brighter, louder, and more joyous?

I shall unleash a whole army against Europe, so that it bleeds from its side, from its breast, as never before. I shall destroy Normandy for its own good, and it will hate the very people who come to deliver it from shame and subjection. I shall make every chimney, every wall, every alley, shriek with pain. I shall be a liberator—don't ask me of what: it will all be in ruins. I shall give back liberty—don't ask me to whom: there'll be nothing there but shrouds and common graves. I shall speak of truth— but don't ask me where: children with their heads blown off no longer listen. I shall sing a hymn to freedom—don't ask if I'll be alone: even the elm trees will have lost their trunks and their roots. I shall impose peace by means of bombs, by sending fighter planes into every window as if throwing grit into someone's eyes—don't ask me what I feel: the hamlets will be left flatter than tablecloths ironed for village fêtes. I close my eyes at last. My only morality is to prepare the death of millions of men; it's no longer a mere duty—from now on it's my very nature. I lean out the window beside you in your tenth-floor apartment in New York. The Japanese cherry trees are in bloom; three barges go by on the Hudson River, making for Staten Island; above them the clouds rush past so swiftly their shapes dissolve into chaos. Father tells us we'll catch cold. You put on a Chopin record and talk to me about Rachmaninoff. All sighs are light as air, carpets never wear out, souls rest in peace again, the stewed blueberries taste delicious.

Paris, April 1952

My living arrangements in Paris were very modest. After the luxury of Berlin I had to lower my sights, limit my expenses to about twenty or thirty thousand francs a month. But I didn't have much trouble exchanging one illusion for another: no longer an international civil servant endowed with very ambiguous powers, I would now be an out-and-out candidate for literature, trying his luck between the Deux Magots and the Café de Flore. I told you of my decision, and you immediately offered to come and join me in Paris: you'd find me a studio and help me furnish it elegantly with the little nest egg I'd managed to put away. I had to make up all sorts of reasons to stop you from coming; I intended to complete my studies and at the same time write a novel, and as the Sorbonne was overcrowded I'd have to choose another university —Lille perhaps, or Bordeaux, or Grenoble. I also begged you not to leave Father, not even for two or three months; he was at the age when work starts taking its toll, and if he was to grow old without feeling it too much he needed someone there to make him take things easily. My arguments were pretty vague, and your replies revealed your disappointment: in Berlin I'd accepted your parcels and thereby entered into a certain complicity with you, but in Paris I had no scruples about keeping you at arm's length. Keeping other people at a distance had become a permanent necessity with me, and you seemed to realize and resent it. You asked me specific questions which I took great care to evade. I hadn't quit my job in Germany because of some serious disappointment, and neither the English nor the French nor the Russians had given me the sack. I'd simply decided of my own free will that my education was incomplete and it was time to acquire a few degrees. As a veteran of the American forces I was eligible for a modest three-year study grant, and I wanted to take advantage of it. Your letters—eight or ten of them a week— showed you didn't really believe me: there must be deeper reasons for this sudden change of direction.

Sometimes I left your homilies unanswered. Then you'd return to the charge: if a mother was to be useful she needed to know all. This would annoy me, and I'd send you almost threatening telegrams. "Very tired. Going to the mountains." "Sitting exams. Writing later." "Considering all alternatives. Love." You'd allow me a short respite and then tell me how you'd met some young man who'd fought in the Pacific and who, having had experiences similar to mine, was able to give you some insight into my state of mind. Or you'd seen some lady just back from Rome, and your eyes were suddenly opened to the state of post-war Europe, so wounded and wretched and hungry. You coaxed me, you tried to get around me, you were quite monstrously patient. You cross-examined me about my private life, which I never so much as mentioned in my letters. I was thirty-two now: wasn't I thinking of getting married? But in your next missive you changed your mind: all things considered it would be better for me to get to know women not as a conqueror or as a member of an occupying army, but with all the sagacity I must have acquired from experience. I scolded you severely: you'd made no progress at all in psychology since 1939, and still talked to me with the same uneasy mixture of sanctimoniousness, commiseration, and unrequited devotion as before. You protested by return mail: how could a boy of yours possibly be so cruel? I must either be very ill or under the influence of someone who wished me serious harm.

I smiled. I'd been living with Maria for nearly a year and was about to inform you I was going to marry her. To tell the truth, you were in my way—you had no real place in my life. I didn't feel any hostility toward you. I acknowledged the part you'd played in my childhood. But now I didn't have any use for your sentimentality or your devotion; at the most

I might think once or twice a month that it would be nice to spend an hour with you. But you weren't buying that; I had no right to eliminate you from my thoughts just because I was embarking on some new adventure. In every line of your letters I detected resentment, imperfectly disguised as almost hysterical solicitude. In the end I skimmed through what you wrote more and more swiftly, paying attention only to the twenty or thirty words that Father added at the foot of the page: they gave me the gist of the unremarkable events that made up the dull existence you both endured. Had any of it affected either of you at all—the Russian Revolution of 1917, your going into exile, your settling in Belgium, the war fifteen years later, your departure for the United States, the relative comfort of your life together in New York? I envied you both your serenity, and suspected my father knew, somewhere deep inside, that it had only been won at a price, whereas you had adapted yourself to it quite involuntarily. I compared his stoicism with your lethargic renunciation, and concluded that you were right to doubt me. From then on, all my solicitude was directed unobtrusively toward my father.

You wanted to know about my daily life right down to the last detail. My eyes weren't all they might be—did I have enough light to read by? Was my bathroom properly equipped? I must be careful about what I ate and avoid cold cuts; the best thing would be to employ a woman to cook and look after the house, and if I couldn't afford this minor expense—it wasn't a luxury, you insisted—I could pay for it out of our joint bank account. Above all I must steer clear of the subsidized student restaurants: a year of them was enough to give anyone stomach ulcers. You knew what you were talking about; you took no care about what you ate and now had an ulcer yourself. My thanks for your advice was very halfhearted, but you kept it up: only a mother could be bothered with such trifles. Philosophy, literature, and turbulent ambitions were all very well, but you claimed authority over neglected colds, bad coughs, and constipation. I sent you photographs of my apartment—two undistinguished rooms on the quai Louis-Blériot; a view over the river was their only attraction. But that didn't slake your curiosity: you detected a woman's touch in the drapes and the tablecloths. You couldn't help yourself: you accused me of hypocrisy and said you knew less and less about my private life as well as my thoughts. What had you done to be left out in the cold like this?

This broadside plunged me into uncertainty. My need to be free was so intense that even the people closest to me loomed like obstacles all around me, blocking every avenue by which I might communicate with myself. I couldn't stand them for long. Sometimes, scared by my own solitude, I'd try to draw near them again, but they'd learned their lesson and it was my turn to be hurt by *their* aloofness. Why wasn't I completely frank with you? There was nothing reprehensible about what I actually did or about what I vaguely wanted to do. Being Russian and Belgian by birth, Bulgarian by early upbringing, American by chance, and German through my hastily acquired maturity in Berlin, I felt torn between several nationalities, and my overriding desire was just to provide myself with more stable roots. At the time I was coming to regard French literature as my one true homeland. I wrote you several letters saying my studies took up only a small amount of my time: what really mattered to me were my relationships with two or three poets, novelists, and playwrights. But I couldn't find the right tone of voice; it seemed to me I sounded too angry, too tense. We'd been apart for many years, and our brief reunions hadn't helped much, being both overwrought and inhibited. I no longer knew you very well, and had no desire to figure you out for myself. My affection was merely theoretical, my solicitude abstract, and my interest blunted by boredom. You were forever making advances, but I was suspicious of them. Maybe I was finding it so hard to size myself up that I didn't have time to cope with my image of you, always being scrutinized in vain and abandoned with a sigh of relief.

I organized my days with method and determination. As soon as Maria left for the office at about eight-thirty in the morning (she worked for the Marshall Plan, in the economics department), I sat down at my typewriter and wrote exactly three pages of a novel. Never more, for in my view quantity was the enemy of spontaneity, and it was better to stop short leaving much unexpressed than to end up with the feeling you'd said it all. That way, at least, I'd find myself with plenty of things clamoring to be clothed with words the next day. Just before noon I'd shave, go down to the boulevard Exelmans, and come back with some grated carrot or cucumber salad, which I combined with the previous day's leftovers for my lunch. I topped it off with a yogurt, some fruit, or half a bar of chocolate. Between three and four I went over my lecture notes and read from the works of such authors as Sartre, St.-John Perse, Henri Calet, and Marcel Arland. Every other day, before dinner, I'd take the métro to Saint-Germain-des-Prés, where I'd join the poets sitting in Lipp's as if in judgment on the rest of the world. I often made myself unpleasant by talking about the nuclear threat and praising the atom; sometimes I predicted that existentialism would come to an end eventually, just as surrealism had before it. I took the temperature of people's minds and souls, telling myself I was getting to be accepted. At least they couldn't accuse me of upsetting an established order: intellectual chaos was universal. I would set out for home at about eight, and then was the time for caresses, abandon, and love. My lectures at the Sorbonne were the only thing I permitted to interrupt this routine: the least I could do was obtain a piece of paper enabling me to teach French wherever I wanted. If I couldn't make my way in literature, I could always fall back on being a teacher.

There was no reason why I should conceal my hopes and doubts from you. On the other hand, why take the risk of sharing them when everything was so uncertain? What would I look like if one day I had to give in and admit that my literary aspirations were as unfounded as my father's once were? I was extremely proud, and as things were I could tell you about my victories and avoid admitting my defeats. I preferred to evade the issue, to seem uncertain or weak and keep my hesitations and enthusiasms to myself. Later on I wouldn't mind playing the historian and giving you brief accounts of events that had affected me. But for the time being I had nothing to boast about: even my relationship with Maria was quite ordinary—or would have seemed so to you. I realized I was afraid of being judged by you: I knew your verdict would be merciless. You'd never forgive a mistake, or only in order to paralyze me and bring me back into line. Your letters became wilder and wilder, as if you didn't bother to read them over anymore. You filled them with all your grievances, all your annoyances and irritations. I felt I had to be a bit less

119

tolerant. I wrote pointing out that dialogue called for a certain amount of dignity on both sides. And for two or three months I wouldn't tell you anything about the things that mattered to me. I was in good health, I had nearly enough money to provide for my modest wants, I was pursuing my studies: what more did you need to know? I made good use of the photograph technique: if I sent you a snapshot of me standing by my desk wearing a sweater, or in a raincoat by the Eiffel Tower or the Sacré-Coeur, or by the Odéon intersection carrying a newspaper, you could work things out for yourself. I had no time to waste. You had nothing else.

But your complaints and demands finally had their effect. Of course you had the right to know more about your son. I wasn't a coldhearted monster—it was just that my caution sometimes became obsessive. Maria told me her bosses were sending her away for ten days on a trip to Austria and Turkey. I took the opportunity to phone you (a thing I never did): why didn't you arrange for friends to keep an eye on Father and come over to Europe right away? The weather was fine, things were inexpensive in Europe, you'd meet the young woman with whom I was currently sharing my life, you could stay with me while she was away, and then you could go on to Mondorf for a cure, just as you used to go to Vichy or Bad Neuenahr before the war. You were devoted to the memory of your mother, so you could stop off in Brussels to visit her grave—maybe you'd meet some old friends. Ten days later you landed at Le Havre, in excellent form and great good humor. Back in Paris your first priority was to visit all the museums. Your hotel was only a modest place near the Madeleine, but you found it charming. You told me you'd wasted years going over and over the same old sterile ideas and now you wanted to bring yourself up to date: painting and sculpture were the fields that attracted you most. Your musical education had been completed long ago, and as far as that was concerned the radio met your needs. The advantage of the plastic arts was that they obliged you to move about, to go on little trips and modify your tastes. You told me you'd already visited the museums in Philadelphia, Washington, and Cleveland: you weren't quite the passive dimwit I supposed. I went with you several times to the Jeu de Paume, where you paid your tribute to Monet's cathedrals, and to the

Museum of Modern Art, where to my surprise you recognized paintings by Rouault, Juan Gris, and Dufy without a moment's hesitation.

It wasn't until the fifth day that you started to ask questions. You'd probably been expecting me to confide in you, and guessing I felt awkward about doing so, had waited—in vain—for me to take the initiative in the form of little hints. I thought that instead of inviting you to our place it would be safest to introduce Maria to you in your hotel, over a coffee or a glass of lemonade. You were all dressed up, and I'd asked Maria to wear one of what I considered her prettiest outfits. It was, after all, a rather solemn occasion. You both behaved with perfect politeness and a good deal of reserve. Beyond your curiosity I soon detected a patient hostility. Of course you went into ecstasies over the roses Maria had brought you, but I could tell from the look you gave me that you thought it had been my idea. You chatted away with each other about this and that: Paris seemed poorer since the war, people weren't dressed so well here as in New York, everything was gray, but after all the charm of the place outweighed any defects or difficulties. You went on to clothes: the price of hats, shoes, and nylon stockings loomed very large in the conversation. Designers provided you with common ground: you recalled the great pre-war names—Poiret, Chanel, Patou; she was more at home with Jacques Fath and Christian Dior. You agreed quite straightforwardly to come to dinner with Maria and me the next day. Neither of you said anything particular on that occasion; you yourself merely wondered if there was enough room in the apartment for me and my desk and my books. I realized you were saving up a great many suggestions and maybe a great many criticisms too. You were registering every word and gesture, and would certainly serve them up again later in a partial and inevitably incomplete form. I felt uncomfortable: you and Maria were still strangers to each other, and I couldn't help thinking I'd interrupted a chapter of my novel for the sake of these pointless formalities. You'd go back to the United States, and Maria either would or wouldn't become my wife—I didn't want to decide anything yet. I was expecting specific questions, perhaps an out-and-out assault. I was sure you'd ask Maria to tell you about her family, her social background, her education, her ideas about the world in general and me in particular. I'd imagined you making use of all kinds of traps and maneuvers, and when I couldn't detect any I was almost ready to conclude that you were now indifferent to my fate. On the one hand I was relieved: if true that would mean I'd be freed of a lot of pressure. But on the other hand it was insulting to occupy such a small place in your concerns. You were moderately complimentary about the meal, and wished Maria good luck, but you didn't make any reference whatsoever to the fact that we were living together. Maria, for her part, showed you every nook and cranny of the bedroom: she'd be delighted if you cared to use it while she was away—I could sleep on the couch in the little living room. Both of you sounded completely natural and yet rather cold; it's not impossible that both of you were speaking quite sincerely. I'd forgotten you *could* be quite calm and amiable when you liked.

As soon as Maria had gone, you moved in—not, you explained, to save money or to meddle in my private life, but to cook me some of the things I liked to eat. You told me in passing you wouldn't expect me to keep you company from morn till night: I mustn't let you interfere with my studies, my engagements, or my writing. You began by moving a few things around: a mirror in the bathroom, a vase, a bedside table, some cushions, the telephone directories. Before long you attacked the knives and forks, the dangerous and unhealthy gas-heater, the color of the fitted carpet, the elevator, and the building as a whole. I was amused. After a couple of days nothing found favor with you anymore: the apartment was undistinguished, the street unworthy of me, the view of the river blocked by ugly and depressing factories. But words and minor adjustments weren't enough: you moved on to epic exploits. You threw away half the saucepans and replaced them with new ones from the Printemps which you said were easier to keep clean. You ordered a more luxurious stove and brighter lamps—the latter would be better for my eyes. I had to call a halt to both your zeal and your spending. I informed you, with icy sarcasm, that material considerations meant nothing to me. I hadn't left behind the high life in Berlin in order to come here and bother about my furniture. You immediately set about proving that if I wanted to be a great writer I must have a soft pillow, a stainless steel frying pan, and a tap that didn't make any noise.

Nor was this lesson in *savoir-vivre* enough for you. One morning at breakfast you asked me point-blank whether I really meant to marry Maria. "That woman," you called her. I could feel my temper rising, and deserve some credit for restraining myself. Instead of counter-attacking and praising my partner, I merely said I couldn't find any obvious fault with her. You answered that even if I were right a man married a woman for her good qualities, not for her lack of bad ones. And you hadn't seen many good qualities in Maria: she was energetic—i.e. calculating; decisive—i.e. unscrupulous; hardworking—i.e. full of secret ambition; realistic—i.e. inacapable of understanding the things of the heart and the mind. I let you go on. I even poured you more tea and passed you more croissants. Once I'd gotten over my initial surprise I was highly entertained by your harangue. I saw in it every aberration a mother is capable of when she guesses her only son might be in danger of dividing up the affection that once was all hers: now she'll have only a quarter or a third, and the rest will go to a stranger, henceforth the most cruel of usurpers. For the first time I told myself you'd make a very good character in a novel. I made a clinical study of your behavior. You were amazed to encounter so little resistance, and plowed on with your argument: Maria was just an ordinary secretary; her manner was merely superficial, an attempt at concealing her true nature. You didn't go into what that was. She wasn't a match for my own inner richness—she was too well organized in her everyday life to have any room left for imagination or the soul. They call for dreams, or at least a modicum of emotion. She didn't understand what I was like deep down, and was bound to bring me bitter disillusionment. I wasn't to ask you for proof: your feminine intuition was infallible.

I interrupted you only long enough to tell you you'd strayed into pure fiction—a good example to set a future novelist. You didn't deign to notice my quip, and resumed your attack with fresh vigor. Maria was an American, and thus unaware of the invisible dimension of life. Some day she'd come to be ruled by self-interest alone, and I'd have to put up with her unalloyed greed and ambition. She showed every sign of this already, even if at present she did pretend to love me. The state you'd found the apartment in was enough to prove it: anonymous, too neat and tidy, without any of the carelessness denoting true magnanimity. I congratulated you again on your literary talent—the ease with which you moved from the novel to poetry, and thence to philosophical exegesis. Then, to overcome my immovable composure, you produced a really incontrovertible argument: Maria wasn't Russian enough. This time my manner did change and I let rip with a few home truths: *you* were much *too* Russian, much too Slav, much too incoherent and undisciplined for my taste. For twenty years I'd been thinking this, and now it was time to say it straight out. My resentment had been building up: who asked you to pass judgment on other people and draw far-fetched conclusions when a little reticence would be more seemly? You were just an ageing old gossip, blinded with jealousy, and so lazy that instead of asking me a few honest questions you preferred to base your behavior on unreliable appearances. The instinct you were so proud of had been drowned in your irresponsible blather; your dignity had melted away like a bar of soap.

We were both silent for a while. The best thing to do was forget our quarrel and go and make it up in front of some modern pictures. So we took off for the avenue du Président Wilson and compared our likes and dislikes in front of the works of Fernand Léger, Van Dongen, Mondrian, the Cubists, the Fauves, and the Surrealists (whose technical skill you admired though you didn't really understand them). Perhaps it was in a kind of shared joy in the presence of Delaunay that our minds came closest together. I was just about ready to forgive you your excesses when you saw fit to start up again. It was quite commendable for me to go in for literature: I was only following in my father's footsteps a generation later on. But I must build my future on a foundation of genuine feelings, and not let myself be led astray by the first female who came along, just because she was attractive and good in bed. By this time we were sitting at a table in Rumpelmeyer's, the tea-shop in the rue de Rivoli whose old-fashioned charm and chestnut purée reminded you of chatty gourmandizings in Odessa and Brussels. I gave you a formal lesson in psychology, speaking of myself as of a perfectly understood subject. I wasn't a spontaneous person, and rarely acted impulsively. I was seriously in love with Maria, even though I wasn't consumed with passion

for her. We weren't very much alike, but that was an advantage: our characters complemented each other. Her stability and equable temper made
up for my volatility, while I could develop her taste and make her feel
she was sharing in the dangerous but thrilling venture of launching me
into the world of literature.

You weren't overly impressed by my explanations. You nodded, savored
the aroma of your China tea, sighed and took refuge in silent skepticism.
These subtleties flustered me; I'd have preferred a direct attack. So now
I was harsh, excessive, and unfair. You had no right to pop up all of a
sudden from America, which had made you vulgar, and try to change my
life as if I was just another piece of furniture, to be shifted around until
it was finally carted off to the refuse dump. You'd never been tactful
enough to keep your distance, and flaunted your prejudices without making any attempt to understand other people's point of view. You regarded
yourself as infallible, which gave you a peremptory manner that absolutely
drove me wild. As for me, I had enough experience to be able to tell the
difference between a whim and a real emotion, between love and a passing fancy. My own assertions soon struck me as no less disagreeable than
your reproaches. We both had a tendency to go over the top and indulge
in petty recriminations. I suddenly declared I might not marry Maria: I'd
taken her on approval and liked her well enough, but I hadn't decided
anything. It might be better after all to have some other affairs, to live a
bohemian life as a writer—independent, unpredictable, and unattached.

But did this picture make any more favorable an impression on you?
Perhaps you suddenly had a vision of me as a down-and-outer, a drunk-
ard, a prematurely old young man staggering from one lamppost to the
next as he might from one heart to the next, charming but a pariah, talented but unable to ward off the blows of fate. But my tactic wasn't bad
in itself: you'd rather see me settled down even in the wrong way than a
prey to my own demons. Somewhat put out by the alternative I'd just offered, you soon thought of a third solution. Why didn't I, as you'd asked
me to do several times since 1945, go and live in the United States? The
chances of success there were better than in France. I launched into a
fresh dissertation: America had been just an incident for me, an inter-

lude for which I wasn't responsible. I didn't dislike the place, but my future lay in Europe, and in particular in Paris; of this I was absolutely convinced. And I'd put up enough of a fight to try my luck there! My true language was French, and nothing could make me change it. I seemed so determined you abandoned this front and renewed the offensive against Maria, and in the course of the verbal duel that followed I got carried away and told you some fantastic lies. One day, I said, during the famous blockade in 1948 and 1949, when the Soviets were besieging Berlin, I'd been arrested by some East Germans while I was on my way to HQ at Pankow in an official car. Maria, learning of this through some mysterious double agents, had used bribes and threats to get me released after five or six days' detention. You distrusted the Russians so much that this pathetic soap opera struck you as perfectly plausible. Drawing yourself up with a sneer, you asked what the world would come to if we had to marry everyone who saved our life! This enormity reconciled us, and on our second visit to the museum we exchanged learned and subtle impressions in front of Picabia and Jacques Villon. Our good humor lasted—by dint of a great deal of effort on both our parts—until you left for Mondorf three days later. I didn't think there was any point in telling you that if in a crisis I had to choose between you and Maria, Maria would win.

Paris, July 1977

Is it done to cut one's mother up into chapters? Does one distort her by clothing her in words? I'm embarking on a dubious and uncertain operation: that of trying to resuscitate you by telling your story as if you were a character in a book, no truer and no more false than those to whom I sometimes give life in my work but who have never really existed. I'm beset by scruples and reservations in the face of this need, this urge to re-create you in the name of fairness too intensely desired ever to be quite free of error. But no sooner do I feel I'm making a mistake and being false to myself as well as to your memory than I'm confronted by another point of view: how can I possibly give a faithful picture of you when everything has to pass through the unreliable filter of words? Writing is my life; I am conscious of having written; everything else, though I'm about to enter my sixties, is poor and ordinary. Whatever I may say about myself is bound to be convoluted and strained, so little do I trust my idea of myself. It's always paralyzed by the facts, and they strike me as immeasurably tedious. The world of the imagination suits me better: but as it fosters dream rather than awareness it, like other evasions, provides only intermittent inspiration. What I say about you must correspond as closely as possible to your mind and your physical appearance: as the fog of fiction fades, it's my duty to depict you as you really were. My own peace of mind is at stake: I mustn't beat about the bush—I must paint a portrait of you that is recognizable.

What's really needed is a good memory, but I'd be wrong to put too much faith in what mine is like now—sometimes strangely clear and smooth, at other times all crumpled up, or as full of holes as an old mess-tin on a battlefield three years after the last casualty expired. Either the too shiny surface irritates me, or I try to mend it as best I can: but the result's never more than a botched job. Do I see you again as you were, or, by a supreme irony, is it myself as I was that I see? You are my mirror, unless, as you fade into the past and its deceptive reconstructions, I become yours. Our images echo and contradict each other, and will soon be no more than inaccurate reflections of models that are both gone forever. Then emotion comes to the aid of impartiality, and I tell myself writing is just as good as experience: you are what I succeed in saying, after your death, about your being. I resign myself to there being a kind of inevitable vibration which distorts everything, and which, because it is sometimes painful and sometimes liberating, infuses something of you into what I write. The image you gradually assume in this book bears only a distant resemblance to that which other, less prejudiced observers, may have seen. But it is the one that will last, while countless other memories disintegrate inside heads too weak to give them permanent form.

Memory is an absentminded lady out for a walk. A stray veil from her hat falls in front of one eye, while the sun dazzles the other. She tosses her head free, catches a glimpse of certain recollections, loses sight of them again, and keeps repeating the process. Some of her memories seem quite close, but she doesn't trust herself and wonders if they aren't really very old. As for other, more recent ones, she tries so hard to make them out in the clearest possible detail that she alters them out of all recognition. I think about you at the time when I was a child: everything is simple, radiant, and serene—but what barren wastes between the scenes! I think about you during my adolescence, in the 1930s, and you fade into the shadows: others are in the foreground—friends, girls I hankered after, teachers, famous men in encyclopedias in whose footsteps I almost followed. I think of you in the 1940s, and then perhaps I think of you as a distant consolation for a terrible spate of events during which my mind could retain only misfortune. Try as I may, my memory of you in the fifties and sixties is completely vague: it's as if I had to be satisfied with faded photographs, indecipherable letters, and a few movies projected in reverse onto a dingy screen. But was I really so free of you then? Had adulthood already left me alone and prey to my own inconsistencies, with you unable ever to intervene? In your last years, however, you're restored to me intact—tyrannical, solemn, persistent. Every time a memory from that period comes back to me I feel an almost unbearable pressure on both sides of my head, as if an enormous boxer, drunk with his own triumph, were squeezing my skull and trying to split it open like a watermelon.

But memory obeys no rules. It's like an anthill disturbed by an earthquake, with the inhabitants scrambling in all directions. Images succeed and generate one another without regard for chronology. Sometimes they make me think of a plane exploding at forty thousand feet: a suitcase whizzes past after a disheveled old man, followed by a bottle, a pair of spectacles, a pregnant woman, a plane seat, a diplomat, a pair of twin sisters, a trolley—all swallowed up pell-mell in space. Sometimes, even if the images are quite different from one another, they merge together into new ones, artificial or outlandish. Time and space meet and disappear, and I link something that happened in Sofia with a forgotten incident in Brussels. Then I have to try to sort out words and gestures which really have nothing in common, and memory is corrected, mended, repainted, copied. It's like an old master at the mercy of a forger, or a piece of period furniture reproduced in worm-eaten wood. I dip you in and out of memory as if such alchemy could give you back an authenticity lost forever. But when I manipulate you like this, am I giving you new life or a second death?

A strange osmosis takes place. From a distance of twenty or thirty years I really can make out a smile of yours or something you said all that time ago. Yet when it comes to feelings, the ones I ascribe to you are my own. I suppose, by a kind of oversimplified logic, that makes some sense: after a hundred pages of mimicry you wind up resembling me. If ever I speak of you with enthusiasm or repulsion, I invariably find I'm speaking about myself. After half a book, can we still be separated from each other? What becomes of objectivity when you wallow in another soul that you've come to regard as imaginary, and all you find, there in the mud, is your own? Are you supposed to reshape it, watch it dry, and give it a specific meaning? Everything I say about you applies to myself. It's shattering. Sometimes I feel I must run away from you, tear up all these pages, liberate myself by means of some simpler heroine, whom I only have to make up and who wouldn't pursue me with questions about her plausibility. But the harm is done: I'm no longer master of my words. They're as full of you as fleas gorged with blood after a night-long feast on their victim. But words are my very substance now: who am I to give them orders? They ill-use me, rule me, lead me astray. I lend them a feeble murmur, and they take all my breath away: my lungs are empty, my chest transfixed—they won't let me breathe anymore. They shove against one another like a frantic herd of primitive bison, each struggling to be the first to take shape and send the others crashing down on the prairie. Once upon a time my fingers could make the syllables shape themselves as I wished, but now the rules have changed and only the words themselves have the right to unfold a plot or carve out a character from nothing: you are what *they* decree, regardless of us both. Of course, I could punish them and simply shut up the book. . .

But I have to admit they transcend me and my inadmissible motives. Dare I claim *I* could feel, as fervently as they, what *they* express? They outstrip me, authenticating in advance whatever I'm able to think about you. If they betray you, don't hold me responsible. Between you and me there's no longer any room for truth: imagination alternately sets us at odds and reconciles us. I arrogate to myself the right, a very debatable one, to conjure you up; I no longer have the right to bring you to life again as you really were. I keep retouching your portrait: on one page it takes on unforeseen depth, on another it founders in wan approximation. In any case, what I'm working at is inevitably a self-portrait.

Ostend, summer 1933

Your behavior was simple and inflexible. I was about to enter what your fashionable friends called the awkward age, during which I would be nervous and unpredictable. There was no need to keep lecturing and rebuking me: instead of bothering about the growth of my mind, you had to make sure my physical equilibrium was beyond reproach. I ought to eat lots of spinach and chicory, and above all plenty of ox-liver, as underdone as possible. I must also shower twice a day, for this stimulated the circulation and cleansed the mind of any unhealthy thoughts. But in your view three weeks at the beach in August was the healthiest measure of all. What could be better than sunshine, ozone, and swimming for a growing boy who read too much and didn't get enough exercise? You and Father—though he was acquiescent in the matter rather than keen—had settled on a villa at Mariakerke, a family resort with the advantage of being only four kilometers from Ostend. While Father and I were swimming, you could attend tea dances at the Palace Hotel and indulge in nostalgic reminiscences of Odessa with your Slav—mostly Polish and Serbian—cronies. Admittedly it took some imagination to summon up Odessa nights, sitting under pasteboard palm trees over iced coffee strewn with petals of candied violet. The illusion must have been hard to sustain amid sighs and hand-kissings performed in the most ponderous Flemish style, coarse as caresses in a painting by Jordaens.

I must have met Cécile Dewaet one morning when the tide was out and the sand still damp. It was a dull day, and instead of going in swimming the children of my age improvised various ball games. Boys and girls formed teams and rules were decided on, with interesting variations. For instance, points scored could be exchanged for shrimping nets, or—if parents turned a blind eye—for furtive kisses. This sort of thing was highly popular, and parents, prizing their own peace and quiet, intervened in extreme cases only. We weren't allowed to go into the beach huts for more than a minute at a time: after that, someone came to see what we were up to. Cécile Dewaet was tall and slim, cheerful and nimble. Her height and agility meant she was extremely good at catching a ball of any kind; the rest of us envied her. She was two years older than I and regularly outpointed me, so for a long while I looked on her as an enemy. Sometimes I merely sulked; often I'd have liked to stick out my leg and trip her. Once, when she was about to win a baseball match with particular ease, I accused her of taking advantage of the wind, which happened to be against me. She burst out laughing and gave me a smacking kiss on the lips by way of consolation. I wiped my mouth ostentatiously.

"I *can* kiss much better than that, you know! Would you like a sample?"

I didn't know what to say. I went on playing with such fury I nearly won.

"The next time you do win," she said, "I'll wait for you in the yellow beach hut!"

That kept me awake all night. The next two days I played so badly the others howled at me and considered kicking me off their team. All I was good for was building sandcastles with the younger kids. At about five o'clock on the second day, Cécile Dewaet came over to me.

"Shall I cheer you up?" she said, and took my hand.

The yellow beach hut—to which I crawled with some difficulty, imagining thousands of people watching and making fun of me—contained two campstools, a few brassières, some bathrobes, a beach umbrella, and a big straw hat. Cécile locked the door on the inside. We were in the dark.

"Do you want to undress?" she said.

I preferred to put my hand on her firm little bosom, then on her knees, which were too bony for my taste. She let down her swimsuit to the waist and asked me to put my arms around her. As I did so she put her lips on mine, which she soon pried apart with a warm greedy tongue. I was at once agitated and furious with myself at not coming up to scratch more eagerly.

"It doesn't matter, it doesn't matter," said Cécile.

Time seemed to stand agonizingly still. I was frozen with fear. She took her own swimsuit right off, then helped me out of mine. Her skin was soft and warm and deliciously paralyzing. I felt horribly awkward, and ready to jump out of mine. She placed my hand against her belly, and I explored areas that felt damp, furry, and slippery. I told myself I ought to be experiencing enormous joy and wonder. But in vain—my impotent imagination couldn't supply me with the slightest pleasure.

"Is this your first time?" she whispered.

Instead of answering I took refuge in the hollow above her collarbone, then under her armpits, protecting myself both against her and against myself. I felt as if we'd been there a whole hour. She had felt me all over and played with my penis. I blessed her inwardly for being older than me and taking initiatives of which I was quite incapable. She rubbed herself vigorously against me, and suddenly the smell of her gave me a strange kind of relief. I found myself on top of her, about to penetrate her; she was helping me and pushing me away at the same time. Then with her knees up by my shoulders and her claws around my waist, she shoved me against the door of the hut and called out:

"Next installment tomorrow!"

That evening at dinner you remarked on how pale I looked, and objected to my fidgeting and my sulkiness. I wasn't hungry, and merely toyed with the prawn salad, usually a favorite of mine. Even the greengages we had for dessert seemed tasteless. You asked me if my digestion was all right. Had some of the other boys been nasty to me? Had I caught cold bathing when the sea was rough and the temperature of the water only sixty degrees? Had I overtired myself playing games on the beach? I wasn't in the mood to answer with more than monosyllabic grunts, from which you concluded that I should go without my usual evening stroll along the promenade and be in bed by ten. I tossed and turned all night, but seemed so cheerful in the morning your suspicions were allayed. But Cécile Dewaet didn't show up, and the beach hut remained locked throughout the morning. To your surprise, I expressed a wish to go with you to Ostend; you decided to stay at home instead and keep an eye on me. This made *me* suspicious. If *I* had secrets, I thought, *you* must have some that were much more shameful than mine: you didn't go to the Palace Hotel to see your lady friends but to meet gentlemen who were more alluring than my father and took you to gaming rooms where children weren't allowed. Perhaps they invited you up to their apartments for amorous frolics like mine, conducted with a know-how I envied but couldn't quite imagine.

I passed a more peaceful night this time, though I did lie awake from time to time, pondering the mysteries of Cécile's body. What with the dark in the hut and my own panic, I hadn't looked at the rings around her nipples properly, and had only a vague memory of the shape of her breasts. Her hips, too, were still an enigma; I couldn't have said whether they were wide or narrow, rounded or bony. I hadn't even thought about her hair. She might well be a brunette, verging on auburn, but I couldn't have sworn to it.

When I saw her again, wearing a curious swimsuit with black and yellow stripes, I hailed her with a boldness which I made sound as vulgar as possible.

"Hallo, stranger! Are you a brunette all over?"

She started to run like a hare, and I followed her along the edge of the waves, noticing she could have used a bit more flesh on her bones.

"Shall we go to your hut again?"

"Who said you were the only one, infant?"

"Do you change them often?"

"All the time!"

"I love you."

"So what?"

"Will you?"

"Tomorrow morning at ten my mother's going to Ostend to buy undies in the sales. So is yours."

"Promise?"

"Do you want me to swear?"

"May I kiss you on the forehead?"

"Don't be such a dope—do you want the whole beach to come running? Why don't you come horseback-riding with me? We'll go slowly. I bet that'll be your first time too, eh?"

"I don't have any money."

"Not even three francs? A fine lover I've picked for myself! Oh well, I'll pay for you."

That night was delightful. I dreamed about birds sliding down hillsides covered with millions of orchids. Next morning you said how right you'd been about the virtues of sea air: I was obviously getting my strength back. I didn't look at all like an overworked schoolboy now.

This time Cécile kept her word. We greeted each other with an unobtrusive wave of the hand and a wink quite free of guile. She didn't trouble to bolt the door of the hut. In fact she left it very slightly ajar, so there was enough light for me to check the color of her skin in the most intimate places. The tide was coming in swiftly too, and if we'd had time to take stock of the situation instead of just plunging into it, the sound of the waves might have made us feel we were in tune with the universe. But we were more modest and more absorbed. She gave me quiet but precise instructions. I was to kneel down, make a long slow journey between her ankles and her thighs, and then stop, advance again, retreat a little, then go forward again, all this involving both my hands and my mouth. We had to be quick but not too quick. She told me my maneuvers were conscientious and effective, then suddenly took my breath away by ordering me to apply them to another area. To her spine, from top to bottom. I did as I was told, though I had to concentrate hard. I took advantage of a lull in her moans to make a grab at her: I had the right to some pleasure too! She gave a loud laugh and a forceful demonstration, ranging from my legs to my chest, of the skill of her fingers. We were panting by now, and I found myself not hating her. Both my body and my mind were willing. Cécile, very red, opened up. My flesh entered hers, and moved, and felt itself on the brink of a terrible explosion.

"Withdraw," she said.

I obeyed. She asked me if I had a rubber, and when I hesitated she took one out of her bag. Now she was even more tyrannical.

"Put this on!" she said impatiently. I wasted precious seconds. My reason, with its long procession of bogeymen, paralyzed me completely. Cécile understood my predicament, and seized hold of my flesh to give it back its firmness. I entered her again, and we merged into each other amid jerks and spasms resembling both rage and receding waves, both abandon and deliberate toil. After a few moments I lost all sense of where I was. I wasn't me; I was an abstraction, moving about in a kind of void. The most minute cells in my body, my Achilles tendons, the nape of my neck, all sent a series of shudders to the center of my being. I felt an immense fire being kindled within me, a terrible volcano demanding release. I found it difficult to breathe, and suddenly thought of you. When the eruption was over, it seemed to me you had taken Cécile's place.

"Not bad," she murmured. "Not bad."

That evening you found me unusually lively. I praised everything I saw. I compared the street, which was dull and gray, with the landscapes of Polynesia, which I knew nothing about. I said I was going to become a great man, probably the inventor of flying submarines and planes that traveled at the speed of light. I kissed you without being asked. I even said the veal, which was burned around the edges, tasted perfectly delicious. On the days that followed, Cécile Dewaet and her mother came and sat with you on the beach, and you exchanged friendly, insignificant conversation. I was puzzled: those friendly glances, that calculated politeness, those vague but cordial invitations all looked suspicious to me. Cécile's mother was much *too* friendly with you: perhaps you both shared unimaginable secrets. Gradually I came to think the pair of you knew about my escapade: you'd plotted the whole thing together so that I should lose my virginity under favorable conditions, without any need for solemn and embarrassing injunctions. My former satisfaction gave way to gloom. Maybe I deserved no credit at all for seducing Cécile. Maybe she'd been instructed by both our families to teach me what a young male needed to know. I avoided her for the rest of the week. It was *she* who asked *me* if we could go and shut ourselves up in her hut again. I resisted for a couple of days, then desire got the better of me. Once again I thought of you at the supreme moment, and wondered whether this unfortunate association mightn't eventually impair my prowess. But I made a great effort and told myself sternly that I mustn't allow my mind to put you in the place of my partner: I wasn't responsible for the incongruous images my flesh came up with in such circumstances. Cécile assured me my caresses and my muscles were all very satisfactory, but when I asked her if she loved me she just gave a rather patronizing laugh. She'd see about that later. Meanwhile she'd give me a chance to make a small place for myself, even if only temporarily, in her heart. Was I annoyed or relieved? Her technique had allowed mine to make rapid progress: why bother to burden myself with pointless sentiment? I met her again in our hideout three or four times. Perhaps you knew, and did nothing about it. Then the vacation was over, and it was time for me to link arms with Jean de la Fontaine, embrace Charlotte Corday, run my hands over Charlemagne and make love to Louis XI and Colbert, before going on, the following semester, to Marie Antoinette and Madame de Pompadour. It wasn't certain I'd meet Cécile again next year, and she came to take up less and less room in my daydreams. That fall you said we wouldn't be going back to Mariakerke: Father's business had been looking up, and we could now afford to spend August on a more fashionable beach— Knokke-sur-Mer, for example. The memory of Cécile Dewaet gradually faded, though it didn't disappear altogether: I felt a mild sort of gratitude toward her, though it didn't last very long. Perhaps the loss of my virginity wasn't all that catastrophic. You too were proud it had happened that way. My sex life hadn't caused you any bother.

Paris, December 1976

You confess you've been for a walk on your own, and I scold you gently: you fainted twice last week, and the doctor expressly forbade you to go out alone. You say if you were to die in the elevator or on the sidewalk it wouldn't be any more tragic than dying in your bed. I notice the fifteen or twenty different medicines standing on your bedside table: are you sure you can tell which is which? This makes you smile: what's wrong with dispatching oneself into a better world by taking the wrong pills, if that's what fate decrees? I pass you a letter that arrived by the eleven o'clock mail. You glance at it vaguely and put it down on the table: you're not expecting to hear from anyone special, and conventional greetings from old ladies—once friends but now forgotten—don't interest you. This morning you felt strong enough to dress, which is already something to be proud of. The top of the Eiffel Tower can be seen through the window, so you conclude that the weather can't be too bad. You stand up, and your arms start to tremble as though they might suddenly fall off. You tell me not to be alarmed: you find it hard to control your muscles— or rather, it takes a great effort to do so. Soon you won't be able to get as far as the bathroom. The other day you were caught short and wet the carpet, and you were embarrassed at having to explain to the landlady. Old age is a curse: it's a terrible thing to live too long. We totter out of the room; you hold on to the walls, not wanting me to help you. Trying to make a good impression, you call out a cheerful good-morning to the cleaning lady as we go past the kitchen. If you don't make them think you're reasonably strong, you explain, they'll throw you out. Then you'll have no alternative but to go to an old people's home, with the women shouting and bawling and getting up at night to suffocate the person in the next room.

You're terrified of the elevator: you cling to me and huddle in the corner as though you expect the cable to break at any moment. The four steps leading down to the street are not so bad; you can manage them with your cane. Outside you stop every ten or twelve yards, and only your eyes seem to be functioning normally. The first halt takes place a couple of store windows along the street, on the same side as the turning into the rue de Grenelle: some travel brochures are on display, advertising an Australian airline and some turquoise blue mosques in Pakistan. You ask if that's not in the Asian part of Russia, but almost at once you tire of my explanations and say there are too many governments in the world, too many new towns, too many old cities that have been renamed. You heave a sigh and repress another, trying to catch my eye and make me bear witness to your physical decline. Your left leg is almost useless: only by fierce determination can you move it along, with little flicks of the hip. Five or six gilded cherubs in an antique dealer's window intrigue you for a moment, then give you a chance to philosophize. Anybody can buy anything these days, and people have lost the instinct for quality. Most experts are crooks, and their customers ask to be robbed for want of anything else to do. We press on, and at the corner of the avenue de la Bourdonnais you take a lively interest in the rows of postage stamps fixed inside the glass door. I explain that this is one of the places where philatelists can buy the stamps France prints for its former colonies, now independent states. You answer with some asperity that I set myself up as a know-it-all in order to expose your ignorance. But a few yards further on you change your tune, and I'm your darling son who knows everything and hasn't a single fault. When we come to the traffic lights you shrink back, and I have to use both arms to help you across. Once on the other side you nod with your chin at a bench where you'd like to sit down; you insist on dragging yourself to it, no matter what.

Finally we get there, and when you've settled yourself and calmed down a bit you tell me late autumn is milder here than in New York. The leaves may be yellow and dying, but they're still beautiful: when *you* stop breathing you won't be as serene as they are. I think of things to say to distract you. Do you remember Sacha Guitry? Well, he had a house a hundred meters away from here. More than twenty years after his death people are discovering that his plays and films are not so negligible as they were made out to be. When Yvonne Printemps, one of his wives, left him for Pierre Fresnay, he told a friend, "That gentleman will soon find out how easy I was to please!" This anecdote makes you laugh, reluctantly at first, then with more abandon. For all their meanness, you say, the French are the wittiest people in the world. I glance unobtrusively at my watch. The torture will soon be over. All I have to do now is see you home.

But you have other ideas. You take a couple of oranges, already peeled, out of your capacious bag: would I like one? I advise you not to take off your gloves or unbutton your coat. Oh! you exclaim: I do still love you a little, even if, when you're all alone, you often wonder about it. But now, for the rest of the day, you won't doubt it so much. Anyway, I'm the one who ought to be careful about the cold, and cars, and life in general. One can never tell what may happen. We are silent for a while, each munching an orange wrapped up in a handkerchief to protect our clothes. You let out a long sigh. Those postage stamps! They follow you, persecute you, wherever you go. Your eyes waver, an expression of terror spreads over your face; you look as though you're going to faint. I turn up your coat collar. You push it down again. You're too hot, you want to go home at once. I'm about to take your arm but you pull away: no, you're going back to that shop to ask if your husband has been in for his stamps yet today. I explain, very cautiously, that Father won't be coming today, or ever. You give a short laugh: of course, *I'm* your husband now! You're straining forward, and if I didn't snatch you back you'd measure your length on the sidewalk. Once more you straighten up. Your face is calmer and you apologize for getting confused about people and things and recent memories. I can't help admiring your tenacity. You consider this walk, exhausting as it is, as proof that you're still alive. Without it you'd be no more than a misshapen body letting itself be slowly invaded by death. It's too soon to go home, you say: let's go on for a bit, as far as the avenue Bosquet. We pass a barbershop, and you tell me the youth who works there as an assistant goes and meets the girl who runs the local grocery store—she's probably Portuguese—at four-thirty every afternoon. They disappear down the rue de l'Exposition, and go and have a good time in one of those hotels where they're not particular about who they take in. The fruit is wonderful: the apples so red, the bananas so yellow, the oranges so orange. France may not be serious, but it has irresistible charm! You're almost cheerful, though every so often you walk more slowly and press the knob of your cane against your heart. There it goes, all aflutter, this old ticker of mine! . . . Now it's relaxing, but soon it'll start to thump again: it usually takes two or three minutes to settle down afterward.

Would you like to go into the café? But you're feeling better now and prefer to go on. The customers there are mostly down-and-outers, and the owner looks like a coal delivery man. He wears a pullover with great sweat-marks under the arms: we're not going to stoop to having a cup of *his* coffee! The world's always making progress: when you were young, people couldn't buy strawberries all year round, and they had to wait until at least April for decent radishes. It's quite depressing—there'll be even more wonders and new inventions when you and I are both dead and gone. I agree; what else can I do? You say you know you're boring me—it's obvious I'm exasperated. If I wasn't so damned polite I'd just ditch you there and then in the middle of the street. Then you'd have to try to get home by yourself, but you wouldn't have the strength. You'd lose your balance, fall over, and break your hip. You don't know why you have to keep living on and on like this—it's obscene. I try to change the subject. What about going into this tea-shop and having a few pastries? What?—it's the worst of all the four bakeries in the neighborhood! They must use lard instead of butter. Or candle droppings, more likely. I laugh loudly at this: I've no choice but to pretend it's very funny.

You say you want to make a new will, and ask if it's better to be buried or cremated. I say we'll discuss the matter again in five or six years' time. You tell me not to be foolish: am I afraid to face facts? I try to look serious again: one of an individual's most sacred rights is that of choosing how to dispose of his or her own body. But by this time your thoughts have strayed to something else: you'd like to read Pasternak again—meanwhile, could I get you the latest number of *Paris-Match?* You love the articles about Aristotle Onassis: he was a gentleman, generous and full of vitality, whereas Jackie Kennedy was just a skinny bowlegged schemer with a face like a frightened fox. If only Onassis had met Marilyn Monroe, what a fine couple *they* would have made! We turn back: you're getting breathless, and the excursion is starting to tire you. You can't understand how it is that for the last couple of months kitchen utensils, saws, pliers, and other items of household equipment have all been on sale at reduced prices in the hardware store. Things can't go on being marked down twenty percent for ever! Do I think there's anything sinister about it? The night club next door to the apartment block where you live doesn't look very appetizing; according to the photographs outside, the guitarists who play there have terribly long, unkempt hair. This irritates you extremely: real musicians don't go in for such affectations. Did anyone ever see Jascha Heifetz or Toscanini or Bruno Walter as sloppily turned out as this lot?

You dismiss me quite gaily by the elevator: I've wasted enough time already today with my old ruin of a mother! You're strong enough to go up on your own: you must show your landlady you're still able-bodied. I insist on coming up with you. We ring the bell, call out to the cleaning woman again—yes, your walk has done you a lot of good!—and arrive back in your room. You unlace your shoes and collapse on the bed. You're exhausted. I sit down in your armchair and pour you a glass of water. Would you like a spoonful of one of your tonics? You're torn between a green medicine and a red one, then settle for just an aspirin. The skin under your chin twitches every so often, and the swollen veins on your hands reach as far as both wrists and fingers. You point to a suitcase on top of the chest of drawers: we haven't much time—the train leaves in an hour and a half. I ask gently, though I'm very shocked, where you're thinking of going. You say the move's all arranged and Father is waiting for you in New York. Or somewhere—you can't quite remember the place.

I say you must rest first—a little sleep will help you get your strength back. Anyhow, I say, as if joking, this is your permanent home. You persist: Father let you take a vacation, but now you're taking advantage of his kindness. You gradually become more and more incoherent, and shrink back inside yourself. We gaze at each other. Haven't we said all we have to say to eachother, and said it too many times? I'm sure you take me for somebody else. Perhaps a doctor; perhaps—your eyes are so full of fear—a murderer. You warn me writers have an unfortunate tendency to drink and gamble, and I'd better not follow the example of Pushkin and Lermontov. Tolstoy's another matter. You want to ask me a favor: when you speak about Father as if he were still alive I must correct you—you're strong enough to bear the truth. Isn't Romy Schneider one of the loveliest creatures to be seen in the international cinema? But she shouldn't associate with such a hideous fellow as Jean-Paul Belmondo. O for the days when actors were as elegant and distinguished as Ivan Moschukin, John Barrymore, and Adolphe Menjou! Everything's going to the dogs: a glance at you is enough to prove it. You're going to rest for a while, then get ready for dinner. It's always much the same: vegetable soup, a piece of stewed veal, stewed fruit. But it's all the same to you so long as it's not too difficult to chew. Triviality is the strongest bond between us now. You don't like my tie—it doesn't go with the color of my suit. A civilized man should be careful about details like that! You'll get me a new one; you're sure I'll be delighted with it.

143

Brussels, autumn 1939

As soon as the doctors said definitely that your mother was suffering from generalized and inoperable cancer, your resolution was unwavering. You called together your father, your husband, your son, your brother Armand and his wife Mathilde, and told them you meant to take immediate steps to make sure your mother was comfortable and surrounded with more than physical care. The spiritual dimension was very important in such cases, and you meant to put your whole soul into this. All hesitation and weakness must be swept aside; in particular, there could be no question of leaving your mother in the hospital, where she'd be surrounded by strangers and soon realize her life was in danger. You started by asking the others for their opinions, as if you hadn't already settled exactly what must be done. There were great lamentations from my grandfather, who was visibly shattered by the news and didn't know how to face up to it. You turned to Mathilde: she was less directly concerned than the family itself, so perhaps she could take a more objective view of the situation. She had the good sense to reply that you and my grandfather would know best: feelings came before practicalities in these circumstances. You now focused on Armand: he was rather volatile, you said—not the sort of person one could rely on to stay the course. You weren't criticizing him—just summarizing the general opinion of his character. My father protested mildly: we weren't there to analyze one another but to arrive at a common decision. But Armand was allowed to make a suggestion: he thought your mother should go home to be with your father; if necessary, a nurse could come in every day, or a nun—consolation was her profession. But this was a solution you absolutely rejected, and you couldn't suppress your sarcasm. Your mother had never never liked Armand; he'd been the laughing stock of the family for thirty years; he'd married a housemaid who didn't know how to behave; he was a cretin who made a living selling wireless sets. You'd paid him the compliment of consulting him on a serious matter, but it was clearly a matter of indifference to him.

Mathilde and Armand rose from their chairs: further discussion was impossible. My grandfather wagged his beard gravely and muttered "Children! Children!", thus restoring a semblance of calm. You went on chairing the meeting, but with a sudden circumspection that belied your real feelings. You even apologized to Mathilde for insulting her. Of course you hadn't meant a word you said—it was just that Armand's bored looks had gotten on your nerves, which were in a bad state because you hadn't been able to sleep last night: one can't be expected to be very cheerful when one's mother is dying. Mathilde didn't say another word all the time she was there. Armand, whom the preceding row suited down to the ground, lit a cigar and disappeared from view amid blue smoke rings. Besides, he said a little while later, he had to go to Cologne on important business, and he'd leave the rest of them to decide for him. After a few uninspired phrases, my grandfather soon bowed out too: at the age of eighty-one, crushed by disaster, he was neither strong nor lucid enough to know what he really wanted. He'd like to make himself useful, he said, but he didn't know how. All he was afraid of was being lonely at night, when it's unbearable. You took advantage of his maunderings to put forward the only plan you were prepared to tolerate: your mother must end her days in your house, where no one could doubt she'd be looked after a thousand times better than anywhere else. But you reassured my grandfather, with a kind of contempt that shocked me, that you'd go and see him as often as you could. I too would visit him frequently, and you were sure Armand and Mathilde would do their duty by him. You also offered to muster up some friends, some distant relations, perhaps some neighbors: the old man would gradually get used to the idea of becoming a widower, and after all his tragedy was the tragedy of us all. I thought your argument monstrous and cruel. I even spoke up and said I didn't feel I was limited by it. In situations as serious as this, I said, a person had to act according to his conscience, without arranging some kind of tribunal to let him off lightly. Armand, struggling with the recalcitrant butt of his cigar, was the only one who agreed with me. If I called in at his office when he got back from Germany, said he, he would treat me to lunch at the Taverne du Passage: their saddle of hare was delicious.

So you had your way without Father saying anything. All he could do was agree with you, down to the last detail. After she'd had the necessary tests done, my grandmother spent five or six days in her own home. She was weak but serene, and spent her time knitting, doing a few undemanding chores, and giving herself temporary comfort with endless cups of herb tea. Meanwhile you turned your own apartment upside down. Your room, including the bed you and Father slept in, was to be given over to the patient, and you and Father were to move into the drawing room, where a hastily chosen iron bedstead was to be installed. This meant you wouldn't be able to have visitors, but never mind—this was hardly the time for entertainment! Several pieces of furniture were to be crammed into Father's study. Only my room was to remain unchanged, but as it was very small and I now lived in a student residence hall, it would come in useful as a closet to store things in. Once these arrangements had been made, you set about redecorating the main bedroom to make it more agreeable. You put up some new lace curtains, took away the mirrors so that your mother wouldn't be constantly reminded of the progress of her illness, and replaced them with reproductions of Mediterranean landscapes. The workmen spent three days repapering the walls: they'd been light brown before; now they were pink. Then you put bowls of flowers everywhere and scattered a few house plants around. All that was missing was a rocking chair, which you bought on the installment plan so Father wouldn't object to the expense.

Once your mother was settled in this virginal setting you did your best to make her think her health was on the whole very good. But she needed to improve the condition of her blood, which had been undermined by an unsuitable diet. She would have to be patient, because the chemical process involved in such cases was bound to be slow. Your mother swallowed this complicated untruth, backed up by pseudo-scientific arguments, but her strength was declining and after about three weeks she was obliged to take to her bed. The doctor came every day. You didn't go out anymore, and even gave up cooking the meals. Father could manage well enough: there were plenty of cheap restaurants in the neighborhood. You made special dishes for the patient, and kept a close watch over her moral well-being. Your behavior was a masterpiece of delicacy and tact. You mapped out the days with the utmost care. After her morning toilet you brought the patient a substantial breakfast: toast, a soft-boiled egg, coffee and hot milk, and a different kind of preserve every day—blueberry, strawberry, raspberry, quince, or an English mixture of orange and lemon with a smell and taste of its own. On fine days you would pull the drapes back and open the window: sometimes a bird's song would mingle with the noise from the trams. If the weather was bad you would hide it behind an arrangement of flowers set on a low table. When the meal was over you gave your mother an expurgated version of the latest political news: Europe was safe and sound, and Monsieur Daladier, with the help of Mr. Chamberlain, had made Adolf Hitler see reason. If our armies were being mobilized on the frontiers it was just as a precaution and not because war was imminent. There would soon be elections in Germany, and the Nazis would be replaced by decent people. As for Stalin, he would remain neutral: despite its present régime, Russia was fundamentally peaceful.

Having administered this little lesson in optimism, you fetched the wool and the needles. As your mother was too weak to knit now, you knitted for her: she could give you instructions as you went along, and you could discuss who the sweater was to be given to: your father, who felt the cold but didn't like mauve, or me—the student hostel was damp, so I'd need a pullover next winter. Or perhaps it should go to Armand: he traveled a lot, and risked catching cold at railway stations and in hotel corridors. At about ten-thirty you'd leave: you didn't want to over-tire your mother, who dozed off every so often, and if anyone stayed with her all the time she might become alarmed. You managed to strike a subtle balance between casualness and too much solicitude. Just before noon the doctor would arrive, check the patient's pulse, take her blood pressure, and prescribe some harmless tablets. But toward the middle of October it became necessary to administer intravenous injections, and this gave her a fright. You found a reassuring explanation: she was getting stronger, so they no longer hesitated to use a more radical kind of treatment. The midday meal now took the form of a little party, on which no third person was allowed to intrude. You'd put a carnation or a wallflower on your mother's tray beside the invalid dishes and purées. Or perhaps the surprise would take the form of some knickknack—a Dresden statuette, an antique key, a thimble studded with jewels, a musical snuffbox. They weren't really presents—just things designed to set off a harmless conversation, all devoid of any connection with suffering or despair. You would claim that the statuette had been given to a distant member of the family in the 1880s by a prince from Württemberg who was in love with her. Then the pair of you would pretend to make out the exact relationship between you and the lady in question, invoking in the process all kinds of forgotten people—Russian and Moldavian, Tartar and Ruthenian—and taking a conspiratorial pleasure in exploring what you both knew was a purely mythical past.

By this time the food had been finished, the prunes eaten, the herb tea drunk. It was flower time. You would compare the virtues of mignonette and peonies, orchids and laburnum, fuchsias and pansies: though since there's no accounting for taste, no conclusion was possible. But what did that matter? It gave you the opportunity to talk about a park in Odessa, a government forest in Kherson, an unforgettable garden in Simferopol, my grandfather's native city and the setting of his assiduous and lengthy courtship. You gently brought the conversation around to the subject of your mother's approaching convalescence, and said you thought a spa would be the best place for it. This new fable gave you an opportunity to talk of places which you didn't know yourself but of which friends had spoken highly: Karlsbad, where the mountains are blue and the springs very healthful; La Bourboule, where motorists are forbidden to sound their horns lest they disturb the people there to take the waters; Monte Carlo, where every millionaire hires three or four private detectives to stop him from committing suicide in the early hours of the morning after he's lost all his money at roulette. My grandmother would gradually fall asleep during all this, and you'd creep out of the room, pleased with yourself but exhausted. Then you'd secretly shut yourself up in the kitchen and have a good cry, emerging pale but a little more relaxed.

Early every evening you'd go back to your mother's room and offer to read to her. You'd choose some passage from Griboyedov or Zénaida Hippius—neither too stupid nor too clever—and read it out a bit at a time, going back a few pages and starting again if you noticed she'd lost the thread. At seven o'clock you brought her the last meal of the day: almost always a light soup and some breast of chicken. Then you plumped up the old lady's pillows and put the little hand-bell within easy reach on the bedside table so that she could ring for you if necessary. But in any case you got up at least once every night, at about three o'clock, to come and open her door and make sure she was breathing regularly. All these rituals were kept up without variation. You showed the same patience and determination in the matter of visits: no one was allowed to disturb the timetable you had established. In your opinion it was my grandfather who needed disciplining the most: you figured he had the right to see his wife every other day at the most, but the interview should last no more than ten minutes, to avoid whining, lamentation, and mutual pity. To prove your point you referred to the doctor's orders, which you invented on the spot with a composure born of steely resolution. Nothing must be allowed to endanger the patient's nervous stability or put a strain on her heart; in her present state, any emotion was dangerous. Grandfather finally accepted these orders: in fact, he was resigning himself to never speaking freely to his wife again. You didn't ask yourself if this was painful to him: you couldn't be bothered with such subtleties. As for my father and me, you said we'd be allowed brief incursions of a minute or two, just long enough to smile and tell the invalid she looked wonderful. But as neither of us was very eager to follow your instructions—Father because of his natural sense of decency and I because I didn't want to be away from the university and my studio too often—we didn't perform our rôles very satisfactorily. Sometimes we were as awkward as any other reluctant recruits; sometimes we overdid the affability.

Armand and Mathilde were instructed to come twice a month: too much solidarity might seem to portend the gathering of the vultures. Only distant friends and chance acquaintances escaped such precautions. You could control them more easily, and as your mother wasn't especially fond of them their visits weren't too significant. Their kindness wasn't sinister, and they had a great advantage over the rest of us in that they created a useful diversion. I gradually realized you wouldn't tolerate anything unexpected: you meant to hold undivided sway over your mother, having made up your mind that no one else could look after her so well or so devotedly. But after about ten weeks, fatigue began to leave its marks: you were becoming shrewish, jealous, and nervous. Your mother was getting thinner every day, her once plump face grew gaunt, and her breathing, now rarely normal, was often more like a metallic snore. The doctor prescribed morphine, and you realized the end couldn't be far off. But your mother's pain must be relieved, even if it meant depriving her of her last lucid intervals. At the beginning of September you told me she probably wouldn't hold out past Christmas, and made me promise not to tell her that war had broken out: she was conscious for only ten or twenty minutes a day now, and they mustn't be marred on any account. But I suddenly rebelled—not against your instructions as such, but against your behavior in general. I accused you of monopolizing Grandmother's deathbed and taking over the future corpse. Your dictatorial ways didn't deceive anyone. You must have some serious lapses on your conscience—errors dating probably from your youth, before I was born—and now you were trying to expiate them. You were treating your mother like a commodity that had to be protected from thieves: were the rest of us predators, then? You needed to suffer, so you acted as if *we* weren't worthy to share in the pain and despair. I, assuming the right to speak for all the rest of the family, was being just as unfair as you.

You didn't react to my reproaches at the time: your mother took up every moment of your day and nothing else counted. But as the days went by your attitude changed. Through a strange compensatory mechanism you stopped devoting yourself exclusively to your dying mother and turned hungrily to me. Was it because, realizing that one prey was about to escape you, you wanted to make sure of another right away? You'd begun to see that trying to prolong a life which was almost over was an illusion. Why not apply yourself instead to protecting with all the fervor at your disposal a life which was just beginning to unfold, but which until now you'd merely brooded over and coddled? You told me I ought to make the most of the priceless gift of being nineteen. You spoke of the war: what lay in store for us? Next spring would probably be disastrous. I detected a spark of universal consciousness in you which I'd never seen before. Your mother was going to die, your husband could be relied on for a sort of balance between serenity and deliberate blindness; in this emotional context, didn't I represent a bet on the future? But what did such a thought amount to in the days of Hitler, Mussolini, Franco, and Stalin? You held out a couple of thousand-franc notes, telling me not to ask where they came from. I was to go where I chose, spend as much as I liked, have my fill of girls and thrills of all kinds! Life is short and sad; you wanted me to take it by the throat. Movies, the theater, trips to Paris, every kind of intoxication—why shouldn't I revel in them all? In the days of Marie-Jeanne Flot I used to play poker—had I lost the taste for it? There you were, calmly encouraging me to indulge in debauchery: and, within me, patience, good sense and affection suddenly gave way to fury. You wanted me to be sensible and wild at one and the same time. Had you stolen some of your mother's morphine, I wondered, or were your nerves on the point of giving way?

You were conducting two crusades at once. About to lose the battle for your mother, you were committing yourself every day more deeply to the fight for me. You sold a necklace and two rings to pay for my escapades. You made Father double my pocket money. Couldn't he hear the noise of the jackboots which would soon submerge us altogether? Didn't he realize I might be called up a week or two from now, despite the fact that

as a student I'd had my military service deferred? One evening in November you gave me another envelope, containing a few gold coins which
had belonged to your mother: what use were they to her now? Didn't you
ever think of yourself? In just a few days, all my suspicions disappeared.
I no longer knew how to interpret your behavior. Had the demon of devotion redoubled his influence on you, or were you being undermined
by despair? I realized my own conduct had been reprehensible: I'd been
trying to get my own back for having to love and respect you less than
I'd have liked.

Then all of a sudden you told the whole tribe they could visit your
mother whenever they saw fit. She was in a coma nearly all the time now,
and there was no further point to taking precautions. You sought the trust
of those around you once again: you were letting go of your prey. I'm not
even sure that during your mother's last hours you still regarded yourself as irreplaceable. Grandmother died in her sleep early in December.
You took no interest in the funeral arrangements. Armand saw to everything. In the cemetery, you didn't shed a tear.

Paris, 1972

The only time I think of you is between two books I have to write, two urgent articles, two lectures I'm due to deliver in Lisbon or Florence, Edinburgh or Toulon, Liège or Madrid. When someone is his own man and has come to terms with his own inconsistencies, what use has he for a mother? My feelings for you are utterly dull and trite. My own way of life is a mere matter of choice: the only virtue I lay claim to is persever-ance, made up of some rather lame acts of defiance, judicious impulses, and a few whims and fancies, suitably toned down and managed. I'm haunted by a consciousness of the absurd and a sense of the ridiculous, but they never dare confront me head on, and I consider I counter them satisfactorily by the savoir-faire of my writing. I'm more a man of letters than an author, and take some pride in saying so. I feel it would be un-seemly to claim to be inspired; I'd rather be accepted as a writer open to all kinds of ideas. And open above all to dialogue—which transforms people's minds and rushes them into evanescent certainties. Fifteen years of practice and compromises—some of them quite justifiable—have left me with a fairly simple idea of literature and my place in it. My first rule is to avoid exploiting my obsessions: I like to take myself unawares some-times, outside my own psychological grooves. I value the unpredictable, the fantasies that visit one briefly and then are gone. I don't lay down rules, nor do I bind myself to a strict discipline. My respect for the reader is enough to make me meticulous in the matter of style and language; to remind me that even the wildest content needs ultimately to be justified by form. What am I writing? What should I be writing? I have a horror of messages: a writer isn't a clerk in the service of morality. Poems don't come to me often, but when they do they reflect a physical need. I'm not wholly in charge of a poem's birth: it takes place through me, and to a certain extent in spite of my reason. And yet I'm not its victim; I accept it on condition that at some point in the process of writing it I may give it a logic acceptable to others. The fact is that the incubation and writing of a poem come naturally to me: I can't boast of having deliberately sought it out. But I can't pass it on to others just as it comes to me. I have too much respect for work, and even though an idea requires little effort I always do my best to transform it into a work of art. I take my revenge on inspiration through labor: could that be because I see the former as too hazy, and the latter as more consonant with a certain idea of duty? This attitude has the advantage of increasing my ambition: the harder I toil over a poem, sometimes rewriting it twenty or thirty times, the more I see it as a kind of practical venture. As such it descends to the level of everyday tasks, requiring unremitting care. But at the same time I secretly hope it may also raise me to the topmost heights of mystery. I speak of the elements, the comets, and of strange affinities, and in particular of man as he might be if he obeyed no laws. For me, poetry is a controlled fantasy, a beckoning dream of revolt, something to savor surreptitiously, in one's egotistical reveries. But what does it really mean? That's what I'd like to know, though I reject the idea of a single interpretation, preferring to regard the power exerted by poetry as a kind of magic. If, to avoid being seen by my contemporaries as a clever trickster, I'm forced to say what a poem of mine actually means, I take pleasure in telling people it represents a bone of contention between the absurd and the absolute. By means of this outlandish and ambiguous profession of faith I provide my readers with a good set of tools with which to rethink the world, a process which, if they are free spirits, costs them nothing but their habits.

Have you ever understood my poetry, I wonder? Have you ever tried to guess who I am as I wait for it to provide me with a revelation, both sudden and false, of myself? But you've never strayed an inch away from bourgeois psychology—for you I'm only the shapeless sum of my words and deeds and discernible intentions. The rest either doesn't interest or bothers you: how can literature be valued for anything beside its usefulness, or any small and obvious charms it may possess? The world of the imagination strikes you as uncouth. You think it's unhealthy to regard it as a second nature, truer than the first. I suspect you of a deliberate determination not to follow me on to this difficult terrain. When you used to play the violin, and even during the brief time when you imagined yourself a sculptor, you understood quite well the kind of disembodied state experienced by Beethoven, Mozart, Rodin, or Bourdelle on the brink of some transcendent act of creation. But your own son couldn't acquire such power, could he? If he did, wouldn't he also acquire a superhuman stature that put him beyond the reach of his mother? I think you grant me talent and skill, but you'd hate me to be a genius, or even to have desires too tortuous for you to grasp.

But you needn't worry—I'm not a genius! Nor am I a poet twenty-four hours a day. I know myself, and my limits, and they don't bother me unduly. Poetry is a painful but relatively rare necessity, but I need to write all the time. I like to express myself, I like to sit down like a robot in front of my typewriter, I like to take a piece of paper out of my pocket in a café, on the subway, by the sea, by a stream, on a mountain, in the presence of a naked woman or a derelict or a managing director or a minister, and to cover it with scribble that's as necessary to me as breathing. My work as a poet is outside time, even if it's still-born, but I back it up with a more dogged kind of labor, like that of a teller in a provincial bank or a junior seamstress in a badly lit workroom. So I write novels, in which I settle my accounts with the age I live in. I know there's no point in this kind of struggle: either I'm right and my victory vanishes into oblivion, or I'm wrong and my words are made ridiculous by defeat. I don't like my stories very much: they're more like scenarios for imperfectly thought-out movies. But I tell myself they keep me busy when I'm not writing poetry, and they keep my poetry from being too prosaic. This consideration makes them seem less despicable than if I had to judge them objectively. You accuse me of being too complex, of arguing too deviously; but you must admit that my point of view, for all its show of sophistication and the fact that I take a perverse pleasure in formulating it, contains a touch of pathos: I write novels full of impurities in order to be pure when I write my poems, ten or twelve days a year.

My prose works owe little to the imagination. Whether the facts are heavily or only lightly disguised, my novels are all autobiographical, if you agree that an introvert may graft his ideas onto his skeleton so successfully that the joins are invisible. My body is also the sum of my whims, obsessions, and aberrations: it's between my pleura and my spleen, my small intestine and my duodenum that I locate my likes and dislikes concerning the twentieth century. In other words, what I feel about Charles de Gaulle, John Kennedy, Willy Brandt, Indira Gandhi, Moshe Dayan, and Fidel Castro. They're much closer to me than you'll ever be. And let me tell you this: in moments of panic or pleasure it's not you I think of but the Biafran war, the conflict over Bangladesh, Nixon's trips abroad, the wealth of Saudi Arabia, the frightening growth of the world's population, Neil Armstrong's few faltering steps on the moon. In my mind, which is more ordinary than you think, my true family consists of these men, who will never know me but in whose name I tease and even torture my uneasy sensibility. I can't let you be one of them: a kind of universal etiquette forbids. And naturally you pay me back in my own coin: you understand my novels, superficially at least, but you refuse to accept their gist. They strike you as cruel, unnecessarily sardonic, hopeless, depressing, more likely to annihilate the reader than reassure him. Sometimes, when you say things like this, I send you the works of Kafka or Beckett or Buzzati and such. You read a dozen or so pages, decide they're just as off-putting as I am, and send them back. I'm the one that's at fault, though: is it right to ask an old woman to share in the tragedies and fears she's always made such praiseworthy efforts to ignore? But it's only occasionally that I hanker after your sympathy, and I'm always glad to realize how impossible that is. I might as well ask you to perform on the flying trapeze, or sing the *Valkyrie* at Bayreuth to an audience of three thousand!

But neither poetry nor the novel earns me a living. Journalism pays better and permits me to make ends meet so long as Maria agrees to sacrifice eight hours a day to a boring job in a government office. I work for two daily newspapers and a few weeklies, writing columns on poetry, novels, and modern painting. Every so often these publications fold or acquire a new owner, but it's not too difficult to adapt to a new public. Where keeping the wolf from the door is concerned, I'm not too fussy: I'm just an intermediary between the producer of good writing or esoteric painting and the preoccupied consumer. My job is to explain, and sell, the former to the latter, even if this involves a certain amount of oversimplification. Pimps and panders do the same, and their profession is generally regarded as honorable. Every day I set out to do battle: if you don't read Obaldia, Pinget, and Barthes you're a hopeless philistine, and if you waste your time with Roger Peyrefitte or Françoise Sagan you ought to be hanged. If you like genuine painting, run as fast as you can to see Matta and young La Yaouanc; if you detect any merit whatsoever in Bernard Buffet or Yves Brayer, you're just one of a flock of sheep being led to the slaughter. My articles hector the reader, and as I don't have much time to write them I enjoy them for the challenge they throw down. But this is just what you dislike: my attitude could make me lots of enemies, and men of goodwill ought to be left to live in peace, even if they happen to have no talent.

You make less objection to my job as a literary salesman: you rather like the idea of my giving lectures all over Europe and America—I've worked up a number of connections in the Middle West—especially as this enables me to come and see Father and you at least once a year. You can tell your friends your son writes books, and though this information may not overly impress them, their smiles open up like paper chrysanthemums when you mention that I'm frequently invited to Yale and Harvard and Columbia to talk about French culture, as you put it. These trips do bring me certain short-lived pleasures: I travel, I get to know a lot of little out-of-the-way places. I linger over a gargoyle in Évora, in Portugal; I pick up an ancient rock on the way from Liverpool to Manchester; I swim in a first-class pool between Denver and Memphis, I discover a statue in Piacenza or a retable in Cremona; I sample a thirty-year-old cheese in Gouda, or perhaps Deventer, I go into ecstasies over a Baltimore millionaire's manuscript by Diderot, I listen to church music in Novi Pazar and Split, I lunch off pigeon stuffed with prickly pears in the house of one of the leading citizens of Marrakech, or eat salmon with a shady lawyer in Aberdeen. I spend the night with a schoolteacher in Heidelberg because we share the same tastes in Latin poetry; with a lecturer in Catania because our tastes are different; or with a student in Toronto because she doesn't quite know what she wants to do and asks me for advice about it in the small hours of the morning. Of course, I stand at one and the same time for French intelligence and Parisian loquaciousness. My audiences lap it all up, and go away with the impression they're going to go on loving France and hand down their veneration to their children. But they're wrong: a knowledge of French is no longer a vital necessity. My accomplices in this pedantic charm offensive are ambassadors, consuls, cultural attachés, university chancellors hungry for decorations, retired professors dreaming of honorary degrees, widows who still remember the subjunctives of their husbands killed in the war: they're all the same, whether in Belfast or Porto, Saragossa or Messina, Salzburg or Baton Rouge. In return for my fee I serve up—together with sighs of nostalgia if my listeners belong to the aristocracy, or with a show of egalitarianism if they're rebellious students—a slice of Voltaire, a consommé of Lamartine, a Sartre in aspic, some Montherlant trifle, a Mauriac ragout, a St.-John Perse omelette, steak à la Jacques Prévert, and a cup of decaffeinated Louis Aragon. Food of the gods to delight the chosen few.

Naturally, I'm always in a hurry on my merry-go-round. I drop in to see you between planes. If you come to listen to one of my talks at New York University, say, or the Alliance Française, your admiring comments really get on my nerves: you like me as a hypocritical show-off, but you're afraid of my more profound aspects. You instinctively make it plain that nothing about me is more than skin-deep. It upsets me even to see you, and I'm soon on my way again. You are a mother between suitcases, between time zones, between Gide and Valéry, between Apollinaire and Daudet, between Villon and Ronsard. In any case, I have to get back to my typewriter. I dispose of Georges Braque in fifteen minutes and seven hundred words on the front page of a weekly; of Thomas Mann in eighteen lines and three compliments; and of Maurois and Jules Romains in the time it takes to write half a dozen sarcastic remarks. André Breton's dead? Churn out your article first and weep afterward. At such moments I feel as if I were being pleasurably flogged: to sum up a person in a few words, without time to think them out properly, gives me a perverse thrill. It's as if words were making use of me without my knowledge, and emerging triumphant. But what a life, eh? When they're not in their paper tower, poets and novelists ought to be doctors, procurers, builders of cathedrals, engineers, furniture dealers, pork butchers, ministers, unemployed laborers, activists of the left, fascists, sea captains, gynecologists, sellers of urinals—it's quite right that they should have another job as well. But not as a journalist! Not as one of the pariahs who live by turning their pen to anything, anywhere! How can he be sincere in his own work when he wears out his integrity on sensational *faits divers?* And if he dashes off obituaries or praises a painter in a coarse, unsuitable style, isn't he a sham when he tries to assume something better? When a journalist sets himself up as a writer he becomes a cheat, a man not to be trusted even with an empty soul.

But I practice both these professions. When you're twenty, literature is a game. A fellow can learn to play hopscotch and to ride a bicycle, so why shouldn't he learn to write and give Mom and Dad and the rest of the kids a surprise? When one's thirty, literature is still a challenge, if the game hasn't yet lost its charm. It's a kind of habit, like poker, or hashish, or betting on horses. It can be cured, but not without a lot of effort, and it always leaves scars. If a man's still at it when he's forty, what other possibility remains? He has to sacrifice to it an arm, an eye, or a few inches of intestine: if he amputated literature itself he'd be paralyzed, incapable of anything. Now that I'm over fifty, I have no other truth left: any others I might have had have been swallowed up in it. I live only through my books; apart from them, I myself am unremarkable. My pages are my body and my mind: my physical existence is nameless. But could I ever talk to you like this? I'm not a good son: I don't even know what that means. I'm not a good husband: ask Maria if words aren't meat and drink and shelter to me. I'm not a good lover: as soon as I've captured my prey I'm chasing after some unusual or dissolute expression to apply to it. I'm not a good citizen: if France were to disappear I'd just be in a hurry to get my work translated into Russian or Chinese. Is this reprehensible attitude due to naïveté or to insufferable pride? But I don't judge myself. Even if I could, I'd still maintain that my identity resides in the words I write. Most of them don't deserve any attention, but if just a half or a quarter of a poem survives after I die, I won't have lived in vain. It's a pathetically small consolation, but it's enough to keep me going.

You're not a nuisance to me anymore. Sometimes I feel a bit wistful and seem to see your face for a moment, until I shrug it off. I won't confide in you: you spoil everything with your moral imperatives, as if each day were a kind of obstacle race in which a man had to negotiate prohibitions on the one hand and facile emotions on the other. You instinctively approve of my behavior because I'm your son and can therefore do no wrong. But you also object: if I'm your son, I ought to act as you would if you were me. Beneath its mild exterior, your love for me is devouring. My knowledge of you is as fragmentary as yours of me. When we meet, which we do more and more rarely, you hide your hopes and fears and troubles, if you have any, so as not to spoil the pleasure of our reunion. So when we're together we indulge in empty outpourings, and when I think of you I'm obliged, like it or not, to reinvent you more every year. You try to be perfect every time we meet, and I try to be acceptable, but after a few moments of unbridled emotion we see that separation has made us unnatural. But do I really care? I'm more interested in ideas than in people now; sometimes I find myself saying I love humanity but don't love men. I allow myself this aloofness in order to make the most of my talent, though I know it's nothing to write home about. I have a real understanding with Maria, but without the intoxication and ecstasy that involve psychological upheaval. In this way I've given up anything that might stand in the way of my books, sacrificed it in the name of middle-class compromise. I never give myself completely—not even to myself. I sometimes make friends, like everyone else, but I soon realize they're becoming either suppliers or customers, even if the stock in trade we deal in is stupidly called affection. Literature is the only venture of mine that has any chance of success. All the rest consists merely of petty joys, petty whims, petty tricks, petty distractions. Physically I'm both passionate and cold; mentally, both shaky and nimble: you must forgive me. I keep you up my sleeve as someone I can always love, for want of anyone better; or whom I might pity, if such a sentiment could help my writing. One day, when I'm fed up with all the rest, I shall turn you into a character—as no doubt you've guessed. My attitude, which calls for neither praise nor blame, makes me immune. Whatever the people I care for may do—whether they betray or idolize me, go or stay, suffer or die, exasperate me or make me miss them—I always end up bending them to my will, turning them into pages of a book. You're no exception; you'll never be so dear to me as when you're translated into words. And so, if I disappoint you, at least remember it's because of my love of writing. And if I myself am not satisfactory, turn to the author. Perhaps, in a chapter or two, he may be able to make amends.

Sofia, 1924

First you scolded me: I mustn't play in the street with boys I didn't know. All Bulgarians were savages, especially the Macedonians, and since Kotcho had relatives who came down from the mountains it was quite natural for him to want to hurt me. What sort of figure did I cut, always ending up the loser in our games of cops and robbers? This time I'd been tied up with barbed wire, my wrists had naturally started to bleed, and if you hadn't intervened I might have gotten gangrene. Did I realize what I was doing? Every Bulgarian was a bit of a Turk, and they'd all decapitate a man at the drop of a hat. Did I promise not to play with them anymore, or would I rather spend the rest of my life without a head on my shoulders? Without a skull, or hair, or a mouth? I shed a few tears, not knowing how one could go on living in such a state. You only wanted to frighten me, but I soon saw the flaw in your argument and reflected that maybe you weren't so clever as I had thought. Then you began cleaning up my wrists. The iodine hurt me worse than the scratches themselves, and I accused you of being more cruel than all the Bulgars and Turks in creation. You realized I needed other consolations besides your kissing and cuddling, which always embarrassed me. But it wasn't easy to spoil me: I didn't like candies and cakes, and I demolished other presents in two or three days, especially if they bore any resemblance to dolls. But I didn't dislike stories, especially if they were about your or Father's past.

You didn't need asking twice, but sat me on a big mauve cushion, between the chest of drawers with your violin in its battered case on top and the rustic table my father used as a desk, with its transparent envelopes and black folders. I used to classify the anecdotes you told me according to the years in which they happened. I had a rather good memory for figures, and divided up the century accordingly, though I didn't always join up the years in chronological order. That day I asked you to tell me about 1910. You thought for a while, then launched into a long account that started out gaily enough but gradually became more and more emotional. At the time you were speaking of you were a very happy young lady. Your father sold leather in many different countries, some of which, like Montenegro and Serbia, no longer existed now. Your mother insisted on your continuing your studies after high school: as I would realize later, parents always know best, and if a person thought he knew everything, well, he'd soon find out he was wrong! And so you went to the Odessa Conservatoire, where you made excellent progress, though this didn't stop you from having fun. Fun, kept within proper bounds, is a good thing at any age. You went to parties and fancy-dress balls and fashion competitions, and sometimes you laughed so much your parents were quite upset. The house was always full of friends: it was in the middle of town, between the boulevard Richelieu and the boulevard des Français, so writers and artists and painters would all drop in casually.

Then you started to describe the city where I was born—I couldn't remember it at all. Yes, of course, you sighed, I'd left it when I was still a baby, but one day I'd go back and see how splendid it was. In spring the lilacs there smelled more sublime than anywhere else in the world; the sailors told tales, in their hoarse but irresistible accent, of adventures which, even if they were imaginary, couldn't have befallen any captain of antiquity; the evening air was so clear it was as if night didn't want to fall; the flights of steps by the harbor were so steep it looked as though the whole city was about to slither gently into the sea. I didn't understand all you said, and perhaps it occurred to you that instead of making the place sound attractive you were changing it into something monstrous and frightening. So you blew your nose gently, as if to check a tear, then altered your tone of voice and began to talk about my father. In 1910 he was a wealthy man, five years older than you and without a profession. He lived off the fortune amassed by his forebears, who'd come, mostly from Belgium and Alsace, to build railroads in the Ukraine. You introduced a little digression in praise of locomotives, with their connecting rods and thick smoke; you spoke of the signals, the rails, the stations, and the excited friends come to meet or see the passengers off. I made you repeat all the strange new words so that I could remember them; every sentence added to my vocabulary. You told me Father's parents had a huge house in Kiev, where Father's father was an honorary citizen. He was a leading figure of considerable power, a handsome man and a despot. The family owned other opulent mansions in Kharkov and Odessa. But, you warned me, wealth is not a virtue, and well-off people may be mean and stingy and selfish. They deserve to be punished by the poor, which was what happened in the two years before I was born. Revolution was sometimes justified, and not all revolutionaries were criminals.

My father knew other languages as well as Russian and French: German, Italian, and Norwegian. He'd made the mistake of scorning English as low and fit only for dealings between grooms and valets. He was rounding out his education by getting to know Europe: in those days you weren't necessarily expected to work if you belonged to a family of a certain rank. Perhaps he was searching each country and town for happiness. Another digression informed me one should acquire this priceless gift in one's youth: otherwise one might not recognize it, let it escape, or be afraid of it when it does come. This philosophy struck me as very complicated, and I politely asked you to go back to my father's travels. He'd studied literature in St. Petersburg, and one day was struck by similarities between the life of Lermontov, whom he admired, and those of Alfred de Musset and Alphonse de Lamartine. So he packed his bags and went off to Paris to study at the Sorbonne. In the same year he visited Heidelberg and Prague, where he lived in the same style, poor and conspiratorial, as the local students. Perhaps it was in 1910 that he was expelled from Bohemia. Was I able to keep up with you in this itinerary, which took in Bergen and Christiania, Leipzig and Liège? You must have no-

ticed my perplexity, for you went and fetched a large atlas. But it was a
recent one, which infuriated you: for the map of Europe had changed.
You told me there'd been a terrible war which had ravaged the Continent like a long illness. All wars are pointless, you said, and lead to the
same thing: sons go away, mothers grieve, and sometimes they never see
each other again. You swore to me there'd never be any more revolutions
or world wars in my lifetime—only peace and well-being. But your emphatic promises sounded suspicious to me. With the aid of blue and green
patches, continuous and dotted lines, you sang the praises of the old, the
vanished Europe, the one my father roamed through to satisfy his whims
and refine his taste. In 1910 there was a great dual empire in the middle
of Europe, with a charming if rather gloomy emperor who was very old
and very bald, with bushy whiskers. His name was Franz-Joseph, he was
a man of goodwill, and his court was full of artists and musicians, with
balls where magnificently turned out officers danced with highly accom-
plished ladies. There weren't many republics in those days, and only the
French one cut any sort of a figure. Elsewhere gracious manners were
kept up, sometimes rather stiffly, as under Kaiser Wilhelm II of Germany
with his sword-like mustaches, sometimes more affably, as under plump
Edward VII, ruler of India as well as of the British Isles. You leafed
through the atlas, and I added to my knowledge of Asia.

Suddenly my father's youth seemed less fascinating than the oddly
shaped islands that appeal so strongly to the imagination. I asked you if
we'd ever go to Borneo, and you just smiled. Then I said I wouldn't eat
anything anymore unless you took me to Tasmania. You replied sternly
that a big boy like me shouldn't talk such nonsense, so I measured the
distances on the map and suggested a compromise: I'd make do with a
trip to Baluchistan. You pinched my cheek and we rejoined my father on
the roads of Livonia, Baden, and Tuscany. Sometimes, you told me, he
was sent to such places on assignment, for he was a good diplomat and
his father would dispatch him to draw up contracts with industrialists and
even government ministers. Such missions might take him to Warsaw (then
a Russian city), or Kaunas (the republic of Lithuania didn't yet exist), or
Agram (since renamed Zagreb), or Pressburg (a name the Czech patriots

had changed to Bratislava). Poor Europe, once so prosperous and peaceful and pleasant—what had they done to it, Joffre, Shchedrin, Clemenceau, Masaryk, Lenin, Lloyd George, Wilson, and the rest? I grew sulky: you were throwing too many names at me, and I didn't know what to say. But I did find a way of getting my own back: I collected pictures of movie stars, and was sure you'd never heard of names like Conrad Nagel, Pola Negri, Emil Jannings, Edna Purviance, and Max Linder. So we were quits: my knowledge of the cinema stemmed your torrent of contemporary history. You told me Father had written some rather lightweight poems, poems of happiness, and it was in 1910 that he began to give readings of them in drawing rooms in Kiev and Odessa. His audience was often very appreciative, but he thought that might have been mere politeness. He met with other young writers who introduced him to the avant-garde: he was about to start taking life seriously. This took you back to your own girlhood, and you painted an idyllic picture of your school, your love of music, your concern for your dignified and taciturn father, and your noble-hearted mother, who could always tell the difference between assumed sincerity and the real thing. There was a moral in all this: I was supposed to conclude that the heart was superior to the mind, which in turn was superior to overweening ambition. When it came to choosing between personal well-being and the conquest of the world, there could be no hesitation. You didn't press me to make an irrevocable choice there and then—I was only five—but you did intend to influence me.

Then you remembered how impressed I'd been by the atlas. You explained why Father was so interested in geography: he was a dealer in postage stamps, and at the same time a bank employee. No doubt it was amusing to get to know the past, but that mustn't stop me from understanding the present, which was slightly less merry and more painful. The good old days were over long ago, and the revolution had temporarily banished us from Russia. We'd go back soon, but meanwhile all our property was lost, my grandparents had returned to Belgium, and we had to live in straitened circumstances. My father had started collecting stamps long before 1910, and had contacts in that field. In those days he also collected butterflies, rare manuscripts, antique pipes, and—a shadow seemed to pass over your face as you said it—pretty women. I was fidgeting about on my cushion and looking puzzled. With a wave of the hand you dismissed any strange ideas I might be entertaining, and went on with your story. After going into exile, Father borrowed some old stamps from experts and sold them for a small commission. At first he worked for other people, but in due course he did so well, thanks to the correspondences he maintained all over Europe, that he was able to set up his own business, which he carried on in a bedroom where his statuettes, files, and catalogs took up no more than six square meters of space.

I had seen postage stamps before, though Father always took care to keep me out of the way when he was preparing to mail them to his clients. But now you set out, systematically and with unexpected zeal, to complete my apprenticeship. Stamps were just fragile little bits of paper that people stuck on letters, postcards and ordinary or express packages, which a postman on a bicycle or with a horse collected as soon as the train or boat that was carrying them arrived, so that they reached the person they were addressed to as soon as possible. They all had a picture on them: usually it was a portrait of the king or queen of the country that issued them, but stamps might also depict coats of arms, famous places or buildings, or men who'd rendered distinguished services to their native land. Their colors varied according to their face value, which was indicated in figures relating to the local currency and the rates in force at the time. If a stamp still had a thin layer of gum on the back that meant it hadn't been used; they were sold like this in post offices, and once affixed to a letter they were cancelled with a black or mauve mark. This might make them look less attractive, but it didn't necessarily lessen their value. I showed some signs of fatigue now, but you made me repeat every detail. The lesson continued the next day, and you promised me a scooter if I'd keep it a secret: in a week or two, when I'd become a real philatelist, we'd give Father a wonderful surprise! Now I must learn the right way to handle stamps without damaging them. You either moved them carefully to the edge of a flat surface and then got hold of them very delicately with your fingers so as not to crumple them in the middle or bend the edges; or, better still, you used a pair of metal tweezers. After twenty or thirty attempts I succeeded in performing this feat, and was very proud of myself! I'd soon show Father which of us was best equipped to be a stamp collector.

I learned to measure perforations, and to recognize watermarks by soaking the stamp in question in a little black dish of benzine. Later on I took an almost passionate delight in cutting stamps off envelopes, soaking them for a while in warm water to detach them from the paper they were stuck to, then laying them face down on blotting paper to dry. My vocabulary expanded enormously. I was no longer satisfied with saying a stamp was brown or blue; now it was ocher or bister, ultramarine or turquoise. I even came to think it a sign of gross ignorance to say a stamp was red: something much more accurate was called for—crimson, carmine, or vermilion. I examined every little picture closely through a magnifying glass. The first thing to do was identify the country it came from, and as the name wasn't always written in French or Russian I had to learn a few foreign words, though this led to some confusion. Sweden was called *Sverige* in Swedish, and Finland was *Suomi* in Finnish. Switzerland chose to be known by its learned appellation, Helvetia. France loftily expected to be recognized by the initials of its political régime, R.F., while Great Britain, ruler of the waves, went even further and dispensed with both name and initials. Some challenges to my imagination had even more lasting effects: vanished countries, not to be found on any map, had left charming images behind them: Karelia, Epirus, Julian Venetia and Eastern Rumelia. My explorations ranged far and wide and included Polynesia, whose many tiny islands I counted with delight. I was sure they couldn't be much larger than their stamps: I had to use a magnifying glass to find them in the vast blue expanse of sea in the atlas: Elobey, Horta, Nauru, Nevis, Penrhyn.

Thanks to the stamps my education made great strides in just a few weeks. I found out how beautiful Queen Victoria had been, and how she gradually grew old; this made me very sad. I compared the likenesses of George V and Nicholas II and could see they were related. Did all great men have the same stern expression as Louis Pasteur in his red portrait? Judging from the profiles of Franz-Joseph on the stamps of Bosnia-

Herzegovina and of Ferdinand on those of Bulgaria, I concluded, somewhat hastily perhaps, that all kings and emperors ended up bald and fat;
this made me sadder still. It was on a stamp from Nyasaland that I saw
my first zebra, looking very thoughtful against a background of elegant
palm trees, and on one from Tanganyika that I met my charming friend
the giraffe. It was love at first sight, and I wouldn't eat until my father
had promised to buy me the whole series: Tanganyika, numbers 1 to 14,
in the Yvert and Tellier catalog. This tome gradually became my Bible,
and I got into the habit of referring to stamps by their catalog numbers.
Some stamps were too rare or expensive for my father to acquire, and I
came to think of them as stately and formidable characters. I had great
respect for Bavaria number 1, all black, and France number 2, dark green
and with a bust of Ceres wearing a laurel wreath. Not to mention Basel's
embossed three-colored dove. For a long time I regarded the captain of
the German cruiser *Vineta* as a hero, a benefactor of humanity: finding
himself out of 3-pfennig stamps one day when he was far away from his
home port, he took six hundred 5-pfennig stamps, cut them in two length-
wise and marked each half with a mauve 3. This deed of courage and
determination, performed on April 13, 1901 off the River Plate, struck
me as much more epic than some of the victories you'd told me about:
Napoleon in the shade of the Pyramids, or Hannibal and his caravan of
elephants confronting snowstorms in the Alps. You didn't try to stifle my
enthusiasm.

Brussels, May 1940

For twelve years Dr. Isphording had been my father's best customer. He specialized in Balkan stamps, and with Germanic regularity bought whatever my father offered in the way of variants, errors, or rarities in good condition. Sometimes he came to see us, bringing small presents for you. In Hanover, where he lived, leather handbags were very solidly made, and fabrics exceedingly hardwearing. You referred to him as a lousy Prussian, but made an effort and smiled nicely at him for my father's sake. You said the discounts Father gave him were really worth more than the useless bits and pieces the Prussian brought you. Teutonic taste— what a joke! You also accused him of being on the side of Hitler and his gang, perhaps even a secret member of the Nazi party. But this time Father put his foot down: 1940 had begun badly, and the various censorships were hindering the free circulation of goods, so serious clients must be treated especially nicely. You accepted these commercial arguments, and even phoned me at the residence hall to insist on my coming to dinner in a couple of days' time: I hadn't forgotten, had I, that Dr. Isphording had given me a 20-mark gold piece for my tenth birthday? I didn't share your dislike of him, and duly joined your little party so that the family could present a united front to the barbarian. After the usual courtesies Father took Dr. Isphording aside to offer him some philatelic marvels at exorbitant prices, and judging by the two cigars that emerged from the negotiation, our friend allowed himself to be persuaded. The dinner itself was dull and slightly tense. I dropped the first brick, deliberately, by asking Dr. Isphording when his fellow countrymen were finally going to make up their minds to launch a real offensive against France and England: the "phony war" wasn't worthy of a thousand-year Reich.

Our friend took his time answering. It was over coffee and a second cigar that he treated us to a detailed lecture. To begin with, he apologized. He was no Nazi, and his family belonged to a liberal élite that had shown its worth in the various 1848 revolutions. But the steel magnates had chosen to follow Hitler, so he'd had to toe the line, purely as a matter of form. However, he didn't regard himself as a hostage of the Nazis; on the contrary, it was they who'd always have to answer to the big industrialists. After Germany had won the war—as he was sure it would, even if Russia should join in one day on the other side—the German patriots would get rid of Nazism and reestablish a democracy at least as remarkable as those in England or France. Still, he wasn't here to talk politics: he'd come for two special reasons. Before he went on he looked around rather nervously, then asked point-blank if we were Jewish. You were extremely upset, and Father, seeing this, decided to step in before you could say anything. He poured himself and Dr. Isphording a glass of cognac each, and, with exemplary calm, told his guest our Aryan purity was indeed compromised: his own father had married a Jewess, and your father was a hundred percent Jewish. We weren't in the habit of discussing our racial or ethnic makeup, but since this kind of conversation seemed inevitable these days, we accepted it with a good grace. I found Father's calm somewhat forced. In his place, *you* would have flown off the handle and no doubt insulted, and lost, a good customer. I wasn't very proud of my own attitude: my identity, which I equated with a slight and harmless spiritual rebelliousness devoid of any religious element, suddenly seemed an anachronism. The second third of the century I lived in was going to judge me on my place of birth, my foreskin, the quality of my blood and the shape of my nose. All at once I could no longer deny the evidence of my body; as for my mind, if it took too long coming to a decision it would be taken over by someone else. I didn't belong to myself anymore: I was being forced to take risks, and the most serious question I had to face was no longer if I preferred Latin to English, medicine to architecture or dream to reality. I was being warned that a uniform was waiting for me; either I'd put it on and become a natural target, or else I'd refuse to put it on and be a traitor, someone who deserved to die without ever encountering the enemy.

Dr. Isphording left us with no illusions: if Belgium were occupied by the Germans, we'd be persecuted. You started at this: how could he talk about occupation when Belgium was neutral? Our guest gave a wry smile and made us promise never to divulge what he was about to tell us. He had it on good authority that the Wehrmacht, having won a fairly easy victory in Poland, was going to attack western Europe in the early spring. The first assault would be directed toward Scandinavia; but we might be sure that some twenty-five or thirty days later the Maginot Line would be circumvented by a fierce offensive against Belgium and the Low Countries. We had been warned. We had time to go and make a life for ourselves elsewhere—in the United States, Africa, or Australia; anywhere we liked. Your lips began to quiver; you had to struggle not to burst into tears. My father was more philosophical: his life had already been broken up by one exile; another couldn't be any worse. That, at least, was how I interpreted his rather sad politeness to our visitor. Bitter though he might feel, he probably thought he was being offered a respite, as if by a miracle. As for me, I was trying to project myself into the future, which I saw in images at once wild and abstract: amid the ruined remains of the British and French armies, the victorious German Reich was turning liberal, European unity was at last a fact. I even had a sardonic vision in which, instead of awaiting the enemy attack, I abandoned my Belgian uniform and volunteered to fight in the German army for a strong and radiant Europe. But my daydreams were interrupted by Dr. Isphording's grave words. Rummaging in his little attaché case, he produced a green cloth bag from which he took first a few chocolates, and then, hiddden by the candies, another bag containing twenty gold coins—marks, ducats, and louis. He asked my father to accept them, as a gift to a good friend who was bound to be in financial difficulties before long. In any case, German citizens weren't allowed to own precious metals, and he didn't want to break the laws of his country any more than he wanted to make it a present of this little nest egg. You showed signs of impatience: you would never accept charity from an invader! Father was at a loss. Once again it was our friend who found words appropriate to the occasion. He wasn't making us a present—he was merely asking us to be good enough to keep the coins for him until after the war. In the midst of this unbearable tension, Father had the bright idea of opening a bottle of champagne, and our grimaces turned to sickly smiles as we drank a toast to friendship.

After Dr. Isphording had left, Father, with unusual gravity, asked me to leave the residence hall and come live at home again. He agreed to my going on with my studies, for the worst wasn't absolutely bound to happen, but he was going to need me for three or four hours a day. He roped you in as well: no more pointless excursions, no more gossiping tea parties! We must close our ranks and follow a plan he'd already worked out in detail. You hemmed and hawed, as if it were still possible to lead a normal life. You even cast doubt on Dr. Isphording's predictions: the man positively enjoyed acting as a cross between one of the herald angels and an emissary of the devil! Father objected to this comparison: his client was beyond reproach in business and must be credited with the same honesty in other matters. For once Father would take no denial from anyone. The warning included me too, and if I myself showed any signs of rebellion, he would cut off my allowance. His strategy was quite simple and involved four or five weeks' work. First he was going to transfer to London the small amount of money he had in the bank, and realize the Belgian government bonds in which he no longer had any faith. His stock of ordinary stamps was too bulky to bother with: he'd abandon it without regret if the Germans invaded—but to save half one's property gave one a right to survive. These Spartan principles shocked you so much you wrung your hands and allowed yourself a few hysterical squeals which Father and I regarded as untimely. You had to get a grip on yourself and show you were equal to the difficulties awaiting us. You soon thought of a distraction, and went every day to pray at your mother's recently dug grave. I roughly dissuaded you: the dead couldn't help us, and you had other duties that should come before indulging in foolish lamentations. In the end you obeyed your husband's instructions, torn between many doubts and the need to set an example. You weren't your own mistress anymore; life was cruel and unpredictable, unfair and capricious, and demanded too much of you. Awful events occurred one after the other with pitiless rapidity, and you became depressed. Several times you told me, with a sort of morbid calm, that you wished you were like your mother, at peace in a graveyard six feet under the mud. I couldn't think of anything consoling to say. I thought you were failing to live up to the situation, and repeated Father's instructions: we ought to observe strict discipline and eschew all sentimentality.

Father had removed all the stamps of any value from his files, and you and I were given the job of sorting them out according to country and date. Then he'd look them over and show us how to put them in transparent envelopes, penciling on each one the relevant number in Yvert and Tellier. As there were about four thousand stamps to be identified like this, the work was slow and mistakes were frequent. Meanwhile Father consulted the lists setting out the names and addresses of his best foreign clients, and dispatched slim packages weighing one or two hundred grams all over the world, each with a note asking the person concerned to keep the enclosed stamps safe for him. His correspondents, he explained, would be honest enough to act as he would himself in their place: trust is the essence of all commerce. Here too he was taking a calculated risk: one tenth of his packages would be lost, another tenth would be confiscated, and a third tenth would fall among thieves. In letters sent separately he apologized without obsequiousness to his colleagues: though he hadn't had time to consult them, he was venturing to send them some stamps in anticipation of a war much more total than the skirmishes on the Alsatian front. He sent between sixty and eighty of these registered letters to colleagues in Lisbon, London, New York, and Buenos Aires, not to mention a younger brother who'd settled in Rio de Janeiro around 1930. This strange task was unaffected by the invasion of Norway, which justified our confidence in Dr. Isphording and encouraged us in our work.

Effort of this kind always calls for a kind of blindness. You saw nothing absurd in cataloguing little bits of paper: for you and Father the march of History was reduced to the dimensions of fragile postage stamps. To save them was to save all three of us; to lose them might mean dying in exile somewhere in the vast expanse of a Europe being put to fire and the sword. I had no inner resources to help me view the situation more sensibly. I had serious but abstract ideas about what might happen after the war, but no real opinion about the opposing sides in the conflict. Defending democracy seemed dull, boring, and uninspired: how could I work up any enthusiasm for men like Edouard Daladier, Paul-Henri Spaak, Neville Chamberlain, Chancellor Schuschnigg and Eduard Beneš? But could I, out of defiance or romanticism, sacrifice my body and mind to some ideal that echoed the ideas of Hitler, Mussolini, Stalin, or Franco? I wanted a swift, decisive conflict; I had perverse dreams of terrible holocausts. Paris destroyed in one week, London razed in two, Moscow burned down as in the days of Napoleon, Berlin blown up house by house and street by street. What these nebulous fantasies of mine called for was an unchallengeable leader, a general rather than a politician, who by wiping out at least half of Europe would be able to impose his will on the ruins and the survivors. Since the Germans had won the advantage, I was prepared for them to keep it and get on with the good work of unification. The idea haunted me, though my imagination always came up against the same clichés. But where Frederick II and Charlemagne hadn't succeeded, was there any reason Hitler should fail? People change: Napoleon had nothing in common with Bonaparte, and I told myself—not very convincingly—that Hitler in his sixties and sated with victories might become a good German again, fair, responsible, benevolent, and magnanimous, like Goethe or Johann Sebastian Bach. My political notions were childish, perhaps already concealing my habitual inability to see events in their true light. On the other hand my helplessness, though I knew it was shocking, suited me very well. After a few months' brief enthusiasm I took no pleasure in my studies. The war would force me to act without having to take the responsibility of choosing to do so. In my most lucid moments I had visions of polite and starchy generals dismissing Hitler and giving power back to the civil authorities—holding peaceful elections, and instead of promising Europe a German Empire destined to last a thousand years, guaranteeing the whole continent a kind of Athenian well-being, brought up to date by modern humanism—something no one had earlier dared to hope for. It seemed to me quite reasonable that fifteen or twenty million men should pay for such a happy state of things with their lives.

Amid the succession of shocks and surprises our life now consisted of, you didn't suffer such qualms: you were simply helping your husband to organize, quite coolly and calmly, our survival. You were docile, uncomplaining and quiet. When you spoke it was usually to express a vague hope after hearing some communiqué on the radio: perhaps the Narvik expedition would succeed; Churchill seemed more solid than Chamberlain, who looked like an umbrella that was stuck and couldn't be opened. By the end of April most of the stamps had been sent off: all that was left were three pocket albums containing Father's most classic and valuable specimens, small and light enough for each of us to carry one of them away on our person. We were ready for the inevitable. Then you did begin to weep over our fate and say how much you loved the furniture, the settee, the carpet, the trees in the street, the passing clouds. You had time now to think about what we were reduced to. You had to wait, but you didn't quite know what for. This period of dull, unspoken regret was followed by one of active imprecation. You'd never really liked Belgium, with its continual rain and lack of color and grace. The people were either stuck-up or unbearably coarse, and their uncouthness was reflected in their clothes, skimpy as their souls and shabby as their perpetually faulty speech. You covered the whole range of hysterical attitudes from sentimentality to injustice, from effusion to hatred, like someone trying on one dress after another and unable to decide between them. I too was nervous, and the more I realized this the more I saw how alike we were: I'd have to watch myself. I was really leaving it to coming events to guide me: they would act for me. I was a coward, restless in my indifference.

The first raids and anti-aircraft fire woke us up at twenty-eight minutes past five on May 10th 1940, a radiant spring day of lush new leaves beneath a cloudless sky. I switched on the radio: not a sound for about ten minutes, then the announcement of the German invasion. I felt strangely elated; I'd been waiting for this day, and it was going to decide my future. You made coffee and slices of bread and jam in silence, wearing a green and blue dressing gown. Father and I shaved without haste and at a quarter past six went out for a walk. We were away for about twenty minutes; we'd never done such a thing before. There was no need for us to talk: the fronts of the houses, the tram-lines, the trees, the chimneys were enough. We knew grave events were about to take place and that we'd make many mistakes. Our silent stroll took on a deep significance: each of us would act bravely if necessary; we were equals now in the face of danger, and irrevocably loyal to one another though the question of vows and promises never even arose. When we got home you'd gotten out four or five suitcases and put them in the drawing room. Did we have to be in such a hurry? The radio announced that Verviers had fallen and Liège was partly surrounded. I checked the state of my uniform, laughing as I did so: was I suddenly going to be transformed into a buffoon? You darted around the whole apartment, making odd calculations: no, we wouldn't be able to take the silver and the china; and your furs and evening gowns would have to be left behind too. You examined the suitcases: you could easily manage to lift twenty pounds, but would you have the strength to carry that weight very far? Father seemed very serene: even if there was a lightning offensive and the Albert Canal was taken, we'd still have five or six days. I stayed by the radio, but it wasn't until ten-thirty that night that the order came through: reservists were not to join their units but to await further instructions, which would be issued shortly.

To hide my real feelings I put on my uniform, then I too drew up an account of my meager wealth: I wouldn't miss my clothes, apart from one nice lemon-yellow silk necktie; nor my curios and trinkets; nor the Monet prints on the walls of my room. At most I'd miss a few books: volumes of poetry by Supervielle, Eluard and André Breton, and especially Jean Cocteau's *Cap de Bonne-Espérance*. I called up Leclercq and Livchitz, and we decided to meet at midday in a café in the Chaussée de Water- loo, on the edge of a wood called the Bois de la Cambre. Leclercq was in uniform, like me. I thought Livchitz looked haggard and drawn. We hadn't met for over a year, and our paths had diverged: Leclercq was interested in politics and administration; Livchitz was reading medicine. Could we, on this historic day, re-create the friendship we'd had at school? I was hoping both the others would adopt the same attitude, so that I would merely have to follow. But a few sentences were enough to disillusion me. Livchitz had made up his mind to fight to the death against the barbarians, no matter what. Leclercq, more prudent, thought it best to wait and see what Leopold III, and the French government, and the British high command, intended to do. Belgium might become a battlefield, but on the other hand it might, more prosaically, just be used as a crossing point. He'd join his unit, of course, but if there was a retreat he reserved the right, if he had any choice, not to sacrifice himself in vain. We didn't agree. At that point I tended to side with Leclercq, though I lacked his calm and adaptability. But the friends of one's childhood aren't necessarily the friends of one's youth: we had to admit our meeting was a mistake. We talked about our studies, and then, as another air raid took place to the east of the city, we started discussing our conquests. There was a cigarette girl in one of the seedy night clubs on the avenue Fonsny, over by the station, who was prepared, in the back of the premises. . . We instinctively kept everything very low-key. We were citizens of small country which History didn't consult: either we had allies and obeyed them, or we didn't have any allies and no one asked our opinion. We were subject to the law that might was right, at the mercy of the first assailant who found it convenient to take a shortcut across our territory. But we did our best to ignore this fact: the bosoms and skin of girls, whether respectable or for sale, were more important to us than the fate of our country. We knew—none better than Livchitz himself, despite his fury and determination—that sacrifice would be absurd. At best we'd do our duty—a duty imposed on us by others.

When I got home my grandfather was there, prostrate: you made him take away a suitcase filled with toilet articles and spare linen. The afternoon passed amid official recriminations: Nazi Germany was treating the western countries the same as she had Austria and Czechoslovakia, but she wouldn't get away with it. She was breaking all the rules, including the rules of war. The Belgian government was asking the French and British armies to join with the Belgian troops to defend the West against the Huns. The reservists, including my unit, were to assemble either near Ostend or in the La Panne area on the coast, two miles from the French border. From this I concluded that after less than ten hours' fighting the government was already thinking of surrendering practically the whole country. Should I say goodbye to my family right away, or, since my orders allowed it, wait until dawn tomorrow? I was inclined to choose the immediate solution and take myself off as fast as I could, thus avoiding all the heartrending embraces and solemn words. You begged me to spend one more night near you, and Grandfather backed you up. Only Father left me free to choose for myself: for him, we were separated and scattered already. It was a sad, tense evening: we had to listen to the radio broadcasting from London to find out that the Germans had achieved a breakthrough between Antwerp and Liège, and there'd been parachute drops over Amsterdam and Utrecht. You disappeared for half an hour, and came back with a tin of caviar: why shouldn't we turn the painful business of separation into a bit of a party? You were quite sprightly. Sometimes you invented cheerful if unlikely theories. The Allies would save Belgium—the current offensive was merely a small diversion, and envoys were bound to be discussing peace terms already somewhere in Switzerland. Sometimes you appealed to our courage: yes, we'd soon be setting out in all directions, but we'd remain united in our hearts and minds. I made no comment on these pitiful platitudes: I was probably quite capable of producing them myself. Father suddenly went to a cupboard and took out a couple of bottles of champagne. He hadn't thought to cool them, so we put crushed ice into our glasses. You scarcely touched yours, and ruled out all attempts at toasts or any other theatrical gestures: this was no time for grandiloquence. Your father wondered whether or not it might be a good idea to go back to Russia: Stalin was now Hitler's ally, and we might all find safe refuge there. One horrified look from you was enough to make him fall silent again: he was as good as inviting you to hell! There were still two bottles of champagne left. I opened them, and probably drank three-quarters of their contents myself. All those solemn faces took on a comic dimension; I was seized by an almost irresistible desire to laugh, which I only just managed to stifle. But one doesn't scold a recruit

setting off for the wars, and you all accepted my sarcastic remarks with resignation. When, at about three in the morning, the effects of the champagne
had worn off, I didn't even repent my behavior. On the contrary, I congratulated myself for having responded as I did to our lamentable play-acting.

We left our apartment the next day—on May 11th 1940, at nine-thirty
in the morning. The train to La Panne was less crowded than I'd expected;
most people who'd decided to leave Brussels were probably heading south.
We didn't speak, but you were very shocked when three young women,
one after the other, offered me their seat: perhaps I was returning from
the front, perhaps I would soon be dying for my country. I was the target
of many preoccupied glances. Rumors were spreading like wildfire, caus-
ing confusion and panic: German parachutists were in Bruges, Tournai,
Calais, Lille. You rented an apartment for two weeks in the little seaside
resort of La Panne: there were no hotel rooms available. I went to the city
hall: a few army officers were installed in tents six hundred meters away,
and they directed me to my regiment, which had just left for the Dunkirk
area. I was on the point of following them there right away; sudden breaks
are best, and I'd have been spared your lamentations. But something drew
me to my father: he had the right to a handshake, a manly glance, and a
few words which finally would remain unspoken but through which we'd
nevertheless convey to each other something of our most intimate feelings. The day's news no longer concerned me: the Germans were advanc-
ing either in the Campine or in Brabant, and if the British tanks were making a triumphant entry into the country in the opposite direction they were
probably doing so only to seal a gap in a front that was already unten-
able. I knew I was going to be overwhelmed by an immense apathy, a sense
of ignorance and doom. In a few hours' time I'd be with other recruits,
and we'd all have just one object: to obey our superiors' orders, but without any enthusiasm. All I was sure of was that I wasn't going to desert;
that was the beginning and end of my choice. Not very heroic. In that
sparsely furnished apartment facing the beach, you asked me if I could
stay with you one more night. The crowd outside was growing by the hour;
the eastern provinces were emptying of their inhabitants.

Holland fell to the Germans, and by dawn the ten thousand or so refugees in La Panne were seized by a kind of psychosis. As for me, I'd shilly-shallied enough and now I really was going to leave you. All three of you—Father, Grandfather, and you—got dressed slowly to see me off. I told Father, with some relief, that I could take my little package of stamps with me. He was grateful to me for thinking of his affairs. Would I at least accept some money? This dialogue was so absurd I didn't even answer, and he slipped a few notes in my pocket. All around us as we walked along, children were nibbling at waffles dusted with granulated sugar. My suitcase was very light: it contained some warm underwear, a toothbrush, some soap, and a pair of shoes. Your eyes were full of a mixture of anguish and stoicism which I couldn't quite interpret: I longed for this walk to end. Grandfather mumbled something incoherent, and I was grateful to him for not being able to get the words out. A passerby asked me where the French frontier was: why didn't I tell him it was closed, and that anyone who tried to cross it illicitly would be sentenced to death? Fiction suddenly seemed the only defense against reality. I slowed down and suggested we all have a last coffee outside a sidewalk café. You agreed: ten minutes more with me was like gaining an eternity. We sat there as if tons of suppressed regrets and emotions were weighing down upon our heads and breasts. With the forced serenity he always assumed in emergencies, Father announced that he'd reserved seats for you and himself in a bus that was leaving for Rouen in a few hours' time; from there you'd go on to either Paris or Toulouse, depending on the military situation. I was startled: weren't you taking your father with you? You said you'd thought about it carefully and decided that such a long and hazardous journey would be too much for him. He agreed, with an emphasis that seemed to me designed to conceal enormous grief. You tried to tell me he'd be better off in Brussels, living in our apartment and looked after by Armand and Mathilde. But you could tell from my silence that I totally disapproved. Then you saw fit to add that the Germans wouldn't harm an old man over eighty years old. You were about to lose your son in the maelstrom of war, and in these circumstances your father had become a useless burden: from now on, your only duty was to save your husband, and you wouldn't accept any others. I pondered the mean deceits perpetrated by the human race, and on the pettiness all four of us were all guilty of, deep down. I almost cried out, "Vile woman! You're abandoning your own father, a Jew, to the Nazis, who'll exterminate him! I'll never forgive you!" I didn't say anything, but you knew the meaning of my harsh expression and clenched jaw. Father paid for our coffees; my farewell embraces were formal and predictable. I didn't turn around after I'd walked away. I had no family anymore. I was twenty, and the century I lived in was twice that age. With a little help from forgetfulness, I was going to make a new life for myself or hurl myself on death. I was carrying no baggage except myself, lighter than my empty suitcase.

Paris, 1977

I see you again, every gesture, every breath, an image three-quarters blurred or else warped by some distorting scruple: by turns exact, incomplete, fluid, moving, and hateful. My lady mother. And I go on amassing variants of this portrait as if you were never anything but the sum of your sighs and your words. What is the fidelity that paralyzes me so? I keep trying to restore you to yourself, and yet there you are in a suburban cemetery. And you've been there for six months, surrounded by other corpses, lying beneath flowers and indifference, in the shade of a few poplars whose slow fluttering doesn't disguise their symbolism. It would be all the same if they were fluttering beside a brook: nature is no consolation to me. I'm within my rights in trying to say who you were, to reconstruct the story of your life, that portion of your past that can be found. Alas, it's not much of a privilege! The abnormal feelings I've repressed so long seem suddenly changed into a desire to distort you. And I allow myself to do so because I can't help being aware of the poisoned treasure of forbidden thoughts I keep inside me. I need to let them out, and yet, whenever they seem gone, writing renews them. And so, Mother mine, shall we enter those dark labyrinths? You'll emerge madder and more animal: but won't that be an improvement for someone who was always so limply reasonable, so conscientious to the marrow of her bones? I cause you to be born again, and you agree, don't you, because now I'm the only one who knows and possesses you completely, pore by pore, syllable by syllable, shudder after shudder, vowel after vowel? You're young, and it's my pen, my typewriter, that decide upon it. I won't let you object. You're twenty-six or seven, for example—a bit younger than when you were carrying me in your womb. You're beautiful in the old way, which is the way I like. You're a little over five feet tall, with thick fair hair that sometimes strays and curls around the nape of your neck and falls over your shoulders. Your face is exceedingly mobile, as if you were trying out a range of expressions and choosing the most emphatic, almost a grimace. Your black eyes don't go with the rest: they contradict the small nose, the plump cheeks, the full but pursed lips, the often quivering chin. But you know very well I don't find your face all that attractive. So what's your skin like, Mother mine: silky, smooth? If I make an effort, all I can recall is something resembling rather rough parchment: get thee behind me, memory! But I command you to have first-rate skin; otherwise, how can I be expected to desire you across half a century of imagination? Thus I decree that all the men turn to look at you because of your skin, but above all—let's not beat about the bush—because of your breasts, which manage to be at once seismic, ample, and shy. They hide only to reveal themselves the more, a provocation typical of that time! You don't aspire to easy conquests, and yet what else are you really capable of thinking about from morning till night? I'm one of the men who hover around you; if you don't mind, I'm the same age as my father was then, though I make myself someone much bolder. I have no intention of marrying you, as you know. You're wearing perfume—a good move, as not much can be seen of your waist or hips. Your gown is loose, and while it permits a few nicely calculated twirls, it reveals nothing of your frame itself. But surely, beneath these masses of material, you must be very well built? Are your legs slim or rounded? Are your kneecaps such that an aesthete can contemplate them with a pleasure devoid of desire, or does one's hand want to grasp them at once en route to more exciting regions?

I could, my lady mother, drink a few vodkas, interspersed with kvass, like the moujiks in Gogol or Leskov, and then, like Rasputin, pin you to the wall of your room. Oh, but I was forgetting—I introduced myself into your father's house on the humdrum but not very plausible pretext that I

Paris, 1977

wanted to show him the hide of some beast killed far away in, say, Turkestan. But as he keeps me waiting, I give you the once-over, and my blood, under the influence of alcohol, becomes rather heated: a nice little rape would just suit me—your respectful son transformed as if by magic into a kind of merchant, older than you are. You begin to struggle already, torn between horror and the attraction of that same horror. But not so fast: fiction, if it's to be properly enjoyed, needs to be more subtle, more European, more civilized. So I abandon my first, brutal scene, and replace it with another, for this novelist's skull of mine contains a whole dusty repertoire of scenery, like the sets of the Comédie-Française. If a line shocks you, or if you find an actor unimpressive or overzealous, hey, presto! we change from Marivaux to Shakespeare, from de Musset to Lope de Vega. But we'll stick to the same period, shall we, for the sake of convenience? You are this nice enticing little personage waiting for love, fame, and intelligence—commodities which you've seen little of till now. As you go around Odessa you look both mischievous and melancholy. Good!—I've got it! I was referring to the wrong playwrights just now: the one that fits you like a glove is Anton Chekhov! You're reserved but ardent: what use would a mother be to me, in my psychoanalytical, Freudian argument, if she were't consumed with enormous desires? Everything is graceful and relaxed: the pale-faced students in the avenue Preobrajenskaia are like the dandies in Lermontov; the fishmongers and other stall-holders don't yet know they're members of the proletariat; the officers of the czar are not making ready for two terrible conflicts, one of them a civil war. The young gentlemen are gallant but vexingly do not importune you. Oh, if only one of them would make up his mind at last to take you in his arms! Virginity, that priceless treasure, is as heavy a burden as a trunk full of gold rubles.

Still, you have a choice. It lies between a hussar, my father, and me, whom we'll call the stranger, as in the books you read: Edgar Allan Poe, Prosper Mérimée, and the young Leonid Andreev. If you didn't restrain yourself, you'd agree to the rendezvous suggested by the hussar. But good breeding inhibits impulse: the handsome soldier would possess you with admirable passion, but how long would he stay? One day he'd leave with

185

his regiment for Khabarovsk, or for Vladivostok on the other side of Siberia, or for Helsinki in the north of purple Finland. So you'll do without his siege and his military assault, my fortress mother! But the other one, now—he'd be a good match: no one would reject my father. He's got a certain amount of money, a lot of savoir-faire, and a charming tightrope walker's personality. You'll certainly yield to him after a lengthy engagement. But to whom will you give yourself before that? Because I'm not letting you wait until you're married, my lady mother! I dislike professional virgins as much in 1907 as in 1977. So you meet the stranger at a ball—I leave you to choose the music: waltz, quadrille, or mazurka. But you're already very musical, and I bet you pick Tchaikovsky, in some cheap arrangement specially made for the dancers of your native province. I invite you, and you hesitate for a moment: you don't quite like the look of me. But one has to be broad-minded if one wants to mix with other people, doesn't one? After telling me the next three or four dances are spoken for, you finally let me take you in my arms. You're not as light as I'd imagined. There's something solid about that twirling body, and are the little gasps that animate your bosom due to fragility or emotion? The small talk doesn't last long. I ask if you often come to these places, where the girls are watched over by caricatures of parents; if you have a lover; if you live in the town. Such civilities over, I turn to compliments. They can't be addressed to your soul, which is beautiful by definition; it's your body that attracts me. I might as well admit it enchants me, for we'll get on faster after a couple of sentences in which you try, in vain, to put me in my place. That's no way to speak to a respectable young lady. . .

My hands stray over your hips, slip inside your bodice, linger beneath your armpits. Like all flirts, you push me away and retain your hold on me simultaneously. I tell you straight out that my tongue, which is very expert, is extremely jealous of my fingers: I don't have to draw you a picture, do I? You address me as Monsieur and tell me I'm an impertinent wretch, and I say you shouldn't speak to your own son like that. You insist on observing chronology, but I completely disregard the time element. You believe in keeping up appearances, while the laws of literature let me do as I please. I want you: even during a polite conversation, typical of the turn of the century, this kind of advance shouldn't faze even the most stuck-up young woman. I grow more insistent: will you please think about how I feel? Deep calls to deep, and you move closer to me than is quite correct. You're going to be mine, Mother mine—my lady mother—I feel it, with a manly satisfaction not far from conceit. As for you, what else can you do but surrender? I desire you in words to make sure I desire you in reality, but you have no need of such artifice. You're going to give yourself to me, as they said in the days of your youth. It's up to us both to decide on the setting. I can scarcely, even at night, ask you to smuggle me into your father's house through a back door in the basement: that's not how they carry on in Pushkin or Balzac, is it? And although, by means of a rather unpleasant fiction, I turn myself into your seducer, it would be going too far to identify myself with the devil. We could take refuge with one of your girlfriends, a fellow student at the Conservatoire: you must be able to lay your hands on a few accomplices, ready to give you alibis by the dozen. I could always suggest a first-class tumble on the steps leading down to the harbor; but you'd say nonsense, one can't make love in the middle of the town. Then I solve the problem: I take you down to the seashore and hail a horse-drawn cab—I'm sure a ride in one of those will do the trick. Soon we're in a quiet spot, the nearest house three hundred meters away. It's a vacant lot; the ground is sandy and relatively clean.

Don't help me, please, my lady Mother. Button by button I uncover your skin, which is almost as I imagined it, though perhaps a bit less dry. Groan a bit better than that, for goodness sake! Hey, are you in more of a hurry than I am? I'm not going to tear your clothes off on the excuse that they get in the way of this sort of thing, though we're both pretty clumsy at it. I enjoy taking my time, the better to admire you while still on the brink of pleasure. We go through the whole ritual. Now your bosom is bare and I cover it with kisses, some brief, some lingering, some dry, some very damp. The rings around your nipples contract. I, obeying another convention, say nothing: it's not done to spoil what's known as happiness by inopportune words. You lie down on the grass, and I do the same, after first looking down on you coolly, for of course you're going to yield to me—you're in a terrible hurry to do so. Other articles of clothing are removed, and all of a sudden you're vexed with me for being less naked than you. Your fingers convey that if I don't undress you'll rip off my shirt and trousers yourself, and to hell with etiquette! My phallus, red and erect, is now on a level with your chest, moving back and forth and hesitating to enter you. Here's your beloved son's penis, my lady mother, knocking at your door. Give it a welcome. You've already given him your pain, your milk, your affection, and then your quiet patience; to make his debt to you complete, give him your vagina. You pant, you wriggle, you're about to weep tears of rage and pleasure. You lightly cup my testicles in both hands, as if holding a sunflower. You bite your lips, forbidding the slightest word to break from your parched throat. In the midst of my intoxication I suddenly break away. We mustn't forget your future fiancé, my lady mother—the man who'll one day be my father, and who ought to take part in our coupling. Let's invite him to be the witness of our irresistible love. That absentminded and irresolute young man will some day become a dealer in postage stamps: the most ridiculous of professions. He'll use tweezers and a magnifying glass. So allow me to use them too: in my hallucination I've got a pair of each in my waistcoat pocket. I tweak out a few little hairs between your groin and your thigh—they were marring a little area that's simultaneously soft and vibrant. With the magnifying glass I examine your vulva, boss by boss, viscous membrane after retracted membrane, secretion and saliva, marsh and abyss, oyster and orchid. Thus will your husband, my father, scrutinize his stamps, perforation by perforation, picture by picture, watermark by watermark. You can't wait any longer, and beg me to enter you. But it's not a reprehensible breakin: I'm only going back inside my native flesh after being too long away. You ruffle my hair and kiss me on the lips: our tongues mingle with sublime fury. The world disappears: you take me back again. Your legs open as if you're willing for me to tear you apart, as if you'd like to die of it. But then you shove me away. There's been a misunderstanding. It wasn't my phallus you were opening yourself to; it was my head. I must go back into you via my brow and my ears, just as I came forth out of you nearly sixty years ago. In your womb I am to be present at my second birth, a birth in reverse. I don't know you, my lady mother, and I sleep with you in order to know you better. You agree to be raped so that I may lie in you forever in a changeless and delicious sleep.

Montpellier, November 1941

Despite its size the farm, standing on the hillside below the yews and cypresses, looked frail and rickety. It had fallen in on itself, and looked as if about to shrink even further. In the kitchen garden, pumpkins and cabbages stood out among a few meager leaves—onions, perhaps, or lettuces. The straggling vines were slowly turning into burned-out matches, wild and twisted. I paused outside the heavy door. I'd changed in the last eighteen months, and I imagined you'd be gray, and more frail, and probably stooping a little. The first few moments are always awkward: one has to try to find the right words, the right tone, the right rhythm, and whatever one says seems false and quite different from what one wanted to say. Did we really have to meet again? Perhaps it would be better if we remained apart, seeing each other only in our imaginations? I felt tired, and suddenly unable to face up to reality. I gazed at the valley, the water tower on the nearby scrub, the trees surrounding the farm. I had to make up my mind, and I chose not to ring the bell. I went back through the gate and out along the road for a hundred meters or so. Now I had a better view of the place as a whole, with its henhouse and its mossy roof. I tried to imagine your life here, and my father's: how could a couple of town dwellers ever get used to this landscape, with its toil, its slowness, its awful long-suffering? I'd be glad to see you again, but what good would that dubious happiness do me? Something held me back: was I about to rush into an ambush of inextricably mingled joys and regrets? I'd lived in want and fear, and in a few minutes I'd be adding your and Father's sorrows to mine. I'd looked for you both, with determination at first in September 1940, and then, later, with less and less conviction, until the day I found you.

Father opened the door. He'd put on weight and shrunk a little: he sounded quite cheerful, but not excessively moved. You came running from somewhere inside the house and threw yourself into my arms. At first we didn't know whether just the physical pleasure of being together was enough, or whether we should start at once to tell each other about all that had happened to us. Uncharacteristically, you didn't press me to have something to eat. You wanted me to go up and see my quarters right away: two huge, rather rustic rooms, newly whitewashed and with solidly built windows. One room looked north, over a jumbled expanse of low hills; the other faced east, over a village: Montferrier, with its church tower. There was a primitive chest of drawers, an enormous table and a vast bed; you could have done the household washing in the sink. I laughed. I had only four kilos of baggage; not only would I have plenty of room—I ought to have brought my horse. You were not amused by this feeble joke, though Father smiled at it and asked me if I'd like to look over the rest of the house. Your quarters, on the ground floor, had slightly more furniture but were just as Spartan as mine; the log fire was the only thing that didn't strike me as absurd. But I pretended to approve of everything, though my exaggerated praise must have given the game away. The kitchen too was large—big enough for a whole tribe of wine growers. Father then showed me the cellars, which contained enough fuel for another three winters. The mistral was terrible, and although the local authorities didn't encourage the use of coal for domestic heating, they'd probably turn a blind eye, as they had last year. The kitchen garden and henhouse were my father's domain; he boasted about his squash, and if only I'd seen his cucumbers last summer! But he disliked fowl, and if on occasion he'd had to kill a chicken, he preferred to leave the job to the farmer's wife who came in twice a week to help with the housework and shopping. To shop one had to go to Plan-des-Quatre-Seigneurs, take the tram to Montpellier, and then stand in line for twenty minutes or half an hour, sometimes in vain, because for all the good that food coupons and the rations they provided did anyone. . . ! He left his sentences unfinished. I was astonished at how he'd taken on southern ways, and when I said as much, he put on a beret. Yes, he'd gone completely native. He reminded me that his own father, Joachim, had retired to Grasse in 1928, a little while before he died. The south of France had an easygoing philosophy, a joie de vivre that shouldn't be underestimated, especially in between two versions of hell. But it wasn't time yet for recriminations and complaints; as far as vegetables and other crops were concerned, all was well. In addition to the hens there were also a couple of white rabbits. Father lifted one up gently by the ears: it was called Rainer Maria Rilke after his favorite poet. Current events were so grim, he said, they needed livening up with a few jokes. Was he trying to put me at my ease, or to pretend that everything was all right?

Your silence made me uneasy. You were just standing aside and leaving Father and me to the superficial sprightliness of our reunion. I looked at you more closely. You'd aged more than I'd realized, and your eyes were more mobile than ever: they darted from left to right as if in constant fear. Perhaps you suspected our meeting wasn't going to last long. You spoke in monosyllables, repeating what Father said and leaving him to tell me you were both well. He started with a stream of anecdotes, as if anything serious was now quite unimportant. The neighbors on both sides were simple, obliging folk: above all they were very good-natured, and that was a rare thing. For the first few weeks everyone had been very cautious, but an excellent modus vivendi had been worked out once you'd shown you were independent. You were neither refugees who'd lost everything and would be a burden on them, nor profiteers who'd tried to buy their land for a song. Your aims were modest, and the rent you paid them for the house came in very useful: they declared only half of it on their tax returns. But they were an immeasurable help to you in other ways: they sold you a little butter, and occasionally half of a slaughtered animal, for something between the legal price and the black market rate. This gray market made an excellent foundation for friendship. And it was real, genuine friendship, over a bottle of good wine or a stew. After all, said Father, there was nothing wrong in mixing with people for whom sun and rain, wind and snow, good drinking water, seed and harvest were more important than the plans of Marshal Pétain or Dr. Goebbels.

I went along with this attitude, at least for the first evening. You agreed with what Father said and waited for me to make momentous revelations. We drank some pastis—the occasion for another demonstration of *savoir-vivre*. Father said how much he liked it, and went on to praise the beneficial effects of *pétanque*. On my admitting I didn't know how to play, he roped me in for the following morning at ten, by which time the morning mists would have cleared. He knew one or two places by the side of the road where the ground was especially suitable for beginners: firm, smooth, neither too large nor too small. He took a pipe from his pocket and asked me if I minded if he smoked. He'd gone back to a habit acquired in his roving days, forty years ago. A pipe was conducive to spiritual peace, he explained, and as he intended to achieve that state he'd purchased at least the symbol of it. Then came some bold comparisons: wasn't the south of France like the southern Ukraine, with its clear skies, picturesque accents, and its people who overcame even the direst troubles with the gift of the gab? With a little imagination, one could detect similarities between Marseilles and Odessa. Then I asked him if he could really be content with himself and his fate, now, at the end of 1941, with the Reich occupying half of Europe and France reduced to the rôle of a slave who asks to have his eyes blindfolded before he commits his crimes? He answered that there are times when any attitude is bound to seem theatrical: he was just trying to play-act convincingly. Then, without a pause, he said he'd cook the dinner. You had some eggs, and his great specialty was a very lightly cooked omelette with chicken livers and onions. We didn't speak of anything serious until the following afternoon; perhaps we'd unconsciously agreed on the need to protect the happiness, part genuine and part feigned, of our reunion.

You questioned me about my health: wasn't I working too hard? You said my sudden gestures were signs of nervousness, and probably of a weak digestion too. I should be careful about what I ate: food substitutes were often of very poor quality, so it was better to make do with an apple or some dried fruit. You realized, yourself, that these concerns were ridiculous and my answers pure politeness. We had more important things to say to each other, but we couldn't find the courage. You preferred to take refuge in trivial worries about my comfort: you hadn't put drapes in my room, nor a bedspread. I must tell you what my favorite colors were now: they'd probably changed since we lived in Brussels. You had a sewing machine and would be glad to run some things up from odds and ends: it was amazing what you could do if you had to. You remarked that my shoes needed repair, and I could see from your face that you took this as evidence that I was very hard-up. You apologized for the fact that neither you nor Father had any leather coupons left, so we'd have to wait till the spring to get me some decent shoes. . . Unless. . . Of course, you were forgetting your friend in the Hérault prefecture: Monsieur Marcorelle was a man of his word and very generous—he'd get me all the shoes I wanted. Father had made lots of contacts among the philatelists in that part of the world, and for a stamp or two he could obtain almost anything you needed. Did I mean to continue my studies? I could sign on at the university of Montpellier, or, if the worst came to the worst, at Aix-en-Provence. Maybe it was time for me to settle down, after eighteen months of traveling around. Had all those journeys been really necessary? you wondered.

Now at last I recognized you: your silence and preoccupation were giving way to aggression. You were still careful, but outright reproaches wouldn't be long coming. To delay their arrival, I began to ask you both about all that had happened to you since May 1940. Father wasn't keen on talking about it: he preferred to erase these events from his memory and minimize their importance. He had been badly affected by having to leave Russia long ago, and had vowed to make this recent exile as undisturbing as possible. As he told it to himself, he'd gone on vacation to the south of France and rediscovered the attractions of simple landscapes and simple people. It was important to cling to this idyllic view of things despite all the denials and adjustments forced on him by facts he couldn't help seeing. But were there other reasons for this willful blindness? Were you, his wife, seriously ill, perhaps with cancer or some other illness that you were both hiding from me? I myself had so many secrets

to keep from *you*, I couldn't believe you two were being any more truthful and spontaneous than I was.

I eventually managed to piece your travels together. You got to Rouen
safely, you said, and rented a room near the cathedral. But four days later
that part of the town was bombed while you were having a meal somewhere in the suburbs. The hotel was damaged, and Father and you lost
some of your things. You threw a fit of hysterics and had to be given one
or two injections: you talked about your dead mother, and how you had
to go back to Brussels to be buried in the same grave. The Germans had
taken Arras, and Dunkirk was about to fall—Father decided to set off
again, but the roads were crowded with refugees and there was danger
from Stuka bombers. Somehow a convoy got together consisting mainly
of people fleeing from Belgium and Luxembourg, but with a few Dutch
and British. Gasoline cost from ten to twenty times its normal price. At
every stop along the way some member of the convoy would abandon a
suitcase that was too heavy or an elderly relative who couldn't keep up
with the rest of you. There was another air raid in Poitiers, but this time
it didn't affect you. You were exhausted, you couldn't sleep, you no longer
had any idea how far you'd come. Father could have told you you were
almost at the Spanish frontier—you'd lost touch with reality and wouldn't
have known the difference. But you were both almost safe for six or seven
days in Montauban: apart from the bugs, you were getting used to the
situation. It was at this point that you suffered a severe nervous breakdown. You refused to eat, you only left your bed to sit in an armchair,
you saw yourself as very old and helpless. Gradually you started to praise
the Germans: it was foolish to yield to panic and keep running away from
them like the hordes of refugees. Off and on you implored my father to
abandon you, to go back, or to poison you: you were a mass of impulses
and contradictions. Then Father had the bright idea of keeping you away
from the crowds, and took you from village to village through Auvergne
and the Cévennes, as if merely to enjoy the coolness of a river or the
whorls of smoke rising over a thatched roof.

You interrupted your narrative several times to see that I had everything I wanted. Little by little you became more natural, though perhaps

not entirely so. Father took over the tale, though he told it with some irony. Your flight turned into a kind of tour through the treasures of the French countryside. You were robbed in one hamlet where you had stopped, losing a shirt, some provisions, and a few francs left in a pocket. Sometimes you were overcharged for very inferior food, and probably you'd been given horse or ass's meat instead of beef. But when the world's falling to pieces all around one, such misadventures can seem quite amusing. And it's wrong to get angry about them and exaggerate one's own importance. Fatalism has its advantages: you live from day to day, with no other object than to be forgotten. As the terrors grew worse, so occasions of pleasure multiplied. You had no duties toward anyone but yourselves, and life lived without a timetable can be very pleasant. Occasionally you would read the newspapers or listen to the radio, but in places like Guéret or Millau that was almost an insult to the leaves, the ferns, and the birds of passage. Neither of you had much difficulty in erasing the past from your memory—you had too much to gain by the maneuver. Father got the better of the march of History, and you, too weak to oppose him, had gradually come to follow suit. Chance took care of the rest. One day in August 1940 you came upon this hamlet on the outskirts of Montpellier, and you took to it at once. You had a little money left, together with Father's stamps, and these enabled him to start work again: he still had some clients in neutral countries with whom he could correspond. Other collectors answered the advertisements he put in the papers. As stamp dealing was subject to quotas and he had no permit, he had to make use of some government officials in Montpellier who acted as intermediaries in return for a small commission. The mail to and from Switzerland was still regular, and that with Portugal and Argentina was almost as good.

You told me about your own withdrawn existence, taking care not to dwell on your anxieties and doubts and the apprehension that seized you whenever you thought of my father's strange serenity. I suppose you expected me to make some harsh comment which would have forced both of you to take a less optimistic view of things. But you were very inconsistent, and let yourself be influenced by Father's gaiety. I soon saw through this dual misunderstanding: he'd set himself the task of reassuring you at all costs, and you'd decided not to cast any shadows over his cheerfulness. So you both constantly vied with each other in acting a part. What should I be—a spoilsport, an arbiter, or an accomplice? At least you didn't read me moral lectures or extract impossible promises: I'd stay as long as I wanted to, and no longer. I didn't belong to you anymore: I was merely granting you a precious interlude in your usual illusory routine. You soon put me at my ease— I was to eat my fill, enjoy the fresh air, make the most of the pleasures of country life and forget the far-off wars. I became interested in the recent grape harvest; I listened with bated breath to theories about preserving olives; I shared your views on local recipes for cooking rutabagas and Jerusalem artichokes. I tended Rainer Maria Rilke and his hutch-mate with exemplary care. After a long inner struggle, I decided the earth nourished the mind as well as the body. And as all I had to give you was my temporary presence, I could refuse you nothing.

But how was I to tell you of my recent past? I'd had too many fantastic changes of fortune to see any meaning or connecting thread in my experiences. In my own opinion I was neither more heroic nor more cowardly than the next man, and I didn't expect others to think any better of me. I'd set out in search of a phantom regiment in May 1940, but whenever I almost reached it, it disappeared again. I narrowly escaped some German scouts between Dunkirk and Gravelines. When I got to Calais I was ordered to report to Saumur two days later. During the débâcle I was with a group of twenty Belgian soldiers, some of whom, like me, were eager to fight, while others were only trying to escape capture after an inglorious battle. Should I tell you about all that confusion?

I preferred a version less complex and less humiliating: I said my regiment, which I'd finally managed to catch up with somewhere (unnamed) in Artois, had made an orderly retreat to the outskirts of Saumur, where we learned that King Leopold had surrendered. We swore to kill the traitor and asked to be incorporated into the French army. I wasn't lying— merely embellishing a confused truth and simplifying what had struck me at the time as a deplorable series of irrational impulses and hysterical decisions. Had I been a defeatist, already beaten before it was certain all was lost? My words were the only truth I had, even if they didn't accord with the facts: surely I had the right to make the best of my own past? We regrouped at Uchaud in the Gard, and were given a brief training. A few days before the armistice I was fighting with the 615th regiment of mountain infantry against the Italians, near Sospel and the Charles-Albert Bridge. Those skirmishes were symbolic of my whole war: like being at a rifle range at a fair without hitting one clay pipe! In the last hours of the war, to avoid being taken prisoner in the German offensive, I demobilized myself. I had the nerve to inform my captain of what I was going to do. He just wished me good luck.

Apart from this, nothing that had really happened to me seemed worth telling, so I relied on fiction rather than fact. I romanticized a few events, either because they weren't presentable or because you'd have found them farcical. One doesn't tell one's mother one heard Marshal Pétain announce the armistice over the radio in a brothel in the rue d'Alger in Nice, between a very fair blond with a Hungarian accent and a very dark black girl with a Creole accent. Nor that at every quaver in that ancient voice, one drank champagne out of a red satin slipper, as in a "naughty" film in the late twenties—both to thumb one's nose at the twentieth century in its darkest hour and to congratulate oneself on still being alive. I stayed drunk for four days, but the madam was generous. Her place would probably be closed down for a few weeks because of the defeat and money would be worth nothing, so she might as well oblige a few lusty soldiers full of good intentions! I told you I rested in a little hotel in Cimiez, contemplating the parasol pines, the mimosa, the pretty blue sky, and the distress of France. But one had to live, or in other words earn some money. I happened to find favor with one of the girls in the brothel, a platinum blond from Alsace called Jacqueline Kolb, with a broad brow, long legs, and a studied smile. Was it because she was feeling guilty about something, or simply because she found herself at loose ends after the brothel was closed? At any rate, she lost no time in offering to share her two-room apartment with me, an ex-soldier, and such an unexceptionable young man. It suited me to act as a cover for her while I waited to decide my own fate, if that were possible. Jacqueline wasn't entirely converted from her old ways. She did some dressmaking and mending, and

went on errands for the elderly and infirm. But this wasn't enough to provide for our modest wants, so she occasionally pulled her weight by seeing a few former customers, preferably those in their fifties. I wasn't living off her ill-gotten gains: I counted up all she spent, and intended to
reimburse her one day for my share. It was understood our liaison wouldn't
last long. Three or four months at most—the time it would take me to
find a niche in Vichy France. The fact was, I wasn't without a new kind
of ethic. I saw Marshal Pétain and Pierre-Étienne Flandin as men determined to save what millions of soldiers lacking both the material and
moral wherewithal had not been able to protect. Jacqueline was a wonderful technician as far as love was concerned, and owed it to herself to
spread her skill around. I took a certain pride in maintaining, six or seven
times a day, that I didn't know the meaning of the word jealousy. But I
made certain changes when I told that story: Jacqueline became a refugee from Alsace whom I'd met on my way across the Alps. I'd helped
her carry her baggage. She was penniless; her parents had just been killed
in an air raid. I got taken on by a garage owner who was shorthanded,
and he taught me how to weld auto bodywork and mend tires. I earned
just enough, with the odd tip, for us to get by. Naturally we came to love
each other in due course, but in the middle of December 1940 Jacqueline
got a pass for the Occupied Zone and we had to part. The story, as touching as any serial in a woman's weekly, ended in much sweet sorrow.

All this time, I went on, I hadn't ever forgotten about you and Father.
I went every day to police headquarters and the city hall to look at the
lists of refugees. But I couldn't submit the proper forms because I wasn't
supposed to work or live in Nice. I was strangely certain, however—
whether by intuition or out of incurable naïveté I couldn't have said—
that both of you were alive and well. At this revelation, which after all
was not entirely untrue, you came over at last and clasped me to you. I
realized the history of my wanderings was of much less moment to you
than the tale of my feelings, worries, and speculations on your account.
All I'd really needed to do, I thought, was say that all the time we were
separated I loved you deeply, and that my love for you helped me in my
struggle against adversity. But how could I be satisfied with such a sac-

charine platitude? I wasn't a good son, and having to recognize the fact a little more each day didn't make me feel any better. I reproached myself, accused myself of deceit, invented fresh evasions to replace the previous ones, reasoned with myself beyond reason, wished you to the devil, then wished myself there too to get you back. I interrupted my confession for a week to arrange and, where necessary, add to or modify the scattered details of my past, introducing some kind of coherence into what had really been a meaningless drift, sometimes painful though sometimes bearable enough. My father saw through what I said: he knew an ex-soldier of my age had to make certain dubious compromises in order to survive. He began to turn over his own memories of the 1914–1918 war. On the Austrian front, near Lvov, looting had been a matter of honor and rape a proof of determination. Later on, after the retreat to Estonia, desertion in the name of revolutionary ideas had been seen as a demonstration of solidarity with a people on the march toward the light. He laughed, and drew at his pipe. Then suddenly you began to shake all over and shout incomprehensibly. We had to half-carry you to bed. My father gave you a sedative and you fell into a long, exhausted sleep. You had these attacks every so often, he explained, but the doctors all agreed they'd wear off: you needed peace and quiet, and had to avoid strong emotions. Next day you were much better. You just looked at Father and me with a strange and solemn expression and made us promise not to talk about the war anymore. We were at peace now, and even if we had to force ourselves to believe that, your health depended on our doing so.

I kept my word and turned my attention to the tomatoes, the last of the season and pretty tasteless. I also gave my opinion on the grape jelly which had taken the place of sugar despite your local contacts. I became fond of going for little walks and doing my lungs good with the fresh air. I was even exquisitely polite to the neighbors when they came to dinner—especially to the local carpenter, whose language was enough to make a gendarme blush. He compared sausages to bull's penises, and said that women's brains were between their legs. But as he had a cousin who was a market gardener and a brother who was a fisherman in Palas, you overlooked his vocabulary. You realized such compromises irked me,

and soon asked me to go on with the story of my wanderings. You had to
know all about my life, however much it cost you. But as, deep down,
you really accepted only the pleasanter revelations, I had no scruples
about recounting merely the less disturbing episodes of my checkered
career. So, said I, one day my boss at the garage asked me if I'd like to
drive one of his vans: he delivered goods in Narbonne, Toulouse, and
Montélimar. Without asking any awkward questions, I accepted the job
as a temporary measure—though what wasn't temporary in my restless
life? I described the job to you as hard but respectable. I didn't mention
the police searches, the official warnings, the times I had to prove I knew
nothing about my boss's dealings with the black market. I was just a rather
inexperienced but resourceful traveling salesman: did that image reassure you? Anyhow I'd gained some time, and wasn't that something in
this monstrous hand-to-hand fight between giants? But I'd forgotten our
agreement about not mentioning the war.

The winter of 1940–41 wasn't too uncomfortable, and I began to think
of embarking on a less passive way of life. My frequent journeys had prevented me from looking for you and Father as thoroughly as I'd have liked.
One day, as I was delivering a cask of wine in Decazeville, I happened
to meet a former major in the Belgian army. We got along well together
and he asked me if I'd like to work for him. He had a little shed where
he was helping to make a list of all our fellow countrymen now living in
the Unoccupied Zone. I accepted with glee: at last, instead of acting as
a porter-cum-removal man, I was going to do something useful. I wrote
some reports, distributed some aid, and arranged a few repatriations.
Sometimes I would be sent on a mission, and so my wanderings began
again, taking me from Limoges to Nîmes, from Carcassonne to Pau, from
Tarbes to Mont-de-Marsan. The frequency with which I referred to places
close to the Spanish frontier should have given you a clue: but no, you
must have told yourself I was satisfied with helping my compatriots. My
father didn't smell a rat, either. So I didn't bother to mention that I went
from one Belgian to another on the orders of agents in London. There were
people in the Pyrenees who smuggled them over the border and sent them
on their way to Lisbon. From there they could get to England. I knew

that two out of ten of these trips ended badly, but the odds seemed reasonable. I wasn't motivated by patriotism: I was paid six hundred francs for every fellow countryman I delivered into safe hands, though sometimes it took what might be considered some rather heavy persuasion. I had no need to look on this traffic in men as either repugnant or heroic: the only people I could persuade were those who'd made their minds up already, and my fee was proof of my impartiality. For five or six months I was a kind of underground recruiting sergeant, not very well paid. Was I sending those young men to their death? Or might I, after thirty or forty operations, have followed their example and tried to make my way to London? I wasn't so sure now that Germany was going to win. The Nazi terror had finally undermined my former philosophy—scarcely changed since the beginning of the war—which had assumed that Europe would swiftly be unified, and that this would be followed by a return to democracy. But as far as you and Father were concerned, I'd been a hardworking official. So I spared you my more murky adventures. And you didn't ask for any proof of what I did say.

In the consulate at Marseilles I found a complete list of all the Belgian citizens in the Unoccupied Zone: I wrote to you at once, and rushed to see you. You and Father hadn't been able to find any trace of me: I was often away on official trips, and what was left of our HQ probably took the precaution of keeping such movements confidential. I was issued three different identity cards in case the network I belonged to was dismantled by the Vichy police or denounced to the German armistice commisssion. In actual fact I'd known where you were living for six or seven months before I came to see you, but what was the point in telling you that? I'd already made my confession, with all the shady abbreviations and corrections I'd always intended to make.

For two whole weeks I'd been in tune with your moods, your work, your reserve, your heavy silences. I'd come to admire my father, whose only, untroubled concern now was to become, rather late in the day, a moderately hedonistic and philosophical southerner. I wondered about my own future between the turnips cooked in goose grease and the abstract threats of fate, the map-like barks of plane trees and the distant summons of invisible wars, the first night frosts and the need to take my place once more among the nameless, frightened actors performing a totally unpredictable drama. One day I received a letter without a postmark: it must have been slipped under the door by some mysterious messenger. It summoned me to a rendezvous the day after next in a café in the cours Belzunce in Marseilles. There I would receive instructions to go to North Africa. My life of wandering was about to begin again, with all its risks, its tragicomedies, its crazy illegality. Was this a genuine mission, or was I walking into a trap? I was under stay of execution, subject to the orders of unknown superiors. I felt a certain elation, though apprehension made me extremely cautious. Father, more observant than you, asked me to go into the kitchen garden with him, among his chervil and leeks. He told me that after much research he'd managed to trace an uncle of his in Chicago who'd made his fortune in the meatpacking industry. This excellent fellow had agreed to send you both the necessary papers for you to go to the United States. Father didn't want to tell you about it yet in case anything went wrong, but as soon as the papers arrived, which should be soon, you'd go to live there as regular immigrants. He had no doubt you'd make good there. Europe, he said, was finished for a long time, and his optimistic act was only to make life easier for you. In exchange for this confidence I told him I too was about to leave mainland France, unless I was being lured into an ambush. When I finally made up my mind to tell *you* I was leaving, I didn't say anything definite: I just had to go away for a few weeks, maybe months, but I fully intended to come back. Yes, in the early spring of '42. We didn't even pretend to be sincere anymore, except when it didn't matter. I embraced you at length, and sadly.

But I was much more demonstrative with Rainer Maria Rilke, to whom I fed fifteen or twenty nice juicy carrots, one after the other.

Paris, summer 1977

You're reconstructed page by page; you disintegrate page by page: so what becomes of fidelity to what you really were? You're no longer there to say gently, but with a tinge of irony, "That's not how I used to react, my boy—I was much more spontaneous than you give me credit for."

One after the other the witnesses disappear too, and those who are still alive sink slowly into decrepitude. You never spoke to me of Bercoff, your first husband; I don't even know his first name. I'm not sure my father ever mentioned him either. The only thing I can really remember about him is something your brother Armand told me some time around 1936. One day, after you and he had had a violent quarrel, he said Bercoff was the only person who'd ever been able to see you objectively. When did you meet this mysterious character? To answer this question I'm forced to resort to invention, and as there's no reason to suppose your way of life before you had me was anything like your way of life when I knew you, my speculations are bound to be full of doubts and hesitation. Be that as it may, I have to try to imagine your youth in Odessa between 1908 and 1912. Why, even if decorum forbade that I, as your son, should learn too much about your early emotions, didn't I ever insist on your confiding in me a little as a writer? There are plenty of contemporary photographs, but of course they're stiff and affected. They show you as very pretty, if a little chubby in the face. In some of them you have a very short hairdo instead of braids, from which I conclude you're impulsive, and anxious either to make yourself appear attractive or to suggest hidden depths. You like music; I seem to remember you find the Romantics more inspiring than eighteenth-century composers. You probably think Massenet superior to Mozart. You don't know anything about the Italians: they're too frivolous compared with your god, Tchaikovsky, whom some of your teachers at the Conservatoire actually knew: they say he was both insufferable and irresistible. You take your studies very seriously. Your French, though you have a slight accent, is as perfect as your Russian; to your parents' surprise, you do like chemistry; you're very good at all practical things, from dressmaking to cookery. Do your elders keep a careful eye on the company you keep? Your father mixes a kind of sardonic indulgence with genuine severity. It goes without saying that your mother understands everything, and expects your sexual awakening to be accompanied by some shocks.

Should a girl from the middle classes be encouraged to go out a lot, or should she be kept on a tight rein? A difficult dilemma: it would be foolish to miss out on any matches that present themselves, but at the same time one doesn't want to give the impression her family wants to marry her off as fast as possible. The only thing to do is vary one's policy according to circumstance. Manners in Odessa are not so pretentious as those in other big cities in the Ukraine: Kiev is more lavish and ambitious; Kharkov tries to uphold tradition. A great deal of laughter is heard around the Black Sea, and jesting is a virtue in itself: there are too many sailors around for bigotry to have much chance. Trade brings crowds of merchants this way: Turks, Asians, Caucasians, Greeks—all are welcome, few doors are closed to them. The citizens of Odessa are different from those of St. Petersburg and Moscow in shunning extremes: elsewhere people may pass easily from debauchery to mysticism, from the most tyrannical rigor to the most unbridled license, but Odessa maintains a stolid skepticism with regard to all cravings and shams. You go dancing once a week, and are invited to lots of parties. You're not shy: you learned early on how to dismiss the bores and protect yourself from the predators who, as in cheap novelettes, lie in wait for such as you—poor little innocents kept awake at night by morbid curiosity. Neither naïve nor stupid, you're a dainty morsel, fit for a king. The leather trade is profitable, and your family's pretty well-off. Bercoff—I think I'll call him Nicholas: Vladimir and Fédor are so old-fashioned—can be thought of for present purposes as a promising young engineer. He talks about the state of technology in Russia, especially in civil engineering. He means to work far away in Siberia, between the rivers Ob and Lena, mastering the elements and helping civilization advance by giant strides. The whole continent needs to be awakened and forced to catch up with history; at present it lags at least three hundred years behind Europe and Asia. Bercoff goes to dances too; you couldn't meet him anywhere else, since none of your friends or relations knows him. I've decided he's three years older than you. He's neither a ladykiller nor a bully—just a guileless young man who reveals his ambition as soon as he opens his mouth, as if he were presenting letters of credit. He's ruddy, robust, and rough and ready; he inspires confidence; he doesn't whisper the obsequious and sweaty nothings your other dancing partners utilize, while you're waltzing, to win hidden rewards in the form of sighs, perhaps of stolen kisses, among the succeeding shadows. Does he appeal to you? As far as your upbringing allows, you dream of leaving home and going to live in a large house with an influential husband, a lot of children, and an adequate staff of servants. You share the aspirations of your class, and devotion seems as valuable to you as passion. Armand, who has taken it upon himself to keep an eye on you, doesn't think Nicholas Bercoff a bad sort, and strikes up a superficial friendship with him—one which involves a tolerable amount of spying.

You get used to Bercoff, a sound fellow whose open and artless courtship reflects his basic decency. If he's ever had any fleeting affairs, they've left him devoid of shiftiness: Bercoff is no cheat. Armand, who has decided that the young man passes muster, urges you to embark on semi-official exchanges. Perhaps Nicholas could come to tea, and if that's a success a little concert could be gotten together in his honor: he already finds you attractive—your musical talents will make you seem even more so. You would like your suitor to be a bit more eager and passionate; on the other hand, his lack of imagination is reassuring. What's more, you have faith in your own powers: whenever you feel like it you can transform affection into something more tumultuous. Which of you takes the initiative? You are too intelligent to leave it to Bercoff. Besides, Armand, a past master at lightning conquest, gives you excellent advice: what you ought to pretend; when to feign innocence, make a few grimaces, profess astonishment; how ardor and reserve may be alternated to good purpose. He supplements feminine strategy with masculine tactics: a most obliging brother. Girls give themselves to him as if in jest, and to prove that thanks to him they know how to avoid pomposity even in bed. You'll soon become engaged. I don't foresee any problems, and need not bother with Bercoff's family: a young fellow like him, with a fine future beckoning, who speaks of Siberia and Turkestan as promised lands, doesn't need to consult his parents. He can just inform them of his intentions; they won't object. Things are peaceful, business is good, and the abortive revolution of 1905 hasn't had any lasting effect. Even surprises are predictable, and your marriage to Bercoff is one of them. You're spared the usual formalities about the contract; there's not even any haggling over the dowry. Where will you go for your honeymoon? Bercoff's a practical man: you'll go to Lake Baikal, near Irkutsk, the area he hopes one day to transform and civilize. You're doubtful: isn't the middle of Siberia a kind of penal colony, inhabited by undesirables? But you give in: an immemorial tradition requires that a wife follow her husband. Besides, the Trans-Siberian Railway, with its huge drawing rooms, is quite fascinating, and Nicholas's wooing very flattering even if his lovemaking can be rather rough. You discover a new landscape, convoluted yet vast, with peasant huts, hides of animals, purple heather, and tundras where sparse vegetation reaches up vainly toward a steely sky. I don't mind using these stereotyped images. Let the setting of your journey recall Eisenstein's and Pudovkin's cardboard and celluloid: there's no escaping platitude. At least I've spared you the clichés of snowstorms, troikas, and samovars!

But your happiness fades—I can't make out why. Perhaps Bercoff's a brute in private life, his lovemaking coarse and devoid of charm. Perhaps he took a wife just as he might take a house, to provide for his physical needs and be free to concentrate on his career. Maybe he's unfaithful to you, because he doesn't believe pleasure and marital duty mix. You find him slow and too down to earth. At home in your house halfway between Odessa and the river Bug, he turns out to be a tyrant who manhandles the gardener and the servants and treats you like a slave, not letting you even arrange the furniture except in your own room. You start dreaming again about the heroes in Pushkin and Lermontov. You miss the people who used to listen to your playing, and compare you, with some exaggeration, to the great virtuosi of the age. Though it's comfortable enough here, there's no one with whom you can rhapsodize over Brahms, Delibes, and Verdi. Bercoff never talks about anything but building roads through the dust: the pair of you aren't suited to each other. You yourself aren't ready yet for realism. Three months later, without any dramatic scenes, you go back home to your parents, who welcome you tenderly, as if you were a little wounded animal. Disgust with Bercoff is followed by firm decision: nothing in the world would induce you to go back to him. But divorce is no easy matter in the Russia of Nicholas II: it will take your father long months of complex negotiation before this chapter of your life can be closed. Sometime after that you meet Alexander Bisk, in whom, having burned your fingers over Bercoff's graceless strength, you see nothing but virtues. He's casual, he knows lots of poets, he's a writer himself, he speaks of Europe with rather languid enthusiasm, he's not very sure what he wants, he sails blithely over his own surface as if afraid to assert himself. Why shouldn't you give yourself to him? The contrast is all in his favor.

I embroider, invent, extrapolate. Everything I've just written is utterly banal, conventional, and mawkish. But I've no right to let my imagination dredge up anything so hackneyed and idyllic. I don't know anything about the complexities of your personality when you were twenty or so. I've been treating you like a character spirited out of the pages of an eighteenth-century novel by someone like Richardson and into an equally insipid one written in the late nineteenth century by someone like Marcel Prévost. You deserve better, but I don't feel capable of painting a portrait of you as you were then without introducing some of the sentimental excesses of a literary tradition I find absurd. Nicholas Bercoff is a mere supernumerary, a walk-on part, and there's no reason why I should try to make a rounded character out of him: it would be simplest and most honest to forget all about him. And yet I can't help being angry at the thought that I never really questioned you properly about your puberty, your obsessions, your physical yearnings. I keep retouching my sketch. It's getting covered with violent crossings-out. The pretty pink pastel portrait is turning into a caricature, and the animal side of humanity peers out through that still chubby face. To the rescue, Zola and Maupassant! How do I know you met my father *after* your divorce? And I could ascribe all kinds of vices to you, or, at the least, masses of unfulfilled desires. But allow me a little vulgarity: people don't usually have the nerve to question their mothers about what they did before they bore them. It's so easy to hide behind decorum and tell yourself that in 1910 people didn't experience the pangs of sexuality. But how did *you* find pleasure? You gave yourself to my father in your own marriage bed, while Nicholas Bercoff was chasing over the Siberian wastes looking for suitable construction sites, a poor man's Potemkin mistaking his illusions for cities of the future! Don't you delight in the pleasures of adultery, as they are called in the works of Octave Feuillet, Tchedrin, and Paul Bourget? What's more— let's have a few more clichés, let me be your Rasputin!—you're insatiable: if a groom or a peasant dared approach his mistress, he'd find her already lying on the straw in the stable, eager and willing. Come on, Ibsen and D'Annunzio, lend a hand! . . . It's not *you* who leaves Bercoff: on the contrary, he, while finding you pretty dull in other respects like most young women of your generation, knows you're very good in bed: skillful, greedy, docile, completely unbridled. *He* repudiates *you* precisely because you're too fond of lovemaking, and in your transports, your bitings and droolings, you forget that your partner exists as an individual. And no husband in Holy Russia is going to stand for that. I have a vision of you being turned out of house and home, an Anna Karenina or Emma Bovary of the dives on the banks of the Moldavanka, being taken in by my father. He has a weakness for fallen women, and on his travels to Altona, Genoa, and Liverpool, in sleazy dawns amid the cold cigarette butts, daydreams of their pale bosoms. How can I guess what feelings were involved—lust or

love, wonder or pity? All truths seem equally improbable. I'm simply re-
sentful that I don't know anything about the intimate physical details of
your sex life during the ten years before I was born. You'll never tell me
whether I was conceived in ecstasy or mere routine. And Bercoff wasn't
called Nicholas. No first name really suits him—neither Serge nor
Constantine, Pavel nor Dmitry. A journalist like me is always bad at his
job. I ought to have interviewed you before you got old. You'd have held
out for a while, but in the end you'd have given in: there's bound to be a
moment some time when a mother tells her son all. I'd have told you I'd
already put to the question such men as St.-John Perse, Chagall, Ionesco,
and Beckett, and they told me their life stories without making a song
and dance about it. The interview might have gone like this:

"Berthe Turiansky, how many times did you make love every night to
Alexander Bisk, my father, while you were engaged?"

"My God! . . ."

"There *is* no God. Answer!"

"Three or four times."

"Be more accurate."

"Three times on the average."

"Including Saturdays?"

"Four times on Saturdays."

"Was it good?"

"It was natural."

"No moralizing if you don't mind."

"It was wonderful."

"Better than with Nicholas Bercoff?"

"It wasn't the same."

"I don't doubt it. Describe it!"

"Bercoff was brutal."

"But it was a better lay?"

"Yes. I felt I was being crucified."

"Crucified or torn apart?'

"Beside myself. Crazy."

"How long did it take you to have an orgasm?"

"I don't understand."

"You understand perfectly well."

"It varied."

"Which did you like best: being insulted, being told he'd love you forever, or making love in silence?"

"I wasn't really conscious enough to know."

"I need a precise answer."

"I didn't mind being insulted."

Of course, the interview might have been less squalid.

"Mother, as a journalist whose job it is to be curious, I'd like to suggest a little game. I don't know anything about your distant past—we've never gotten around to talking about it. Would you mind if I pretended to be a young reporter interviewing some celebrity, with you as the celebrity?"

"If you like, silly boy."

"All right then, let's go. Where did you meet Nicholas Bercoff?"

"You've got the name wrong. He was called Vassili—Vassili Borissovitch. I met him at my parents' house, of course. He was the youngest son of my father's main supplier. He came every month, bringing leather and hides direct from Voronezh and Saratov."

"He wasn't an engineer?"

"Not at all. He was a very good businessman, and he played the violin. We used to play duets."

"Was he a boor?"

"He was well built, but he looked very vulnerable."

"Were you happy with him?"

"Perfectly."

"But your marriage lasted only six months."

"I've done all I can to forget him, and I've succeeded. He had a cough—his lungs were weak. We went to the Caucasus a couple of times, hoping the altitude would do him good. But he only got worse. His family begged me to leave him and make a life of my own instead of staying on and having to endure the agony of his decline and death."

"And Father. . . ?"

"He was a consolation at first. And then I came to love him."

Paris, May 1973

I'd come, as I did every year in April or May, to see you and Father in
your apartment on Riverside Drive. You'd made it into a charming place,
adorning it every few months with two or three more painted clay busts
of your friends and of favorites like Gorky, Churchill, Pasternak, and Don
Quixote. You didn't have the energy now to work at your sculpture very
often, but you kept at it with a mixture of resignation and regret, partly
so as not to turn into a half-cooked vegetable, as you put it, and partly to
honor the memory of your master, Archipenko. You talked to me at length
about him this time, and showed me some complimentary letters he'd
written you. He was, you said, the most unassuming and disinterested of
men. Surrounded as you were by people who were loud and pretentious,
you valued modesty, tact, and all other delicate virtues. Didn't I agree?
You looked sweet, but extremely frail. Instead of answering, I looked at
my father. Although he was over eighty now his memory was as good as
ever, and apart from a touch of deafness he was in excellent health. But
I was puzzled: quite suddenly he'd just sold all his stamps, and he had
no more chores to enliven his quiet life. It had occurred to me that old
people die very quickly when deprived of the one activity that involves
some duty or discipline. I couldn't shake off this thought. Each of our
meetings might turn out to be the last for one of you, but how could I
speak to either as if he or she might soon be the sole survivor? Because
of this our conversations were becoming quite anodyne and abstract. You

yourself questioned me at length about the lectures I'd just been giving in Buffalo and Rochester on the French theater since 1945, the young European novelists and their fascination with nothingness, the atom bomb, world poetry. Father stuck to trivialities. He told me how he'd begun going to the movies in the early afternoon as he could get a reduction then as a senior citizen. Comparing the curves of Brigitte Bardot and Sophia Loren or the acting skills of Robert Mitchum and Peter Sellers made it easier for him to forget the real world. Apart from that, the most he'd talk about was a few distant memories: his discovery of Khlebnikov, his fondness for Jukovski, and the one time he met Alexis Tolstoy, in a seedy tavern in Sochi. I used my own volubility to disguise my uneasiness. For the first time, perhaps, I gave you a true account of my lecture tour and the college course I'd given the previous year in Milwaukee. As a way of avoiding painful confidences, I entertained you with a stream of insignificant evasions, ranging from a detailed description of a modern library to a comparison between the behavior of black women students and that of the Swedish masses (the latter now as inarticulate as the former as a result of listening to recordings of Elvis Presley and the Beatles). I told you about some odd conversations I'd had in the '50s and '70s: with an Arab notable in Fez who spoke Latin; with a government minister in the Congo who wanted to throw off all European influence; with a German priest just back from Tibet and Katmandu who was looking for a change of soul. I set up all these vapid anecdotes and tedious characters as a barrier between us, a sort of television screen emitting images and noises which distracted and dissolved our real selves.

You persuaded Father to take his younger brother Michel, who'd just lost his wife, to Lakewood, a village in New Jersey where you both used to go to relax. There, among the beautiful trees, in peaceful surroundings, the two old gentlemen would be able to talk about the past, get to know each other again, and heal the breaches that various squabbles had caused between them over the years. Michel, though short-tempered and cantankerous, wasn't really a bad sort, and even if he wouldn't admit it to himself, he needed his brother. You weren't going with them: peace and harmony would be restored more easily if they were on their own. You

asked my opinion. Yes, you were right, of course: Lakewood was a good
place for a reconciliation. But there was work waiting for me in Paris. Once
again I had to leave you, and once again our farewells, which prudence
made ever more impassive, were overshadowed with vague apprehensions.
On the way back across the Atlantic the Boeing I was flying on hit a couple
of air pockets, three or four passengers were injured in the tremendous
jolts that followed, panic broke out on board, and I experienced some
rather alarming palpitations. I was given a couple of injections the following evening, but they weren't entirely effective. I was only in my fifties, and somehow such reminders of mortality made me feel disgusted
with myself. The following night sleeping tablets were no help. At ten
o'clock next morning, just as I'd decided to go and see my doctor, a phone
call from New York knocked me out completely. Michel was sobbing almost incomprehensibly on the other end of the line. The story eventually
emerged. A few hours ago, the hotel in Lakewood where he'd been staying had caught fire, and five people had been killed. He'd had to jump
out of the window onto a sheet held out by the firemen. Here he paused,
groaned, and said he felt terribly guilty, it was a dreadful shock, but unfortunately there could be no doubt: although his body couldn't be identified, my father was one of the victims. Because of his slight deafness
he couldn't hear the fire alarms, and the flames were too high for Michel
to get to him. Then my uncle began again about how grief-stricken and
guilty and shocked he felt. In a strangled voice I tried to comfort him.

I spent the next hour getting in touch with all the people in New York
I knew were close to you: a male cousin, a niece, some friends, a few of
Father's colleagues. I asked them to contact one another and arrange to
meet at your place, all at the same time: the main thing was not to leave
you alone and to see that a doctor prescribed you some sedatives. They
promised, as I'd hoped, that they'd stay with you for at least a week, until after the funeral. I then managed to get hold of Maria, who was abroad
on a mission. I asked her to take my place at your side and act just I
would have done myself: I was so shattered my strength had completely
failed me. I was covered in sweat, and trembling from head to foot. I decided not to call you: only someone more in control of himself than I was

could find suitable words. I shut myself out of that pain, that loss, that tragedy. I fainted in the passage between the kitchen and the drawing room of my apartment. I didn't regain consciousness until four hours later. I felt an unbearable loathing for myself: I was getting old, I was a coward, I was away from you just when you needed me more than ever. Would I be able to muster the courage to get on a plane and go back to New York? My pulse was still irregular and I decided to go and see my doctor instead: let my body decide for me. But remorse was choking me more and more. It turned out that my nerves were affected, but a few showers and some sedatives would put them right in a week or so: the doctor wrote out a fairly ordinary prescription. But I was anxious and unsettled, and asked him if it was all right for me to go back to the United States. He said I'd get better more quickly if I could avoid it. I pressed him: would he advise me to go to my father's funeral or not? I detected a tinge of contempt in his reply: moral questions were none of his business, and in any case it didn't make much difference whether I stayed at home or followed the treatment sitting on a plane.

I hesitated until late that night, and didn't take any of the tablets I'd been given: perhaps I was still waiting for my body to make up my mind for me. I was probably hoping I'd have another fainting fit, and my wish was duly granted. I swooned away again and came to next morning, weak at the knees, my chest racked by irregular thumpings. So I finally decided not to leave Paris. I needed to be strong in order to think of your future and persuade you to take the proper course. I was overcome with a kind of perverse pleasure: I was getting myself out of all the painful duties, the pointless tears, the funeral ceremonies, the condolences, the stupid flowers, the hateful words, the sorrow—all the things that were bound to lay me low again. Yet I was failing in my most sacred duty. I had to take refuge behind some hastily summoned theories: funerals are a horrible concession to society, forcing close as well as distant friends into the hypocrisy of seeming afflicted; the priest conducts the ceremony only because it's his job—a quarter of an hour earlier he didn't even know the name of the corpse he prays and sermonizes over. I was rebelling, or trying to rebel, against routine, convention, mediocrity. Was this a time to take part in all that play-acting? And indeed I couldn't help weeping there and then—weeping for my own cowardice and distress. To make up for all this cravenness, I wrote to you the next day. It was a beautiful, though somewhat muddled letter, saying my three doctors had categorically forbidden me to fly. And who could say?—if I'd disobeyed them, given my present state of health together with the effect the shock had had on it, I might well have had to be taken straight to the hospital as soon as I landed in New York! I said that as long as I lived I'd never forgive myself for not being able to pay my last respects to my father, kissing his brow and joining you in silent vigil over him. I was solemnly adjuring Michel and his family, and Maria, whom I was sending to be with you, to do all they could to help you. I was staying in Paris against my will, and just as soon as I was strong enough my one idea would be to prepare for your coming over. After thirty-five years of separation it was time for us to live together, remembering and venerating my father. I assured you my heart was as irreparably broken as yours: we now shared a fathomless and never-ending sorrow.

Had I overdone it? Did my words betray a desire for forgiveness? I didn't know what to do. But the simplest solution was to put my rash protestations into practice. I kept to my resolution: you would come to Paris and live with me. As chance would have it, there was a small apartment for sale in the block where I lived. I used up all my savings to buy it, and Maria and I were to move in there, leaving my former apartment to you. But I didn't foresee clearly enough the drawbacks inherent in this arrangement, didn't realize what serious quarrels it would give rise to. I was clear-sighted enough to see the problems, but so headstrong I assumed I'd eventually get you to toe the line. You'd dwindle into a docile old woman and do as you were told. Anyhow, my mind was made up and I wasn't going to change it. I hadn't had a chance to consult Maria, but she'd soon see it was the only decent solution for the suddenly dutiful son of a recently widowed mother. At the same time I wanted you to choose your own future: in every letter I wrote I said you *could* stay in New York, among your friends and possessions, without having to change your habits at all. I was showing myself in the nicest possible light and having the best of both worlds: I was ruining myself in Paris in order to give you a quiet and comfortable home, yet at the same time leaving you free if you wished to end your days in a setting where you and your husband had led a peaceful and on the whole happy life. Where practical matters were concerned I issued definite orders, knowing you were far from competent in such things; Maria would see to it that you carried out my instructions. Some bank accounts had to be closed and others opened; the tax situation must be borne in mind; there was a list of documents to sign, bureaucracy to be endured, surplus furniture to be sold and a lease to be temporarily renewed. At least such minor chores gave you new responsibilities and prevented you from brooding on your tragedy.

In the few lines you sent me, in handwriting that had become almost illegible, you wondered at my refusing to come to New York even after my health was back to normal. Surely it would have been natural for me to visit my father's grave and discuss your future with you? I replied curtly that I was still busy preparing an acceptable home for you, and that anyway I wanted to avoid influencing your choice so as to be spared any future reproaches. I was being truthful, in a way: it was necessary that your move should seem to you to be your only possible choice, unaffected by any pressure on my part. I guessed that you were really begging me, somewhere in your subconscious, to impose a definite decision on you. We vied with each other in prevarication, empty protestation, and certainties that suddenly changed into resentment. I was less affected than you were by what had happened, and counted on the support of your friends. They were unanimous: you'd aged ten years in a few weeks and should obviously come and live with your only son, who could surround you with comfort and affection. Four months after my father's death you were ready to come to Paris. Everyone thought I was sure to take the place of the husband you'd lost. You set sail on the *France*, accompanied by enormous trunks containing odds and ends you'd had since your youth, the sculptures you'd produced yourself and some odd manuscripts written by my father. I'd insisted that you ask one of your women friends to come with you as far as Le Havre: you said you preferred to travel alone. But you were changing continents, and it was a mistake on my part to think you had the strength to make such a change at the age of eighty-three. You resigned yourself and let yourself be persuaded, but deep down inside you a strange lethargic anger was building up. Fate had been hard on you. As soon as I saw you on the ship, landing in France, I realized you now cherished a frenzied desire for revenge. You had three enemies: Maria, who had a claim on an affection that should have been exclusively yours; myself, because after forty-five years of your thinking I was someone exceptional I would now be revealing myself day after day, with all my defects and all my virtues, as someone completely ordinary; and above all yourself, whom you sometimes assessed quite clear-sightedly and sometimes looked on with loathing. Hadn't you sent my father to Lakewood, or in other words to his death? Expiation would come to be second nature to you, and you'd drag me down into it with you despite my affection, solicitude, patience, and assumed good humor. Your first impulse was to open your arms to me, but then you suddenly repulsed me: instead of giving you these roses I should have laid them on my father's grave. You were responsible for your own misfortunes, but if ever you gave yourself a short respite from blaming yourself I naturally took your place: from this time forth, I would be held guilty for everything.

Brussels, 1933

You can't just leave it to the high school to teach me about life! Education is useful and even necessary, you quite agree, but all these strangers who keep telling me what to think—are they any better than robots? What do they know about the heart, with its torments and desires? A mother is the only possible teacher for such delicate subjects, and as I already have a tendency to value knowledge above intuition, precautions must be taken to prevent me from turning out to be too cold and circumspect. With that endless succession of lessons and books, might I not gradually lose my childlike charm, together with that faintly sad smile for which you'd give up your very life if necessary? School is a kind of factory: I shouldn't take it too seriously, though at the same time I should work hard to stay at the top of the class. Oh, how difficult it is to be a perfect mother, as you consider yourself to be! The proper division of labor is quite clear, and you have no wish to change it: my father provides me with the material elements necessary for a peaceful and healthy physical development; school furnishes my mind, though in your opinion it is so efficient as to be dangerous; but you alone are responsible for seeing that I remain a sensitive boy, alert, delicate, open to the beauty of things and souls. You're not yet sure whether you'd like me to be an artist when I grow up, or a doctor, or a merchant. You're not even sure that what you want will have any influence on my choice. Secretly you'd like me not to get any older, to stop growing, physically and psychologically, before I start to show the inevitable first symptoms of revolt. You allow me a lot of freedom: I play games, I go on excursions with my friends, I like swimming, and although the cinema isn't always exactly nice or proper, you don't insist on accompanying me to the movies. You even learn to calculate your demonstrations of affection so that they don't upset me too much. But you can't help fussing over me, and you know that in a few months' time, a year at the most, I won't put up with it anymore.

I'll be chasing the girls soon, you're sure, judging by my antics at the seaside every August. Why shouldn't you choose a perfectly acceptable girl for me? We could have tea together, attend the same dancing class, and gradually become indispensable to each other, all with your unobtrusive approval. You consult your friends, Madame Meltz and Rosa Rom: you're sweetness itself, and dream, a little too loudly perhaps, of an encounter, neither accidental nor calculated, between our family and other people of the same social standing. They don't necessarily have to be of Russian origin, even though the Slav soul is the most generous in the world. The girl herself should be well brought up, rather shy without being timid, and beautiful though capable of not showing it right away. Rumor has it you're already looking for a girl for your son to marry, and that though you're not in any great hurry, at least you're making long-term plans. You're invited to parties to meet distant cousins, neglected sisters-in-law, or young ladies somebody once met taking the waters at La Bourboule or Wiesbaden, and you have indulged in apparently idle chatter with all of them. Your friends unobtrusively draw up lists of eligible damsels. You still say you're in no hurry, and as you persist in this attitude, everyone concludes your intentions are as before. One day Madame Meltz introduces a lively but nervous lady who possesses the signal virtue of being married to a charming lawyer from Orel. Her daughter is a year younger than I, and cannot but be charming, wellbred, intelligent, and modest. You're shown a photograph of her: she's not a beauty, of course, but aren't good looks a snare? You manage to persuade yourself she's elegant and refined, or at least that you shouldn't reject her out of hand.

You exchange visiting cards, and Tatiana Lopato's mother invites you to visit her in a glorious villa near Stockel. The husband is slightly paralyzed, but the house radiates order and affluence, with its neat lawns, vases that must be antiques, rugs from Asia Minor, and tasteful Limoges china. Your hosts suggest a game of whist, and when you say you don't play cards are delighted at the prospect of teaching you. You're perhaps rather disappointed in Tatiana, who could be more vivacious; and her photograph is certainly flattering. But you hold to your purpose: just give your will a push in the right direction and you're certain that in a year or two the young lady will become prettier as well as more lively. Meanwhile you're also having some difficulty with your cards: the kings of diamonds and sevens of spades don't mean a thing to you. But what does it matter! The Lopatos are very hospitable; they'd like to widen their circle of friends and are enchanted by anything remotely connected with the old Russia. However, you don't think it's necessary to introduce me yet. You talk about me, embark on a subtle propaganda campaign on my behalf, and even make my father go with you to Stockel one day. He comes back bored, but agrees to see the Lopatos again—they're no dimmer or less amiable than most. As they keep inviting you, you have to make some spectacular return, though our small apartment isn't suited to the occasion. The party will have to take place in a restaurant. Father, usually rather careful about money, indulges you in your whim, and all six of us have a real feast at a restaurant on the harbor in Namur. I'm too interested in the foie gras and the canard à l'orange to pay much attention to young Tatiana, who strikes me as insipid. Her mother, with her ample curves and the regular tremors of her décolleté, makes a much greater impression on me, and my imagination, heated by a whole glass of wine, constructs an orgy in which that lady is the main attraction. It's in order to see her once more that I agree we should all meet again. Everyone praises my reserve with regard to Tatiana; a recognized sign of good breeding. They think I'm waiting for the young lady to form an opinion of me before I say what I think about her. In such circumstances girls model their judgments on those of their mothers; and Mme Lopato thinks, without a moment's hesitation, that I'm the sort of young man they can happily associate with.

There are no more whist lessons, though. You say you have no memory for cards. They suggest other games, such as backgammon and checkers. The time comes for you to issue another, less extravagant invitation, and you ask Tatiana to our place. But the Lopatos have a more complex notion of friendship: why shouldn't the two families go on an excursion together one Sunday? They own a very good automobile—a rather old but indestructible Minerva—and the lawyer finds it relaxing to drive it himself. There are some places in the forest of Soignes, or over toward Wavre, which are really delightful, and you can go for long hikes there. The children can walk three or four hundred meters in front of the others, and get to know each other without interference from the grown-ups. I don't say anything: I rather like the idea of seeing new places, and the prospect of playing hide-and-seek or doctor with Tatiana is a small price to pay for a picnic. The grown-ups send us off among the trees to pick wild strawberries—six months out of season! I finally take a good look at my playmate. Only her eyes are passable: cold and gray, but with a tinge of green. Her lips are too thin, she's got too many freckles and a protruding chin. The rest of her isn't any better: scraggy waist, square back, stiff legs. What can we talk about? Jules Verne, Alphonse Daudet, the Cid, Jackie Coogan, Laurel and Hardy, Victor Francen in the Karsenty Company's visiting production of a comedy by Henry Bernstein, or Mistinguett's triumph at the Summer Palace? Since I'm expected to be bold, I ask Tatiana if she's ever been in love, and I suddenly find she's been well initiated into the rules of hypocrisy and elementary seduction: she leans back against a beech tree with a blade of grass between her teeth, simpers about how hot it is and fiddles with the neck of her dress. Then she gives a laugh like the squawk of a startled hen, and says that she'll tell me about her experiences if I tell her about mine. I say she'd do better to show me her thighs: her skirt's so long I can hardly see her knees, which are unattractive anyway. When I press myself against her by way of persuasion she doesn't push me away. Instead she just stands there rigid, as if I were the kind of boy who doesn't need any encouragement to take pseudo-liberties. We both feel so ridiculous we're paralyzed, and just go back to the grown-ups.

You keep on giving parties and thinking up schemes to put the two families on an intimate footing. We're all friends now rather than acquaintances, aren't we? And someone's only got to mention Russia for our friendship to be further enriched by the thought of the ancient roots we so providentially share. I don't say anything when you question me about Tatiana. I'd like very much to see her mother again, but all the rest gets on my nerves, though not enough for me to rebel. I keep rolling my eyes on each of the three or four occasions that Mme Lopato comes to dinner, but she thinks this is due to inexperience and directed at her daughter. Tatiana is more astute: she knows youths of my age dream of violent transports in the arms of alluring ladies like her mother, who at thirty-eight or nine, with the help of a dash of perfume, is irresistible. But in the end I give up on the visions of thrilling caresses, because Tatiana starts seeing me alone. Alternately at our house and at hers, we eat ices, ask each other riddles, plan to go to the movies together. I become more and more disagreeable. One day I refuse to peel an apple for her when you ask me to: why doesn't she have a banana, which she can easily peel for herself? Another time I won't let her borrow a novel by Pierre Benoit: I don't like other people marking up my books. She finally telephones and invites me to go with her to see Magda Schneider and Jan Kiepura in some comedy. I say such twaddle doesn't amuse me anymore, and anyway I'm going to see a Pabst film next Saturday with some boys from school.

But for all my recalcitrance you go on with your machinations. You tell me the Lopatos are wonderful people and could be useful to my father in his business. I object, with a mixture of irritation and amusement, that this doesn't mean I have to find their daughter attractive when in fact she's ugly. But you're so disappointed by my attitude, I decide to give Tatiana a last chance. One morning I put on an ingratiating voice and call her up on the phone. After making sure her mother's out shopping, I invite her to a very dimly lit cinema, well adapted to the petting that goes on in the back rows. I know I refused her invitation, I say, but she can accept mine: it's for me to take the initiative. I go on to tell her my conditions: she's to touch me on the knees, the groin, and the thighs, and give me a bit of pleasure. She needn't worry—no one's going to see, in the dark. In my lewd and vulgar effrontery, I describe the martyrdom I have in mind for her, but she betrays no signs of aversion: the poor thing isn't even capable of telling me how disgusted she is. Expressing scarcely any outrage, she suggests another form of entertainment: tomorrow we could go swimming in the pool at La Glacière, which would give me a chance to see her in her bathing suit. And she'll bring a friend called Elfride whom she's sure I'll like: she's more developed than Tatiana, and a year older than I am. I succumb to the temptation, though not without a few regrets for Mme Lopato. Elfride is indeed a well-rounded morsel, and I'm fascinated by her bosom and her behind. We laugh before we get to like each other, we get to like each other before we start to smooch, and we smooch for some time before we lie down together, first by the water and then in it. Tatiana is our accomplice in all this: all she asks is to share our secret. Then come dances, boating expeditions, visits to night clubs near the Bourse. I'm sure I'll have my way with Elfride. Tatiana is a good pal; she'll smooth over any mistakes I may make and explain away any misunderstandings. Elfride is of course divine. When these minor events come to your ears, your attitude is that of astonishment mixed with pride: instead of bewitching one highly presentable young lady I'm captivating two. I'll turn out to be a real Don Juan. You're usually much more severe when I foil your little plots. So instead of being angry with you, as I'd intended, I just give you a few hugs, together with a caution: I'll choose my own sweethearts from now on, all right? Our pleasure at this temporary agreement is translated into an addition to my pocket money: I really do have a very nice mother, when she doesn't take it into her head to dispose of me as if I were a slave. Mme Lopato's backgammon suddenly strikes you as very tame. But Elfride is a goddess opening up like an enormous raspberry: for now, for the first time, I'm making a serious study of Hieronymus Bosch's *Garden of Earthly Delights*.

San Francisco, October 1942

"Midway, the Coral Sea, Guadalcanal—from now on these names are drenched in blood, mixed with a drop of milk from a coconut. I'm writing to you, my dear Mother, because I'm alone on a Saturday evening in this city of blacked-out lights, where it's been drizzling for a week, dampening down body and soul. I haven't been a very good correspondent lately: just the occasional horribly monotonous note, dashed off to give the gist of what was happening to me: yes, I'm back in the war again, but from a distance; yes, I'm well, like any other soldier who hasn't yet been sent back to the front; yes, there is some hope—where would I be without it? There's no reason why we shouldn't try to cheer each other up, you and I, even if it involves a few fibs. But today I can't stand the idea of such deception; I'd rather open your eyes to the truth, even if it's only this once. You fled from Russia, you fled from Belgium, and once you got to New York you shut yourself away by the Hudson River as if the flames of the world could never reach you again. As for me, I was drawn into the war and lost it twice before I was twenty-one, though I was never allowed to play a real part in it. After that I sold—yes, sold: I want you to know the truth at last—I sold some poor helpless Belgians to the services in London, to swell the Legion's meager ranks. Later, when you and Father were preparing to emigrate to the United States, I was sent—with false papers, like a double-bottomed suitcase—first to Oran, and from there to Casablanca. Once there, I was on my own! I had to spy

224

on some refugees from Austria and Poland and lie to some idiotic Brits
in exchange for a passage to Cuba on a typhus-ridden Portuguese ship.
For you everything was official, of course, with a trip across the Atlantic
on a nice liner, starting with waving handkerchiefs and ending with petty
triumphs and respectablity. But the only country I had was my own dirty
little alien's skin; and do you know whose side I was fighting on? I know
only one regiment: the one in which you survive three seconds longer than
in the regiment opposite. How splendid and moving and limp and cloying it was, our reunion in New York six months ago! You wept for joy,
and I wept with you: I'd wet my pants with fright so often in the past,
why shouldn't I shed tears now because you and I were suddenly together
again, safe and sound?

"And now, would you believe it, I'm frightened again. Where do *we*
stand in all this conflagration? The Japanese are hanging on, and so are
the Germans. We'll win the war in the end—we have to keep telling ourselves that if we don't want to go crazy—but meanwhile where will I be?
By the end of the war my remains might be at the bottom of the sea, unless they end up in a hole in the mud among the other bones, with a little
cross on top worth four dollars and seventy-five cents. The scene here is
inexpressibly awful. They've made me a hospital nurse specializing in
radiography—don't ask me why. I've attended the courses I was told to
attend, and been given a certificate signed by a general. So now I spend
all day long X-raying badly wounded men, back from the enchanted isles
with a palm branch in the brain, a flying fish in the chest, or one pearl
too many in the eye. So much for their fine trip to Bougainville and the
Cook Islands! When my photos are dry, one of the medicos operates:
three-quarters of the heroes die on the table, and half the rest are paralyzed for life. The people around me aren't men anymore—they're shapeless bits and pieces, with genitals groping about of their own accord as
if to find their owners! Imagine the sort of conversation I can have with
a lumbar vertebra, a pancreas, or a larger intestine leering at me through
its pus! And I—crushed by this dreadful job, though I should at least
remember it makes me useful in a way—what's become of me? I landed
in the United States really determined to fight against the Krauts. I

greeted Pearl Harbor as a victory over all my petty tricks and hesitations. I hid a few things from you then, as usual. It's true I joined the armed forces of this huge continent, but after how many vicissitudes! The Free Belgians wanted me, and so did the Free French, on the grounds that I'd been working for their paper in New York. I told them to go and liberate themselves without me: I knew too much about how de Gaulle had Admiral Muselier arrested! I had to ask for protection from the United States both against my own country, Belgium, and against France, the only country in the world where I'd have liked to be born: United States law prohibits the conscription of foreign nationals on American soil by governments which the men in question don't recognize. This move didn't let me off the hook, however: I was told I'd be mobilized in the next month or so by the Americans! My heroism consisted in enlisting beforehand. This easy gesture enabled me, in theory, to choose which of the services I wanted to be in and where I was to be sent. But the Intelligence corps is still waiting for me, and as for Europe—my preferred battleground, since I'm beginning to get to know it—well, for the moment, Europe seems to be situated on the other side of the Pacific from Tokyo.

"So I suppose the fate that's being prepared for me is to die for Hawaii and the oranges of California. How absurd. Some days I tell myself I could buy some suitable clothes, bribe a truck driver, and cross over into Mexico via Arizona. It should be quite easy: the Americans don't understand the attractions of desertion—they're too stupid to think of it. What I did between between Tarascon and Port-Vendres a couple of years ago I could do again wherever I ended up—in Nicaragua, say, or San Salvador. I'm sure someone could find a use there for a dealer in arms and cynicism like me, who's also a specialist not only in postage stamps but also in green fevers and indigo poxes! At the age of twenty-three, my dear little Mother, I've seen hell so many times I'm quite at home there. Do you know what I'm going to do in a minute, to stop myself from thinking of you, or Father, or myself, whom I feel like shooting every time I catch sight of my reflection in a mirror? I'm going to drink two or three cans of warm beer, followed by a zombie, a cocktail made up of several different kinds of rum which makes you keel over before you can say Jack

Robinson. If I sober up again, I'll go and mix up a few X-rays at the hospital: I'll switch the labels so that Jones's jaw is ascribed to Smith and Farrow's lung to Williams. I'll then have four more deaths on my conscience without lifting a finger. Then perhaps they'll send me too to the mangrove swamps.

"I meant to write and pour my heart out to you, but I see I've poured out my revolting innards as well, not to mention my thoughts, more disgusting than any common grave. I usually tell you about my more tender feelings; why for a change shouldn't you share in my disgust, despair, and incurable fear? San Francisco is debilitating: everything makes one think of invisible shrouds, quiet winding sheets and clandestine burials. Soldiers march across the square for the last time; beyond the horizon, threatening in the gloom, lies death. There are probably five hundred thousand of us either back from the Pacific or about to go there. We don't say anything. We even get into the habit of chewing our hot dogs with studied slowness: after all, it's very like us, this lump of minced meat, which is what we'll soon be too. But there's one important difference: we'll never be so clean and healthy again. As you see, frankness and sincerity don't really suit me. I usually play down my feelings so as to avoid painful exchanges and make you think my mind's full of sweetness and light. This time I've gone to the opposite extreme, and I might as well go all out. I'm no better balanced than you are, and if you're blinded by lethargy, I'm blinded by repressed anger, anxiety, and uncertainty. The year 1942, if I survive it, will have aged me inside by a quarter of a century. I love you, Mother dear, and at the same time, because I can't tell you everything, I hate you."

I read the letter over to tone down some of the more offensive passages, but in the end I didn't send it. Instead I wrote another which seemed to me more what you expected—marshmallow and sloppy sentiment:

"Dearest Mother,

"My work at the hospital—mostly reading aloud to officers and men on leave from the Pacific, some of them slightly wounded—leaves me with some spare time. Today I went for a walk under a clear blue sky around the most beautiful city in the world. Its combination of majesty and charm derives from its little apple-green and lavender-colored houses, climbing up the slopes so that the roof of one forms the basement of the other. From the top of the hills there are the most marvelous sweeping views: you can see at a glance the harbor with its gray ships; the chaotic and ever-changing masses of the wharves; the smooth and gentle bay; the bridge, like a giraffe lying down for you to climb up on its neck and ride over to the islands and the north shore—red and ocher, disheveled, drowsy, dappled with cobalt blue. And behind all this the Ocean, now lordly and imperturbable, now seized with sudden green wrath. The faces on Market Street and Telegraph Hill open on another landscape too, a continent far away and belonging to another age. I imagine I'm in Hong Kong or Peking; the notion of time gradually disappears. Sometimes I go to the library and bury myself in the aphorisms of some philosopher from a thousand years ago, and this reassures me. The war can't go on forever. Admiring the example of the little old-fashioned cable car that climbs up and down Powell Street, squeaking like a toiling insect as if to ask the passengers to help it turn around at the top, I tell myself *we* need to cultivate an Asiatic wisdom. We'll come out all right in the end. You can imagine how fondly I think of you and Father. I'm sure I'll be over to see you before the end of the winter. I'm looking forward to it already."

Paris, April 1975

"I owe all that's beautiful in my hellish life to you."

"Have you noticed how many petals there are on these roses?—the ones that merge from crimson to gold. They always have unusual species here at Bagatelle."

"Yes, my boy. How nice it must be to be able to forget everything and dissolve into a flower. Memory is the most devastating of cancers."

"I've always thought chestnut leaves look like frogs' feet when the buds start to open."

"Paris! I hate Paris!"

"Once upon a time you used to look forward. Now you prefer looking back. It's perfectly natural."

"Why don't you say straight out that I'm senile! You and your wife think I'm only an old crock, who'll fall to pieces altogether any day now—and good riddance!"

"Don't you think these formal French gardens look rather like poodles that are taken to be trimmed too often?"

"I think it's wonderful, magnificent—and it leaves me cold!"

"You seem very jumpy today. Why don't you take a pill?"

"What for? The long sleep will come soon enough. Or rather it'll come too late. I've lived too long. I'm useless. I should have passed on after your father died. That was only a pinprick of grief to you. You could have felt twice as much and hardly noticed it. Will you at least come to my funeral? You didn't go to his."

"How many times do I have to tell you?—I was ill! I've even shown you my doctor's prescriptions!"

"For a hundred francs a doctor will say anyone's got anything."

"Why don't you just enjoy the trees and the grass?"

"Yes, you're right. You always are—that's the trouble with you."

"Can we make peace, then?"

"Who's going to give peace to my broken heart, eh? Do you ever ask yourself that?"

"Don't you think the tritomas and the gazanias go well together?"

"The what? You know everything, don't you?—it gets on my nerves! You've got too many things in that head of yours. As for your heart, you shut it long ago—shut it, and threw away the key. Knowledge, knowledge—that's all you care about. My mother always said overeducated men are monsters."

"Would you like to go home?"

"You don't like what I say, so you shut me up. I know your methods."

"If you don't enjoy my company this afternoon, let's continue our walk another day."

"You haven't bought me just because you brought me here in a taxi!"

"Don't let's make everything personal."

"I'm not interested in what the birds and the bees think!"

"But you do love nature—you know you do."

"I don't know what I love anymore. I'm falling to pieces, as you can see, and there's nothing you can do about it."

"Next time we come here we'll go to the Shakespeare garden—it's quite near here. Some eccentric Englishman listed the names of all the flowers and trees in Shakespeare's plays and poems, and got specimens of them from all over the world—India, Sumatra, Japan. . . Then he bought some land to plant them in, and later on presented the whole garden to the City of Paris."

"Another intellectual! Lilacs out of books!"

"I'm an intellectual too, in my own way."

"And take yourself for Shakespeare sometimes, if you ask me! That's all you're good for—turning out books!"

"Thank you. . . Do you want to take a little stroll on your own?"

"So that you don't have to listen to my maunderings? How considerate. . ."

"This really is difficult, you know. . ."

"I suppose you'd rather have a nice, obedient mother—like a doormat. But you won't get the better of me, you and that wife of yours."

"We only want your own good."

"I could puke when you say 'we'!"

"You never have been able to accept that we get on well together."

"Just a façade!"

"You've never been able to accept that any member of the family can be happy if you haven't had a finger in the pie. You're always sitting in judgment on other people, but you never stand back and have a good look at yourself. Do you think you're without sin?"

"If only you knew! At night—"

"That tragic tone doesn't impress me."

"Am I allowed to finish? At night I keep tossing and turning. . . . I accuse myself of having been a bad wife and a negligent mother. I eat my heart out."

"There's no need to go to the other extreme."

"I suppose you'd like to stop my being Russian?"

"I'd like to stop you wallowing in it."

"Of course. You two are just the opposite. Cold. Calculating."

"Life is hard in Paris. I can't afford to be too sensitive."

"And your wife has made you harder still. You're like granite, the pair of you."

"You do exaggerate!"

"Let's walk over to the fountain. . . . Look at the sun dancing on those bushes!"

"They're rhododendrons. The peonies are late this year."

"What was your last book about?"

"It's a fantasy. About an anti-hero of our time who wants to give himself to a cause but can't find one worthy of him."

"What you write is as harsh as you are."

"Perhaps it's a kind of defense mechanism."

"As for your wife. . ."

"Let's leave Maria out of it. I've been married to her for twenty-one years—couldn't you start regarding it as an established fact?"

"It's quite easy to get a divorce these days."

"She and I get along very well in every way."

"Your pride will be your undoing—I've always told you so. You always had to be top of the class at school, and if anyone else got the same marks as you did you wouldn't eat for the rest of the week."

"We all have our own versions of the past."

"That's how you justify not coming to your poor father's funeral. Your precious imagination distorts everything. You'll soon be saying you were taken hostage by bandits and never knew anything about how he died."

"Now you're the one who's letting her imagination run away with her. Anyhow, if I've done wrong sometimes, so have you. I'm speaking quite dispassionately. You abandoned your father at La Panne in 1940, and he died four years later, carried off in a cattle car. No one—no one, I tell you—ever forgave you for it. Not Armand, not Mathilde, and not Father either."

"Thank you, my son."

"Put your handkerchief away in your bag!"

"This lovely garden, that clear sky, the mild air, children playing—you choose a wonderful day in spring, my last spring, to accuse me of all the crimes you can think of."

"I don't accuse you of anything. We're both in the same boat."

"You're uncomfortable—because you're being unfair and you know it. Let's go. I'd have done better to stay in America. Nobody there talked to me the way you do."

"Let's have a glass of lemonade, anyway."

"I want a coffee."

"The doctor says coffee's not good for you."

"He says the scenes you make aren't good for me either! They shorten my already wretched life! If only you knew. . ."

"You can insult me and kill me by inches, and I'm supposed to treat you like a plaster saint?"

"You're as cold as a lizard. If you really want to know what I think, I figure you're worse than your wife—"

"Whom you've bad-mouthed ever since I married her."

"With reason."

"Of course: you're always right. Let's compromise—let me order you a pot of tea."

"And a cream cake."

"Four!"

"Talk to me about flowers."

"It was in 1953 in the Borromean Islands in Lake Maggiore that I first saw flowers which eat flies and bumblebees—close up on them like rat traps so they can't get out however much they struggle. Their meals are brought to them at regular intervals. At Funchal in Madeira I saw whole hillsides covered with orchids, every color of the rainbow, growing in a foul-smelling mixture of mud and dung. And in San Cristóbal in the south of Mexico I was completely dazzled by the flame trees, which earn their name by lighting up the sky with their blossoms. I was lucky enough to be there during the parrots' mating season: they perch on the trees and sometimes fight to the death—you can't tell whether it's feathers or petals flying."

"My angel!"

"You say that, and yet you walked out of my house."

"I'll never live under the same roof as your wife again."

"What have you got against Maria?"

"That look of hers. Did you ever notice the way she looked at me?"

"Perhaps she was afraid of upsetting you."

"If you believe that. . . !"

"She was a great help to you when Father died."

"She was just trying to make herself indispensable. I call that cunning, and wrong."

"You needed someone to sort things out—all the other people around you were hopeless."

"Oh, she was efficient all right! Like a jailer."

"If people help you they've got ulterior motives. If they don't, they're monsters of indifference. We can't win."

"Well, you're not going to change me at my age."

"And at my age I don't have to think everything you do is wonderful! First you flounce off to a hotel, then I have to find you a retirement home in the suburbs. Three months later you moved on from there and went to Vittel for eight weeks!"

"It's my fate. You and your wife just couldn't keep me with you."

"I don't deny it."

"Send me back to America!"

"You're not strong enough to make the journey—the doctor wouldn't let you go."

"Do whatever you like with me, then—but do something!"

"I see you every day. We're strolling through a beautiful garden at this very moment. You've got friends coming to see you tomorrow."

"Old wrecks at their last gasp—I can't put up with their blather for more than half an hour. All we've got to talk about is the dead. People we used to love who are now dust and ashes. What sort of a life do you call that?"

"Would you like me to go to Cannes and find a nice little family *pension*? You might like it there, amid the mimosa."

"You *are* saying it with flowers today! But I see through it all. If I went to Cannes you'd be a thousand kilometers away."

"I'd be five times farther away if you went back to America."

"There you go again—an answer for everything. Always right. And cold as ice."

"I'm the only person you've got, so you might as well make the best of me. And I always go along with your whims in the end, even when they're completely unreasonable."

"You'd like me just to do as I'm told, wouldn't you? Living with a jailer for a wife has turned you into a policeman. You dole out my pocket money. Soon you'll be rationing my fresh air and telling me how often to breathe. I know you!"

"You must be in pretty good shape to go on at this rate!"

"And you never cry. You don't have enough feeling left!"

"I deliberately try *not* to feel! Things would be so much easier if I could be indifferent. But I can't."

"You're making great progress."

"Sometimes I think my mother's gone away and I'll never see her again. You're like someone else altogether. You're not at all close to me, yet I have duties toward you that I do my best to discharge. But my love is dead. Even my affection's completely exhausted."

"I suppose you think you'll make me angry by saying such dreadful things? But you're wrong. *I* could just as easily say you're not my son anymore. But I'm going to leave you everything—everything your father left me."

"Enough to live on for three years! I'd rather be on pleasanter terms with you."

"Don't play the millionaire with me! That wife of yours has turned you into a snob. . . I haven't seen any carnations or tulips here today—I love those tulips that are striped like the parrots you were talking about just now. All they need is a beak."

"Bricadabasipoussis."

"Mincratapasmic."

"Chtamchipro."

"Don't you think we're a bit too old now for that game? We've been playing it for fifty years."

"Yes, Mother, you're right. We *are* getting old. Come, take my arm. We'll think of some other parks to go to. And next week we'll go to the zoo, shall we? I'd like you to meet the okapi. He's one of my best friends: gentle as a gazelle, striped like a zebra, and nervous as a baby giraffe abandoned by its mother under a baobab tree."

Berlin, autumn 1948

In a shrill and tearful letter you implored me for the hundredth time to leave Berlin: the cold war was probably going to get worse, the Russians had become bloodthirsty monsters under Stalin, and I had no right to sacrifice myself for my work: I ought to think of you and Father, who worried day and night over what might be happening to me. I couldn't help smiling at your hysterical solicitude, to which as usual I'd reply in a couple of days' time with a few cheerful lines saying I was quite well and perfectly safe. I put your letter away and went back to business. First I phoned Soviet HQ: in an hour from now I'd be in the office of my Russian opposite number, Major Fradkin, handing over the bulletins the three Western occupying powers had just brought out. And he'd give me an envelope containing the equivalent documents, equally meaningless, from his side. Perhaps, the routine exchange over, we'd talk about the two East Germans arrested by the Americans for attempted sabotage—a vague accusation which would end up as usual in agreement between us on some more crucial subject, such as supplies of heating oil or cement for the three sectors of West Berlin. I added, before putting the phone down, that I'd told my superiors the route my car would be taking, so there was no point in the Soviets' ambushing me. These precautions were not enough, however. Just as we'd left Friedrichstrasse and were heading for Pankow, my driver just avoided running down a sort of derelict who'd thrown himself in front of us. I protested to Fradkin: I was the only Western official who'd been in regular contact with him and his staff since the beginning of the blockade, and if he managed to get rid of me where would he find another liaison officer so well disposed? Anyhow, did the top brass know about these wretched little tricks? They were unworthy of the Red Army! After this the conversation grew more friendly, though still with the usual touch of cynicism on Fradkin's part. He'd only recently arrived from Moscow and was doctrinaire, fanatical, and cold: he didn't understand anything about the fraternity recently forged in battle. I had to tell him it wasn't done to indulge in hostilities against one's former allies three years after the war was over. He asked me if the West could endure the blockade much longer. I burst out laughing, trying to seem as sardonic as he was. Young he might be, but he really ought to know there never had been a real siege; compromises were being made all the time; we lived in an age of half-measures. The Russians didn't shoot down our aircraft or cut off our water supplies; the subway went on running; the gas works were functioning almost normally. I even allowed myself the luxury of telling him the Western powers were in the wrong over this matter: in order to carry out monetary reform in their sectors they'd unilaterally ended the Potsdam agreement, so what did they expect but reprisals such as the absurd obstacles Fradkin's compatriots were putting in the way of people and goods trying to move from Berlin to the three Western zones of Germany?

On the way back I stopped off at the racetrack at Mariendorf, and put thirty marks on Xanthia, a trotter I liked but who came in first only once in every ten races. The driver was a talented young man called Gerhardt Krüger. Then, after dictating a few letters and reports around five o'clock, I was free for the evening. It wasn't the right time of year for tennis, so to get some exercise I was in the habit of going for a walk—though naturally, given the nature of my work, I had to be careful about possible attackers. Before dinner, vendors of all kinds came to my house to propose bargains. Would I like to buy a Paul Klee in exchange for twenty kilos of coffee? Or a stamp authenticated by Richter and Müller-Mark— a Brunswick number 3 with cover and excellent margins, or a Cross of Savoy designed by Diena—for between fifteen and eighteen cartons of

Camel cigarettes? Then I'd dress for dinner, usually in the traditional style: dinner jacket, patent leather shoes, silk handkerchief in my breast pocket, fancy cuff links. Sometimes I'd read for half an hour. I'd been making a systematic study of Expressionist poetry since I'd met Gottfried Benn the previous year: I particularly admired Georg Heym and Alfred Lichtenstein. Sometimes I'd have to fob off a regretful ex-mistress begging for one last kiss or yet more tearful farewells: instead, I'd give them a glass of champagne and some caviar on toast, and dismiss them without a qualm. On this particular evening Maria—tall, red-haired, sculptural—arrived at eight-thirty. Should we have dinner at my place or in one of those little night clubs, candlelit because of the power cuts, to be found in certain courtyards between Fasanenstrasse and Uhlandstrasse, where you could pretend you were back in the Berlin of 1925? But why decide before we'd made love, giving ourselves to each other with a persistent passion which might make us plunge into the abyss or scale invisible heights, encompassing gentle tremors and the most delicious collisions? We decided that love should be followed by cold chicken at home, accompanied by a recording of Johann Sebastian Bach. Just before midnight we went out for a stroll in the dark, interrupted by the planes of the airlift, like so many motorcycles hurtling across vague patches of cloud. Did I think much about you during those weeks of feverish activity? I was all tangled up in myself, involved as I was at one and the same time in diplomacy, administration, blackmail, gambling, making love, making an impression, infatuation, poetry, and official documents. I changed personalities and points of view several times a day, not troubling about what they all added up to. I was made up of various incompatible characters, all doomed to have me settle scores with them, but at the same time furtively determined not to recognize one another. This situation gave me a curious pleasure, which I didn't spoil by speculating as to where it would all end. At thirty, I was in control of my own diversification and often gloated over the fact: wasn't I born for paradox and misunderstanding? I took back to the Russians four of their soldiers who'd gotten drunk on cheap orange liqueur and broken a lot of plate-glass windows in Steglitz. Would my generous act be understood, or would the culprits be sent to prison? Or would I be accused of having gotten them drunk in order to create an incident from which I emerged with credit? I went to see Bertolt Brecht, recently back from the United States and now working on a production of *Mother Courage*: of course I'd translate a selection of his poems! We talked about whether a writer ought to defend some political cause, and our conversation ended in an unsatisfactory compromise: conviction without talent wasn't enough, as in the case of his friend Johannes R. Becher. But talent without conviction, as in the case of a chronic pessimist like Gottfried Benn, was even more pernicious in these days of national reconstruction. He was useful because extremely well-read and lent me some books by Paul Zech and Franz Werfel that dated from just after the 1918 war and were so rare I hadn't been able to get hold of copies myself. Skipping from literature to politics at the request of Generals Clay and Ganeval, I wrote an ultimatum from the three Western powers to the Czech government: on several occasions their aircraft had overflown the occupied territories and the air approaches to Berlin, and if these violations were repeated they could expect severe reprisals. As my office was responsible for protocol and for liaison between the Allies, it served as the official channel for such friendly exchanges. My superiors had told me the tone of my letter should reflect the contempt in which the West held Czechoslovakia since Jan Masaryk's suicide.

I also had to give my driver a severe dressing down. I'd told him he could supplement his wages by taking part in minor black market operations, but I wasn't going to lend him my own car for that purpose: as my employee he ought to set an example of discretion and ingenuity. A typical Mecklenburger, he didn't understand such subtleties, and I upset him further by saying straight out that if I ever caught him in the act I'd fire him. However, I also asked him to sell a few cans of coffee that you'd sent me, for as much as he could get. Your letters might be something of a nuisance, but your food parcels, which could be converted into money or stamps, made up for them. Given all the bother my duties involved, I had a right, I told myself, to spend the occasional half-hour being mercenary and looking after number one. I saw this self-indulgence as praiseworthy lucidity. I needed conquests as well as dangers, even if some of them were imaginary. The fact that I loved Maria without reservation needn't prevent me from pursuing a few other shadows. It was only natural to tire of one woman after fifteen or twenty nights, or to switch girlfriends around so as to compare bodies, skins, souls, and the cries or silences of pleasure. But just as one may almost lose consciousness for a moment by breathing in too deeply while making love, so, in the same circumstances, I would suddenly feel a pang. Some faces I'd known had left me; others I'd driven away too abruptly. And now I longed with all my heart to have them back, to look at them more carefully, without even touching them. So I wrote to Heidi, Ilse, Liselotte, and Clara—all of them just a pair of lips to me, or the back of a neck, a heaving breast, or the close-up of a thigh. But who answered? And even if I saw those lips or that hip again, I quailed and was unequal to my dreams: we'd have a brandy or whiskey together, wish each other luck, and part friends for life who would never meet again. With Maria I was more serious: I asked her to forgive me for loving her more than I had meant to. This evasion allowed me to mount my mental merry-go-round again.

One morning on the way to his office, Marshal Sokolovski drove across the Western sectors at almost 70 miles an hour, and an American patrol made up of inexperienced recruits from Oklahoma or Wyoming forced him to get out of his car to identify himself and account for his speeding. At first he was rather amused, but he lost his temper when one of the Americans, hearing his name but unable to recognize his rank, said, "Sokolovski? My name's Skolkovski—are you Polish too?" The commanders of the Allied forces, in consultation with the allied high commissioners in Germany, dispatched me to the Marshal's HQ to offer him their apologies. He talked to me for five minutes, not very graciously, then dismissed all his staff except one. He needed me, he said, then deputed General Krivoï to speak for him. I was very intrigued. Krivoï struck me as rather like Fradkin: loftily polite, very sure of himself, cold. He asked me how long I'd been in Berlin and what front I'd fought on. I said there was a file on me containing all the details right down to my great-grandmother's maiden name, which I didn't even know myself. He smiled, and these preliminaries were to lead to a relationship between us of perfect frankness based on courteous mistrust and a delight in taking risks. The Soviet high command was about to repatriate a large number of their troops and replace them with other units. Unfortunately several thousands of them, who'd earned their demobilization, had contracted venereal diseases: heroes and victors couldn't be prevented from seeking their pleasure among the vanquished. But under existing laws this practice made them guilty of illicitly consorting with the enemy. The law might eventually be made less stringent, but meanwhile Marshal Sokolovski would rather send the men home cured. To cut a long story short, could I get him some penicillin? I told General Krivoï I'd have to consult my superiors: I didn't know anything about medicine, and penicillin wasn't for sale in either France or the United States. Such minor obstacles shouldn't stand in the way of a resourceful fellow like me, he said. I could get the stuff in England, or even from British HQ. There was no point in alerting the whole military hierarchy, so I should conduct the negotiations with the utmost discretion. He gave me a list made out in German: it would tell a pharmacist all he needed to know. All *I* had to do was show my usual resourcefulness: the black market held no secrets for me. Krivoï wanted me to agree, and make a solemn promise to help them, then and there. But as this was an arrangement between friends, he allowed me twenty minutes to think about it. He also poured me a cup of hot tea with his own hands, to help me make up my mind. Whatever our current differences, he was sure I'd do this favor in the name of our common victory over fascism. Power went to my head. I grinned mockingly and asked for another vodka, to which General Krivoï kindly added a piece of lemon peel. I said that since in a way I was his prisoner I would do as he wished, since his reasons for asking it were also reasons of State. But I couldn't guarantee success. He said he was sure I'd manage. What was he offering in return? He congratulated me on my bargaining skills, and said I had only to name my demands. I made some quick calculations. It would take me three or four weeks to get hold of what was required. I'd also need some money; a few civilian go-betweens, preferably Berliners who had relatives in the Soviet zone and whom I could have arrested if necessary; and more information about the units in which penicillin was available in injectable form. There were countless other unpredictable factors. Then, tense and uneasy at my own effrontery, I painted a pathetic picture of the British, French, and American troops in Berlin, sacrificing themselves to keep the citizens of the capital properly supplied, but unable to get any gasoline for their own tanks. Krivoï tossed his head impatiently at these platitudes: he knew very well that if there was any actual fighting a single Soviet regiment would be enough to wipe out the whole of the three Western sectors. The blockade, he told me condescendingly, was a political weapon. Without more ado, I asked for a hundred thousand liters of Russian gasoline in exchange for every gram of penicillin. It took my interlocutor no more than a couple of seconds to close enthusiastically with this offer and clasp my hands so warmly I could feel the bones grinding. Now all I had to do was try to live up to his flattering expectations.

How much could you have understood of the life I was leading—the life of a reckless predator? Many of my expolits were shady, and professional secrecy forced me either to disguise them or to keep them entirely to myself. I was accumulating a lot of spicy memories, alternating with brief excursions into a farcical kind of heroism and a variegated series of infatuations and enthusiasms. Meanwhile your sermons were becoming more and more urgent: I was too absorbed in my work to realize the disasters Stalin was plotting; we were heading for a third world war, and I'd be one of its first victims; there was still time, though only a few weeks, perhaps only days, for me to resign from my post and go to live in New York, where I could grow up at last in propitious circumstances. As I didn't answer what you said in your letters but just sent a few reassuring phrases, you changed your tactics. It was all very well for me to neglect my own safety, you wrote, but I had no right to put you in danger: because of the risks I was running, your health was being affected. Your heart was now at the mercy of the slightest emotion, and my obstinate insistence on living in the lion's jaws was precisely what did it most harm. In the end I wrote and said that I'd stand back and consider your situation and my own with the proper philosophical impartiality; I asked you to realize that I had what's popularly known as a ringside seat, and knew better than anyone what the Russians were up to. I then launched into a wild diatribe: the blockade was only partial, and the capitalist world was distorting and exaggerating the whole thing. It was in the so-called free press's own interest to overdramatize the situation in a scandalous manner. I concluded by declaring that in my view the Soviet régime represented the hope of mankind, even under Stalin, and if it had gone astray it was the fault of the democracies. I did add one cheerful note: should the present tension degenerate into armed conflict, I'd be taken prisoner in the first fifteen minutes and be a distinguished hostage who'd be exchanged for a minister or an ambassador. So I'd be safe and wouldn't have to fight while airborne Russian troops descended on Belfast, Lisbon and Seville, before deploying infantry divisions all over Europe. Did my bravado show you there was no point in trying to tell me what to do? In any event, your letters became calmer, though at the same time more disillusioned and abstract: you just went on imploring me, without any hysterics now, to come away from Berlin.

I resumed serious business. I exchanged twenty-five kilos of suet for a 1909 painting by Chagall depicting a green isba, a cyclamen-colored roof, a bearded moujik walking among the stars, and an upside-down cow. I promised Friedrich Dürrenmatt, a young Swiss writer, to get his first story published in a good journal despite the current difficulties; I'd already made a similar gesture to Paul Celan, another beginner who'd sent me some of his poems. I asked Wilhelm Furtwängler to come to my office and advised him not to play any more Mendelssohn: the fact that he'd been banned under Hitler didn't mean he was a genius. I also asked him not to exclude the works of Dmitry Shostakovich from his programs: his belonging to the Communist Party was no reason why he should be ostracized, even during the blockade. Furtwängler's assistant and probable successor, Sergiu Celibidache, struck me as very rigid and clumsy, and I told his boss to postpone his official nomination. I bought the remains of seventeen American and French airmen from the Soviet authorities for five thousand dollars per corpse: they'd crashed in the Baltic States and been buried in makeshift graves, and their families wanted them back. I took delivery at an abandoned station in Treptow: two generals and three colonels were waiting for me in a red-carpeted railway carriage containing a lot of lengthy documents, some wooden pens and a few grimy inkwells. The temperature was below zero, the ink had frozen, and my pen broke when dipped into it. The resulting roar of laughter removed all solemnity from the proceedings, and I presented my co-signatories with a capitalistic Waterman. Then I came away to repatriate the dear departed, while the Soviets went off with the much-coveted foreign currency.

The head of the Polish military mission made ardent efforts to get to know me. He'd read some of my poems, he knew I'd worked with some of his colleagues in London, he didn't have many friends, and wanted to surround himself with new faces. I kept my distance; he kept inviting me to lunches and cocktail parties. His name was Vladislaw Borbeck, and he was the son of a small Lithuanian landowner. He behaved flamboyantly and talked recklessly, letting everyone know that he regarded the English as hypocrites, the French as fuss-pots, the Americans as children, and the Russians as barbarians. It wasn't until we'd met for the seventh or eighth time that he revealed what he was after: he wanted to go over, bag and baggage, body and soul, to the West, judging freedom in a muddled society preferable to slavery in an ideal one. I told him he'd gotten the wrong guy. I wasn't a double agent, and in my opinion the future of communism was more promising than that of the capitalist democracies. He gently accused me of willful blindness. I could tell my superiors of his plans: he'd make an excellent recruit, he assured me. But he required certain favors in return for his defection—a well-paid job in Washington or Toronto, for instance. We met again several times—either in a garden or at the movies or in the officers' mess at Soviet HQ, in order to avoid suspicion or to throw people off the scent. But Borbeck was greedy: he wanted me, with the aid of some carefully chosen accomplices, to smuggle his whole family out—five people in all—together with their furniture from Warsaw, the family plate, and a Saint Bernard with a coat like a weeping willow. Treason was being transformed into moving house. I didn't hesitate to tell him how skeptical, not to say disgusted, I was about his scheme. But I was under orders to do whatever he wanted;

Vladislaw Borbeck was a renegade of importance. Once all the preparations were made, I explained to this dubious hero that he and his off-
spring, his mother, his sideboards, his hunting boots, and his knickknacks
would fill the whole plane, and there wouldn't be room for his mutt. He
was shattered; I told him to take it or leave it. Then I went back to
officialese and instructed him to be in my office, with the dog, in an hour's
time: by the end of the afternoon he'd be flying through the air at an altitude of two thousand meters. He panicked for a moment and asked if I
meant to denounce him to the Russian authorities. I took great pleasure
in telling him, savoring every syllable, that he did indeed deserve the
punishment usually meted out to traitors. When he presented himself in
my office with his enormous hunk of dog, I handed him a cyanide pill
and told him to give it to the Saint Bernard in a dish of food I'd had prepared. I must have looked very threatening, because he did as he was
told. The dog twisted and turned, threw up, and after a few minutes was
laid out cold. Then I confessed to its master that one lousy hound more
or less didn't really make any difference; there was still plenty of room
on the plane, which after unloading its cargo of supplies for the people
of Berlin would take off again empty for Frankfurt. I'd just wanted to see
a death like the one he himself deserved.

For a change, in the days that followed, I lost a lot of money at poker,
then spent a fair amount of time consoling Ingeborg, whose pear-shaped
breasts had been haunting me, for having left her six months earlier, probably prematurely. The consoling process included many favors, for I was
determined to leave her again in due course, but I shall never forget that
skin, those hips, those caresses: I applied all sorts of ecstatic adjectives
to them, which wasn't at all like me. It was at this point that your letters
grew urgent once more—up to five or six of them a week. And I suddenly changed, both in what I wrote and in what I felt. I told you quite
calmly I'd come to agree with you: the siege had been affecting my nerves,
and I was grateful for your advice. In a few weeks' time—the time it would
take me to put my affairs in order and find a replacement—I'd leave for
Paris and take up my studies again at the university. I asked you to be
patient, and told you the blockade of Berlin no longer served any pur-

pose and would soon be lifted. That letter wasn't a sham: literature had suddenly supplanted all my other appetites, and the comic opera of the life I'd been leading was starting to get on my nerves. I promised Maria I'd live with her—perhaps go as far as marrying her, one day. I asked her to go and live in France, where I'd join her in a year's time at the latest. I'd experienced a pre-war period, a war, a post-war period, and a cold war: now it was time for me to learn about peace.

New York, October 1957

I was on my way from Toronto to Virginia, so I had decided my forty-eight hour visit was to be a model of affection. To begin with our exchanges consisted of charged silences and few words, so as not to fritter away our accumulated warmth. You were quite well, Father was extremely well, and my health was satisfactory enough. We were happy and natural. Problems and embarrassing questions might come later; with a bit of luck we might avoid them altogether and have a reasonably pleasant, if not very lively, reunion. We exchanged presents: I'd brought you a Chanel dressing gown and Father a Lanvin scarf, a mixture of wool and silk. You had a surprise for me: a bust of myself which you'd worked on for several weeks and cast in bronze. Although you could catch a likeness quite easily with your friends, you'd had to try much harder in my case. I found the result rather lifeless and not much like me, but that didn't stop me from being very enthusiastic about it. We had some light refreshments soon after I arrived, then I quickly suggested going to the movies: we needed to erect a screen between us, and a cinematic screen would suit the purpose very well. Father thought this a good idea, and I left you and him to choose between two comedies, one with Alec Guinness playing the lead and the other with Rex Harrison. You yourself didn't like intellectual or tragic films, but either of my two suggestions seemed to you quite suited to the occasion. Next morning at ten we left Father hard at work and I took you to the Cloisters. We both went into raptures over the copper and gold tones of the Indian summer, which gave me an opening for lengthy descriptions of the New England countryside in October and November, when the maples are Delacroix red, the greens more intense than in the Venetian masters, and the browns as rich as any in Van Dyck. I calculated that these rather forced allusions would lead smoothly to a tour of the galleries and museums. I kept up the good work as we looked at the Catalan crucifixes in the cloister. I observed that in the second third of the eleventh century Catholicism gave birth to a delightful kind of popular art, inspired and ecstatic, unparalleled in the history of sculpture. I went on to run down Greek sculpture, which I loathed, as I did the overly demonstrative giants of the Renaissance, Michelangelo and Donatello included.

Coming down to earth a bit after this tirade, I showed my solicitude by asking how much you'd got out of your lessons with Archipenko, and whether Father gave you enough money to buy the clay and other things you needed for your work. If not, might I help, so that you could cast your favorite pieces in bronze? Or were there other, more manageable materials I could send you from Europe? Nothing would give me greater pleasure, as you must know. These offers improved the atmosphere still further. Then we both showed off our knowledge of modern sculpture by discussing the order of our preferences, our likes and dislikes. By now it was almost lunchtime, so we had a snack at Reuben's on Fifth Avenue: I loved their toasted sandwiches with sauerkraut, pastrami, and mozzarella fillings. This interlude, which I was careful to keep light and impersonal, gave me the chance to expound upon the subject of gastronomy, which of course was one of the criteria of civilization. I treated you to detailed descriptions of dishes I'd sampled at Point's in Vienna and Gordon's in Baltimore: I wasn't sure if the best French restaurants, which I didn't know all that well because they were usually beyond my means, were really any better than places in the United States which specialized in shellfish—giant Alaska crab, for example, and crayfish stuffed with clams. These sententious bromides were soon succeeded, in the Museum of Modern Art on 54th Street, by more subtle rhapsodies.

Besides revering Archipenko, you admired all the sculptors of the early '20s who resembled him, though that didn't stop you from liking Maillol and Despiau as well. But Pevsner and Brancusi didn't attract you at all. From all this I drew various conclusions about women and art: for deep-seated, visceral reasons, I explained, women were the enemies of abstraction, whose products they saw as cerebral anomalies. Women were comfortable only with children, trees, faces, sunsets. Toward the end of the afternoon, to complete your education, I showed you the work of Moore and Chadwick, and told you about César and Ipoustéguy, French sculptors whom I admired but who were as yet unrepresented in MOMA. I'd send you some catalogs and articles about them: an artist with your talent owed it to herself to know more about the work of her contemporaries. In the evening, after a brief siesta, I took you to a concert: didn't you think Emil Gilels a worthy successor to Vladimir Horowitz and Walter Gieseking, your two favorite pianists? Music having replaced sculpture as our subject, we now contemplated, through mists of shameless sentimentality, Purcell and Debussy, Haydn and Berlioz, Smetana and Bizet, Pergolesi and Ravel. We found we hated some of the same things, loved others almost equally, and simply couldn't agree about others. You wouldn't admit that Erik Satie was a genuine composer; I refused even to discuss the antipathy I felt for Puccini and Rameau. Ours was simultaneously a heated and heartwarming battle, still going strong at midnight while we were having a cold supper with Father. You were exhausted by now; I had succeeded in not telling you anything important. Perhaps the best way to ward off our quarrels was to scale filial love down to camaraderie and swathe it in shallow aesthetics.

The next day didn't go so well. I'd decided to devote it to painting, and we started off at the Whitney Museum. You asked me what one was really to make of the new American painters, and with some effort I managed to find one I thought worthy of interest: Arshile Gorky. I didn't know what to say about Jackson Pollock or Robert Motherwell. My sense of proportion prevented me from admiring them: to me they were mere daubers whose spontaneity had won out over conscience. I wasn't yet forty: had I been overtaken by the avant-garde already, or had I always been a reactionary without knowing it? A cloud now overshadowed my goodwill toward you, and it was without any sensation of wonder that we stood in front of a Bonnard, a Max Ernst, a Feininger, and a Kupka. I had to force myself to exclaim and admire. The freshness of the previous day had worn off. You wanted to go home early. I was going to leave again in a few hours, and you were growing tense. You asked me about my writing, but without waiting for my answer you told me what you thought: I'd made a good beginning and shown some sparks of talent, but five years later I had to admit I'd reached my limits. All my moving about was proof of it: I gave lectures and taught courses; I was a sort of traveling salesman of French culture. This was at the same time flattering and rather humiliating. I replied, with an assumption of dignity, that I liked this way of life: I met useful people, made lots of contacts, saw no end of interesting things and places. At little cost to myself I'd visited Mexico, Andalusia, Morocco, Austria, and the remotest parts of Apulia. All *you* knew was that I wasn't happy. So then I had to ascend to the spiritual level and the vast perspectives it lent itself to: what does the notion of happiness signify in a period which has just emerged from existentialism and the idea that life is a makeshift; a period when people move about in the midst of the absurd, with a constant feeling that everything is stupid, uninteresting, and in any case doomed in an uncertain but ever menacing future to be blown to smithereens? In the heat of the argument I mentioned Hiroshima, which I called humanity's second original sin. Another Landru, another Rasputin, another Himmler and the whole planet could be shattered to pieces like a watermelon in which some mischievous urchin has hidden a firecracker.

You now became determined: if I couldn't be bothered with it myself, *you* were going to think about my future and do what you could to improve it. You weren't at all sure Paris had been good for me: too many of my activities seemed to consist only of window-dressing. I had some very good degrees; I was always being asked to teach at American universities; so why didn't I make a new life for myself somewhere nearby? Then not only would I be able to see you once a month but I'd also have a sounder intellectual base to work from. Where was France going to end up when it had a new government practically every week? I listened, feeling no hostility, to what you said. I told you I had no prejudice one way or the other. I'd never had a real native land, but I felt most at home in the country that spoke my own language: over the years, my books had made the choice for me. But I hadn't forgotten what I'd promised myself: on this visit I had to be nice and charming. So I said that I might be tempted to come and live in the United States if I ever found a job there that was worthy of me. People change, their tastes alter, disappointment may make them settle down: I was leaving you a glimmer of hope. You couldn't help but praise my wisdom and patience. No doubt, deep down, you thought that if you could somehow find me the sort of job I'd referred to, I'd come around to your way of thinking. We were both ready now for another bout of form, color, and visual excitement, and this time neither Picasso nor Tanguy, Derain nor Kokoschka struck us as obstacles keeping us from confronting more important matters. We managed to merge ourselves gradually into the paintings, so that when we came to the surface again after our bath of beatitude we felt purer, better disposed toward, prouder of understanding each other. You told me yet again, but almost affectionately, that you loathed Maria, and I reassured you by saying human beings weren't perfect, and sometimes one needed a change. This encouraged you to risk a few rather salacious remarks: you supposed my wife must be rather good in bed, which was reason enough to keep her on for a while, but in the long run I owed it to myself to do better. As I didn't protest you confessed, under the seal of secrecy, that you knew some very attractive and cultivated young women with whom I might find happiness. I roared with laughter and said I'd be glad to try out any fiancées you might produce. And we parted with shows of affection in which no one could have detected the slightest trace of play-acting.

Paris, February 1977

I pause at the corner of the avenue Bosquet and the rue de Grenelle: shall I take you the sort of almond cake that you like, or some chocolate truffles, or some fruit? The day before yesterday you went into raptures over a pot of mauve gloxinias: they must still be in flower. There's a timid little drizzle falling, just enough to hide the top of the nearby Eiffel Tower. I walk past several store windows; it's the vegetable stall that attracts me most. Inside the store I notice some kiwis, but they're a bit overripe. The Mexican strawberries look shriveled: they probably haven't ripened in the open air. I finally pick up a pineapple by the tuft: it's as finely carved as an objet d'art—I tell them not to wrap it up. As I go up in the elevator my not very interesting thoughts jostle one another: I've got an article to finish on Gombrowicz; I must call in at *Le Monde;* I'm supposed to do a talk on the radio about the younger Canadian poets; I have an appointment with my dentist; you seem to be fairly well: you walked as far as your usual bench yesterday morning, and your doctor doesn't think your state of health any more alarming than it was last week. Your landlady opens the door, puts her hand to her mouth, and says:

"I've been trying to get you on the phone for a couple of hours. Your mother is dead."

I take off my raincoat, hand her the pineapple, and tell her to take it into the kitchen—it's hers. I don't know whether I ought to sit down, rush into your room at the end of the passage, or check my pulse. I brace my-

self, but I don't know what for. I can feel a pain between my jaw and the
roof of my mouth; a determination not to lose my self-control; a kind of
relief too, with my first lucid moment, at the thought that you haven't had
to suffer long. I slump into a chair, and your landlady discreetly disappears into another room. I try to pull myself together, make myself take
things calmly. I'm really thinking only of myself: for a start, I have to get
through this crisis alive. I must make myself feel as little as possible;
later on I'll tell myself that the inevitable, which had been coming for a
long time, has finally happened more or less as I'd imagined it only two or
three days ago. I detach myself: it's absolutely necessary that I detach myself right away. I decide not to go in and see you for another quarter of an
hour. I quell any sign of panic. I am calm. I simply must be calm.

I go down to see your doctor, who lives a couple of floors below in the
same building. He lets me in at once, and writes out a death certificate
on the corner of his desk, pushing aside a stethoscope.

"There was nothing to be done," he says. "Her general state of health. . .
the weakness of the heart. . ."

I ask what I owe him. He waves his hand.

"My dear sir. . . !"

I go upstairs again and try to call Maria, but she's still out shopping,
and in a way I'm glad not to have to share my distress. I call up a funeral parlor and a smarmy voice solemnly takes down the address: at 7:45
this evening they'll send a very experienced and considerate gentleman
to give me all the necessary information. I feel sorry for myself, I try to
console myself, I congratulate myself for not getting into a panic. But now
I have to contemplate your dead face, to face up to my first impression
of you after you are no more. Your forehead's smoother than usual; your
closed eyelids bluish; your mouth rather twisted, as if in a smile cut short.
Your nostrils are so pinched they pull at your chin, but the flabby jowls
resist. Your fingers are visible below the sleeves of your turquoise dressing gown, painfully clenched, and your thin legs seem not to belong to
the rest of your body: they look as though they'd always lain there inert.
I don't know what I'm feeling, and tell myself I need to get into a turmoil
so as either to fight against it or deliberately give in to it. I could press

my lips to your brow. Or I could just sit down as if to store up a kind of sorrowful eternity, reduced for the moment to seconds of intense sadness. What I actually do is brush your hand with my lips, avoiding any symbolic gestures. What is it I feel? Peace? Emptiness? Relief? Or a grief that will gradually get worse? I note without surprise that I'm not suffering at all.

The landlady returns. I pluck up my courage and question her, but she doesn't say much. You woke up late and complained about pains in your chest and legs. You refused to eat or drink anything but a mouthful or two of hot tea, and even then you had great difficulty holding the cup. A few minutes later you asked for the doctor, who promised to call in as soon as he could on his rounds. Soon afterward you began to tremble all over. You clenched your hands over the upper part of your chest, and became so agitated you couldn't breathe. You uttered a few incoherent words in French and Russian. Then the doctor came, ready to give you an injection, but he changed his mind. After a final spasm, you suddenly relaxed and lay still: he could see you'd stopped breathing. They both propped you up on your pillow.

I don't say anything. I seem to be submerged by something at once profound and indistinct. Why didn't I catch one last word, one last gesture, one last glance that I might have made live on in me? It's always a crime not to be there when one's needed, but wasn't that absence of mine worse than most? But again, is this the time for remorse? I must try to calm down and be on guard against my own reactions. It would do me good to go for a walk: wherever one goes there's always something to see—a series of therapeutic images. I wring the landlady's hands and apologize for all the trouble your death is giving her. I go to the city hall to declare your death. I sign my name in a ledger and my grief becomes official, a matter of record, witnessed by a bust of Marianne, symbol of the Republic. Now there's nothing more I need to do; a female official, whistling a Gilbert Bécaud song, tells me she'll inform the medical authorities and a burial certificate will be forwarded to the funeral parlor. You are catalogued, numbered, and listed. I make no objection.

The funeral director's an amiable fellow, not sinister in the least. He presents his condolences, together with a form that has spaces for questions and answers, which he fills out briskly as we speak. I have to choose from a number of photographs the sort of coffin I require: I select an expensive but not ostentatious model, slightly baroque, with artistically carved handles. Absurdity mustn't strike twice: you'll rest in a decent box that's neither too plain nor too rich. The color of the lining, which may be either silk or velvet, depends on the age of the deceased: white for a virgin, sky blue for a child, red for an adult, mauve for an old person. Red will do for you: but what an odd compromise! At the last moment I make them leave out the crucifix: you weren't an orthodox believer and you never prayed to your own god, who put in only an occasional appearance. The director removes the crucifix from his estimate: a plated silver one, buried with the deceased, costs three hundred and thirty francs. Shall I be there tomorrow to see the body placed in the coffin? I say yes. He advises me to come after the body has been prepared. It's a painful business, and it's best for me to see you again after you've been washed and made up. One last thing: the funeral procession and the flowers. I ask how many roses are usually placed on the grave. He says one can make a reasonable show for five hundred francs. I tell him to spend two thousand. "That'll be lovely!" he exclaims.

Yes, it will be perfect, all those flowers dying on top of you. I sign the estimate: I needn't pay right away, they don't mind giving credit. All I need to do is give the name of my bank and my account number. I offer the funeral director a brandy. He says he admires my poise: his job can be very unpleasant. I don't inquire about his family, his social security benefits, or how much annual leave he gets. We're both paid-up members of a caring and well-ordered society.

It's only at dinner that between a couple of mouthfuls I say to Maria: "My mother is dead."

She rushes over to put her arms around me, but I push her away. The sound of what I've just said upsets me more than your actual death: formulating reality gives it enormous significance. I go on eating, though rather more slowly. Maria doesn't know how she ought to behave. I look at her with a kind of cold hostility: I used to have a capital sum of affection, of which she owned three-quarters or nine-tenths and you had the rest. But now your share comes to her, and the visceral rivalry between the two of you is over. I don't feel like going into detail: Maria will come to the funeral with me the day after next, and that's that. She asks if I'm having dessert, and I say there's no reason why not. I go back to my desk: anything absurd or mean gives me a strange satisfaction. At about eleven o'clock I listen to a Bach recording; its mechanical sobriety irritates me. I consider putting on some Beethoven or Mahler instead: a bit of frenzied romanticism might at least stir me up. But no, I'm immune—gloomy and imperturbable. Will I be able to sleep? Will my nerves hold out until the funeral? I have to think of myself. Maria's being there is no help. When one loses one's mother one needs either to be alone like a prophet on his mountain, or lost in a crowd, one indistinguishable face among a thousand. I swallow a couple of sleeping pills; they'll take effect in the small hours and I'll get about four hours' sleep.

The next day is nothing unusual: the mail, a talk on the radio, an article I have to write. I dictate a few letters to Maria, five or six at most, to distant relatives, a couple of your nephews and a few childhood friends. I tell them all how fond of them you were, and how affectionately you used to speak of them. I tell them you didn't suffer much before you died. I call up your acquaintances in Paris—half a dozen of them at the most. I encounter tears, lamentations and inarticulate cries, which make me decide not to invite any of these old fogies to the funeral. I'll go alone. I even intend to forbid Maria to come with me: you and she didn't get along, and in such circumstances it's indecent for someone to go through the motions of paying their last respects. But I change my mind: if I should feel ill, or faint, I'd like her to be there. The best tranquilizer in the world is utter selfishness. I move around a lot; I invent things to do, as pure camouflage. In spite of myself I can't help making a few calculations. Your going so suddenly, without any major illness or hospitalization, will have cost me less money than a protracted deathbed. At what point does an inevitable tragedy become a relief? I don't feel any self-pity; I may be a poet and a novelist, but I'm just as worldly as the next man. My conscience doesn't trouble me unduly: I just need to threaten it a bit and any qualms soon quiet down. My character includes both self-discipline and weakness, and the first gets the better of the second. My day is coming to an end. It's been as stupid and as nervous as the one before because my imagination hasn't gotten to work on your death yet and the fumes of the intellect aren't bothering me for the moment. The evening is less serene. I take Maria to dinner in a bright, noisy little restaurant: we mustn't miss the chance to celebrate the miracle of still being alive.

And now I'm looking at you for the last time. The funeral parlor has done its work and you're lying in your coffin. Only your head is visible: you look peaceful, unreal, as if carved out of some material that's neither transparent nor opaque. In spite of myself I feel time is standing still: centuries of morals and literature have made this moment into a symbol of pious meditation. But my mind, spurning such commonplaces, prefers to wander in realms of its own: yes, it's a mere replica of your body there in front of me, perhaps a work of art, part sculpture, part illusion. But I feel rather embarrassed, probably because Maria, the landlady, and the attendant specialists in bereavement all indulge so freely in platitudes. I leave the room as they prepare to nail down the lid of the coffin. Outside, the cold offers a salutary resistance. Store windows live longer than human beings. I walk as far as the grocer's, to gaze at the pineapples as I did a couple of days ago. Perhaps I could buy another one: it's easier to commune with fruit than with people. The coffin's now in the black hearse. A passerby raises his hat. I feel like asking him if he'd do the same for a newborn infant: the dawn of a life should command more respect than the twilight. The roses are beautiful, like a scar. Maria and I get into a car with tinted windows. Paris never changes: why should I be seeing it with new eyes? I think about the grave and how my heart is going to react to it: whether I like it or not I'm in my fifties, and tired. I'm grateful to Maria for not saying anything to comfort me. The southern suburbs are dirty and gray. When we get to the cemetery another team of attendants takes over. The new lot might be working in a factory, the way they shake hands and exchange a few words, glad to sign off work, reluctant to punch in. I have more respect for these nameless, necessary, serious people than I have for you—certainly more than I can feel for myself. I see your name neatly handwritten on a little board, between a hole in the ground and a heap of freshly turned earth. I suddenly wonder if we should have had a priest: but no, he and his ritual phrases would only have detracted from the deliberately understated, not to say clandestine, nature of the occasion. The coffin is let down on its ropes. Won't the grave diggers catch cold, naked to the waist in this treacherous February weather? Someone hands me a rose. I push Maria forward. If we have to observe this sort of convention, at least let me not be the first. I take a poem out of my pocket: I wrote it for you when I woke up this morning. I'm going to throw it on the smooth lid of the coffin instead of the statutory flower. But I hesitate, then put it back in my pocket: what would be the point of such a gesture? I wish I were invisible; tear off a rose petal and let it fall to the ground; then, outraged by the slowness of the ceremony, hurl the rest after it. I'm given a kind of receipt: the earth certifies in the presence of witnesses that it has safely received you back again according to the rules. I tip all the attendants. In the car going back to Paris I say angrily to Maria:

"Sorry, but I just don't feel anything."

Your only tomb is this book: you'll never have another. The people you knew grow fewer and fewer: the older ones sink into incoherence, the young acquire attachments of their own. I can't swear that all these scenes and sentences and words, with so many large gaps between them, give a faithful account of you. Literature has different requirements from those of biography, and obeys other laws. I've just spent a sometimes unbearably intense few months living with you, pen in hand and typewriter within reach. But is that long enough to do justice to half a century of filial love, of often intermingled distaste, neglect, and apprehension? You're now a strange amalgam of things that have been written down: your body isn't in your real body anymore, nor is your soul anywhere near your real soul. I pass these reinvented scraps of you on to a few readers, who, whether absentmindedly, by way of amusement, or—more probably—with indifference, will reconstruct you in their turn. You used to have form, weight, a way of breathing, a tangible presence: now you exist only in the dimension of words. Have I made use of your truth? I'm inclined to think, on the contrary, that my writing has gradually trans- figured you in accordance with its own rhythms and habits and whims, sometimes deliberate, sometimes careless and to your detriment. Some- times my concentration flags and I fail to analyze a memory or develop a half-buried image as I should. But I'm going to separate myself from you at last, and if ever I feel like coming back to you—or need to do so— some vaguely melancholy evening, I won't consult my unreliable memory. I'll open this book, in which everything will square with my own past, undifferentiated from yours. The dividing line between fiction and fact is almost invisible. And now with every month, every week, every sen- tence, I too am growing old. You are dead, and this book I've just fin- ished is dying too in its way. I won't be adding anything more to it: nei- ther more thrills nor more sorrows. All that remains of you is here, modi- fied by every vowel, mummified by every comma.

Is a writer motivated by anything other than his own physical need to express himself? I was suddenly overwhelmed by this necessity when I thought of you, and since I couldn't shake you off, since you clung like a leech, I tamed you by changing you into a character. Was what I felt a perverse excitement, or a vague kind of remorse that I had to get rid of? I don't know. I was never a model son, and I never thought you a won- derful mother. Instead of canceling each other out, the difficulty inher- ent in my feeling for you and that inherent in your feeling for me simply joined together. We were sorry we couldn't live nearer to each other, and we were sorry distance didn't make us love each other better, In the ab- stract, when we were apart. I judge you harshly because it's not in my nature to tolerate anything too emotional; nor does my writing admit hand- kerchiefs waving, tears flowing, or hearts on the point of breaking. And there's no point in my panicking now that the portrait is finished: you'll remain as I've painted you, and I can't improve matters by adding a few would-be sympathetic touches like someone adding sugar to sour lem- onade. I consider a touch of hostility more admissible than too much in- dulgence. We are even now, you and I. Alive, you were free, suspicious, brave, and possessive. I have obliterated everything about you that isn't contained in this book. It will act for me as a balance sheet, a photograph album, and a foil. I shall also remember your rare aphorisms. For example: "I don't believe in God, so the day your father died I turned him into a saint"; "A mother is always right after she's dead—you'll see"; "To understand is good, but to love is better: it makes you give yourself"; "Don't ever reproach yourself, my son—you're perfect, because I'm your mother." I transform your words into literature, you see: that's all I'm good for. Spare me the hell of affection.

Odessa, summer 1918

I've had to gather together a number of disparate and sometimes vague elements in order to reconstruct an episode that occurred in your life before I was born. Your father, my father, your brother Armand, my uncle Michel—in this connection, all were unanimous in their praises of you. Odessa changed hands more than eight times that year. It was soon occupied by the revolutionaries, then recaptured by the Whites, who lost it again. The situation became fluid when the Greens and the Reds started ripping each other apart: Petlioura's nationalists and the Bolsheviks didn't see eye to eye over the future anti-czarist society. The Western powers interfered; at one point, even the vanquished German army entered the city. There were summary executions. For one side, to utter the names of Denikine or Kornilov was a capital offense; for the other, mention of Lenin, Trotsky, or Kamenev brought the same retribution. The inhabitants of the city took refuge in cynical neutrality: they knew the next occupant of the Hôtel de l'Amirauté, whoever it might be, would soon have blood on his hands. Then the people of Odessa decided to make the best of things: because one occupying force followed another so swiftly, the harbor was packed with shipping; soon everyone came to disregard the occasional burst of gunfire; to hail the latest temporary victor, wine and kvass flowed like water. The avant-garde wasn't only political: in literary circles there was talk of the changes being brought about in poetry by Babel and Akhmatova, and even in language itself by Khlebnikov.

You'd been married to my father for no more than a few weeks, but you were nonetheless an ardent defender of such new concepts as futurism and acmeism. My father sometimes took the floor himself: in reaction against so much pretentious theorizing he defended art for art's sake, and spoke of his fondness for symbolism as represented by Balmont, following the ideas of Rimbaud and Mallarmé.

But he was often reckless. The Bolsheviks took Odessa again, but this time they were more skillful than on the previous occasions and managed to hold on to the city long enough to reorganize it. The OGPU, the secret police, covered every block in every street, showing no mercy to any roisterers. The literary groups moved to new, more discreet premises, then gradually, for fear of informers, faded away into obscurity: literary theories could be as subversive as social or political ideas. But despite the risks you went on giving parties where passionate texts were read aloud and stirring manifestos distributed. Father hastily gathered together his poems and wrote some new ones. He soon had enough for a book. His friends approved. The volume was to be called *Scattered Harvests*, and a small local publisher undertook to get it printed. At this point the Communists, after an energetic period in power, were replaced by the Greens, who set about looting the lower part of the city and confiscating such necessities as wheat and coal. Their egalitarian anger once assuaged, they took to debauchery, and the Reds were able to oust them within a few weeks. But this time all traitors, reactionaries, and members of the bourgeoisie were arrested. My father was one of them: he owned a house and his parents were known to be wealthy. He didn't mind going to prison: he sympathized with the new régime, and anyway had come to be somewhat more careful than before in public.

You, on the other hand, realized at once that the situation was serious. You couldn't get any information out of the local police, and the city hall was no better: it was full of the wounded and dying, and the mayor himself had fled. So you changed your tactics and went to see the publisher. He was evasive. Paper was scarce, the printing press had been requisitioned, prices kept going up all the time. You made him swear the book would be ready in a week, in exchange for four times the agreed price.

But there was no time to be lost. Armand had an old school friend in the Communist militia: you roped him in. Then you rushed to the party cell dressed as a poor student and offered the man in charge your services in the revolutionary cause, together with some of your jewelry. He didn't accept right away: he wanted proof of your sincerity. You said your father, now a merchant dealing in leather and hides, had started out as a shoemaker. You were familiar with manual work; they could employ you in the mess, for example. He said he'd have to think it over, but in any case the liberation of your husband was a matter for his superiors. You explained how iniquitous and unjust it was that Alexander Bisk should have been arrested: he was a man of the left, even though he might have failed to understand right away the glorious epic of the revolution. You were fervent, passionate, a little crazy, and your fin-de-siècle vocabulary amused the official. He asked you how far you were prepared to go for your husband's sake—and you fled in terror. Fortunately Armand's old friend had been found, and met you in a derelict soap factory, where on a scrap of paper he wrote down the name of a member of the OGPU. This was Chervenko, the real ruler of the city. Back you went to the publisher. He'd kept his word, and the book was due to appear in two days' time. You asked him to hold up the printing for a few hours, and when he looked puzzled told him it was a matter of life and death. Now you sought out Chervenko, who happened to be in a good humor because he'd just shot a few enemies of the people. He said he knew you well: your brother Armand had been a close friend of his when he was still a poor man. He asked how old you were—you must have been nearly thirty but didn't look more than eighteen. He said he wouldn't make advances to you despite what he called your sparkling beauty: one couldn't make revolutions and love at the same time. He opened a file.

"'Alexander Bisk,'" he read out disdainfully. "'Bourgeois, and son of a bourgeois.' What could be worse?"

You launched into a long and breathless argument. Men like him changed society, but men like my father changed literature, poetry, philosophy—all the things that were most fundamental in a nation. He didn't promise anything, but told you to come back tomorrow.

The second interview was more stormy. Chervenko had had a university education too, but while this hadn't stopped him from sharing the aspirations of the workers, my father merely lounged about in drawing rooms reading foreign poets who enthused about birds and flowers instead of hammers and sickles. Chervenko was a poet himself—Armand would certainly be able to remember his work. But that was all over for the moment: the revolution came first! Then you had an inspiration: poets didn't kill one another, you said. Such a thing had never been known in the whole of human history. You said you were partly responsible for my father's error: you ought to have given him better guidance. But if he were set free you would take it upon yourself to make him change his attitude. If Alexander Bisk owed his freedom to Chervenko, he would show his gratitude by becoming a revolutionary poet. Chervenko looked at you with a mixture of admiration and scorn. You pressed on: Odessa had changed hands so often, what was the point of burdening his conscience with the death of a poet who could be converted? You touched a sensitive spot by telling him how my father had entertained Mayakovski, Essenin and other poets revered by the Communists. You were lying, but for the first time it seemed to you that Chervenko was taken in.

"I find you amusing, lousy bourgeois," he said. "Come back tomorrow."

Back you rushed to the publisher, whom you asked to replace page 5 of Father's book, which should have consisted of a dedication to you, with a new page reading, "For Kostia Chervenko, my brother in arms." Alarmed by your own audacity, you explained that only fifty copies of the book need be altered in this way. The work would be finished in a few hours, but the book still had to be bound. Two more days to wait!

The third encounter with Chervenko was disappointing. He seemed ill at ease, and you wondered if he was in trouble with his superiors: in such an unstable situation, he might have been outflanked by the extremists. Neither of you had much to say, but he didn't seem to mind wasting precious time with you. He offered you tea and made you listen to him brag about how powerful he was. His activities consisted mainly of distributing among the various prisons the hostages seized by the riffraff under his command. You were bold enough to recite one of my father's poems

to him; it was about homesickness. This startled him. He too had a loving image of Russia, not as she was—pitiable, ill-defined, drunken, stupid—but as, thanks to him and his comrades, she soon would be. You
implored him point-blank to set my father free. He didn't answer, which
you interpreted as a good sign. Then for a moment you lost your head: if
he must have a scapegoat from the Bisk family, what about one of Father's
younger brothers, Michel and Georges? He gave you a stern look, and
you pulled yourself together again after your unworthy lapse. Then it was
his turn to let his hair down: he knew what he was fighting for, but couldn't
justice soon turn into terror, then into famine, and finally into a dictatorship in which the proletariat would have to delegate its powers to a
tyrant? He was at once ardent and confused, realistic and mystical. He
brought the interview to a sudden and bad-tempered end.

"Come back at five in the morning," he growled. "Then we'll go and
see your poetaster together. He's down in the basement."

During the next twenty-four hours you were radiant. You took the publisher a bunch of gladioli, and he handed over the first copies of *Scattered Harvests*, warning you to be careful with them because the glue
wasn't yet dry. You practiced on the violin, surpassing yourself as you
played Vieuxtemps and Paganini, and thinking that one day you really
would become a celebrated virtuoso. You dreamed of having lots of children, some of them first-class painters, others distinguished lawyers. You
were happy for no particular reason: the trees were motherly, the sky
friendly, the ships in the harbor promised wondrous voyages, the passersby were airy as balloons about to fly away, the soldiers looked as if
they ought to have flowers in the barrels of their guns, the stores were
full of invisible treasures, the streets sang under the horses' hooves, the
squads of militia were crisp as freshly baked bread, the sea deeper than
the skies reflected in it. You drank fig brandy. You didn't go to bed. You
packed a suitcase; then another with some of my father's things in it. At
the appointed time you went to see Chervenko. He was swearing and pac-
ing up and down his office, his hair disheveled, his tunic creased. Before he'd done all he had to do in Odessa, he was being sent to Kursk, to
purge the whole region. He hardly recognized you. What did you want

with him so early in the morning? You had tears in your eyes. You held out Father's book. He read the dedication, then shrugged and said:

"I ought to shoot you too, you stupid bourgeois."

You sat down on a bench, your face buried in your handkerchief. He came over.

"Perhaps they'll give me something pleasant to look back on—these idiotic poems that have got my name tacked on to them. If I ever get the chance to read them! People like me end up either on the barricades or in a common grave."

He looked into your eyes, full of all the suffering and all the hope in the world. Then he muttered, as if still lost in his thoughts:

"Put 'em all up against a wall—that's the simplest solution."

Then he grabbed you by the arm, took a big bunch of keys out of a drawer, and pushed you toward the staircase leading down to the cellar. Followed by a guard with a pistol in his hand, he opened a door leading into the cell containing my father and a dozen or so other prisoners. Father and you and Chervenko were soon going back up the stairs. Chervenko gave Father a dig in the ribs and opened a concealed door. When you'd gone a hundred meters and were at the corner of the street, Father opened his book at the page with Chervenko's name on it. No explanation was necessary. You just said:

"We've got till noon to leave the city."

That was your finest hour.

Paris, June 20–August 31, 1977

AFTERWORD

In the late 1970s and early 1980s Alain Bosquet, by then well established in European cultural circles as a poet and "man of letters," told and retold the story of a past which *A Russian Mother* (*Un mère russe*, 1978) sought to recapture. This was followed by a fictional trilogy, also autobiographical, entitled The First Thirty Years.[*] A final novel in this series, Letter to My Father Who Would Now Be a Hundred Years Old,[†] 1987, was written in the more intimate vein of *A Russian Mother*, and these two titles in themselves convey a striking difference in the writer's relation to his two subjects.

In Letter to My Father Who Would Now Be a Hundred Years Old, "letter" expresses a form of communication with the person to whom it is addressed—a person who, when identified as "my father," seems to enjoy a privileged relationship with the letter-writer. As readers familiar with the other volumes of the ensemble know, and which can be glimpsed in *A Russian Mother*, the father-son relationship gradually becomes highly positive. But in *"A Russian Mother*," the adjective "Russian" distances the mother from the son-author-narrator-character and

---

[*]*Les trente premières années*: the first volume, The Child You Were (*L'Enfant que tu étais*, 1982), covers much the same ground as the opening sections of *A Russian Mother*. The two following volumes, Neither War nor Peace (*Ni guerre ni paix*, 1983) and Cruel Games (*Les Fêtes cruelles*, 1984), recall the strangely unsettling and grim atmosphere of the mid-century years, formative years for Bosquet in his adolescence and young manhood.
[†]*Lettre à mon père qui aurait eu 100 ans.*

suggests a somewhat judgmental approach. Bosquet wanted to come to terms with the intricacies of his past as reflected in his memories of both parents, and the startling opening of *A Russian Mother* throws some light on the process. The setting is Paris, the date October 1976, just four months, the reader is carefully told, before the death of that mother in 1977. As the narrative moves toward that final point, the reader becomes aware that those two dates recur quite prominently throughout—narrative "markers" as it were. So, we might be tempted to conclude, Bosquet's obsession with the past was initially linked to the trauma caused by his mother's death.

In fact, the initial episode as presented, suggests a more subtle psychological disturbance: the anxiety caused by the emergence from the writer's unconscious of the ambiguous sentence which, in the form of a perfect "*alexandrin*," as the writer notes with satisfaction, is repeated four times in the short three-page opening, "You're my mother, you're dead; all I feel is relief." The task of writers, of course, is to transmute their experience of reality into literature, a kind of personal exploitation, even though, as in the case before us, the transmutation is fraught with rage and guilt; here the "truth" uncovered proves to be, in some manner, unbearable. The book then may function for the writer as an "exorcism," another form of deliverance, in this case, from the ambiguities of the fifty-year emotional confrontation of the son with the now dying mother.

In spite of a frequently expressed contempt for any indulgence in the emotional vagaries of the "I," Bosquet has never been reluctant to speak of his past, generally in deliberately deprecating terms, factual and preferably ironic: "Born in Russia, growing up in Belgium, fleeing to the United States; learning about peace in Germany, living in France, seems frivolous. It is my fate." And that fate defines him in his eyes as a man without roots "from everywhere and nowhere."* Certainly, not an excep-

---

Alain Bosquet in "Poètes d'Aujourd'hui" v. 117 (1964), Pierre Seghers Editions. In the series as a whole, the editor presents the poet and an outline of his biography. Although for this volume the editor was the poet Charles le Quintrec, a friend, Bosquet, typically, asserted his independence by presenting his own account of his life. A "*Métèque*" is a term he often referred

tional condition in our modern world; or again, as he writes in his preface to *Les Fêtes cruelles* in 1984, stressing the fragmentation in time caused by the impact of history, rather than just the dispersal in space due to exile: "I was born of the Treaty of Versailles (1919), I almost died for Danzig. I landed in Normandy (Nov. 8, 1942), then came Berlin, Hiroshima (August 1945)."

These brief allusions situate him in a certain context—in time and space—but do not define his personality. "I am," he notes, "in a way a child of the absurd," a remark which situates him, too, but in relation to a specific intellectual climate. There is no self-pity in his account of a childhood which might have been subtitled "Memoirs of Exile" or "The Book of Separations." And *A Russian Mother* is indeed a book about exile, exile lived as separation, successive separations culminating in the long-drawn-out process of that most tragic perhaps of all separations—the mother's separation from herself through the disintegration of memory due to old age, as observed with almost clinical precision by her son, desperately aware of his helplessness as he watches the various phases of the process. It is within this context that the opening sentence takes on its full meaning. As for the son, we know of course that no real "identity" can emerge for an individual without going through the process of separation from aspects of the given world, interiorized in childhood during which, for Bosquet, his mother and father were the only stable frame of reference he had.

Uprooting and displacement characterized his family life. Born in 1919 into a prosperous cultivated social milieu in Odessa, the brilliant pre-communist cosmopolitan port in the Ukraine, Anatole Bisk chose the pseudonym Alain Bosquet when he became a poet, residing in Paris and writing in French; in *A Russian Mother* he is also affectionately designated by the diminutive "Tolia." The facts as he alludes to them little

---

to in his self-definitions. In the Greek, "*meteskos*" designated a stranger living in Greece who was not a citizen. The word was adopted by the ultra-nationalist French groups around 1894, but inflected to convey a negative image. A "*Métèque*" was seen as an "unpleasant person," says the dictionary; foreign, with bad manners; and the term was often applied to Jews.

by little, are accurate but sparse. His mother, Berthe Turiansky, was a good musician; his father, Alexander Bisk, came from a cosmopolitan family of Alsatian and Belgian origins. Both had Jewish family connections. Like many wealthy young Russians of his generation, Alexander had completed his education rather haphazardly by touring the major universities in Europe. During the Russian civil war, he was arrested as a "bourgeois" by the communists and sentenced to death. It was, as recounted in the family legend, and re-imagined by the son in the last episode of the book, due to the energetic intervention of his then young wife that he was reprieved, but he lost all his fortune. With his wife and son he escaped to Bulgaria where he made a living as a philatelist.

In 1925 the child Tolia was sent to Brussels, entrusted to his grandparents' care in order, in his mother's terms, to get a respectable education. Influenced by a gifted teacher, he fell in love with French poetry; he belonged to a small lively circle of students who launched one short-lived review after another; and he determined to become a poet. In 1934, he became a Belgian citizen, subsequently majoring in Romance philology at the University in Brussels. Drafted into the Belgian Army in 1940, he crossed the frontier into France at the time of the successful Nazi invasion of Belgium, and there he was incorporated into a unit of the French Army.

After the collapse of France, he made his way to America, arriving in New York just after the bombing of Pearl Harbor. He participated actively in the Gaullist *Voix de France*, became a U.S. citizen, and was sent to a military training camp. From there he was posted to London (1943) to serve in the Intelligence branch of the Allied Army preparing the landing in Normandy. After the successful Normandy campaign, Bosquet was posted to Berlin as interpreter and liaison officer with the quadripartite commission of control responsible for the city. In 1951 he left Berlin to settle in Paris and became a French citizen in 1980. One can understand some of the significance of the "first thirty years" he undertook to record some thirty years later.

Certain advantages helped to compensate for the uprooting, such as Bosquet's encounters with outstanding figures, which provided a broader cultural text for the poet. The process began quite early—when he was still in his teens—in Brussels, which was for some years a center of Surrealist activities in close touch with Paris. Two Belgians figured prominently, the painters René Magritte and Paul Delvaux. The young students also had a strong international bent and admired Joan Miró, Max Ernst, André Masson, Yves Tanguy, Salvador Dali and André Breton equally. The group adopted the Surrealist hatred of the "bourgeois" mode of life and its proclaimed goal of destroying the social order; also in the realm of art, the will to break with the given patterns and forms valued by the culture.

It was this small, internationally oriented group which prepared Bosquet well for his encounters in New York with the exiled leader of the Surrealists, André Breton, a friend who, in 1942, helped launch the first small volumes of poems by Bosquet: *The Impardonnable Image* and *Swoons*, the first illustrated by Fernand Léger, the second by Masson, a most elegant beginning! During this period he met many notable refugees and, among the Americans, Langston Hughes, Archibald MacLeish, and John Steinbeck. These literary associations would further develop to include such figures as Samuel Beckett and Dali, Beckett who, in later years Bosquet would count along with prestigious figures such as Wallace Fowlie, Edouard Roditi, and Denise Levertov—among his translators; while he himself translated Beckett as well as his own poems on occasion. Poetry has been Bosquet's major concern and passion over the half-century of his writer's life. He has published many brilliant meditations on the subject to which it would be impossible to do justice within the scope of this Afterword.

For Bosquet, poetry will always hold the highest rank among human activities, although painting, where he is a connoisseur, is a close contender; music, his mother's domain, holds its place in the Panthéon of the arts as well as the newborn art of films. The "space" occupied by the arts in his work shares the non-linear, not partitioned character of time itself. The range of culture in all his writing is immense and precise and can prove disconcerting to the reader. It is part of the task of the artist, according to

Bosquet, to gain some kind of control over the chaos of impressions un-
leashed by the violent changes characteristic of the modern world, and
which, in a sense, constantly challenge his sense of identity. Furthermore,
they also challenge the basic tenets of middle-class Western morality, its
goal to achieve a perfectly tranquil, harmonious, secure life, free from risk.
This theme, closely linked to Bosquet's acute sense of the collapse, in
today's world, of the values of Western Civilization, is the driving motif
underlying Bosquet's fictional world, the nature of the conflicts which en-
gulf his characters and the disasters that they suffer. These are the dramas they have in common with human beings everywhere on the planet,
and in which their creator participates: thus his claim that they are all ba-
sically "autobiographical," "others," recognized as "the same," a way
to break out of the confines of self-enclosure.

Bosquet was already an experienced writer when he undertook to recapture the drama of those years: a poet, a novelist and short-story writer,
a journalist and a critic. As his discussion of the easily blurred frontiers
between fiction and autobiographical narrative shows, he was on guard
against the temptations and snares of dramatizing or poeticizing the frag-
mented memories of his childhood years merely through manipulation
of language. "My biography," he warns, "is also that of my imagination.
I marry dreams and rage." Within this perspective, Bosquet likes to give
graphic details of sexual awakenings which sometimes elicit observations
that a "layer of misogyny" is woven into Bosquet's work. Women are often seen as bodies, to be consumed like exotic fruit—for instance, as
"juicy," "pulpous," and more or less always available for seduction by
male predators. Or, if they fail to play their role in this scenario, they
may be quite violently attacked.

On the other hand, Bosquet can depict an almost "romantic" sensitivity to the feminine presence and the enrichments it can bring him;
this is clearly expressed in a novel like *L'Amour à deux têtes* (Two-
headed Love), in "Poèmes pour Elle" (Poems for Her); in his association with and his book about Marlene Dietrich, *Un Amour par téléphone*
(1992). But in his critical assessments he never pulls his punches when

dealing with a woman writer, even the most popular at the moment, such as Françoise Sagan, a young best-selling novelist fully supported and acclaimed by such prestigious figures in the French world of letters as François Mauriac.

It is a moving experience to follow the three closely-knit main characters in *A Russian Mother*—Alexander, the father, Berthe the mother, and the child—over a period of fifty years as they travel from Bulgaria to Brussels, then under the Nazi threat to the south of France, to New York, and finally, in the case of mother and son, to Paris where Bosquet persuaded his mother to join him after his father's death. When, at the end of World War II, in 1945, Bosquet chose to stay in Paris and try his luck at making his living as a writer, he was taking quite a risk. But the situation in Paris in 1945 turned out to be more propitious than it had seemed. The War had dispersed the main literary figures of the *avant-guerre;* some had left France, some had died; some had been involved in the deep dissensions between "collaborators" and "resisters." The latter only now held their place in the literary community. The dominant figures, Jean-Paul Sartre, Simone de Beauvoir, and Albert Camus were cast in the role of intellectual and ethical leadership. The "existentialist" thinkers, whom Bosquet sometimes designates disparagingly as "crypto-moralists," dominated the scene.

But they were far from reflecting fully the mood of the hour. There was room for other, new voices. Bosquet's was one of these. In very short order he became one of the central figures in the literary life of Paris, a life which was changing as communications opened up, and from all over Europe and the United States travelers and tourists began to converge on London and Paris. Before long Bosquet was serving as literary critic on the staff of such well-known journals as *Combat, Le Monde* and *Le Figaro*; as a member of influential committees responsible for attributing the many literary prizes that punctuate the literary life of France. He himself was, over the years, the recipient of others, one of which, the prestigious "grand prix" of the French Academy, was awarded to *A Russian Mother*; some principally acknowledged the quality of his poetry.

In those years, too, Bosquet drew on his American and British experience: he translated Walt Whitman, Emily Dickinson, Carl Sandburg, and Lawrence Durrell, and published an anthology of American poetry in translation (1956; 1961). In 1971 he took a trip back to the United States. He had started a review, original in format and called *B et B*, co-authored, it was planned, by one of his Belgian friends named Brusselen. It was to take the form of a dialogue so as to avoid any one-voice, one-view account. This was to prove an all too utopian project, but the two young men set off to visit America, which Bosquet admitted "fascinated him." With New York, of course, he was familiar; and he was familiar with campuses where he had taught or lectured: Brandeis, NYU, and the University of Wisconsin, at Madison and Milwaukee. In 1967 he published a set of essays entitled *Middle West* and, four years later, his experiences in Milwaukee and Madison are recognizably evoked in certain episodes in *Chicago—oignon sauvage* (Chicago—Wild Onion), one of his best volumes of short stories. What appeals to Bosquet's imagination are American Indian art and culture, and, beyond Chicago, Los Angeles, San Francisco, Mexico. This contact with Mexico will inspire one of his novels, also a prizewinner: *La Confession mexicaine*.

Bosquet's warm response to the vastness and variety of the American scene was conveyed to some extent in *B et B*. The brilliant group of friends Bosquet had made as an *exilé* in New York later yielded an invaluable book of interviews, Memory or Forgetting (*La Mémoire ou l'oubli*, 1990), featuring such great figures as Louis Aragon, Thomas Mann, Piet Mondrian, Léger, Jorge Luis Borges, Maurice Maeterlinck, Henri Michaux, Sartre, Saint-John Perse, and Breton. Some of these were recorded as early as 1953; others, Bosquet warns, are reconstituted from memory between 1982, it would seem, and 1987. The interviews are often combined with personal reminiscences, and one of the most moving is the recall of the day, twenty years earlier, when, with the French cultural counsellor, Edouard Morot-Sir, he heard the radio announcement of the assassination of President Kennedy.

At times, during those years, Bosquet looks with some misgiving at the accumulation of journalistic material he has to produce, pages and pages. Although he belittles their value, since for him, only poetry justifies the writer's activity, he is nonetheless an excellent essayist. The landing of the astronauts on the moon inspired a delightful meditation—a long essay entitled "Good-bye to the Moon." The moon, so long the inspirer of legends and dreams, we now know is a barren creature, far less exciting than the earth we live on, and the dreams it inspired. Human dreams, legends and myths are the very stuff of which poetry is made, as Bosquet likes to remind us. And poetry is, in his eyes, the breath of human existence. In *A Russian Mother*, in this respect, Bosquet's sophisticated narrative technique raises problems for the reader. At one and the same time character, narrator, and author, where is Bosquet himself in the book? The facts can be checked, but how did they impinge on the writer's sensibility and understanding and affect the tense love-hatred bond between mother and son, and the son's understanding of life? Certainly the narrative does not suggest any smooth transition from the "innocence" of childhood to a harmonious maturity, a pattern often presented in conventional descriptions of the process of "growing up" by nineteenth-century realist writers.

Like the life described and like the unforeseeable pattern of memory itself, the narrative follows no linear consistent pattern leading inevitably from episode to episode. It is not a retrospective construction. Experiences of loss and death consistently impinge on these lives. Thus, the novel opens on a scene of departure and separation and ends with the final separation of death. It presents three deaths: that of the grandmother, later the horrendous death of the father trapped in a hotel fire, and finally the death of the mother. Death, too, is a frightening physical presence in the narrator's "stream of consciousness," cinematographic recollections of the turmoil in his body and mind as he lay, under bombardment, on the beach in Normandy. In contrast, in the early recollections, Bosquet develops with

275

humor the erotic obsessions and perplexities of the adolescent discovering the sensual pleasures and coercive claims of an ardent sexuality. Love and death—the two motifs converge as he reaches the end of a narrative that plunges into erotic freudian fantasy: i.e., the oedipal episode in which, with some complacency, six months after his mother's death, he constructs an obviously *imagined* scene of intercourse with her as a young woman. Eros and Thanatos, love and death, conjoin in that neo-baroque episode. One may detect an element of *bravado* in regard to the theme itself, when Bosquet evokes the somewhat burlesque image of the grown son once again emerging from the womb, *head* first.

Most successful, however, is Bosquet's choice of the narrative technique. The mode of direct address, suggesting the *presence* of the mother, felicitously breaks with the carefully calculated patterns of psychological analysis, unsuited to the vision of a child. The text gives the impression of spoken exchanges, leading to the recreation of patterns of speech. Under their apparent randomness, they trace the emotional shifts in the relations between the child and his "entourage," more convincingly than would an analytical account that would destroy the writer's obvious intent to catch the different unconscious underlying assumptions of the speakers. The interplay of repetition and difference in those speech patterns is highly suggestive and incites the reader to explore the relations between the speakers. In a sense the narrative momentum leads from dialogue to dialogue in what we might call a series of small "comedies of situation" well-suited to the temperament of the author and, by their variety, to the pleasure of the reader.

GERMAINE BRÉE
Kenan Professor of Humanities Emerita
Wake Forest University